Praise for Stephe

REMEMBER BE CLAYTON

"Magnificently compelling. . . . Stephen Harrigan handles these scenes with immaculate detail, an acute ear for fear and cruelty, and an eye for the unpredictability of human behavior in moments of passion. . . .We are knocked flat with admiration."

—*The Washington Post*

"Like the unforgiving bullets that pierce Clayton's flesh, the story goes unflinchingly deeper into the very human failings of fathers, the need for children to forgive and what it means to create art. . . . A tautly written novel. . . . With *Remember Ben Clayton*, Harrigan has created art."

—*Austin American-Statesman*

"A writer of great compassion, Harrigan has infused *Remember Ben Clayton* with a quietly smoldering sense of sadness, 'a welling sorrow,' that manifests itself not only in the statue of a young man taken in his youth in an unjustified war, but in his characters' betrayals and remorse. And yet, there is a glimmering of light throughout this dark novel, a testament to the author's—and his characters'—innate humanity."

—*San Antonio Express-News*

"A stunning work of art. . . . The story builds with determined momentum, providing a grimly vivid sense of place and deep insight into the creative process and family relationships. Harrigan's *The Gates of the Alamo* has become a modern classic, and his latest novel deserves similar acclaim."

—*Booklist* (starred review)

"The characterizations in this story are superb, enhancing this engrossing novel that never plays out as you expect it to."

—*The Oklahoman*

"A solemn, affecting exploration of the effects of devoting one's life to art at the expense of family, friends and love."

—*The Texas Observer*

"As in *The Gates of the Alamo,* Harrigan works on a broad canvas. . . . Lying behind the Texas narrative are the bloody remnants of the Indian wars, fresh enough to reach directly into the lives of the next generation and to provide a mirror to the carnage just concluded in Europe." —*The Austin Chronicle*

"A heartening novel about art, war, and the tug of family relationships." —*Kirkus Reviews*

"Thoroughly engaging. . . . Intimate and compelling. . . . Harrigan transports his readers to each scene, as well as inside the tormented minds of his characters." —*The Southern Review*

"Rich in detail about the Texas landscape and the men and women who live there. It is a telling measure of [Harrigan's] skill as a writer that he seamlessly weaves . . . major themes through this new work without allowing his characters to bear the weight of being symbols rather than real people. . . . Harrigan is a gifted storyteller whose images at times are as rich as those in the best poetry." —*The Washington Times*

STEPHEN HARRIGAN

REMEMBER BEN CLAYTON

Stephen Harrigan is the author of seven previous books of fiction and nonfiction, including the novels *Challenger Park* and the *New York Times* bestseller *The Gates of the Alamo*. A longtime writer for *Texas Monthly* and other magazines, he is also an award-winning screenwriter who has written many movies for television. He lives in Austin, where he is a faculty fellow at the Michener Center for Writers at the University of Texas and a founding member of Capital Area Statues, Inc.

www.stephenharrigan.com

ALSO BY STEPHEN HARRIGAN

FICTION

Challenger Park

The Gates of the Alamo

Jacob's Well

Aransas

NONFICTION

A Natural State

Water and Light: A Diver's Journey to a Coral Reef

Comanche Midnight

REMEMBER BEN CLAYTON

A NOVEL

STEPHEN HARRIGAN

Vintage Books
A Division of Random House, Inc.
New York

FIRST VINTAGE BOOKS EDITION, MAY 2012

 Published in the United States by Vintage Books, a division of Random House, Inc., New York, and in Canada by Random House of Canada Limited, Toronto. Originally published in hardcover in the United States by Alfred A. Knopf, a division of Random House, Inc., New York, in 2011.

The Library of Congress has cataloged the Knopf edition as follows:
Harrigan, Stephen.
Remember Ben Clayton : a novel / Stephen Harrigan.—1st ed.
p. cm.
1. Fathers and sons—Fiction. 2. Fathers and daughters—Fiction.
3. Family secrets—Fiction. 4. Sculptors—Fiction. 5. Art—Fiction.
6. Families—Texas—Fiction. 7. Sons—Death—Fiction. 8. World War, 1914–1918—Casualties—Fiction. 9. Domestic fiction. I. Title.
PS3558.A626R46 2011
813'.54—dc22 2011001859

Vintage ISBN: 978-0-307-94879-3

Book design by Iris Weinstein

www.vintagebooks.com

Printed in the United States of America
10 9 8 7 6 5 4 3 2 1

TO MASON LYNN RANDOLPH
AND TRAVIS HARRIGAN RANDOLPH

And to the cast of CAST (Capital Area Statues, Inc.):
Lawrence Wright, Bill Wittliff, Marcia Ball,
Elizabeth Avellán, Vincent Salas, and Amon Burton

REMEMBER BEN CLAYTON

ONE

They tore at the earth with their entrenching tools and mess-kit lids as the shells burst all around them and in the scattered pine tops overhead. They were already dug in but they needed to be deeper, because there did not seem to be any way to survive above the ground. The concussive turbulence sucked away the air. The men gasped for breath in the vacuum.

Shrapnel pierced the tree trunks and ploughed into the earth with hissing force as the ground heaved and pitched like a malevolent carnival ride. Arthur Fry, a nineteen-year-old feed store clerk from Ranger, Texas, thought one of his ears might have been sliced off but he was not sure. There was a thick pooling warmth below the rim of his helmet but no pain. The blasts had blown dirt into his eyes and when he tried to squeeze them shut it felt as if the insides of his eyelids were lined with broken glass. He had not been under fire before and could not recognize with any clarity the sounds and signatures of the shells. They were supposed to be able to differentiate the smell of mustard gas from that of ordinary high explosive, but in this endless barrage there was no way to tease out one toxic smell from another and the order had not come down to put on their gas masks.

Some of the shells rattled and shuddered like they were tearing the sky apart and some carved a narrow screaming path. In the last few days the Germans had been pushed off Blanc Mont Ridge by the Second Division and now they were engaged in a fighting retreat, using up all the ammunition they did not plan to carry with them in a furious, indifferent barrage of whiz-bangs and jack johnsons and GI cans and other shrieking varieties of ordnance whose names Arthur did not know.

Thick clods of dirt pattered down on his back and then Arthur heard the shell that he was sure was going to kill him, an abruptly withdrawn shrillness somewhere in the sky overhead, a predatory silence as the descending shell concentrated on the terrain below, patiently searching him out. It finally exploded just over the slight swell of land that hid them from the enemy, an eruption whose vicious force seemed to come not from the sky but from deep below, as if the shell had plunged to the core of the planet and detonated there. The inside of his head roared with soundlessness. He could not even hear his own whimpering. He pressed his face still closer to the noxious, gaseous earth. He tried to concentrate on the feel of the cool dirt against his skin.

When he forced his eyes open again it was in response to an odd little brush against his sleeve. Through the haze of gas and dirt he saw an animal he had never seen alive before running about in tight, frantic circles between him and Ben Clayton. In their camions on the way to the front they had passed smashed hedgehogs on the roads, but they had seemed like slow-moving and primitive things and he could never have guessed at their living vibrancy. This one hopped in confusion, its soft quills lying flat and its nose twitching madly as it scrambled around and around searching for a place of safety.

Arthur looked over to Ben. He had the odd thought that he should reach out and grab Ben's shoulder and point out the strange creature to him. He would have liked to impress his friend, to show that his lighthearted curiosity was greater than his fear. But he could not make himself move and there was no possibility Ben could hear him over the roar of the shells. And in an instant the hedgehog straightened out in its flight and disappeared, bounding back toward Blanc Mont.

Another shell exploded twenty or thirty yards down the line and then the barrage ended. The air trembled in the sudden silence. Arthur turned over on his back and looked up at the sky through the swirling chemical vapors and touched his ear. The monstrous wound he expected to find there was nothing but a shallow cut, the bleeding already stanched by a makeshift plaster of gummy soil.

"Jesus God in heaven!" somebody called, and when Arthur looked toward the sound he saw a man lying on his back, his body blown open and his splintered bloody ribs exposed. The dying man stared in fascination at the gaping maw of his own chest and held his trembling hands in the air. He screamed for somebody named Aunt Agnes. Arthur tore his eyes away and convinced himself he hadn't seen this or heard it; it was just some horrible spasm of imagery that his mind had produced. He had no more responsibility to believe in it than he did to believe in the nightmares of his childhood.

From up and down the line they could hear the groans and pleadings of the wounded. It had stopped raining sometime during the night but the ground was still wet and as the stretcher bearers and runners hurried now through the shallow trenches they kept sliding on the slick chalk that lay beneath the thin topsoil.

Sergeant Kitchens walked down the line to talk to the men and steady them, but Arthur could see he was not steady himself. "Keep digging in," Kitchens said, "but don't go all the way to China because it looks like we'll be jumping off here soon enough."

"You think this is really the jump-off line?" Arthur said in an unsteady voice to Ben, who was methodically picking away at the chalk with his entrenching tool. Ben looked up and said he guessed it was.

"Well, it's a lot of open ground to cross, if you ask me," Arthur said. Between them and the village there was a half mile of open scraggly ground with no cover except for almost untraceable dips in the terrain. The marines were supposed to be in possession of the main part of Saint-Étienne but nobody knew if that was really true. In any case the Boche were strongly entrenched behind a cemetery wall at the eastern end of the village, and on the far bank of the little stream, and on a solitary hill, deadly prominent, just ahead to their right. There were also machine-gun nests, Arthur knew, artfully concealed in every contour and pocket of ground.

"I don't expect it'll take us that long to get across it," Ben said. His voice was clear and steady but his eyes had narrowed to a weird focus that gave Arthur no comfort. The change had come over Ben in the last few days, on the nighttime marches across the cratered fields from Somme-Suippe. What he had learned about his dad back home in Texas from one of the Indians in Company E had closed him in on himself. He wouldn't talk much; his friendly open face had turned taut. When they stopped to rest or to eat their cold meals he sat apart from Arthur and fingered the little rectangle of metal, cut from some abandoned mess kit, upon which he had laboriously tapped out with a blunt nail his name and rank and unit along with a pretty decent sketch of a horse standing atop a shallow mesa. A number of the men had made trench art like it. They kept them in their wallets as a backup to their dog tags in case their bodies were blown apart and the pieces scattered among multiple heaps of the dead.

The fact that his best friend had nothing else to say to him hurt Arthur's feelings and made him feel isolated. All right, then, he thought. He would stay silent about things until Ben had the decency to initiate a conversation. He picked up his own entrenching tool again and began to hack away at the bedrock, trying not to think about the blown-open doughboy he had just seen or his own quaking fear and homesickness or the steadily intensifying thirst that he knew would not be relieved until they had taken the village and made their way to the stream that ran behind it. Supposedly the marines had control of a well somewhere in the sector, but nobody in his regiment had yet seen any water from it. The big wooden casks of the water carts had been shot to pieces on their way up to the front, and for the last day they had been filling their canteens with the juice from canned tomatoes. But now even the tomato juice was gone. All Arthur had was a few sticks of the lemon-flavored chewing gum that was supposed to moisten your mouth and blunt your thirst.

It was oddly quiet now up and down the line except for the industrious chocking sounds of the men as they continued to dig in. It was an October dawn in a distant land. France. There was another quick slurry of rain and then the weather hastened away on the wind and the sky was clear. They could hear the Boche speaking to each other in the town they were going to attack, the unknown German words sharp and disciplined and practiced. The enemy was digging in too, getting ready for the rolling barrage that would precede the American assault.

An observation balloon hung in the sky behind the German lines, placidly menacing, its swollen fabric aglow in the morning light. Toward the east, along the Orfeuil road where the 141st was dug in, a solitary German airplane was diving out of the sun. They could hear the distant, earnest pattering of its front-mounted gun, and then a swarm of British aircraft arrived to chase it away.

Something was going to happen soon, Arthur knew. There was too much activity, too many runners sprinting back and forth from wherever the field headquarters were, too great a sense of exhilarating dread, for this heady moment to escape. The thought of the attack coming was the only thing that calmed him. It was a chance to move out of this boggy rut, where the chemical vapors still lingered, mixed in with the smells of shit and tobacco and wet canvas and the dewy morning scent that somehow managed to rise from the ravaged ground. The idea of advancing and taking his chances, rather than sitting here any longer—thirsty and passive and helpless—filled him with a startling surge of happiness.

Nobody was talking much. Everyone was in the same state of somber watchfulness. Arthur studied Ben as he sat cross-legged in the mud with his rifle on his lap, examining his personalized rectangle of aluminum.

"You're a pretty good artist," Arthur said. His own voice sounded dry and thin to him—both from fear and from thirst. "Maybe you could make me one sometime. I'd pay."

Ben looked up at him and almost smiled. His mood had been so dark for so long that his suggestion of a smile warmed Arthur's spirits as much as the sun had. He realized how big a threat Ben's withdrawn demeanor had been to his well-being the last few days, the loneliness and hurt he had been feeling in this foreign land because his best friend could not rouse himself to be sociable.

"You don't need to pay me," Ben said. "What do you want on it?"

Arthur deliberated: the house he grew up in, maybe, or the banks of Palo Pinto Creek, where his grandfather had taught him to fish, or a bobcat, which was the mascot of the high school from which he had graduated a year and a half ago.

But thinking of Texas again made him think of what the man in Company E had told Ben.

"You know," Arthur decided to say, "it's not healthy to be in this situation we're in and you being so preoccupied about your dad. It was a long time ago, he said. But maybe if you wrote your dad and gave him a chance to—"

"You don't know a thing in the world about it so maybe you better just shut up."

Before Arthur could even get offended the shells started rattling and whistling again overhead. It took them all an anxious moment to realize that the shells were going the other direction this time, fired from the batteries behind their own lines at the German positions ahead. The chewed-over soil a hundred yards in front of the American lines erupted once again as the shells landed with impressive coordination, throwing up an obscuring curtain of dirt and debris.

"We're going! We're going! We're going now!" Sergeant Kitchens was suddenly shouting as he ran up the line pounding men on the shoulder and hauling them to their feet. "Fix bayonets! The sonsofbitches have already started the fucking barrage!"

Arthur pulled his bayonet from the scabbard on his belt and fitted it with shaking hands to the lug on his rifle barrel. He had darkened the shiny blade with lamp smoke as he had been told to do, so that a sniper could not see its reflection at night, and now in his anxiety the dull pewterish gleam sickened him. The bayonet blade, the copper hide of the observation balloon, the heaving, upthrown earth—he was surrounded by the suffocating no-color of oblivion.

"Hurry, goddammit!" Kitchens was calling. "Don't stand around here chewing the fucking sock!" If they didn't start at once, they would lose the protective cover of the rolling barrage that was already advancing ahead of the attack. But they didn't know where to go except vaguely forward. They didn't know what objectives to attack. The orders had not come down in time.

Arthur hurriedly tightened the straps of his gas mask bag across his chest, he checked the pockets where he had stashed grenades and mills bombs, he touched the hilt of the trench knife on his belt. He shoved the blade of his entrenching tool down the front of his pants. One of their French instructors had told them to do that to shield their genitals from low-flying machine-gun bullets.

And then he looked at Ben. Ben was composed. He was silent. He stared ahead, his face set as he shifted about in his webbing, distributing the weight of his gear. There was something murderous in his eyes.

"Well," Arthur said. He was thinking maybe he could get Ben to at least apologize before they jumped off. But he was back where he had been, in the dark private mood that Arthur guessed was suited for the work that lay ahead of them.

Kitchens blew his police whistle and the platoon started to scramble upward to the swell of land. Arthur felt Ben pat him firmly on the arm—perhaps in fellowship, perhaps in farewell. It did not make up for his rudeness but it warmed Arthur all the same and gave him a bit of courage.

Arthur said, "Here we go," but Ben was looking forward again, with that frightening, excluding clarity in his face.

They strode across the open ground, moving apart from each other, following the barrage curtain. Kitchens and a chauchaut team from their squad walked ahead of them—Bernie Rutledge carrying the heavy gun, Kyle and Herman Kuholtz, cousins from Amarillo, lugging haversacks filled with magazines.

A whistle blew. They stopped. The barrage moved forward. They started again, the mud caking their boots. No one was shooting at them, not yet. They went another hundred yards. They could see the barrage outpacing them now, the shells landing not in the town but uselessly in the swales beyond. Somebody had made a mistake.

But still the Boche weren't shooting. The cemetery was now only a hundred yards ahead. To the left the steeple of the village church shone peacefully in the sun.

A few paces ahead Bernie Rutledge stopped, caught in something. He tried to lift his foot and back up, and that's when the machine gunners opened up, the bullets splintering the chauchaut and the arms that were holding it, and at the same moment bursting through Bernie's neck. He collapsed onto the strands of wire that had been planted low to the ground in careless coils so that brush and grass would grow up through it and conceal it. The Kuholtz boys dropped too, twitching and howling as the rounds kept hitting them.

"Get over the goddam wire!" Kitchens screamed at the top of his voice. He boldly planted his foot on Bernie Rutledge's back so that he could vault over the wire. He went twenty paces before a bullet ripped through his face.

Ben and Arthur had no choice but to step on the Kuholtz boys to keep from getting snared in the wire themselves. Herman Kuholtz cried out, "Stop it! I ain't dead!" On the other side of the wire they dove into a shell hole. The blade of the entrenching tool Arthur had shoved down his pants gouged into his groin. He glanced back and could see boys still dropping on the wire. And now the enemy artillery had opened up again, ripping open what had once been a cultivated field and raining down unharvested sugar beets that Arthur thought at first were grenades. The firing was most intense from the hill to their right, but he could hear the workmanlike rhythms of a machine gun somewhere to their left supporting the fire from the knobby summit.

Kitchens was dead. He was sitting upright twenty yards away. The bullet that had hit him had blown away his jaw and his tongue hung out the side of his face. He looked like a panting dog. Arthur saw the company's twenty-two-year-old lieutenant, a brand-new sears-roebuck from Wichita Falls, being hauled back to the American lines, screaming as his shattered legs bounced over the clotty earth. There was no one to give orders. The units were already hopelessly mixed. He did not even recognize the nearest men to him, who were cowering in the same shallow depression as bullets tacked away at the ground all around them. Their faces were as white as cue balls. Fear had washed out their features and made them all look the same. As one of the shells made a low trajectory over their heads he thought he could hear the liquid sloshing of mustard gas.

"What do we do?" he shouted to Ben.

But Ben was already on his feet. He had spotted the Boche machine-gun nest to their left and was racing heedlessly toward it. It was not courage that drove Arthur to follow him. It was only the fear of being left alone.

TWO

When Francis Gilheaney received a telegram from the president of the Knights of Ak-Sar-Ben reading "Statue in Danger," he left San Antonio on the first train that would get him to Omaha. The riot erupted in full force as he was standing at the reception counter of the Henshaw Hotel. A couple of young thugs burst into the lobby waving shotguns and theatrically declaring they would kill any and all niggers they saw. Unable to think of any more stirring rhetoric, they ran back out to join the crowds that were rushing down Farnam Street toward the courthouse.

Gil left his bags with the desk clerk and went outside. He had not slept for twenty-four hours but his mind was alert with peril. Thousands of men swarmed in the street. They had ropes to hang the Negro man under guard in the courthouse jail who they said had assaulted a white woman. They carried torches and shot revolvers and rifles into the air. Gil could spot the men who were home from the war, who were unemployed and scared about it and looking for someone to blame. They were not firing their weapons profligately like the others. They had their eyes fixed straight ahead and their course was lethally firm.

All along the street the rioters were throwing bricks through windows and looting the hardware stores, pouring out with guns that had the prices still attached and filling their pockets with shells. Gil did not belong with this crowd and he knew it would not be long before someone gave him a look that told him so. He was not a delirious teenager or a young veteran with a grudge. He was a sixty-year-old man in a good suit, with a scowl of disapproval on his face that his pride would not allow him to remove.

At the end of the block the courthouse where the accused man was being held was on fire. It was eight o'clock at night. The flames in the lower windows illuminated cyclonic columns of smoke, which rose straight into the air and then flattened into tendrils that drifted toward the Missouri River. Up ahead a streetcar had come to a stop, unable to proceed because of the crowd and the confusion. Three or four men dragged a Negro man out of the back and over to the sidewalk in front of a Chinese restaurant.

The man kept his feet after they slammed him into a wall. As they approached he tried to argue them out of their position. He said the man they were after was in the courthouse, not here. He knew nothing about an attack on a white girl. He worked in a photography studio and was on his way home. They had no intention of listening. They smiled with feral satisfaction and kept closing in, taunting him and poking him with broom handles.

Gil had urgent business of his own but the sight of this man, helplessly pleading his case as he was about to be beaten to the pavement and probably hanged, caught him up.

"You men!" he barked out as he walked up to them.

They turned around. They were boys, no older than seventeen. He saw in their eyes that his age and his size and the way he was dressed caught them off guard, that he might be the sort of man they had the habit of deferring to in their unclouded moments.

"I'll take care of him," he said. "You men go on. They need everybody at the courthouse."

They stood there dumbly.

"Go on!" he yelled. "He's getting away!"

They looked to the courthouse. They had not seen the fire yet, and fortunately for the credibility of his scenario it added a new dimension of urgency. One of the boys gave Gil a confused nod and led the rest of them off to join the crowd that was now running at full speed toward the courthouse. The Negro man, assuming that Gil was the ringleader he pretended to be, left his hat on the ground and ran off in the opposite direction, disappearing down a side street a half block away.

Gil walked back into the middle of the street to lose himself in the surging crowd in case the boys he had ordered away came to their senses and returned to deal with him. Above the heads of the mob he could see the flames growing in the courthouse but he could not yet see the statue that stood on the lawn in front of it. Before he got much farther the procession came to a chaotic halt as some sort of scuffle broke out twenty or thirty yards ahead. Men behind him began shoving forward, eager to be in on the commotion. Gil planted his feet to avoid being trampled to the ground and lashed out with his elbows and then with his fists to try to clear a breathing space for himself.

The violent congestion finally broke up and they were moving again. Gil felt his heart pumping with fear and exertion and he tried to calm it with deep breaths. He had no debilitating maladies to speak of, but he was at an age when this kind of excitement should not be courted. It had been reckless of him to intervene in the beating of the Negro on the streetcar, but he had come to Omaha on a mission of salvation and it would have been a poor thing to ignore a flesh-and-blood man in danger in favor of a bronze one.

The telegram had said the statue had been "defaced." Gil had worried over the precise meaning of that word on the long train journey from Texas. Now, as the mob finally reached the courthouse lawn, his speculations came to a despairing end. The statue's patina, which he had worked weeks at the foundry to perfect, was ruined, buried under a slapdash veneer of black paint. The statue was called the Pawnee Scout but you would not have known it to look at it now. Shining out against the black paint were garish circles of white around the eyes and mouth, a crude attempt to turn the crouching Indian into a pop-eyed figure from a minstrel show. And around his neck someone had tied a hangman's noose.

Four or five men stood casually around the statue as Gil approached it. Another perched on the scout's shoulders, yelling encouragement to a group of vigilantes who were slicing the firemen's hoses with axes. Gil felt an almost suicidal boldness as he made his way toward the man sitting on the statue, this underweight tough with his hat pushed back on his head, cawing out to his fellow rioters. He was going to grab him and unseat him and throw him down hard onto the statue's granite base. He didn't think about what would happen after that or care much about it. Rage and revulsion had blinded him.

But when he was ten feet away somebody yelled out that they were hanging the mayor and the kid hopped down on his own. He and his friends took off sprinting across the lawn toward Harney Street to join another faction of the mob that was dragging someone Gil could not see toward a rope pitched over a signal tower. He climbed up onto the base of his statue to try to get a better idea of what was going on. In the light of the burning courthouse he could make out a great deal of fighting and scuffling and then he saw the body of a white man, the man they said was the mayor, twitching madly as he was hoisted on a rope. In the next moment a car slammed into the traffic tower and the man came falling down again with it. Another furious battle erupted as the men who were trying to save the victim from hanging struggled to get his body out of the mob's possession.

The mob was like a school of fish, instantaneously shifting in response to some unseen stimulus. Now they were surging back in front of the courthouse, shooting their rifles in the air, screaming up at the police officers and deputies in the burning building to release the Negro prisoner or burn up themselves.

Gil stayed with the statue. He removed the noose from around the Pawnee Scout's neck and threw it on the grass. He inspected the figure's desecrated face, wondering if he could get the paint off with some kind of solvent without ruining the patina. It was unlikely. In the morning, when he could see better, he could make a more informed assessment, but at the moment he was pretty sure the whole thing would have to be sandblasted, maybe sent back to the foundry, and the patina reapplied.

No matter. For now the statue was safe, it was whole. As the crowd shifted this way and that, following its urgent, unhinged directives, Gil kept his station, standing next to the Pawnee Scout with his arms folded and his eye out for anyone who might care to do it harm. The grass of the courthouse lawn was torn up and littered with broken glass, and as the great building steadily burned, flaming papers drifted out the windows and a foul-smelling ashy film descended upon everyone who had gathered to demand the death of the supposed assailant who was locked inside. Gil looked around and found a discarded two-by-two that was no longer than a yardstick. It would make an unwieldy weapon, but he would use it as such if required. For the moment, events had subsided into a gruesome calm. After the near-hanging of the mayor, the crowd shifted its attention back to the courthouse, watching the flames and listening with nervous absorption to the screams and cries for reason coming from inside.

"They're coming out!" somebody called after a few minutes, and there was another barbarian rush toward the front of the courthouse. But it was just a group of female prisoners who staggered out of the building, their hair and uniforms covered with ash and grime, all of them trembling and gasping for breath. The crowd let them pass. Its attention was fixed on the courthouse roof now, where a hundred or so prisoners and deputies had climbed to escape the flames. The smoke was so thick and the confusion so intense that Gil could not make out what was going on. The man the mob was after was named Brown, and they kept screaming his name until their throats were raw.

Gil was not going to let these people deface the statue again. There was nothing he could do about the rest of it and it was pointless to think otherwise. He did not know the precise nature of the crime this Brown was accused of and he doubted that any of the mad avengers besieging the courthouse had reliable information either. The rage of the mob was as distinct from justice as the force and direction of the winds blowing the black smoke out to the prairies. Some sort of horrible reckoning was brewing and it could not be stilled.

While the prisoners milled about on the roof, something else was happening on one of the floors below. Men were climbing toward a window there on firemen's ladders. But the climbing figures were not firemen, they were white-shirted men who had left their coats and hats on the ground and were scrambling upward toward the window in a way that reminded Gil of spiders rushing to the center of a web. One of the men had a long coil of rope across his shoulders. Someone on the ground had control of a searchlight and the beam played across the face of the building as the men reached the window and climbed through it.

Gil was alone now. Everyone else on the lawn had closed in on the building again, and when a thread of gunshots erupted on the south side they pushed their way forward, trampling the slower or less curious, until most of them were out of sight. For fifteen minutes nothing happened. Then there was a tremendous exultant roar and Gil knew the Negro man had been surrendered. When an even louder roar went up he knew he had been hanged. There was cheering and wild gunfire for a long time and then an open car came around the corner with men in the passenger seats standing and shooting off their guns and the mob trailing along triumphantly in its wake. Behind the car, attached by a rope, skidded the body of the Negro they had just hanged. The man was dead but he was not dead enough. The rioters were yelling, "Burn him! Burn him! Burn him!" and it was clear to Gil that killing this man had only left them more wild, more unsated, more afraid of missing some exhilarating next development. The car moved slowly, and the body behind seemed to move at a processional pace along with it, the eyes and mouth open as if still straining to comprehend the sudden thing that had happened to it. Gil looked away; it was unseemly to lay his eyes on this dead man's public humiliation. But everyone around him was joyous, and he knew at once that the body being towed along behind this Model T was not the resolution of the terror he had been witnessing but only the beginning of it.

He stood closer to the Pawnee Scout. The figure was larger than life-size but because of its crouching position Gil was able to set one hand protectively on its shoulder. The two-by-two, his makeshift club, was in reach. He had not seen the statue in many years, but the sight and feel of it brought him back vividly to the six months he had labored on its creation in his Washington Square South studio, six months of feverish, frustrating, transcendent absorption. The Knights of Ak-Sar-Ben, the civic group that had commissioned the Pawnee Scout, had at first insisted on a hackneyed representation of a lone Indian scanning the horizon. But Gil had argued for a stronger conception, a figure crouching above the ground, his hand lightly touching a hoof- or footprint, his face registering something subtly wrong. Gil had never told himself what was behind that expression, what unfortunate sign the Indian had just come across, but this barely detectable wash of sadness or alarm was what had made the piece work. He did not even know how he had rendered that emotion in the scout's face. It had just come as his hands were forming the clay. Sometimes that happened; you gave a statue a reason for existing. You gave it a soul.

A half hour after the car towing the dead man had disappeared around the corner, the mob came back. They had burned the body of the Negro by then and were looking for someone else to kill or something else to destroy.

"What about this nigger here?" someone yelled, pointing at Gil's statue. "He's awful damn quiet."

"He ain't a nigger, he's an Indian," another man said.

"Well, he's an honorary nigger now."

Gil stepped forward, trying to keep his posture and tone as relaxed as possible.

"It's all right," he said.

"What's all right?" a man with a repeating rifle said. He had a beefy face and was smiling and seemed inclined to be friendly.

"I mean we can all just leave this statue alone."

"But maybe all of us don't want to do that."

"Well, I'm asking you to."

"Who are you?"

"I'm the sculptor."

"What do you mean? You built this thing?"

"That's what I mean, and I'd appreciate it if—"

"Well, then next time you ought to build something worth a shit."

They started laughing and came forward with ropes while several cars backed up onto the lawn. It was too late to reason with them. He held his ground and told them to stop but they didn't listen and began to shove at him without even looking at him, as if he were an obstacle that merited no comment or concern. They tied the ends of the ropes around the Pawnee Scout's neck and trunk. The other ends were already fastened to the axles of the cars.

Gil shoved back hard at one of the assailants. It was one of the kids who had attacked the man on the streetcar. The kid didn't come back at him right away. He just stood there and stared at him for a second instead with his fists up like a prizefighter. He looked like he was just now realizing how he'd been tricked.

Instead of rushing him, the kid roared theatrically at Gil. It was a display of youthful, feral mockery at an opponent he considered old and irrelevant. In the darkness, the kid's screaming face was so drained of blood by hate that it was the color of a boiled shirt. A coil of black hair spilled onto his forehead from under the brim of his hat. His cheeks were drawn and thin, his mouth gaping open, his eyes as blank as the eyes of a cave fish.

The ropes around the statue drew taut as the automobiles were thrown into gear. Gil took a penknife from his pocket, unfolded it, and was starting to saw at one of the ropes when the kid who had been screaming at him lunged and grabbed his hand and with the help of several of his friends pried open Gil's fingers and liberated the knife. The kid held the knife up in the air as if it were a trophy and then threw it down onto the statue's granite base and stomped on it. He was looking down when Gil grabbed his two-by-two and hit him hard on the top of the head. The kid looked up, said "Ow!" in a chuckling tone, as if the blow had been a pathetic gesture, and then Gil hit him again, straight down on the collarbone and driving a splinter into his neck.

Gil took a step back, still holding his makeshift club, readying himself to swing at the inevitable next assailant. But they were all on him at once, grabbing the lumber out of his hand, knocking his feet out from under him. He landed hard on his elbow. He felt one solid punch below his ear but the rest of the blows were ill-aimed or ill-timed or perhaps halfhearted. By the time he scrambled to his feet they had turned their attention to the Pawnee Scout, which was now inching out of its base, the four deep threaded pins that had held it there exposed and bending, until it sprang free and went tumbling across the grass and into the street.

"Somebody go into that hardware store and get some sledgehammers!" he heard someone say.

The mob was in motion again, answering the call for sledgehammers or racing down the street after Gil's statue. They were going to pound it into bits and there was nothing he could do. It was just a pile of metal that had been defaced and seized by a mob, of no more concern to them than the windows they were smashing or the building they had set aflame, just a piece of junk that its creator had tried haplessly to defend.

He turned away from the street and looked down at the empty granite base as if he were staring at his own unmarked tomb. And then, as an afterthought, somebody running past cracked him on the head with some kind of club. As he fell, the ground sprang up at him and struck him with the force of a slamming door. It knocked the air out of his lungs and put his conscious mind in suspension. He stared in confusion at the burning courthouse, trying to remember where he was and what had gone wrong.

THREE

His concussed brain was healthy again, though it continued to emit unexpected pulses of anxiety and melancholy. The hinge of his jaw was still damaged somehow. It hurt just to open his mouth to brush his teeth, and each yawn he could not suppress was a painful event. But all the bruises and cuts were healed, and the bursa that had formed on his elbow had been successfully drained and no longer troubled him.

But the loss of the Pawnee Scout was a deep and lasting wound. It had been his finest work, equal to anything J. Q. A. Ward or even Saint-Gaudens had done, and if there were any real justice in the corrupted tribunals of art this personal judgment would have been recognized by the world. The statue's molds were still in storage in the foundry but he could not trick himself into thinking the city of Omaha or the Knights of Ak-Sar-Ben would have the funds to have it recast and reassembled, not when the city was just emerging from martial law and the courthouse and half the storefronts would need to be rebuilt. And the chances that he could come up with that kind of money himself, at a time when major commissions were scarce and his own reputation uncertain, were faint.

The statue was gone forever and there was nothing to do but face the fact and move on. That was what he was doing today, training his hopes forward as he sat in a parlor car of the Texas and Pacific Railway. The landscape, in its drab infinity, was not helping his mood. It mocked the basic human longing for scenery. Blank cultivated fields alternated with stretches of waste ground that were distinguished only by choking tangles of mesquite and stands of cactus, with now and then a dead coyote strung by its heels along the fence line.

Gil took a handwritten letter out of his pocket and read through it again as he sipped the afternoon cup of coffee the porter had just brought. Then he swiveled in his club chair of green velvet to face his daughter.

"He says nothing in here about a horse."

Maureen looked up from her *Saturday Evening Post* and held out her hand for the letter.

"He stresses the point—" she started to reply, then paused as the sound of the steam whistle through the open window threatened to drown out her voice. "He stresses the point that the boy was an excellent horseman."

"Well, if he wants an equestrian statue he may very well not know he's going to pay double."

"He must have money, Daddy. Otherwise he'd have put us in a day coach and we'd be breathing in soot all the way to Abilene."

"There's nothing easy about a horse. Saint-Gaudens himself had to farm the horse for his Sherman out to A. P. Proctor."

"If a horse is required, you'll do it better than anybody."

He took off his reading glasses and smiled at her, somewhat skeptically, testing whether this was a sincere compliment or just her acerbic recognition that it was time to brace him up. She returned the smile in the same spirit. She was thirty-two, unmarried, unlikely to be. She was a talented sculptress in her own right, though her ambitions in that direction were so deeply withheld from her father—perhaps even from herself—that they amounted to a kind of secret. Maureen had been his studio assistant since she was a teenager and with her mother's death last year she had taken on the role of housekeeper and bookkeeper and emotional advocate as well. When he had returned to San Antonio from Omaha, it had fallen to his daughter to talk him through his despair, to reassure him of the great opportunities still to come, of his monumental works that still stood in public places throughout the country.

"Well," he said as he folded the letter and returned it to the pocket of his suit, "we will find what we will find, I suppose."

She picked up her magazine again and continued to read. If only she had taken after Victoria, Gil thought guiltily to himself for the thousandth time as he covertly studied his daughter's face. His late wife had been his model for many years. It had been her proud jaw and straight nose and unvanquished shining beauty that had animated a dozen or more of his statues, every spirit of Columbia or Democracy or Liberty, every pioneer woman or musket-loading helpmeet. But it had been mostly Gil's features Maureen had inherited, not Victoria's. She did not have her mother's sweeping brow or clear green eyes, and her build—dense and strong like his own, but without his commanding height—suggested power more than fashionable grace.

In New York there had been one or two disillusioning episodes that had never, so far as he or Victoria had been able to tell, risen to the level of love affairs; and when they had first moved to San Antonio six years ago Maureen's heart had been shattered by a young assistant city manager who had courted her indifferently and moved on. Lately there was an English professor from the University of Texas who wore a cowboy hat and a Palm Beach suit and showed up in San Antonio every now and then from Austin to take her to the pictures, but the visits were irregular and often without notice, and if there was anything serious developing Maureen had taken pains to keep it from her father.

The worry that he and Victoria had shared over Maureen's happiness had fallen now to him alone, and it was another burden he carried with him on this train journey deep into the bewitching nothingness of West Texas.

Outside the window, though, the emerging twilight was finally teasing out the allure of the landscape. There were low ranges of hills now, slight but seductive in the failing light, and the scrappy vegetation looked almost sumptuous. He watched a jackrabbit sprinting along near the railbed, the light shining through the parchment skin of its gigantic ears.

"Should we have an early dinner?" Maureen asked after a while. Several of the families that were apparently traveling all the way to California were now heading toward the dining car.

"Don't we arrive at eight?" he said. "Why not just wait and have a steak at the hotel? They're bound to have a good steak in Abilene."

There was indeed a good steak, though by the time they had collected their baggage and walked across the street to the Grace Hotel—

where Mr. Clayton, the man they had come to meet, had made a reservation in their name—they barely made it to the dining room before it closed. Gil was agreeably hungry but he noticed Maureen's appetite was indifferent, and the imagination of the kitchen did not extend past the colossal slab of beef on her plate. She applied herself mostly to the green beans, which had come out of a can but were not terribly overcooked.

"Not such a bad hotel for a cowtown," Gil remarked as he surveyed the elegant marble floors and glanced sympathetically at the attentive white-jacketed waiter who was doing a manly job of not expressing disappointment at the arrival of new customers when the kitchen was about to close.

Maureen agreed that it was surprisingly acceptable. They had both been expecting something squalid and dusty, a town equal to the no-account spaces they had seen outside the train window. But the impression Gil had of Abilene in the brief walk from the train station was of a city of wide streets and stolid office buildings in a brave little downtown cluster.

"I should go back through my Italian sketchbooks," he said, surrendering his plate to the waiter to make room for a slice of chocolate cake. "I once spent an afternoon in Padua in front of that Donatello equestrian—what's it called? Something unpronounceable."

"Gattamelata."

"Yes, Gattamelata. I don't see how anybody could do a better horse. Of course, it's a massive old-world sort of beast, not some cowboy pony. Maybe I should buy a horse to use as a model."

"First let's see if Mr. Clayton even wants this to be an equestrian statue," she said sensibly. "And then let's see if he has the money to actually pay for it."

Gil gave her a mock frown. He finished his cake, sipped his coffee, felt some of his vital spirit returning for no perceptible reason. Worrying about his daughter, grieving over his wife, still sore in tendon and soul over the loss of his statue, he could not deny the expansive mood that was stealing over him in this shutting-down hotel restaurant in Abilene, Texas. He generally still traveled with the enthusiasm of a boy leaving home for the first time, and here he was in a place he had never expected to visit, a place that held no charm for tourists but certainly plenty of other things that would be of interest to men of serious purpose. More than that, there was the prospect of real work ahead, not just paying work but the promise of the yet-unencountered subject, the yet-unformed clay.

AT BREAKFAST the next morning a man approached their table and said that Mr. Clayton had sent him into town to pick them up and drive them out to the "place." He introduced himself as Ernest, which Gil thought an unlikely name for a cowboy. But he was unmistakably a cowboy. His hair had been creased all the way around the circumference of his head by the tight fit of his hat, so that bareheaded—as he was now, deferentially twirling the brim of his hat in his hands—he looked like a threaded jar without a lid.

"Sit down and have some breakfast with us," Gil said.

"Well sir, thank you. I just might do that. I already had breakfast but I guess another one won't hurt me none."

He ordered eggs and biscuits and something called redeye gravy. He had a wide, eager smile and a rather sloping chin and was missing a thumb on his left hand. He wore jeans and a clean work shirt with a frayed notebook and a pencil poking up out of the breast pocket. When his breakfast came he ate with sloppy enjoyment. Gil supposed he was about forty, though his face was so deeply weathered he could have been much older.

"It ain't but a little over twenty miles," he was saying. "Shouldn't take us even an hour to get there."

He turned to Maureen. "Might be a little dusty, ma'am, but I got a couple dusters in the back of the car so you won't ruin those nice clothes."

"That's thoughtful," she said. "Thank you."

"What can you tell us about this statue that Mr. Clayton has in mind?" Gil asked.

"Oh, I better let Mr. Clayton himself tell you about that. He got it in his head to have a statue of his boy, is all I know."

"And you knew the boy yourself, I suppose?"

"Oh, yes sir," Ernest answered, looking down into his coffee cup while his face took on a faint, fleeting somberness. "We all knew the boy."

•

THEY DROVE through the downtown streets and through Abilene's outlying neighborhoods and past a few desolate-looking diners and then onto a dirt road leading to nothing.

Maureen rode in the backseat, sitting forward, listening as her father quizzed Ernest about rainfall and annual cotton yields and varieties of cattle. It was his interviewing voice, his open-handed man-of-the-world demeanor, so different from the private working silence into which he disappeared once a piece was truly under way. Even now she could detect the subtle onset of that feverish distraction. As Ernest talked, her father moved his fingers slightly, unconsciously kneading the air above his lap. This meant, she knew, that he was working already, with nothing to go by: no photographs, no description, no knowledge of whether there was to be a horse included or not. Out of nothing, he was creating a statue of a dead boy.

She shifted her attention to Ernest's own hands, splayed tight like a frog's feet on the big steering wheel. She didn't realize she was staring at Ernest's missing thumb until he took his hand off the steering wheel and held it up to her face with a grin.

"Caught it in a dally when I was workin' a steer," he said. "Popped right off like a bottle cap."

"I'm sorry," Maureen shouted over the grinding motor. "I hope you don't think I'm being rude."

"No, ma'am. I stare at it myself sometimes when I ain't got nothin' else to look at."

She nodded, and mouthed silently to her amused father: "What's a dally?"

They drove on into a subtly changing landscape, the flat agricultural terrain giving way to rhythmic dips and swells that grew more pronounced in the bluish distances, though the far-off hills were not nearly as emphatic as the lovely rock balustrades that loomed above a wonderland of clear creeks west of San Antonio.

When at last Ernest shifted gears and turned off the main road, warning them to hang on as they turned onto a rutted, semi-maintained track, dispiriting doubts started to creep into Maureen's mind, and she could see that her father shared them. She would have assumed a wealthy rancher would mark the edge of his property with an arch or decorative column of some sort, at any rate something more imposing than a beat-up mailbox. The poor road was another bad sign. They swayed back and forth in the hard seats as Ernest navigated around the ruts for another five or six miles, following the road as it led between two shallow peaks and then alongside a creek with barely more than an inch or two of water flowing above a broken limestone bed as smooth as paving blocks.

The ranch house and outbuildings finally came into sight after the road veered off onto higher ground. Gil and Maureen exchanged cautious looks. It was not much of a house, just a fortress-like main room of stacked stone to which a long peaked-roof wing appeared to have been more or less randomly appended. A man stood on the porch, watching the truck drive up. At his feet sat an unlikely ranch dog, a chubby gray-muzzled dachshund. As the car approached, the man climbed stiffly down the stairs and walked out to the edge of a parched circle of grass that marked the end of the caliche drive. He stood there bareheaded, his hands stashed in the back pockets of his trousers, his head cocked, staring at the approaching vehicle as if awaiting not a pair of invited visitors but some dreaded decree of fate.

Gil stepped out of the car and said hello and offered his hand. Lamar Clayton took it and looked back at Gil with an assessing stare and a faint smile that could have been either an expression of welcome or the manifestation of a private judgment. Gil judged he was a decade or so older than himself, a quiet old man with an air of grave self-possession, the tough skin of his face marked by a network of wrinkles and deep vertical creases.

His expression brightened as he greeted Maureen, but he did not have much to say to her besides hello. Maybe the self-possession was just shyness, Gil thought, the evasive, deflective manner of an old rancher unused to being around women. Nevertheless, there was something commanding about his stillness, his patient assumption that it should be others who speak first and say the most.

"Ernest treat you folks all right?" Clayton said, with a sly glance at his hired man, who was already hauling their luggage into the house.

"We were in excellent hands," Gil replied. "And we've arrived at a beautiful place."

"Oh, I don't know about beautiful," Clayton said, "but I ain't got tired of it yet. We get a nice breeze from across the creek there this time of year, and the north wind don't bother us too much in the winter, since we're down here in a kind of draw."

He paused, as if he were planning to reflect some more on the favorable location of the ranch house, but it was just a stalled silence.

"Anyway," he said, rallying to the conversation again, "come on in. George's Mary ought to about have our supper on."

If there was a reason she was called George's Mary—something beyond the obvious assumption that it was to distinguish her from someone else's Mary—nobody explained it as they sat down to eat in the narrow parlor. George's Mary, Gil supposed, was close to his own age, a stout woman in stout shoes and a faded print dress, who set various platters down upon the table with no comment and then disappeared into the kitchen to put a pie into the oven. Was she Clayton's wife? Unlikely. He didn't know much about the mores of ranch life in Texas but he assumed the woman of the house would at least preside over her own dinner table.

Ernest, the one loquacious member of the household, had disappeared to the bunkhouse, so it was just the two of them sitting there, spooning fried beef and potatoes onto their plates and trying to carry on a conversation with no great assistance from their host. It seemed to be Lamar Clayton's attitude that dinner was for eating, and Maureen's dutiful openers—what lovely china, what wonderfully airy biscuits—were met with that same polite half smile and maybe a word or two of explication. The china, he allowed, had been one of his wife's great treasures.

The "had been" confirmed it: dead wife, dead son, lonely inward old man.

"Get out of here, Peggy," Clayton said without conviction to the dog, who stationed herself by his chair and spent almost the entire meal reared up on her hind legs with unnerving persistence, looking less like a dachshund than a vigilant prairie dog. Despite Clayton's surly commands for her to leave, he kept tossing small pieces of meat onto the floor at her feet, which of course only reinforced her commonsense determination to stay where she was.

Gil had no problem with silence when decorum or gravitas called for it, so he followed Clayton's lead and mostly forgot about conversation as he finished his meal. Maureen did so as well, though clearly she was unimpressed with all this manly forswearing of talk, this solemn chewing. It was not until George's Mary cleared the plates and served them buttermilk pie and coffee that Clayton looked up from his plate and seemed to understand that it was time for something to be said.

"She makes a pretty good pie, I always thought."

"Excellent," Gil said, smiling in George's Mary's direction as she hurried off once more into the kitchen.

"Everything was excellent," Maureen jumped in. "It was a gorgeous meal."

Clayton nodded his head and ran his hand across his full head of wavy white hair. There was another beat of silence during which he seemed to be deliberating about what to say next. Gil could hear the ticking of the mantel clock, the creak of the windmill across the yard.

"Well, now, about this statue," Clayton finally said. "I guess you're interested or you wouldn't be here."

"I'm interested," Gil answered. "But of course I'd like to know a bit more about what you have in mind."

Clayton folded up his napkin; he picked up a crumb of piecrust from the table and put it back on his plate.

"Ben—that's my son—was killed over in France. Some little town somewhere called Saint-Étienne. I looked it up on a map of France over at the library in Albany, but there's more than one Saint-Étienne in that country and I couldn't find the one I was looking for. It ain't but a hundred miles or so from Paris, over on the western front. Anyway, they buried him in this Saint-Étienne, pretty much where it happened as I understand, and then he and a bunch of the other boys got moved to a big American cemetery they started up over there. They asked me did I want to bring him home—they said they'd do that for me—but I didn't take to the thought for some reason. Didn't like the idea of bothering him again, I guess. Didn't want to think of that. Maybe that's a little strange."

"Of course it's not," Maureen said to him.

"Anyway, I just thought if I had a statue of Ben, if I had a likeness of him, not just a picture, something I could . . ."

He gripped the edge of the table with his hands and sat there tensely for a moment, forcing back his emotions.

"I seen your statues in San Antone, Mr. Gilheaney, like I wrote you," Clayton went on when he found his voice again. "The Alamo one, of course, and that one you did of that Cabeza de Vaca fella. I don't know much about statues but I seen plenty that I didn't think were any good. Yours have got something special to them. The people seem alive."

"I do my best to make them seem that way. Do you have an idea of where the sculpture would be situated?"

"Oh, yes sir, I got that all picked out. There was a place that Ben liked pretty well, and I reckon that's where it ought to be."

"I should like to see it."

"I'll take you there, if you and Miss Gilheaney don't mind bouncing in the car a little more."

"And I wonder what you have in the way of photographs of your son."

"I got a few," he said, and stood up and walked in his shuffling, stove-up gait into another part of the house, the dog following behind. While he was gone, Gil glanced at his daughter, who simply shrugged, her eyebrows lifted in a wait-and-see expression. George's Mary came in to collect their dessert plates. There was a teary sheen to her eyes but her manner was brisk and silent.

"Everything was delicious," Maureen told her.

"Well, Mr. Clayton ain't too hard to please," she said, "long as I burn his steak till it's tough as a boot." She lowered her voice almost to a whisper. "You'd think a man who lived all that time with the Indians would like his meat on the rare side."

"He lived with the—" But before Gil could finish the question Clayton had come shuffling back, holding a high school yearbook.

He opened the yearbook to a bookmarked page and set it on the table in front of Gil. Maureen moved her chair closer to her father as the two of them studied the photo of Ben. It made no impression: neither handsome nor interestingly ugly, just another in a rank of young men looking indifferently at the camera, their hair tightly combed, synthetic half smiles on their lips, their thoughts hidden.

"There's another one of him on the baseball team, but you can't hardly see him in it," Clayton said, as he turned to the next bookmarked page, where Ben stood in the rear rank of a team grouping, the cap on his head obscuring his face.

"And then we got these Kodaks here," Clayton said. There were a half dozen of them, small and wrinkled from much handling. They were a little better. One photo showed the boy standing with an elegant-looking woman who, Gil supposed, had been his mother. Another had him posing with some of his fellow soldiers, their arms interlocked as they smiled at the camera in front of their barracks.

"That one's at Camp Bowie," the old man said. "Not too long before they shipped out."

Gil and Maureen studied it a moment more and then went on to look at the others. Only one of them showed Ben by himself, and from that one they could get an idea of his bearing and proportions. Though solidly built, he had not been tall, perhaps a few inches shorter than his father and with an apparently unarresting face—the jawline neither particularly firm nor soft, the features regular but not remarkably so. But his smile, in the photo in front of the barracks, was electric in some frustrating way Gil could not pin down. There was some inner quality that seemed to override his features, that made their impact secondary. It was the same with Lamar Clayton himself. Ever since he had met the old man, Gil had been almost unconsciously puzzling over how one could reveal, in clay, that face's hidden burden of experience and sorrow. If he had been handsome, it would have been easy, because handsome faces were built for the display of sweeping emotions. Gil's own wife's powerful face, which he had used so many times as a model for mournful or triumphant women, was an unfailing scaffold for whatever noble mood needed to be set upon it. By contrast, he thought, he could sculpt Maureen for the rest of his life and never truly capture her, never be able to make her bland exterior light up with the complex fire he knew burned within.

"These are all the pictures you have?" he asked Clayton when he and Maureen had shuffled through the few imperfect images several times.

"Yes sir, that's pert' near it."

"I have to be honest, Mr. Clayton. It's not a lot for me to go on. But of course I'd certainly do my best. And I feel that at this point, before we go too much further, I should be honest with you as well about the cost of such a project."

"Well, a statue's a permanent thing. I don't expect they come cheap. How much?"

"I can't give you an answer just at the moment. My daughter and I will have to talk about it. And a lot will depend on whether the statue would be just of your son, or whether you would want it to include some other element, a horse, say, or—"

"Oh, his horse would have to be part of it. Ben would be in the saddle, the way I see it in my mind."

"Well, of course that would considerably—"

"I understand your point. You're the experts, you and Miss Gilheaney. You think about it a while and give me a price and we'll talk about it. In the meantime didn't I hear you say you wanted to see where the statue was gonna be?"

FOUR

Clayton drove them himself, taking them deeper into the ranch along an increasingly problematic road. The little dachshund stood imperiously in his lap and stared out at the passing sights with quivering absorption.

"A motorcar ain't the best way to get back up in here," he told them. "But I didn't expect you folks was comfortable on horseback."

"Comfortable enough," Gil said, bluffing a little.

"Daddy is," Maureen said, looking a little pale from the irrhythmic jostling of the car, "but I'm afraid the spectacle of me on a horse would be a comical sight to Mr. Clayton."

"Well," Clayton said, "I bet the sight of me trying to make a statue would beat it."

At last he pulled to a stop and turned off the motor. They were in a broad, shady declivity above a dry streambed. Off in the distance stood a modestly imposing grouping of flat-topped hills that seemed as evanescent as a thunderhead.

Clayton drew their attention to a gradual rocky slope leading upward from the side of the road.

"This is the highest point on the ranch," he said. "But as you can see, it ain't that high. Won't take us but a minute to climb it, if you're ready."

"Lead on," Gil told him.

A horse trail led up the flank of the hill, and in ten minutes they were at its broad mesa summit, looking out over a landscape that should not have been spectacular but somehow was. The view was uninterrupted by any man-made feature, and the terrain almost pastoral in its overall sweep despite its jagged and thorny components. The sky was clear. It was startlingly vibrant, the vast reach of it as bright and blue as a solid shell, but with a limitless transparency, so that the longer Gil looked at it the deeper it drew him in. A buzzard teetered silently above them, the fringe-like feathers at the ends of its wings clearly individuated, standing out from the brilliant sky vault with a stereopticon sharpness. A few dozen head of white-faced cattle drifted along by the flank of another hill a half mile away, grazing on a thin carpet of wild grass. Gil heard some skyborne bird's sharp whistle—not the buzzard but some unseen eagle or hawk. Otherwise there was nothing but tantalizing silence until Clayton decided to speak.

"This is the place," he said. "It ain't the easiest spot to put a statue, I know that, and I expect to pay the cost of that too. But this was Ben's place. Sarey and me—that was his mother—we used to bring him up here for picnics when he was little. And when he was in a brooding frame of mind—after his mother died, or when he was home on leave right before they shipped him out—he'd tend to saddle his horse and ride off. He never told me where it was he was going, but I'm pretty sure this was the place. Anyway, it's where I want to remember him being."

"It's a fitting spot, Mr. Clayton," Gil said. "Very fitting."

The little dog wandered determinedly across the summit, her tail wagging at the prospect of discovery. Every once in a while, when she was probing too deeply into a burrow or an overhung rock that might have housed a rattlesnake, Clayton gave a low whistle and she backed off and looked up at him, whimpering.

Meanwhile Gil paced off the ground and made notes of the distances in a small sketchbook.

"The sun rises here, I would think," he said to Clayton, gesturing to the summit of the hill to their east.

"Pretty close."

"And how cold will it get in the winter?"

"Can't hardly predict. Down past fifteen or so if the right norther decides to come on through."

"I don't see a road down there."

"Ain't none."

"So who's going to see the statue?"

"I am."

Gil thought about this, then turned back to Clayton.

"Perhaps you and Maureen could wait in the car for me."

"Why?"

"He likes to be alone at this stage," Maureen explained to Clayton. "To get his bearings, so to speak."

"All right. Let him get his bearings."

Gil watched as the old rancher led his daughter back down the hill, his hand hovering beneath her elbow with touching solicitude as the little dog ranged ahead of them.

Left to himself, Gil took out his sketchbook and studied the dimensions he had written down. He stared once again at the open landscape—open but secretive, because it was so far removed from any human habitation or byway. Placing a statue on this hilltop, a site undefined by pedestrians or vehicular patterns, by buildings, by conventional sight lines, by any expectations whatsoever, made no logical sense. And that was what began to stir his interest. It was a deluded, heartbroken dream of a commission, not so much a statue as an apparition. But here was a real chance, he thought, a chance to create a monument that was not carefully ushered into being by committees of city fathers or boards of directors or clubwomen, but by one man's private grief. The challenge for Gil would be to create a piece that could somehow command this summit without calling attention to itself.

But did the old man really have the money? He wrote down some quick calculations in his sketchbook—the value of his time, the cost of materials, the fees to models and plasterers and foundry workers and stonecutters and the workmen who would be required to erect the statue and its base in this remote location. The amount came to almost twenty thousand dollars. He could do it for less, of course; he could factor in less profit for himself. He was not rich, but since moving to San Antonio, he was getting by. There were fewer commissions after the war and they were going to younger men now, or to the so-called modern artists, or to talentless blowhards who got by on nothing but flattery and connections—or simply to the monument dealers who had gotten into the business and were now trying to sell every town square in America a knockoff statue of a grenade-flinging doughboy.

Standing alone on top of this mesa, he felt all of that irritating competition drop away as his excitement about this project grew. The inexpressible thing that had raised the Pawnee Scout to true art could be coaxed forth from this piece as well. He knew it could. He had been in this business a long time and knew what it meant to be stirred in this way, aware that there was some effect, some emotion, as yet unseen and ungrasped, waiting to be revealed. It was his skill and his labor that would reveal it. He was the man for this peculiar monument, this lonely bronze eulogy in the middle of nowhere.

LAMAR CLAYTON was not the sort of man who needed company, and Maureen felt awkward standing by the car with him while her father performed his solitary conjuring act at the top of the mesa. She watched Mr. Clayton roll a cigarette with a bewitching economy of movement and then absorb himself in his smoking, in his calm, unstudied silence. It was social habit, more than awkwardness, that finally compelled her to get him to speak. She asked him to tell her about his wife.

"Ain't a whole hell of a lot to tell," he said. "Her proper name was Sarah but she went by Sarey to pert' near everybody. She was younger than me by twenty years, a hell of a lot more polish to her. She grew up on a ranch near Sweetwater but she'd spent a summer or two in San Francisco when she was a girl. There was some family out there, an aunt who was married to a Portuguese man. He'd been in the whaling business, as I understand it. Sarey had me about half talked into taking her out there to visit them when she came down with the cancer. She was close to forty years of age when she died."

"I'm very sorry to hear it," Maureen said.

"Oh hell, no point in complaining about such things. Ben was still pretty young when she got sick, just eleven or twelve or so. I reckon I did about the best I could with him. But I keep thinking about how I might have done better. Just looking at those Kodaks today, I thought about how if his mother had been alive she would have made sure there'd been a lot more pictures."

"It's clear he was a fine-looking young man."

"He got the better part of his looks from his mother, that's for sure. And his easy nature too. I guess you and your father already figured out I ain't all that comfortable talking to people."

He looked at her out of the corner of his eye with a sly half smile. He was, she thought, serenely bashful. And sad, of course. The death of his son had obviously crushed him, and she suspected he was too old to rise from such a blow. The statue itself was clearly enough a symptom of that, one of those desperate and defiant things that grieving people did when simply moving on was too much to bear. There was a part of her that wanted to talk him out of it, to spare him all the expense and what was certain to be a final, resounding revelation that death was more triumphant than bronze.

"So you help your dad out with his statues?" Mr. Clayton asked as he stared up at the summit, where her father, out of sight, was still deliberating.

"Yes, a piece of this size is quite an operation, as I'm sure you can imagine. I pitch in wherever I'm needed, though it's a point of pride to him that the actual modeling is his alone."

His matter-of-fact nod left her unsettled somehow. There was very little in his world, apparently, that needed to be commented upon. She was used to talkier men. Her father, when not absorbed in the quietude of his work, was a natural conversationalist. Vance Martindale, on the unannounced occasions when he swooped into San Antonio from Austin, would bombard her over dinner with opinions on *Sonnets from the Portuguese* or *Sartor Resartus* or the abject philistinism of the Texas State Legislature. The silence that surrounded Lamar Clayton should have seemed like a natural barrier, but in fact it drew her in, and in an odd way was more revealing than speech.

She watched as Peggy sniffed around at the perimeter of a stand of cactus. The dog looked up and happened to catch Mr. Clayton's disapproving eye and then trotted back on her stubby legs to stand next to his boots. In a moment, with a slight nod, he released her with a warning.

"She's not what I would have pictured for a ranch dog," Maureen said.

"Me neither. Peggy was my wife's idea. She wanted some sort of creature around the ranch that didn't have to earn its keep, that could just sort of be. Ben and that little dog got to be pretty close after Sarey died. Now I guess she just puts up with me."

The dog woofed and the hair along her spine turned dark with alarm, but it was only Maureen's father coming back down from the hill, scattering loose rocks as he walked. Moses coming down the mountain, Maureen thought. His eyes were alight with that familiar charge of creative discovery she had known from her girlhood, those magic moments when he was always at his happiest—the time when pure inspiration was flooding through his mind, before the frustration of real work set in.

"Mr. Clayton," he called out, "I would very much like to meet your son's horse."

LAMAR CLAYTON stood leaning against the corral fence as the sculptor busied himself with studying the little chestnut pony. Gilheaney had taken a tape measure from his jacket pocket and had his daughter help him as he measured off the animal's height and girth and the length of its head. Then Miss Gilheaney walked around in a circle taking pictures with a Brownie. Poco didn't like the snap of the shutter and he was suspicious of these strangers and didn't trust their intentions. He calmed down some when Lamar walked over to him and put his hand on his neck and told him to hush.

Lamar wasn't sure the horse had the wrong idea about Gilheaney. There was something about the sculptor's methodical inspection of Poco that Lamar found irritating, or maybe threatening. Like he wasn't just measuring the horse but taking him over in his mind. Gilheaney was a big enough man he could have been a statue of himself, over six feet tall and framey and turned out in an expensive-looking suit. He was big-headed, with steely hair that he parted in the middle and kept short on the sides, the kind of man who always looked like he'd just walked out of a barbershop. But to judge from his hands, his blunt, powerful fingers, you would have thought he'd grown up doing ranch work. He had a look in his eye that saw into you, or past you, or to somewhere you weren't expecting him to be looking.

"He's mostly a night horse," Clayton said. He felt the need to reclaim the horse somehow from the sculptor's scrutiny. "He's clean-footed and Ben used to say he could see in the dark like a bat. Ben loved this ol' horse."

"He's a fine animal, that's plain to see," Gil replied absently, stepping back to study the horse as Maureen clicked away with the Brownie. As the creature's proportions became clearer to him, he was preoccupied with an emerging artistic challenge. The impression he had from the photos of Ben Clayton was of a muscular young man, with a solid torso and wide shoulders. Since this figure would be sitting atop a diminutive working pony, he did not want the boy to appear to be riding a donkey. On the other hand, he was excited by Poco's musculature and comportment, his pared-down authority. It was more important for the statue to appear real than heroic, but achieving that authentic end would require levels of artifice Gil had yet to gauge.

He turned to Clayton. "What about Ben's clothes?"

"His clothes?"

"Do you still have them?"

"Some of them. What do you want his clothes for?"

"I'll need to get as accurate an idea of his size as I can. They would be very useful, if you don't object."

"Hell, I ain't got no reason to object," Clayton said.

But the old man looked particularly sorrowful, Maureen observed an hour later, as George's Mary brought out the boy's laundered and folded clothes and set them on the dining room table. She put down a pair of boots as well, and a battered sweat-stained hat.

"What did he wear mostly around the ranch?" Gil asked.

Clayton picked up one of the khaki-colored work shirts, frayed at the cuffs and with one of the pocket flaps half torn off.

"I'd say this one here if I had to guess," he said.

"You don't have to guess," George's Mary said. "That was his favorite shirt. I ought to know. I washed it about a thousand times."

"And this hat? This is what he wore on the ranch?"

"Mostly," Clayton said. "He pretty much stuck to that one hat after his head stopped growing. I remember he picked it out when we were at the dry goods store in Abilene."

Gil lifted up the hat. It was high-crowned, the sweatband half-unstitched, the brim rolled up just a bit on the sides where the boy had absently shaped it through years of use. The underside of the hat brim presented another sculptural issue, since to a viewer looking up from below it ran the risk of being a boring flat surface.

"Mr. Clayton," Gil asked, "may I borrow this?"

"The hat?"

"The hat, shirt, trousers, boots . . . everything. Unless you object."

"We'll take excellent care of them," Maureen said. "And return them, of course."

"All right," the old man said after a moment or two. "Hell, pack them up and take them along with you."

THE EVENING MEAL turned out to be a livelier proposition than their solemn luncheon. Lamar Clayton still presided mostly in silence, but this time they were joined by Ernest and another hand, a cheerful, always smoking man who seemed to have survived thirty or so years with the daunting name of Anaxagorus Jackson. "Don't worry," Ernest said, as he made the introductions, "we can't pronounce it neither, so we just call him Nax."

Nax smiled and buttered his baked potato with a cigarette still dangling from his mouth. He sat next to Ernest, and the longitudinal axis of his head—enhanced by a steeply receding hairline—made a somehow harmonious contrast to the foreman's squashed-together features. Gil guessed that this was the way it usually was, Clayton and the hands eating together and talking about screwworm treatments and fence repairs and the working agenda for the next day. The private lunch with him and Maureen had been an exception.

After George's Mary served coffee, the hands sat around chewing on their toothpicks for another twenty minutes or so and then retired to the bunkhouse. It was barely dark. Gil was restless, as he always was at the end of the day when he was away from his studio. At home, it was his habit to work until eleven or so at night, when he could at last exhaust his churning physical and mental energy and go to bed.

"So why do you need his clothes?" Clayton suddenly asked, just when Gil thought the old man was about to fall asleep in his chair.

"For my model. I'll have to find a young man of your son's general size."

"Somebody else is going to wear Ben's clothes?"

"It would make the piece that much more authentic."

Clayton took another sip of coffee, mutely agreeing, though clearly still troubled by the idea of another boy in his son's clothes.

"I'll have a sketch for you in the morning," Gil said. "Then, if you approve the initial concept, I'll make a maquette."

"A maquette. That like a model of it or something?"

"Exactly. A three-dimensional clay miniature. Assuming you approve that, I would then go to work on a scale model and then on the final sculpture itself."

"What's your best price for all of this?" Clayton said. He glanced at Maureen as he asked the question, giving her a faint smile, as if in apology that they had embarked upon some tedious manly subject in which she would have to indulge them.

Gil shot a look at Maureen as well, allied with her in a wordless deliberation about the old man's ability to finance such a project. The twenty-thousand-dollar figure he had roughly calculated on top of the mesa would have been more than a fair price for the client he had imagined when he first received Lamar Clayton's letter—a remote, lordly cattle baron who simply sought out the best of everything without regard to cost. But the evidence of this gloomy ranch house, and the gloomy mood in it, threw him into a hurried revision.

"The cost will be sixteen thousand dollars," he said. "That is a complete price that includes the statue, pedestal, any necessary engraving, and the erection of the work under my supervision."

Clayton looked away for a moment at the blank wall—thinking it over, or pretending to.

"All right," he finally said, without much joy but without any apparent resentment. "It's a deal. You make me up an invoice and tell me how much money you want up front. The sooner you get started on this thing the better I'd like it."

"Good," Gil said. "From my end, the timing is excellent."

"You want to know the truth, I thought it'd cost me double that."

HE SPENT THAT NIGHT in the boy's room, one of the two rooms that formed the original stone core of the house. There was a single small window through which he could see a hazy full moon that looked like a giant dissolving aspirin tablet high in the West

Texas sky. On either side of the window, at shoulder height, were two indentations that passed all the way through the thick wall, funneling down to small circles that were open to the night air. It took Gil a minute or two to puzzle out what they were: shooting holes, to fight off Comanches during the not-so-distant days of the Indian wars.

Ben Clayton's saddle sat on a sawhorse on one end of the room. It seemed a bit old-fashioned in a way Gil did not have the expertise to judge, something to do with the straight, high-backed cantle. There was no ornamentation, no silver inlays or intricate tooling, just solid leather. The working saddle of an earnest, unaffected young man, a plainspoken American martyr. Or perhaps that was the way Gil was already seeing his subject because he preferred to think of his own style, and hence his own substance, as unadorned as well. No simpering cherubs commenting from the ether, no bombast or symbolic blather, a minimum of the decorative vines and garlands that were known in the trade as "spinach." He would use this saddle in the statue, of course, not merely for its authenticity but for the pleasure it would give him to sculpt something so austere and worn.

When Lamar Clayton had shown him to his room after dinner, he had pointed out the saddle and the other vestiges of his son's life that he had been too paralyzed with sadness to do anything with but leave in place. A picture of Ben's mother and father's wedding day rested in a silver frame on an empty spool that had served as the dead boy's end table. In the photograph, Lamar was twenty years younger and a few pounds heavier, his hair streaked with gray but not yet white. But there was no more buoyancy in his expression than there had been at the dinner table tonight. He must have been fifty in this photograph, Gil supposed. Why had he taken so long to marry?

His new wife, dressed in a traveling suit, her hand gripping the crook of his arm, was slender and winning, beaming at the camera as if she were in possession of a wonderful secret about her dour husband. It was a better-quality likeness of Ben's mother than the one Clayton had shown them earlier, and it made Gil rueful to think about how the only people in this little family with a glint of vivacity were now dead.

By the light of the kerosene lamp he sorted through the young man's war memorabilia, scant enough to fit into a shirt box. Most of it seemed to be from his training at Camp Bowie: a pamphlet called

"Songs for the Hike," a blank postcard from the Westbrook Hotel in Fort Worth, displaying a photograph of a not-very-good statue called the Golden Goddess; a "Souvenir Folder of Camp Life," whose cover depicted a group of doughboys engaged in bayonet drill and whose pages were mostly blank. Under "My Division," Ben (Gil assumed it was Ben) had written "36th," and under "My Regiment" he had penciled in "142nd," but after that he must have lost interest or become annoyed at being prompted about what to enter, because the spaces for "My Company" and "My Training Log" were left blank, as were all the rest of the pages.

There were three postcards, all from Camp Bowie. "Dear all," one read, "Well I escaped getting my wisdom teeth pulled by one of the dental students they got here. They said there's no reason to worry about mine. Ortho Cotton got his pulled and now his jaw is swelled up pretty bad. If somebody has the time could you send me that extra quilt after all? These blankets are thin and it would save me having to go buy another one in Fort Worth. How's Poco? Ben."

The other postcards were equally brief and chatty. He enjoyed working in the pit on the rifle range, he was getting pretty tired of hearing the Top's whistle all day long, he finally could manage "right shoulder arms" without knocking his hat off, everybody in his squad had gotten tested for hookworm and passed with flying colors.

And that was all, except for a telegram at the bottom of the box from the Adjutant General's Office deeply regretting to inform Mr. Lamar Clayton that his son Private Benjamin Clayton of the 36th Division, 142nd Infantry Regiment, had been officially reported killed in action near the village of Saint-Étienne-à-Arnes. The telegram was followed by an apologetic letter from the chief of the Graves Registration Service, pledging to inform families as soon as possible "as to the present resting places of their noble dead who glorify the nation's roll of honor."

Lamar Clayton had directed Gil to the shirt box, saying that's where his son's letters were stored. But was this all? Surely the boy had written home from France. Perhaps he had even kept a diary. But Gil could find nothing else. The traces of Ben Clayton's life in this room were sorrowfully palpable, but as a sculptor Gil needed more. He needed to know who this young man had been, and that key knowledge did not seem to be on offer, either in the artifacts surrounding him in this room or in the terse testimony of his father.

Gil wanted his subject to be visible, and it troubled him in an obscure way that an emotional portrait of Ben Clayton had not yet begun to present itself to him. Except, of course, for the profound emotion of loss, the death of promise, which would be the unstated theme of his statue.

From the moment he first stood on top of that mesa he knew that this piece was what he had been searching for. It had the potential to turn his life in Texas from one of artistic exile to one of liberation. Sixteen thousand or twenty thousand dollars didn't matter. This was a theme that had the power to bring forth the greatness he knew was still within his grasp. He was irritated with himself that he had not traveled with a few of his sculpting tools and a block of plastilina, so that he could make a proper three-dimensional sketch. A drawing would have to do for now. He took out his pencils and a pad of paper from his valise and went to work at Ben Clayton's boyhood desk under the imperfect light of the lamp. The statue would be, more than anything, calm. As calm in its way as the beautifully eerie memorial Saint-Gaudens had done for Henry Adams' wife. As a younger man, Gil had once stood in front of Saint-Gaudens' hooded female figure, nearly weeping at its plangent mystery, and at the shivering inspiration that underlay its artistry. He sensed a similar opportunity here, an opportunity for something glorious and enduring.

He sketched rapidly; it was the work of ten minutes. Lamar Clayton's idea of the statue was of Ben on horseback, but Gil swiftly rejected the father's vision and supplanted it with his own: a young man, dismounted in death, standing beside a beloved horse, looking out across the landscape of his childhood. When he was finished, Gil held the drawing closer to the light. It was enough. Not a pencil stroke more. And the finished statue, he knew, would be similarly spare. The challenges were all in the proportions, in the posture of man and horse, in the fidelity and detail of the face.

It was after midnight before he finally turned off the lamp and climbed into the narrow bed upon which Ben Clayton had slept for most of his short life. Moonlight flowed in through the small window and even from the two shooting holes, helping to endow the saddle on the opposite end of the room with a seductive physicality. He heard the profound, reverberant notes of an owl's voice as the bird made its rounds on silent wingbeats from tree to tree around the house. He heard as well the snorting and stamping of horses from the nearby stable, and from the unimaginable distances of the night came the anxious, cascading calls of coyotes. These were the sounds, Gil noted, that would have ushered Ben into sleep from his earliest childhood—so different, surely, from what he had listened to in France during the last nights of his life.

FIVE

Lamar Clayton sat on the porch with the dog in his lap as he pondered the sketch. He was in no hurry to provide a reaction. Gil waited him out, pretending to study the movements of a solitary buzzard in the pale morning sky. Maureen stood against the porch rail, sipping her second cup of coffee from one of the late Mrs. Clayton's delicate china cups.

"That ain't what I had in mind," Clayton finally said. "You got him standing next to Poco, not in the saddle."

"This is a stronger conception."

"I pictured it different."

"I know you did."

"Then why are you arguing with me about what I want?"

"Because I know my business and this is the better approach."

Clayton looked over at Maureen. "What do you think?"

"He could do it the way you suggest," she said, "and it would be very satisfactory, even exceptional. You'd receive fair value for the price you paid. But if you want it to be a work of art, you should allow my father the freedom to make it one."

"I want a good likeness. I don't care about it being no work of art."

"I think you do, Mr. Clayton," Maureen said. "You care about that or you would have hired someone else."

Clayton seemed to take her point, though grudgingly. He looked at the sketch again, then handed it back to Gil.

"All right, you do whatever you want."

"Good. I'll plan on coming back in a month or so with a maquette for your approval."

"That's agreeable." Still in her owner's lap, Peggy twisted over on her back and growled softly until Clayton consented to rub her slick belly. "How much you want to get started?"

"The usual terms are a third on approval of the maquette, a third on approval of the clay, and a third on delivery."

"The clay? What's that?"

"That's the full-size sculpture. I'll make the maquette first, then a scale model, then the finished clay. That's what the plasterer will make a mold of, and in turn the foundry will take the plaster mold and cast it in bronze."

Sensing that this pragmatic cowman would find it of interest, Gil launched into an explanation of the plasterer's process and the lost-wax casting technique that the foundry would employ. He also talked about the pipe fitting and carpentry that would go into the construction of the armature, the stamina involved in hauling buckets of clay or standing for hours at a time at the top of a towering ladder sculpting the features of a monumental face. Clayton leaned forward in his chair, his solemn demeanor eroding a bit as a keen interest began to show in his eyes. He seemed to be regarding the sculptor on his porch as not just an alien conjurer but a man like himself who worked with his hands.

They talked for another twenty minutes while Maureen went inside to pack their things. When it was time for them to leave, Clayton lifted the resentful dog off his lap and rose to shake hands.

"You going to be coming back along with your father, Miss Gilheaney?" Clayton asked Maureen, as Ernest was cranking the balky motor of the car in the dusty driveway.

"If he invites me, Mr. Clayton."

"If I'm doing the paying, I guess I can do the inviting," he said, meeting her eyes for only a moment before looking away shyly. "You come back."

ERNEST HAD JUST DRIVEN off the ranch property onto the main road leading to Abilene when he turned to Gil in the front seat.

"You suppose I could see that drawing you did?"

Gil took the sketch out of his pocket and handed it to him. Ernest steered with one hand as he studied it, lifting his eyes back and forth to the mostly empty road.

"Well, that's Ben all right," he said.

"It's only a preliminary likeness."

"I know, but it's still him."

He gave the sketch back and drove on, not speaking but clearly working something over in his mind. Gil glanced back at Maureen, who sat quietly in the backseat, staring out at the countryside with the borrowed duster buttoned to her throat. The frail magic of the landscape could not stand up to the hard glare of midmorning. It was tangled and dusty again, a spreading rangeland with no tantalizing shadows or contours, just the foundational blankness of the earth itself.

"It's strange," Ernest finally said to Gil, "to think about lookin' at a statue of Ben. Like he was the president or something."

"It won't be so imposing as that. That's my hope, anyway. I want it to feel natural."

"Well, I hope it'll cheer the old man up. He's been pretty daunsey since Ben died. We all have, I reckon."

"What can you tell us about Ben?" Gil asked him. Maureen, hearing this question, leaned forward in her seat to listen.

"Oh, I don't know," Ernest said. "It's hard to know where to start talkin' about somebody you knowed all his life. I still think of him mostly as a little boy. I was just gettin' used to him bein' grown."

He lifted his hand off the steering wheel to wave to the driver of a car heading in the opposite direction.

"Ben was an intelligent boy. Even when he was a little kid, there weren't no way to outsmart him. He was always ahead of what you were thinkin'. He looks a bit like his daddy but I think he come by his nature, the better part of it anyway, through Mrs. Clayton. She was a kind lady. She had a quiet way that drew people in. Kept her thoughts to herself mostly but saw everything that went on around her. Ben had that quality too. When he was pretty young, twelve or so, he'd be out nighthawkin' with us on the roundups. You could surely trust that boy to watch those cows at night."

Ernest shifted his eyes to Gil. "If what you were askin' was how he ought to look in the statue, I guess that's what I'd say: quiet."

Gil nodded, glad to have the vague impressions of Ben Clayton he had been forming confirmed to at least some degree, and glad to know that the attitude of calm he had proposed for the statue was on the mark.

"What is this we heard," Maureen asked, pitching her voice above the motor noise, "about Mr. Clayton living with the Indians?"

They could both see that the question surprised Ernest. He didn't answer for a moment, taking advantage of a low-water crossing to pretend his full attention was needed in working the reverse pedal to slow the car. When he finally spoke again, his loquaciousness had deserted him.

"Mr. Clayton don't like to talk about that much," he said.

"SOMETHING'S NOT RIGHT," Gil said to his daughter in the dining car that afternoon. They had changed trains in Fort Worth and were now on the long home stretch to San Antonio.

Maureen sprinkled a meager teaspoonful of sugar into her coffee. "What's not right?"

"You'd think the boy would have written home. There were no letters, only a few postcards."

"Maybe Mr. Clayton burned them. Out of grief. People do that."

"Yes, I'm sure they do, but I don't think that's the case here. There's just a natural scarcity of information. I don't like the sense of there being something missing. I'm not a detective."

"You don't have to be, Daddy. You have enough to go on."

"Maybe," he said.

Gil folded his napkin and set it beside his empty plate, contemplating the pleasing sway of the dishes and utensils on the table as the train rattled south out of Fort Worth.

"I think I need to go back," Gil mused. "Not just to show him the maquette, but to stay around a while. I need a better sense of the place. I need a better sense of my subject."

"How long a time were you thinking?"

"I don't know. A week or so. If Clayton can stand the sight of me that long."

"It will add to the expense."

Gil waved the observation away, though she had a fair point. The way to get rich and stay rich was to knock out one big statue after another, as fast as possible. He had already caught the mood of this piece, he had already formulated the concept. But he could sense a hidden richness in this statue, an opportunity for greatness.

"A week is nothing," he told her. "If it will improve the quality of the work—and it will—then we'll afford it."

She smiled. "You liked it out there, didn't you?"

"Of course I did. Your father's a cowboy at heart."

IT WAS well past dark when the taxi pulled up to their house off Roosevelt Avenue. Above the rooftops of this low-lying neighborhood southeast of downtown San Antonio, the full moon hung starkly in the sky, illuminating the crumbling bell tower of Mission San José. What a strange world I've come to live in, Gil confided to himself as he paid the driver. It was a thought that visited him often enough. How could it not? For all of his life he thought he would come to ground among the teeming opportunities of New York, or perhaps find a picturesque exile in Europe, surrounded by intoxicating ruins and statues of antiquity for inspiration. The thought of living on the edge of an old Spanish mission field in Texas, among breweries and lumberyards, would never have found an excuse to enter his mind.

And yet here he was: home. Or what was supposed to be home. His wife had been dead for a year, but at moments like this he felt the confirmation of her absence with crushing force. He knew that Maureen felt it too. As they entered the house, she hurriedly switched on the light in the parlor, as if the darkness and emptiness of the house made up some sort of an active threat.

Mrs. Gossling, the housekeeper, had left a pot roast for them that afternoon. After unpacking, Maureen heated it up and then the two of them sat at the kitchen table, eating their late dinner while they skimmed through the newspapers that had accumulated in their absence. Neither felt the need to talk much after the long train journey together, but Gil could not stop thinking about the conversation that would have taken place at this homecoming if Victoria were still alive.

The news of a major commission had always made her beam with relief, since it was she who had borne the burden of managing their accounts, scanning the mail for promised payments or an unexpected check from the sale of a gallery piece. Gil had always had a high tolerance for financial anxiety; it was a necessary trait for a man in his line of work. But the suspense had worn on Victoria, and he missed the opportunity to reward her with the news of a project that would ensure their continued solvency for a year or more. And he missed just talking to her, telling her about the old man who had seemed as poor as he was sad but who had not even blinked at the price Gil had proposed, and about the lonely primacy of the site that made him confident that this statue would be a work of heartbreaking impact.

"I might use the Holloway boy again," he said to Maureen.

She looked up from the *Evening News,* with its screaming headlines about Bolsheviks and railroad strikes.

"He might be a little too slender."

"Maybe a little. We'll see how the clothes fit him."

Rusty Holloway was the young man whom Gil had used as the model for one of Crockett's men in his Defenders of the Alamo grouping. He was the son of a well-known Texas Ranger captain, though he himself was an unadventurous postal worker who had a Class 3 deferment and had missed the war. And despite his father's iconic occupation, Rusty was not much of a horseman, something that Gil would have to take into account, since the human figure would need to imply an easy conformance with the horse next to him.

They talked for a few moments more, about whether he should lease or buy a horse to serve as the model for Poco, and where it could be stabled, and then they each silently went back to the newspapers again until Maureen announced she could no longer stay awake. She kissed him good night and retreated to her room, leaving him alone in the kitchen in a dim pool of electric light.

He turned off the light and walked to his own room, the sound of his footfalls combining with the ticking of the mantel clock to create a lonely recessional tattoo. The haunted stillness of his own house made it that much harder to purge the gloom of Lamar Clayton's lonely ranch house from his mind.

He brushed his teeth and changed into his pajamas and went to bed. The trip to West Texas, as trips tended to do, had broken the continuity of his acceptance of Victoria's death, and he felt her once again beside him, sleeping on her back, her profile looming as sharp as a mountain range. Thirty-three years of marriage had never eroded the fascination he found in staring at that unforgettable face, which still embodied for him everything that was beautiful and heroic and mournful in the female soul. Before she had gotten sick she had begun to put on weight, the broad planes of her face sagging a bit with the added flesh, but even at fifty-four she could have still served as a model for a ship's figurehead.

Her heroic features had implied so strongly an internal fearlessness that it had taken Gil many years to fully perceive how uncertain she could be, how deeply her morale could be shaken when tensions were in the air or prospects were on the wane. The move from New York to San Antonio had been a new start for Gil, but for Victoria it had amounted to a plummet out of a familiar world, a descent caused by her husband's tyrannical artistic pride. She had gamely tried to start anew here, to follow him into the social embrace that greeted an eminent sculptor from New York, but the attentions of all these kind strangers had done nothing to buoy her up. They had sent her, instead, on a slow slide into solitude. Along with Maureen, she had done her share of volunteer work during the war, rolling bandages and putting together relief packages, but she had made no real friends in the process, and after the armistice she was more alone than ever, spending her days in more or less solitary management of the household while Gil and Maureen worked together in the studio. When she was stricken by the Spanish flu—a disease that had mostly attacked vigorous young people—Gil had not been able to banish the thought that the vaporous gloom of her new life in San Antonio had added to her vulnerability.

There was no point in trying to sleep now, not when he was turning over once again in the middle of the night his responsibility for Victoria's lingering unhappiness and shockingly swift death. He got up and put on his working clothes. He made his way through the moonlit hallway to the kitchen to drink a tumbler of limeade from the icebox. (Embracing the Mexican preference for limes over lemons had been one of the easiest adjustments to life in San Antonio.) His throat was dry and he drank the cool limeade in several long swallows while standing at the window looking out at the October night. He washed the glass out in the sink and quietly slipped through the kitchen door. His studio was only fifty or sixty feet away but in the unseasonable nighttime humidity beads of sweat were already forming at his hairline by the time he reached it. Gil did not much mind the humidity, though it had tormented Victoria. It kept the clay moist, for one thing. And it added to an overall vivifying sense of living in a strange and secret place.

The odor of that moisture-saturated clay welcomed him as he walked through the door, along with the smell of lumber from the scrap pile that had accumulated at one end of the studio, where he kept the wood that he used in filling out his armatures. The high-ceilinged barn he had converted into his studio had been made higher by a four-foot-tall panel of north-facing windows installed on solid trestles that rested on the reinforced studwork of the barn walls—and it was through these windows that the moon shone now with such radiance that he could almost go to work by its light.

But it was daylight that mattered in a sculptor's studio, daylight of a certain proportion and strength. The reflected light from the moon lent a distorting, golem-like glower to the pieces scattered around the studio. Gil's full-size plaster of the Yellow Rose of Texas appeared especially ferocious, her eyes lost in shadow and her beautiful delicate brow looking, in this light, as thick as a caveman's. The statue had been commissioned four years ago by the young men of a local civic organization dedicated to the memory of the young maiden (fictitious, Gil was almost sure) who had supposedly distracted Santa Anna while the Texan army marched up to attack his camp at San Jacinto. Unfortunately, the Knights of the Yellow Rose of Texas had never been able to find the funds to have it cast in bronze, and a grocery store had in the meantime been built on the spot where it was to have been erected.

The Yellow Rose was only one piece in what sometimes seemed to Gil a gallery of disappointment: maquettes to enter competitions for commissions that had been awarded to others, busts of bank presidents and board chairmen and the mayors of mid-size cities that he had undertaken purely for money, allegorical tablets commissioned by gas companies and department stores to honor their achievements in the annals of customer satisfaction and free enterprise.

It had been a long time since he stood in this studio with the sense of righteous creative purpose that he felt tonight, addressing a project that was not just remunerative but inspiring. He sorted through the scrap pile until he found a thick slab of pine that would serve as a base for the maquette, blew the dust off it, wiped it with a rag, and cleared off the worktable at one end of the studio. From a deep drawer filled with tangled pieces of thick wire he retrieved a twelve-inch human armature he had built for a previous model, and with a pair of pliers he set to work bending it into the internal skeletal shape of a boy Ben's size. When it was more or less as he wanted it, he set it aside and started to work with more of the thick-gauge wire, fashioning another armature for the horse. At the end of an hour's work he had the two armatures screwed down to the base and standing side by side, the schematic arm of the man resting upon the spine of the horse. That's enough, he thought, though his imagination was racing, charged by the sight of these loops of pliable wire shining in the moonlight, the always exciting first step toward three-dimensional reality. That's enough, he told himself: leave something for tomorrow.

SIX

Months earlier, in secret, Maureen had entered the competition for a city sculpture commission. The piece was to be placed on the Commerce Street bridge and called Spirit of the Waters in homage to the San Antonio River, which passed below. It had seemed natural not to tell her father, though it had been difficult to locate a space in which to model the piece and sometimes awkward to invent excuses to leave the house for the extended periods of work required.

In the end, she had been able to commandeer the studio of a friend who taught art at the Ursuline Academy. The studio was vacant only on Saturdays, but so far it had suited her schedule, and the bulk of the work was now finished and would be ready for the judging competition next week. Her father would not begin the Clayton piece in earnest for another few weeks or so and her presence in his studio was not yet in demand. She had told him this morning that she was going out to spend the day with Vance Martindale, which was not rigorously true but not false either, since Vance had written that he would be in San Antonio over the weekend and wanted to see her.

She had decided to hide her participation in the competition from her father because she knew she would not have been able to abide his enthusiasm. The congratulations, expressions of confidence, and unsought suggestions that would emerge from his interest would, she knew, quickly subsume her own uncertain ambition. She would be not just his daughter but his blood-bound protégée, a role to which her own authentic worth as a sculptor would forever be hostage.

It was a sense of that authentic worth that she was trying to recapture now. Back in New York, she had come close to achieving some sort of independent success. She had steadily applied for commissions, sometimes using a false name, carefully testing the waters to see if she would be taken seriously in her own right and not just politely accommodated as the daughter of a well-known sculptor. None of the commissions had come her way, but she had not really expected them to. She was a woman, which would have made rising to the top of the list unlikely in the first place, and she was young, with no reputation. But there had been enough encouraging comments on her work to make her believe she was being noticed and that with time and patience she might advance into a career.

But her rising confidence had coincided with her father's deepening frustration at the direction his own career was heading in New York and his abrupt decision to move the family to San Antonio to take advantage of the new Texas commissions that kept falling into his lap after the success of his Alamo piece. Maureen could have refused to move, of course. She had even gently aired the possibility to her father, who had responded with reasonable words but with such a hurt and betrayed expression in his eyes that she was astonished at how strongly it was in her power to wound him. And she could not really leave her mother to face the Texas wilderness—as she imagined San Antonio to be—without a daughter's support. If she had been in love it might have made a difference; she might have had the cruelty to remain in New York and abandon her parents to the edge of the known world. But she had not been in love, only mired in an indifferent half-courtship with a young newspaperman who, as it turned out, was interested in women only for propriety's sake. Breaking up with him had involved no heartbreak at all—just more dispiriting evidence that her lifelong fear of being undesired was rooted in some sort of objective truth.

On a Sunday afternoon last summer Maureen had taken a solo San Antonio bicycling excursion, following the course of the river past the old missions, sketching all the way, trying to conjure up something for the Spirit of the Waters piece besides the sprites and maidens and various genii that she knew would be the starting point of most of the other contestants. She wanted to depict the river rather than to airily personify it, and as she studied the almost-finished clay model now, she thought she just might have succeeded.

She had created four tablets, one for each side of a short column, that re-created in relief the things she had observed from her bicycle: noble cypress trunks, moldering Spanish aqueducts, swooping herons, and perching kingfishers. As a New Yorker who had lived in San Antonio for only six years, she believed she had rendered these elements with an outsider's reverence. The coziness of the little river, its spring-fed clarity, its exotic history of Indians and Spanish explorers and filibusters had unexpectedly stirred her. As she stared at the panels, she began to realize she had been drawn to something else as well: not just to the generative idea of the Spirit of the Waters but to the fetid over-abundance of the foliage, to the spectral menace of the cypress knees rising from the water and the loops of grapevine hanging from the trees like snares. Beneath the celebratory business was something darker, a homage to a mysterious and unwelcoming place, the place where her own compliant exile had begun and where her mother's life had come to its end.

She heard bootsteps echoing in the empty hallway outside: Vance Martindale was here. She glanced at her reflection in the window glass and quickly began covering the four panels with a moistened cloth.

"Caught you," he said when he swept into the room. "It must be something scandalous or you wouldn't be covering it up."

"It's something you may not have an opinion about until it's finished," she said. "And maybe not even then."

He took the crooked pipe out of his mouth with one hand and lifted his hat with the other as he stood there grinning at her. For all his natural bluster and confidence he was oddly shy with her, and she still did not quite know how to read him.

"I need to buy a new suit," he said.

"You certainly do." He was wearing a rumpled out-of-season white suit, the side pockets where he kept his pipe and keys and change bulging carelessly. The brim of his hat was floppy with abuse, and he needed a haircut. He was an inch shorter than she was, bowlegged from a boyhood of ranch work in South Texas, and had a proud hayseed grin, which Maureen suspected was a conscious foil for his brilliant mind.

The studied carelessness of his appearance had appealed to her from the first. It was maybe a little put on, but she didn't mind. They had been conspicuously at ease around each other ever since they were introduced at the unveiling of her father's memorial to the Defenders of the Alamo, a piece for which Vance had written a robust appreciation in the *Southwestern Historical Quarterly.* Since Vance lived in Austin and she in San Antonio, their relationship had existed mostly as a fitful flirtation. But he was coming to San Antonio more and more lately, always on the excuse of some bit of academic business or other. If it was true—as she hoped it was—that the real purpose of these visits was to see her, he had not yet brought himself to admit it.

"I'm serious," he said as she gathered up her things and locked her friend's studio. "I'm going to Joske's to buy a new suit and I need you to consult. I've decided to give those philistines in the English Department an opportunity to take me seriously. But if I'm going to look my dashing best I need a woman's opinion."

They walked along the river, following it downtown. Vance said he was in town to interview a Mexican boy healer for a book he was writing on Texas folklore. His scholarly enthusiasms were rooted in the culture and history of his own state, which made him a low-paid eccentric in the English Department of the University of Texas. The donnish professors there, believing the youth of the state should be taught their Shakespeare and Gibbon, had no great affection for someone who insisted on teaching them cowboy songs or tall tales of the open range.

He was extremely interested to hear about Maureen's visit to Lamar Clayton's ranch, and kept pumping her for answers about things she had not thought to notice—how much acreage he had, what variety of cattle he ran, whether he employed any Mexican vaqueros as hands, what his brand looked like.

"I could write a whole book on brands alone," he said as they emerged onto Alamo Plaza. "Cortés, for instance, right after the conquest wasted no time in branding his cattle with Latin crosses. Of course, you could go all the way back to the pharaohs if you wanted to—"

"But I don't really want to," Maureen chided.

He laughed and offered his arm as they crossed the plaza and it felt good to take it, to adopt the pose of a normal woman strolling with a winningly eccentric man, a man who might this very day finally kiss her, who might someday declare he loved her.

Cars were parked up and down the streets and around the perimeter of the little plaza in front of the Alamo. There were palm trees everywhere, a sight that had always been more alien to her than the strange revered ruin itself. In front of the open door of the old mission, a family was posing for a snapshot, the young children squirming and protesting as their perfectionist father stalked about with his camera, searching for the best angle. Other families were lined up behind them, waiting for their chance to record their presence at this great inexplicable shrine.

"Would it embarrass you if I tipped my hat?" Vance said as they walked past the ancient church.

"Yes, very much."

He tipped his hat to the Alamo anyway, to annoy her.

At the edge of the plaza they passed her father's monument to the heroes of the Alamo, four bronze figures crouched behind a palisade wall, Davy Crockett in the foreground urgently priming the pan of his flintlock rifle. The piece had taken three contentious years to complete. At first her father had to counter the charges that an Alamo statue could not be entrusted to anyone but a native Texan, and then he had to convince the city fathers that his conception—a dynamic tableau of frightened men in a desperate fight—would be far more memorable than the stolid portraiture they had originally envisioned. Then of course there had been the all-consuming work itself. Maureen had spent almost a year in research, gathering rifles and powder horns and haversacks from the attics of old pioneer families, consulting with historians about the structure of the palisade wall that Crockett and his men were said to have defended, examining moth-eaten frock coats and beaver hats from the period in order to present her father with authentic options for the clothing the figures would wear.

She paused now in their walk to stand before the statue for a moment, pretending to Vance to be concerned about a shiny spot on one of the defenders' knees where the patina was starting to rub off, but really to admire the feeling and skill that her father had brought to the work. Crockett was depicted as the middle-aged man he had been. There was a fatalistic resolution in his face as he stared down at his rifle. But one of the defenders next to him, the figure Rusty Holloway had posed for, was only a boy, and though his face was proportionately correct it seemed to be elongated with terror, almost as if the sculptor who prided himself on realism had found it necessary to make a concession to the modernist distortion he distrusted. It was the face of a young man who knew with certainty he was about to die, and in staring at it now Maureen could not help but think of Ben Clayton, and wonder if his last moments had been this fearful and frenetic.

"Strong work," Vance said. "Maybe a little too sincere for the twentieth century."

"My father has no use for artistic fashions."

"Nor do I. I write about cowboy songs, remember? Shall we get my suit?"

Joske's department store was at the end of the block. She accompanied Vance as he clomped rapidly on his booted feet through the women's department, past autumn suits and coats, the new blouses of georgette crepe. The end of the war had brought forth a flowering of goods everywhere, and nowhere more abundantly than on the display tables of the department stores. In passing, she fingered the material of a light-blue poplin suit, coveting it despite the certainty that it would not come close to draping as elegantly on her full figure as it did on the slender mannequin.

Vance was not so slender himself, but he was immune to that sort of self-consciousness. She stood there listening as he described exactly what he wanted to a sales clerk in the men's ready-to-wear department. Then he sought Maureen's opinion on various gray or plaid or brown worsteds that the clerk brought forth for him to try on.

Together they decided on a suitably rustic brown check—he said it reminded him of the color of a Nueces River cutbank—and while the tailor marked it for alterations Maureen wandered idly through the busy store, surveying the new belted men's suits, the wider lapels, the straw hats that were back in fashion after the war. She remembered the moment last year when she had been shopping with her mother and a somber bell had rung at noon and everyone—the customers, floorwalkers, elevator boys, cash girls with their hands full of bills—had stopped in mid-action. "May we all take a silent moment," the manager had proclaimed from the top of the stairs, "to pray for victory, and for our young men far away in France and on the seas."

The memory came back to her now with chastening force. During the war she had done volunteer work for the Lone Star Hospitality Service, serving doughnuts and passing out magazines at the train station to anxious, high-spirited soldiers being shipped overseas. Along with the rest of the customers that day in Joske's she had inclined her head and mumbled her prayers for the boys' safekeeping. But somehow the emotional gravity of the war itself had bypassed her. After that moment of silence, she had returned to the concerns of her daily life, fretting about her future, worrying about her mother's unhappiness in San Antonio, calculating her own odds for ever escaping into something resembling her own life.

When had that been? September? October? Could it have been the very day when Ben Clayton was killed in France?

In any case, it had not been long after that day when the city sirens finally wailed in honor of the armistice, when Maureen and her family had joined the rally in front of the Alamo, thinking that not just the war was over but the influenza crisis as well. And it had been that next morning that her mother had woken with a fever.

"I've got the rest of the day to kill," Vance said when he tracked her down. He was wearing his old suit and his proudly abused hat. "What shall we do?"

She was irritated at his assumption that she was perfectly free for the rest of the day as well, free to serve as his companion and verbal sparring partner. But she was not irritated enough to deny herself the rare pleasure of spending the day with a man of her own age, a man whose blustery sense of himself she rather liked. She dared not hope too aggressively that he was really interested in her, that he had something more in mind than a lively, bantering friendship. It was up to him to reveal himself.

She took his arm again as they walked out of the store and into the sunlight. She was still obscurely stirred up, still thinking about the war and the way its effects were coming to rest in her soul.

"Tell me about France," she said to Vance. "What was it like for you?"

"No tales of valor, I'm afraid. I might have had some to tell if our boat had been a little faster, but as it was we got there just before the armistice. All that training, and I didn't have the honor of firing even one volley at the evil Hun. But I very much admired the landscape—those hedges in Breton—and there were times when the battery was doing horse maneuvers and I was galloping up and down the column shouting orders that I felt like some exalted version of myself."

"So it was fun?"

"My shameful little secret. And thanks to the beneficence of the AEF I was able to stay on in Paris for three months studying at the Sorbonne. The finest time of my life. You should see Paris, Maureen."

She would very much like to see Paris, to live there as her father had when he was young, but she left this obvious fact unexpressed.

They went to the pictures. Vance found her a seat and then went out to the popcorn wagon in front of the theater, leaving her to read the deflating introductory title card on her own. "To these Women, and their pitiful hours of waiting for the love that never comes, we dedicate our story."

The picture was called *True Heart Susie.* It billed itself as the story of a "plain girl." But Lillian Gish wasn't plain, not in the way Maureen understood the word. She was a woman you would certainly notice on the street. Her figure was slim, her small face was soft in profile but radiant and beseeching when she looked straight at the camera or into the face of the smug and oblivious boyfriend whose college education she had financed by selling her family's cow.

It was a ridiculous story, of course, as so many of them were. Vance whispered wisecracks into her ear all the way through it. Maureen smiled at his wit, but she couldn't deny that every once in a while Lillian Gish's simpering emoting brushed against a chord of real feeling. Here was Susie in the pew, watching as the love of her life married another; saying nothing of her disappointment to anyone, just collapsing afterward all alone in theatrical sobs. Maureen recognized that element of uncomplaining muteness in herself. It was not pride, as it seemed to be with True Heart Susie—it was just a deflated acceptance, something she had had to fight against all her life.

It was night when they walked out. He suggested dinner. They strolled along Commerce Street all the way past the cathedral and on to Haymarket Plaza, where the Chili Queens had their booths and long picnic tables set up, and where the music from the mariachis blasted forth into the still night air. It was warm, like a summer night back home in New York. The plaza was filled with Mexican families and with Anglo visitors like themselves drawn by the easeful, exotic atmosphere of a more ancient Texas.

"I hear Rosa has the best enchiladas," Vance said, guiding her to one of the rude wooden tables. The trumpets of the mariachis sounded with such piercing force that it seemed to her that the colored lanterns overhead swayed in reaction to the notes muscling their way through the air. Vance had to shout over the music to give their order to Rosa, a sharp-featured, good-humored woman with an entrepreneurial demeanor.

As they ate their enchiladas, Maureen told Vance all about the Pawnee Scout and her father's fruitless expedition to Omaha to save it.

"What a horrifying ordeal," he said. She appreciated the way he could swerve from irony to full-hearted warmth and sincerity. "To lose something like that, something you've given your soul to. I can't think of a similar case, a statue lost before the sculptor's eyes. How is he managing?"

"He was in his studio when I left this morning. When he's in his studio he's usually happy enough."

"I admire your father," Vance said. "In fact, being a poor cowhand turned professor, I'm in awe of the very idea of being able to capture someone's likeness in sculpture."

"You needn't necessarily be in awe," she said. "A lot of it is just technical."

"I don't believe it."

"It's true. On a normal human body, the legs are half of the overall height. The average human figure is eight heads tall. The ear is just behind the midline of the vertical axis of the head, and so on. You can get a long way with just basic knowledge like that."

"But not all the way."

"No," she said.

"I'd be in awe of your work too if you wouldn't cover it up when you hear me coming."

"I have to. You're a natural critic."

"Not of you, Miss Gilheaney."

He looked at her across the picnic table, the paper lanterns swaying above them, the music swelling as the mariachis headed in their direction. If this were a picture like *True Heart Susie* it would be the moment he moved the greasy dinner plates out of the way and leaned across the table to kiss her. He wanted to, she could tell that. He held her eyes unashamedly, making her feel admired, appreciated, almost beautiful.

But he did not kiss her. Instead he distracted himself with a big grin, rose from the table, said, "Nos vamos, Señorita?" and led her across the plaza. They passed the mariachis, who were blasting forth some Mexican folk song at top volume, their singing punctuated with all sorts of yips and trills. Vance handed them a few coins as he and Maureen walked by.

"I'm pretty sure that was one of Pancho Villa's songs," he said as they waited for the streetcar to arrive. "I guess you could say it's an insult to Pershing, but after all, San Antonio is really Mexico, don't you think?"

It was still early, only eight o'clock, but he insisted on accompanying her home. As they rode down Roosevelt Avenue he begged her pardon and pulled out a pad and pencil to jot down some questions he'd just thought of for his interview tomorrow with the boy healer. He told her if he gained the confidence of the boy and his formidable mother he might be coming back to San Antonio two or three times this fall, and it would be a great delight if she would agree to see him again.

"Of course," she said.

"Good. I like you, you see. People tell me I'm rather a blowhard but I'm a good judge of character. And you have caught my attention, Miss Gilheaney."

He insisted on getting off the streetcar with her and walking her to her door. The house was dark.

"Your father isn't home?"

"He'll be in the studio. Out back."

"Well, I'll give you into his keeping, then."

He took her hand, squeezed it for a moment in both of his, and walked back in the night toward the streetcar stop.

SEVEN

"El Gran Escultor!"

Dr. Aureliano Urrutia called out from the darkness of the Menger Hotel Bar. Gil blinked as he closed the door to give his eyes a chance to adjust from the blinding afternoon sun. The bar was a replica of the taproom of the House of Lords Club in London. Apparently it had once been somebody's idea of high culture to model a San Antonio saloon on a posh London watering hole.

Urrutia sat with Walter Sutherland in a booth of polished cherry under the gallery. Sutherland toasted Gil's arrival with an empty scotch glass and signaled the waiter with the same gesture. He was five years older than Gil, a wily enthusiast who had made his fortune in the grocery business and now spent his leisure hours buying up pre-Columbian art and puzzling aloud over the mysteries of antiquity.

"Do me a favor and have a real drink," Sutherland said to Gil as the waiter appeared. "They're tearing down the bar, you know?"

"Tearing down the bar?"

"If this goddam prohibition bill passes they sure as hell will. Ain't that right, Otto?"

The waiter nodded wearily and asked for Gil's order. Gil compromised with a beer. Having watched his father and his uncles drink themselves into early deaths, he had long ago seen to it that he developed into an abstemious man, moderate in all things except for a wild pursuit of glory.

"What the hell good is a bar anyway when the dries run the world?" Sutherland went on. He could be lively and full of striking opinions until his third or fourth drink, when he had a tendency to degenerate into a resentful boor.

"So, my friend," Urrutia said to Gil, "you're in mourning once again. We heard the news about your statue."

"Awful damn sorry about it," Sutherland said.

Urrutia dismissed Sutherland's condolences with an impatient wave. "He's sorry, of course, but he's a philistine and doesn't understand that a good statue matters more than a hundred human lives. A thousand."

Gil had had a superstitious aversion to directly meeting Urrutia's gaze ever since he had heard the rumor that the doctor had killed General Frederick Funston with the evil eye in the lobby of the Saint Anthony Hotel. It was one of many wild stories that surrounded the mysterious physician, who apparently saw no advantage in disputing them.

Urrutia's eyes were in fact mild, not lethal at all. There was something sagging and wistful in his demeanor, the look, perhaps, that once-powerful men develop when they're in exile. It was said that back in Mexico, Urrutia had been Huerta's henchman, that he had surgically removed the tongue of one of the president's rivals, and that it was Funston who had finally arrested him and thrown him out of the country.

About the only thing Gil knew for sure about the doctor was that he was passionate about sculpture, to the point that he was planning a sculpture garden, centered around a replica of the Winged Victory of Samothrace, for the mansion he was building on River Road.

"Don't worry," Gil said. "I've recovered. In fact I've just begun a new commission. A very interesting piece, a sort of memorial to a boy killed in the war."

"What's the difference between a memorial and a 'sort of memorial'?" Sutherland asked.

"I'm not sure I know myself," Gil admitted. He took a sip of the Menger's house beer, soon to be banished from the earth. "I'm doing it for the boy's father, a rancher in West Texas. He's a grieving man, very private. I doubt that he means for anyone but himself to even see the thing."

"Grief," Urrutia said, contemptuously waving away the word he had just pronounced. "I'm tired of hearing about grief. Grief is holding the world back precisely when it must—I am searching for the English word—*roar* forward."

The doctor expressed himself with such cold authority on this subject that Gil wondered if it might really be true after all that he had cut out that man's tongue. He felt unmoored, as he often did during these sociable afternoons. Could it be that this theatrical, perhaps shady man was among those that he now counted as his friends?

Urrutia and Sutherland were part of the civic group that had originally lured Gil to San Antonio for the Alamo piece, and that had ultimately convinced him to stay. The members of the group were direct-speaking men of business for the most part who knew nothing of the poisonous political currents of the New York art world and were happy to steer commission after commission his way, usually without the charade of a competition. They had taken his talent as a wonder from the first, assessed him as a man who knew his business, and were generally too awed or too busy to argue with him about his ideas for a particular statue.

How different it had been in New York, where the announcement of every commission uncovered a seething pit of artistic competition and self-regard. He had seethed in the pit along with the rest of them, of course, until he could bear it no more. He might have had the USS *Maine* Monument if he had been a little more amenable to the commissioners' demand for rearing hippocampi and lounging river gods, but he would rather have starved (so he theatrically declared to poor Victoria) than surrender to the sculptural cliché of yet another shovel-hooved aquatic horse. Piccirilli, of course, had set no such barriers for himself, and so it was his indecipherable sculptures and ponderous allegorical nudes that now stood forever at the entrance to Central Park.

For the international competition to erect a statue of General Gómez, he had sailed to Cuba at his own expense and put himself up at a hotel for weeks while he and fifty other men displayed their clay models in a humid and crumbling exhibition hall. When he saw that the competition was rigged, when it became plain that the commission was to go to a well-connected blowhard who knew nothing about proportion and was ridiculously reliant on enlarging machines, he had packed up his model and embarked for home before the award was announced.

Gil did not have the boiling temper that was tolerated and even cultivated in so many of the monumental sculptors he had known. When he walked away, he did so quietly. Anger was one thing; everybody knew it would cool sooner or later. But an inflexible artistic vision was, he had discovered, a chronic liability. After the *Maine* and the Gómez, word got around about him, but it did not travel as far south as San Antonio, where he had been greeted on his arrival with a banquet in his honor and a band playing an original composition titled "The Gilheaney March."

"What rancher?" Walter Sutherland was asking now, as he peered down with dismay into his empty glass.

"His name is Lamar Clayton."

"The hell you say."

"You know him?"

"Goddam, Gil, of course I know him. Everybody in Texas knows him. Back when I used to dabble in the cattle business I'd see him every year at the stock show in Fort Worth. Hardly said a word to anybody, but after what he went through I guess you can't blame him."

"You mean losing his wife?"

"Losing his wife? Hell, people lose wives every day, and they'll still talk your ear off. You don't know about Lamar?"

Gil shook his head.

"I don't either," Urrutia said.

"Goddam Indians stole him when he was a boy. Him and his sister. Killed their daddy out in the fields, scalped their poor mother right in front of their eyes. Then rode off with the kids. He was raised Comanche, ol' Lamar was."

So that was what George's Mary's mysterious reference to "living with the Indians" had been about. Gil had imagined some quaint interlude, the sort of thing he himself had dreamed of doing as a young man, voluntarily removing himself from the stifling city to seek adventure and wisdom among the uncorrupted natives. This was quite a different thing, and in some way that Gil could not consciously calculate, it explained an air of stillness and sadness in the old rancher that seemed to reach further back in time than the recent death of his son.

"How splendid," Urrutia declared. "Like something you'd see in the pictures."

"They got him home somehow when he was sixteen or seventeen," Sutherland went on, "but he wasn't much good for a long time after that, drinking and so forth."

"He seems sober now."

"Hell, he's been sober thirty years or more now, I'd guess. Ain't no fun to be around but he's a good businessman for sure. Because he'd been a wild Indian when he was a boy he got some nice grazing leases pretty cheap from the Comanches, from Quanah Parker himself is what I hear. That's how he made his money. He don't like to part with it neither. I hear he lives in a sod house, almost."

"Not that bad," Gil said. "But it's not the house of a rich man."

"So ol' Lamar's son got killed in the war? I'm damned sorry to hear it."

"Make sure you do a good job on the statue," Urrutia said, "or this Indian man might—what's the word for when you rip away the hair?"

"Scalp," Sutherland said.

"Exactly! Or he might scalp you."

WHEN GIL LEFT the Menger he walked across the plaza to the post office. He kept a box here for his business correspondence, and the mail today was mostly bills: from Star Clay Products for the ton of clay that had been delivered to his studio last month, from his foundry in New York for the balance due on the casting of a half-dozen portrait busts. There were several letters from friends in New York, though the tide of incoming personal mail had long since slackened. He did not get back home as often as he should, and it was natural for people to fall out of touch with a distant friend whose life in faraway Texas they could not imagine.

He closed the box and his eye fell on the one next to it, his box as well, that he had not opened for several weeks. He had rented it in secret, when they first arrived in San Antonio, for the sole purpose of receiving mail from his mother. She had died five years ago but he had not given the post office box up, partly because it was also the address through which he still received correspondence relating to her affairs—small checks, mostly, from the firm that had published her paintings of martyred saints as holy cards or as illustrations in missals—but also because of a guilty reluctance to finally close off the last secret threads of communication between mother and son.

He should do it today. Give up the box and switch the address. But the line at the counter was gratifyingly long; he would do it next week. Instead he took out his other key and opened the box and gathered up the stray pieces of mail that had accumulated since he last checked it. There was a parish bulletin from St. Joseph's, the old church on Sixth Avenue where Gil had made his first communion and to which his mother in her later years had increasingly devoted her life. There was also a Catholic newspaper with stories about the latest miraculous cures at Lourdes and the Blessed Mother's pleas at Fatima for the conversion of Russia. His mother had subscribed to these periodicals in his name. He did not know why they kept coming, five years after her death. Maybe she had bought some sort of extended subscription, so that she could be sure her influence would reach beyond the grave.

When he got home, Mrs. Gossling was quartering potatoes and dropping them into the soup well of the stove.

"I'm leaving you three meals," she said without turning around to greet him. "You do remember I have to go to Castroville to visit my poor brother?"

"Of course I remember," Gil said. And he did remember, if vaguely. Mrs. Gossling never stopped talking about her baby brother, a good man but a hopeless drunkard who was always dying but then not dying of various ailments. When she first came to work for them, after Victoria's death, Gil and Maureen had felt obligated to pause in the kitchen and listen intently to her catalog of grief, but after a month or so they had both come to the conclusion that Mrs. Gossling was more interested in hearing herself talk than in eliciting pity from them.

"I'll be off in a half hour then," she said, sweeping up potato and carrot peels with the heel of her hand. "This will need to simmer until six o'clock or so. I've set out the bowls for you to put the leftovers in."

"Thank you, Mrs. Gossling," he said.

She replied with a curt nod and he went to his studio, thinking of Victoria's cooking—now mostly lost to them, except for the dishes

Maureen had learned at her mother's side—and of Victoria's presence in the kitchen, which even in her homesickness and melancholy had been so much more warming and welcoming than Mrs. Gossling's.

But he also remembered the times when Victoria had glanced at him as he was entering the house and seen an envelope in his pocket from his secret post office box, an envelope with his mother's handwriting. On these occasions her welcoming smile would instantly disappear. She would not say anything; the argument between them on this point was ancient and irresolvable. She would just turn back to the stove and tell him in a polite voice when dinner would be ready.

He went into the studio and got out the key to the always-locked drawer where he stored his mother's letters. There was no reason to hold onto the parish bulletins and newspapers that kept arriving but he could not make himself throw them out, so he unlocked the drawer and slipped today's additions under the rubber bands that held the growing stacks of back issues.

And then there were the rubber-banded collections of his mother's letters, dozens of them in this drawer, probably a hundred more locked away in a file cabinet. His name was written on the envelopes in his mother's beautiful hand: Mister Francis Gilheaney, the "Mister," he knew, less a form of address than a mother's assertive declaration of her son's worldly success. The letters were typically long, full of boilerplate exhortations for him to make a good confession, to attend Mass, to offer up a prayer now and then to Saint Jude, along with effusive declarations of love and pride and occasional bafflement. He had carefully answered every one of them, taking hours sometimes to compose his replies, groping for language that would be evasive but not dismissive, that would satisfy her hungry curiosity to some small degree without revealing more about his life than he could afford to.

He slipped the last letter she had written him out of the stack. He felt the weave of the paper with his fingertips. Proper stationery had been the first luxury she had allowed herself, back in his family's brief one-year period of prosperity when they had moved from their tenement on Leroy Street to a townhouse on St. Luke's Place. He had not had the steady means to provide quite that standard of living for her in her old age, but in addition to a nice apartment on Sullivan Street he had been able to keep her in stationery and in the paints and brushes and canvases she used to fill her lonely hours. It had been years since there had been any buyers for the religious art she used to paint to help support the family, the images of Saint Teresa of Ávila or Saint Catherine of Siena that were printed and distributed and passed out as holy cards to parishioners all across the country. But she had still sat at her easel producing variations of the portraits of the saints that had so entranced him when he was a boy.

To distract himself from these memories Gil sat back in his chair and fixed his eyes on the unfinished maquette of Ben Clayton standing next to his horse. He could see a hundred things wrong with it already: something awkward about the way the boy's hand rested on the saddle, a thickness in the horse's neck. This was only a preliminary sketch, of course. There was much research still to be done and more models to be made in varying scales until he set to work on the final full-size sculpture. But when he went back out to West Texas in the next few weeks to present this maquette to Lamar Clayton he wanted the old man to sense a power and fidelity in this beginning step.

He turned again to the letter on his desk, intending to put it back with the rest, lock the drawer, and get on with his work. Instead he opened it and started to read it again. With every word his eyes passed over he felt a sharp self-rebuke, the hurt of an elaborate deception that he was responsible for and now could never put right.

His mother had relayed no news of any direct importance in the letter. She wrote that her late sister's son, a cousin almost unknown to Gil, had recently passed out at a lunch counter in Union Station in Chicago but was not believed to have suffered a heart attack. Monsignor Berney at the age of ninety was embarking at last on the trip to the County Carlow he had dreamed of taking since he was a boy. Mary Rose Conroy still went over to his mother's apartment every night before bedtime to have a cup of tea and to say the rosary with her, and when the weather was decent the two of them—vigorous widows in their early eighties—would still venture forth from their building on Sullivan Street and walk across Sixth Avenue to Sheridan Square, and then make a visit to St. Joseph's on the way back. They had finally finished the Seventh Avenue subway and you could tell the difference, she wrote. The horsecars were almost gone now—a shame, when you thought about it—and people were flooding in from other parts of the city with predatory curiosity. The old Elevated trestles still cast Sixth Avenue in their immemorial shade, but someday they would be gone too, torn down, and the people like her who had walked along the gloomy street for decades would be suddenly exposed to the sun like the bugs under a branch that somebody had lifted off the forest floor. And they were tearing down so many of the old buildings to make room for gleaming studio apartments for those uptown invaders. Yes, the tenements were old, of course, and filthy and crowded, no better than rookeries some of them, but still it hurt to see them go. The Italians were moving in everywhere. They were decent people for the most part and good Catholics, she supposed. She didn't mean to sound superior, but it was just different here now. The movie theaters everywhere, the dance halls, the streets filled with young people caring about nothing except having a good time, barely thinking about their immortal souls.

Three pages of this, front and back, circling themes of lament, of loss, of puzzlement and subtle accusation. Like a schoolgirl, she had always written "JMJ" (Jesus Mary and Joseph) at the top of every sheet of correspondence, even sometimes at the headings of grocery lists. Her penmanship was gorgeous but the ink had been pressed hard into the paper, and Gil could not help but think of his mother alone at her desk, alone in the apartment whose rent and upkeep had been a large part of his financial burden, urgently forcing these vague words down.

"What are you reading?"

He hadn't heard Maureen come in and her voice startled him. He jerked upward in his chair, in the same motion grabbing the letter and slipping it back in its envelope.

"Nothing," he said. "Just Senator Grayson's widow writing to ask how much it would cost to have another bust cast for her children."

He put the letter into one of the unlocked drawers in as matter-of-fact a way as he could manage. He would have to wait until Maureen left to transfer it to the locked drawer where he kept the rest of her correspondence.

He looked up at his daughter. She was standing on the other side of the desk. She was wearing her best dress, crisp blue poplin with subtle embroidery along the scoop of the neck. She was smiling, grinning really, her eyes radiant.

"What's going on?"

"You'll never guess so I'll just have to come out and tell you. I've just come from a tea at the Saint Anthony's roof garden."

"You didn't tell me anything about going to a tea."

"It's not necessary for you to know everything I do, Daddy, but that's a separate issue. The tea was a meeting of the Women's Club of San Antonio, the Arts and Beautification Committee. Headed by this very stout, very formidable woman, Mrs. Toepperwein. Her grandfather was a messenger from the Alamo or something, and of course in this city the Alamo trumps everything, so her word is law."

"And the word is what exactly?"

"That I have a commission."

Gil looked at his daughter, still puzzled, but beguiled by the look on her face, by the idea that this moment might at last be the harbinger of her happiness and independence. "Daddy, my design was chosen! For a project on the Commerce Street bridge. And they're paying me a thousand dollars!"

She told him about the Spirit of the Waters competition, how she had entered it without telling him and modeled the piece in the studio of the Ursuline Academy when he thought she was out shopping or was simply too busy with his own work to notice she was gone.

"But why on earth in secret?" Gil asked her. "Did you think I would object?"

"I don't know," she said. "It's been a long time since I've tried anything on my own. And I didn't want you to be deflated if I didn't win. But now I *have* won and so everything is out in the open. Of course, there's still a lot of work to be done. The panels I've made so far are just scale models. But it won't interfere with the real work, Daddy, I promise. I'll just need a tiny corner of the studio. And anyway, the deadline is ages away. The Clayton will probably already be at the foundry before I have to start the full-scale work."

His daughter's anxious expression unnerved him a little. It was as if she was frightened that he would freeze with disapproval and order her to abandon the project before she began, as if she expected him to be jealous.

He did his best to put her at her ease, standing up at last and kissing her cheek in congratulations, proposing that they break out a stowed-away bottle of soon-to-be-contraband champagne to celebrate, demanding to see the models. They sipped their champagne and then before dinner Maureen went into her room and brought out the clay sketches, setting them on a long table and then pretending to stand there with no grave concern as he studied them.

"Marvelous," he said. The work was better than adequate but so strongly did he want to believe that it was extraordinary that he uttered this compliment with an explosive enthusiasm that surprised him—and caused tears of pride to form in the corners of Maureen's eyes.

Maybe it really was the beginning of something for her, he thought. She was intelligent and reasonably talented, she had always worked hard and diligently. She was a woman, but that wasn't so a great a liability for an artist as it used to be.

And if his suspicions were correct and there was something of substance brewing with Vance Martindale, he might be able to put aside at least some of his guilt for moving his family to Texas.

EIGHT

They had been told that the Bois des Vipères was clear, but you could not count on anything being clear. The German prisoners of war who were supposed to mark the unexploded shells, so that they could be carted away and destroyed by the Service de Désobusage, were paid only forty centimes a day, and as often as not when they saw a shell they simply gave it a wide berth and left it lying there.

Vipers Wood was not a forest, it was just a remnant strip of vegetation where the landscape dipped a few feet below a rocky shelf. A mile or so of tangled brush, thirty or forty yards in width. Something you wouldn't even notice unless you had been under fire from the machine-gun nests hidden within it. It was strange to be back here, just over a year later. The forest, and the German trench across the road, had already been taken by the time Arthur's regiment had marched this way toward Saint-Étienne. It had been other units of the 36th, along with the marines in the Second Division, who had been shot apart by the machine guns hidden in these woods. They were the ones who had taken Blanc Mont Ridge. Climbing up the long slope of the ridge a day later, Arthur and Ben and the rest of his company had passed their bodies, shredded and buried in the mud of the shell craters, part of the stinking detritus that had poisoned what had once been farmers' fields. He remembered how the company had paused at the summit of Blanc Mont Ridge. They could smell the dead all around them, and they could see the distant steeple of Reims Cathedral.

Arthur pushed the branches out of the way with his thick work gloves, careful with every step. In only a few yards he came across coils of barbed wire hidden in the underbrush, and beyond it a rusted sheet of the corrugated iron the French called *tôle ondulée,* along with a few broken clay bottles of Dutch schnapps and scattered picket posts that marked where a machine-gun position had been. The shallow trench leading out of the position would have to be filled in, and the *tôle* dragged off and reported to Dervaux, the *chef du travaux.* Here in the Devastated Zone, where all of the villages had been blasted away and the fields ripped apart, where nothing existed anymore except for a few indomitable crows, a piece of corrugated iron was a commodity.

Arthur unhooked the heavy clippers from his belt and knelt down to cut away the wire. The German wire was stout and cunningly designed, with clusters of barbs that grabbed you everywhere at once. It was hard work to cut it up but it gave him satisfaction. It was right that he was here, working for the Service des Travaux de l'État, undoing in some small way what had been done. By an accident of logistics he was with a crew that was moving across the same country in which he had fought. Two weeks ago they had been on the Navarin Farm Road. Then they had come here, just outside the ruins of the village of Somme-Py, and in the weeks ahead they would sweep up to the summit of Blanc Mont and down toward Saint-Étienne, where he and Ben had charged the Germans in their cemetery stronghold. Sometimes Arthur imagined he was rolling up the past, tucking it tightly away where it would never have to be seen again.

It was a pleasant thought and it might have given him comfort if every present moment did not contradict it. Even if there had been no pain from the ragged hollows of his sinuses, where infections were constantly brewing, or from the ill-fitting vulcanite prosthesis biting into always-tender gums and raw bone, an awareness of his face and its effect on others would still reign over every thought. Over every thought, he knew, until the end of his life.

He dragged a tangle of cut wire away from the trees and out onto open ground, beginning a pile for the camion drivers to pick up. German POW crews were at work on the long slope leading up to Blanc

Mont. Arthur wondered what that slope might have once looked like but could not picture it. The image of unmolested fields, of woods and flocks of birds, would just not come into his mind. Beyond the Bois de Vipères there were no trees, there was no color except for the green uniforms of the German prisoners. There was no level ground, only shell holes and blown-up trenches, and twisted phalanxes of picket posts and rebar to tear into your legs if you tried to walk across it. And no sound—that was the strangest thing. Just the crows cawing to each other, and the pumping of a tractor engine, and maybe once in a while the barking of a dog from somewhere beyond the moonscape. But nothing soft, no birdsong, no wind passing soothingly through the leaves. The leaves were all gone, except those that scraped against what remained of his face as he hauled more wire from Vipers Wood.

It took him most of the morning to remove the wire in front of the machine-gun position and then he started in on the picket posts, unscrewing them from the chalky rock. While he was doing so he heard Dervaux arguing beyond the margin of the trees with an angry *sinistré.* They were talking rapidly and excitedly and Arthur's French was still not good enough to make it all out. He thought the *sinistré* was telling the *chef du travaux* that his fireplace had been stolen and that he blamed the men of the Service. It made sense, but of course Dervaux could not acknowledge it.

Arthur glanced through the leaves at the man. He was middle-aged, gaunt and defeated, his patched-up clothes sagging on his frame. He was close to tears. He was telling Dervaux that he had once been a respected man in this village until the war had come and forced him to flee the home he had built with his own hands, and when he came back he had found nothing left of his house but his fireplace, and now that was gone too.

Dervaux listened without saying anything and kept his expression blank and his lips squeezed around his pipestem. He was a fair man and a sympathetic one, but his job was to put the ravaged earth back together and he could not solve the problems of every brokenhearted refugee. He told the man to go find the *maire* and complain to him, and the *sinistré* finally staggered away across the broken ground, yelling curses over his shoulder whose precise meaning Arthur could not understand.

Arthur worked in solitude the better part of the afternoon. There were other crew members in the woods, men with whom he lived in flimsy workers' barracks that had been erected for them outside Suippes, but the thick tangle of trees hid them from view and imposed a meditative silence that suited Arthur's mood. He needed to practice his French as much as possible, but talking was awkward with the prosthesis, and with half of his upper palate destroyed his voice had a parched and slurry sound that embarrassed him almost as much as his appearance.

When everything in front of the sheet of *tôle* was clear he grabbed it and tried to drag it away as well, but the iron was too heavy and unwieldy and the brush too thick. He was about to call out for help to Jérôme, who was working a few dozen yards away, when he noticed that in moving the *tôle* he had exposed an unexploded stick grenade and, just beyond it, a pair of hobnailed boots attached to the legs of a dead German soldier.

Arthur found a stick, tied a ribbon to it, and marked the grenade. Then he gently tugged the sheet of corrugated iron a little more until he had exposed the rest of the soldier's body. He was lying on his back in the little scrape trench, staring upward, his jaw hinged open as if his last act had been to gasp in wonder at something he saw revealed in the sky. There was not much skin left on the skull, and as a result the helmet that still covered his head looked absurdly oversized.

Arthur left the body lying there and went to tell Dervaux. When he came out of the trees he saw the *chef* at the edge of the road fifty yards away, talking to somebody through the passenger window of an autotruck.

"Ah! Fry! Come here!" Dervaux called when he caught sight of Arthur. "These women, they want to talk to you!"

Dervaux took a step to the side and now Arthur could see through the windows of the truck two young women staring in his direction.

Arthur stopped. He looked off to his left, hiding the grotesque half of his face from their sight. From this peculiar stance, he called to Dervaux in French.

"There is a body in the woods. And a grenade. I've marked it with a handkerchief."

"Yes, yes. Very good," Dervaux answered indifferently. "Why are you standing there? Come here."

Arthur walked over to the truck, still holding his head awkwardly to the left, a habit that was as instinctive to him now as putting one foot in front of the other. Of course, he knew he could disguise nothing. They would see soon enough. Everyone who looked at him would see soon enough.

"They say you're an American!" one of the women said, stepping out of the truck and smiling at him. "So are we!"

She was young and bold and righteous. She looked into his eyes with an uncomfortable intensity. People did that, he had noticed, because they thought it made them look unafraid and accepting.

"My name is Missy," she said. "And this is Gwendolyn."

Gwendolyn sat in the cab next to the French driver. She slid across and walked out behind Missy. She smiled as well, but less forcefully, and her eyes moved discreetly from his face to the swell of Blanc Mont.

"We're from the Smith College Relief Fund," Missy said.

They were twenty or twenty-one, Arthur guessed. Close to his age. He didn't know anything about clothes but he supposed they were expensively dressed. Their coats were tightly woven and the blue one that Missy wore looked oddly sumptuous in this landscape where color and texture no longer existed. Some of the girls he had known back in Ranger had been pretty but none of them had been so in this way, with this sweeping, shining confidence. The second one—Gwendolyn—was not as beautiful as Missy in the face, but he could see by the way her slender arms reposed so elegantly at the sides of her body, the elbows bent, the hands clasped lightly in front of her waist, that she possessed a physical refinement that was more commanding than beauty.

"We were in Suippes," Gwendolyn said, her voice as low and lazy-sounding as Missy's was excitable, "and they said there was an American working out in this sector for the STE."

Arthur nodded blankly, his face still turned away, though out of politeness he kept shifting his eyes back in their direction. He had always been bashful around girls but the need he felt now to get away was intolerable. They were trying not to stare but whenever their eyes landed on his face he felt they were scouring him with horrified scrutiny.

"So why the STE?" Missy asked, with a burst of nervous laughter.

There was something in her tone he didn't like, as if he was supposed to share her assumption that an American working to clear the French battlefields was somehow comical.

And now he had to answer, had to use his horrible wheezing, smacking voice, had to feel the vulcanite prosthesis move up and down in his ruined face like the hinged mouth of a ventriloquist's dummy.

"I'm not sure I could tell you, ma'am," he said. "I just reckoned I would stay on in France, I guess."

"Well," Gwendolyn said, "it doesn't matter. We're delighted to meet a fellow countryman. And we've talked to Monsieur Dervaux, and he's given his permission for you to come to dinner with us tonight in Suippes."

"It won't be anything fancy," Missy assured him. "Just spaghetti, probably. But one of the girls with us turns out to be a divine cook, and there's even a rumor we'll have some fresh fruit."

Arthur stood there for such a long time, not answering. He was sorry to embarrass them but he couldn't think of a polite way to say no.

Finally he said, "Well, I thank you for the invitation but I guess I'd better not."

"But why—" Missy started to say, but Gwendolyn put one of her sculpted hands on her friend's shoulder to silence her.

"Just think of it as an open invitation," she said. "We'll be in the sector for a couple of weeks at least. I'm sure all the girls would like to meet you, and we have a doctor with the unit too, Dr. Ford. He's very busy, of course, but he's very kind and would certainly want to make time to see you."

"That's all right," Arthur said. "I ain't sick."

"Well, I didn't mean that you—" She stopped herself, and then took a step forward and reached out and touched his arm just below the elbow. He could feel the pressure of her slender fingers through his heavy cotton jacket. And he knew that this would be the way women would always touch him from now on, with an over-attentive kindness, with a look in their eyes that said they understood and wanted so very much to be able to help.

"We just wanted you to feel welcome. We thought you might enjoy some American company. Please think about it, Mr. Fry."

She knew his name. It occurred to him that nobody had ever called him mister before.

He glanced at her sideways again and saw she was trying not to cry. "I reckon I better not," he said again.

ALL THAT NIGHT, lying on his cot in the temporary barracks room in Suippes, with a cold wind outside charging across the Champagne, he thought about the two girls from Smith College. He wondered where Smith College was. It had been strange to speak to them in English.

He wondered what it would have been like to accept their invitation and sit in a warm intact house somewhere eating spaghetti and maybe drinking wine with them, Missy and Gwendolyn and the rest of the young women who had come to France out of a virtuous duty to help a ravaged country. They probably would have brought the latest sheet music from back home and one of them would have played the piano while the others sang, doing their best to make their guest feel comfortable and whole. But Arthur knew, with the same casual certainty that a cow knows it can't cross a cattle guard, that he could never be at ease in anybody's company again.

The Service des Travaux de l'État was as close as he could come to that, he thought, at least for now. The anonymity of the Service suited him. He did not know or care where most of these men came from. Jérôme, sleeping in the cot beside him, was the closest he had to a friend. He was a skinny boy who patiently corrected Arthur's French as he smoked an enormous pipe that had belonged to his grandfather. Jérôme had been gassed at Navarin Farm and there was something wrong with his bowels and usually twice a night he would have to rise in pain from his cot and go to the latrine, and he would remain there for a long time. But he was uncomplaining and cheerful and did not think Arthur's own grotesque wound was in any way remarkable. Many of the other men were veterans as well, poilu who had somehow survived the war and come home to nothing. Some of their towns, like Somme-Py, had simply been blasted from the earth until hardly a stone remained and a person who had lived there all his life could not even tell where the main street had been. Most of the workers were French, but there were Russians as well, and of course the

German prisoners of war, and Chinamen and Mohammedans from the French colonies who were even farther away from home than he was.

Home was a bad thing to think about. He had been practicing for a year to keep his mind away from Ranger. There was no point in that. Maybe someday he could stand to remember what it was like to be in the fourth grade where his mother was the teacher, the way she would glance at him in his desk as she turned from the blackboard, with an expression in her face that only he could read, a secret look that said all this stern distance was for show, that she had not forgotten he was not just another pupil but her beloved son. Maybe when he was an old man and could no longer feel pain in the same way he would allow himself to minutely recall the bracing thrill of the season's first norther, or the way in summer his father used to scratch Arthur's back on the sleeping porch until he fell asleep listening to the coyotes madly pleading for something in the barren hills beyond the edge of the town.

In the meantime it was good to be in a place that could not be confused with Texas, except sometimes in its forlorn vastness. It comforted him to speak another language, to work more or less in anonymity, cordially avoided by everyone. The task of restoring the soil of France to productivity gave him an abstract satisfaction, but it was not as deep or as genuine as another feeling he could not hold on to for more than a few moments at a time, let alone define. This sensation had something to do with not really wanting the trees to grow again or the birds to be sweeping across the blank gray sky or rising from the reborn fields. He had taken some sort of comfort in the complete deadness of everything, in the silence, in the understanding that the world had been seeking an end for itself and had finally found it. He had been content to share in that stasis of oblivion, and he resented that life was starting to surge again.

He wished he had never seen those girls but they were lodged in his mind now, their clear skin and beautiful American diction, their haunting sympathy. They were part of the earth that would flower without him.

After an hour of not sleeping he started to shiver in his cot. Then he heard Dervaux cursing at the end of the room as he got out of bed and opened the creaking metal door to the stove and threw a few more thick logs into it. Firewood was precious; most of the toppled and blasted trees were so full of shrapnel they could not even be sawed. After a while the drafty room warmed a little, but Arthur could still not get to sleep. It was the prosthesis that was keeping him awake now. Maybe the drop in temperature was shrinking or expanding the object's vulcanite base, because it did not seem to be fitting properly anymore. In the French hospital in Paris they had machined grooves into the bone of what remained of his jaw to hold the apparatus in place, and there were wires and hooks too, which he could now feel biting into the tender skin on the inside of his mouth. Removing it was out of the question. Only the doctors were supposed to do that, and in any case he could not abide the thought of lying on his cot with the open crater of his face exposed to view.

He shut his eyes hard and did his best to push the pain aside. He was pretty sure it would be gone by morning, or at most fade into quiet discomfort. The horrors of the last year had left him with a sophisticated understanding of which sorts of pain could be expected to grow and tighten their grip and which would probably recede. Pain that he could identify as fleeting, no matter how intense, no longer caused him much concern.

He heard Jérôme, several cots away, turn in his blankets and sigh. It was time for him to go to the latrine. Arthur watched him get out of bed and set his feet into his boots and pull on his coat and walk outside with his bootlaces whispering on the wooden floor. The men had complained at first about Jérôme disturbing them in the middle of the night and jeered about the smell, but he had handled himself with dignity and soon they left him alone.

It might take him twenty minutes to come back. Arthur resolved to be asleep by then, but the best he could manage was to enter a suggestive still-conscious state in which he saw images that were not dreams, but that were startling in their detail and specificity. He relived the day in the Bois de Vipères, he saw with enthralling precision the way the light came through the leaves and the patterns in the coils of barbed wire. He saw once more the young women from Smith College and felt so much vivid yearning and regret when they appeared in his mind that he shook himself out of this pre-dreaming state and into stark alertness.

And in the place of these hypnotic visitations there was just wretched memory again. He did not know what sort of shell it had been that had wounded him. He had no memory of anything after the fight in the cemetery. The shell that had blown off half his face had also ripped away part of his clothes and buried him in mud, though there had been enough of his face exposed so that he could breathe through his mangled nose. He never knew how long he had been there. The French had been fighting on their flank and it was French *brancardiers* who had found him. The American part of the attack had moved on by then, and his uniform had been so torn and bloody that the *brancardiers* probably did not even know what army he had belonged to and so had just lifted him onto a stretcher and taken him to the French dressing station.

He had come to in brief waves of consciousness. He lay on the mud-streaked green linoleum floor of the field hospital, watching men writhe under red blankets, screaming so hard the veins in their throats looked as if they would burst, though with his damaged eardrums Arthur could barely hear their cries or his own. He could feel the wooden structure of the hospital trembling all around him as the shells landed along the front. When he opened his eyes again he saw a priest with pince-nez arguing about something with a doctor. The doctor was rubbing his back against a wooden post, trying to get some relief from the cooties. The men were speaking in French and Arthur could not understand a word, but he guessed they were talking about him and about how the doctor resented having to treat an American when there were so many wounded poilu needing attention.

He remembered the hideous smell of the ether as they poured it onto the mask, and the hallucinatory grid that then appeared over his eyes, each square going blank one after the next until he woke again into a postoperative existence of pain and bewilderment and static time. For the long months he was in one hospital or another the smell of the ether never went away. There was the smell of ether but also the odors of disinfectant, blood, putrid flesh, mud, and gas from the acetylene generators that provided wavery light. Wending through the toxic smells was the aroma of the nurses' cocoa from the sterilizing room where they kept it simmering on the boiler. The nurses wore starched blue uniforms and the priests wore purple stoles and the wounded were brought in under red blankets. Red hot-water bottles were everywhere; in his delirium they seemed like sentinels, hanging from nails on the wooden posts and resting at the foot of every bed. Wounded men vomited black blood into white enamel basins.

When his eardrums healed he could hear the pounding of the boilers and the crackling sound of gas gangrene bubbles as the nurses pressed on them, and the shrieks of men calling out to God or their mothers as their wounds were dressed.

A French boy with a facial wound almost as bad as his was in the bed next to him for several weeks, and he taught Arthur a few words of French and read articles out loud in *Le Rire* and *Le Petit Parisien*, pointing to the words Arthur already knew to show him how they were spelled. He said he was an apache, and finally made Arthur understand that the word did not mean he was an Indian but a petty criminal from the Paris streets who had been drafted into the Bataillon d'Afrique. Then one day they took him off to surgery and he never came back.

Arthur's own surgeries were complicated by the impatience of the doctors who resented the fact he did not speak French so they could explain what it was they were going to do to him. Only once had there been a doctor who was fluent enough in English that Arthur could understand him, and what he said only made him more afraid.

"We will take out today a little more of this part of the face," he announced cheerfully as they were getting the ether ready. "There will be some pain afterwards but God will give you strength."

Sometimes it seemed to him he went into surgery in one hospital and woke up in another. He never had a clear sense of what hospital he was in, or what ward he was in, or where the war was. Sometimes he could hear shells in the distance and sometimes there were birds singing, and nurses laughing outside on their breaks.

During the last surgeries he was in a ward exclusively filled with cases like his own, many of them worse. Some of the men had no faces at all, just collapsing holes where mouths and noses had been and a pair of frightened, bewildered eyes staring out at the world. Sometimes the doctors were able to create a semblance of a face for them again, as they did for Arthur, but they always had the look of men wearing a mask, trapped behind some fixed expression, unable as he was to smile or to convey emotions except through the plaintive movement of their eyes.

It was just before they were going to put the prosthesis in, sometime in the spring, that an American lieutenant found him in a garden to the side of the hospital in Paris, where he sometimes went to sit in the sunlight with a child's French grammar book that one of the nurses had given him.

"There you are!" the lieutenant said. "We've been looking for you!"

Arthur was startled to hear somebody speaking to him in English—the exclamatory words sounded like an assault. When he saw it was an officer, he saluted, and when the man saw Arthur's face the heartiness went out of his voice and he set his gaze a few inches above Arthur's head.

The lieutenant was studious-looking, with a spare build and a distracted manner. He told Arthur he had been listed as missing in action until a few weeks ago, when word came that he was alive and with the French. The 36th was in Tonnerre, getting ready to leave for Brest and embark for home.

"If you want to go home with the rest of the Arrowheads," he said, "you've got to get on a train in the next three days."

Arthur said he was supposed to be fitted for a prosthesis and didn't think he could make it.

"Well, I don't know what the hell to do about that," the lieutenant said. "We're all going home and I've got other men to see about before we do."

Arthur said he was sorry and the lieutenant nodded in a distracted way and shifted nervously on his feet. There was an empty chair next to Arthur in the garden but he didn't sit down. He told Arthur he was sorry to have to tell him this but both of his parents and his little brother had died of the flu three months ago.

The news did not seem so bad at first because it could not be true. But then he could feel the reality of it forming and growing, and he knew it was useless to argue against it. After seeing Ben die, after catching a glimpse of his face for the first time in the shaving mirror of the man in the bed next to him, he had developed a swifter acceptance of inconceivable things. All of his family was dead; he could try to rally his imagination against this knowledge but he knew that in the end his imagination would be crushed.

"Can I get a discharge, sir?" he asked the lieutenant.

"What are you talking about?"

"I didn't want to go home anyway, looking like this. And now there's nobody to go home to."

"You want to live in France?"

"Yes sir, I think so."

The lieutenant said he would come back the next day. When he did, he brought with him discharge papers for Arthur to sign. Arthur didn't even read them. He just scrawled his signature where the lieutenant told him to. The lieutenant wished him good luck, put the papers back into his satchel, and walked away, hurrying to catch the train for Tonnerre so that he would not be left behind.

From the first week Arthur had arrived in France he had been homesick and had almost driven himself insane by casting his mind forward to the day they would be boarding the ship to return home. After a few months the feeling had eased somewhat, but he could never have believed the relief he felt now at not having to go back at all. His parents were dead but at least now they were spared from having to see him when he stepped off the train, their son who had left half his face in the mud of Saint-Étienne and who now tried to hide the damage with a frightening apparatus that was almost as hideous as the wound. No one else would have to see him, either: not his brother or his classmates or the people he worked with in the feed store, not the soldiers he had trained and fought with, not the girls he had spoken to at high school dances or camp meetings, not the grandmother who had already buried three of her sons and always had a look in her eyes that said she knew God had worse in store for her.

He had the sense that in France his disfigurement would not be quite so freakish or horrid, because the war had been going on for so many years before the Americans had come that the people were used to seeing men with appalling wounds. It was easier just to think of himself as someone who had died and been imperfectly resurrected in a strange new place, with a new language to learn and foreign manners to decipher, someone who was now free of any expectation of happiness or companionship.

•

IN HIS MOST contented moments Arthur thought of himself as an unfeeling ghost, drifting above all the fear and hurt of the world. Nothing else could be taken from him because all that mattered was already gone. But then there would be an encounter, such as the one today with those girls from Smith College, to remind him that there were still yearnings that could not be suppressed or fulfilled. No matter how purified of emotion he might feel at certain times, there was always something left to be stirred up, some new assault of homesickness that was all the more forceful because he knew in his heart he could not quell it by returning home.

Weeks later, after they had cleared the Bois des Vipères and the nearby trench and Blanc Mont Ridge, and after he had recovered the blank state of mind that was his only source of peace, he found himself standing where he and Ben had stood before, at the jump-off line where the attack on Saint-Étienne had started. It was a cold, cloudy day, colder than it had been this time last year. The village's church steeple was shattered and half the buildings were now rubble. The wire where the Kuholtz boys had fallen was still in place. He and Jérôme spent the better part of two days removing it, then began clearing the machine-gun nests and filling in the scrapes that were hidden in almost invisible swales of the terrain. Arthur realized as he worked what an effective killing zone this had been, the machine guns positioned to reinforce one another and to cover deliberately placed gaps in the wire where the inexperienced attackers had been channeled.

Thousands of sharp-edged shell fragments poking up from the ground made it treacherous to walk. They found helmets and gas masks and spectacles and scraps of paper and postcards buried in the hard dirt, and once the bones of someone's hand that the American cleanup squads had missed. Anything that looked like it might be some sort of personal artifact was tossed in a pile that Dervaux would go through at the end of the day to determine if it was something that should be forwarded to the American army.

It did not look like the same place to him. At the time of the attack the battlefield had been hidden in smoke and fumes and curtains of dirt raining down from the impact of the shells. Even if the landscape had not been so deeply obscured he would have seen little of it, since he had barely looked up the whole time as he clung tight to the ground or moved with cowering dread from one position to another.

Even now, he found himself crouching and looking for places to hide himself, gripped by a fear of standing upright, exposed to fire.

After a few days they began work on the cemetery at the edge of the village. He remembered this place better, it was seared into his mind forever. There was a civilian cemetery and next to it one for the German army, built during the years when the Boche had occupied the village and thought they would never leave this part of France and so interred their dead in its soil. The Germans had left their own cemetery untouched except for a trench running between the rows of crosses, but the civilian cemetery next to it had been heavily fortified in preparation for the American and French assault. The Boche had dug into the graves, hauled the coffins and bodies away, and tied into the deep crypts with their trenchworks.

The villagers had taken it upon themselves to restore the civilian cemetery as best they could, but there were still gaping trenches and shell holes and a litter of broken marble from tombstones and grave monuments. While the men of the Service worked, some of the villagers stood and watched, anxious that the dead still remaining in their tombs not be disturbed further.

The temperature had dropped again, but there was so much shoveling and hauling to do that Arthur sweated through his work clothes and his hands felt numb and clammy inside his gloves. The discomfort helped to deaden his mind. He worked with mechanical intensity, trying to think only of the debris to be cleared and the meal to be eaten at the end of the day and the possibility of exhausted sleep to follow. He worked next to Jérôme and two other men, hauling *tôle* and wire to the scrap heap outside the cemetery walls. He had not told anyone that he had fought in the battle here. He had no interest in speaking about it, in English or in French, and most of the men here had stories of their own of far greater battles, from the dark times of the war before the Americans had come. There were braggarts in the Service, of course, men who could not shut up, but Arthur had noticed that most of the men preferred to talk of other things, or to talk of nothing at all, and that sort of evasive silence suited him well.

Turning over the dirt on the rim of a shell hole, he found a little appointment book for 1918, most of its pages eaten away by the elements, and with German notations written in pencil. In the hole itself there was a Waterbury pocket watch. It was a cheap watch, beyond repair, and there was no inscription on the back, but he added it and the appointment book to the growing pile of personal effects at the base of a monument in the German cemetery.

Many of the grave markers in the civilian sector of the cemetery had been blown to shards, others had been carried away by the villagers for safekeeping, but a few were still in place, their elaborate stonework scarred by shrapnel and machine-gun fire, their crosses and angels broken off. Arthur studied one of them as he worked in the late afternoon under the gray winter sky. It was the grave of a man with his own first name, Arthur Depuiset. *"Décédé le 15 mai 1899,"* it read. *"Âgé de 51 ans."*

He wondered who Arthur Depuiset had been. He wondered what it would like to be fifty-one years old. Arthur's parents had been barely forty when they died, but they had seemed so old to him the last time he had seen them, standing there blank-faced as he boarded the troop train out of Fort Worth. His mother had not cried. She was from harder stock than his father, who had a sentimental streak and shook Arthur's hand with a pleading look in his eyes. He could imagine those wounded eyes looking at him now, trying to understand what had happened to his son, and he felt once again the bitter relief he took in the knowledge that his parents were dead.

Arthur expected he himself might reach thirty or so. He did not really care to live much longer, and would surely be well through with life by then. In the hospital an English-speaking French doctor had come one day and asked him right away if he had had any notions about killing himself. Arthur had told the truth and said he had not, but he remained mildly receptive to the idea of an early death. He would bide his time uncomplainingly, and then a day would come when he would not have to think about anything or endure anything or fight back memories anymore.

He read the inscription on another grave—*"À la Mémoire de Marie Adeline Rossignon. Décédée l'août 1902 dans sa 71e année."* He was thinking how Marie Adeline seemed like such a young name, wondering what it was like to be called that as an old woman of seventy-one, when he noticed two bullet holes in the lower left side of the monument.

He had a shuddering awareness that this was the place. This was where Ben had died. Maybe the bullets that had made those marks were the same bullets that had passed through Ben Clayton's body.

It was odd that he could just go on working today, knowing where he was, but he could. He shoveled dirt into the trench, wrested iron and wood out of the grip of the soil and the permeable rock below. He just kept working like it was any place else.

He tried not to think about anything as he worked but it wasn't really possible. He didn't blame himself if his mind slipped back into the past as long as his body kept burying it. It must have been in the assault toward the positions on the far side of the stream that he had been wounded. He did not know exactly where he had been found and had been in too much pain and bewilderment to ask. Somewhere on this side of the stream, probably. The last thing he remembered was being in the German trench, staring in stupefaction at Ben's already-dead body. Ben's eyes were fixed and blank and it looked as if he were willingly dead, a quality of acceptance that had infuriated Arthur and made him feel as lonesome as a child in a dark forest. He remembered the feeling of betrayal as well, the sense that Ben had purposely left him for some plane of experience that was more interesting.

The memory came back to him now but without, he supposed, the proper weight. His wound had been so searing and complete that it had been impossible for him to see beyond it. He could only imagine the intensity of the grief he would have felt for Ben if he had not entered into such a cauterizing inferno of his own. Even the death of his family, which he knew should have left him howling with sorrow and shock, was something he seemed to have accepted with fatalistic understanding. It was not that he had ceased to feel, only that he had ceased to be impressed.

By the end of the day the sky was sealed in with lustrous gray winter clouds. Night would fall in an hour. He was all right. Being back on this battlefield, back in the cemetery at Saint-Étienne, had caused him no special suffering much beyond what he had already set himself to endure. The work, as always, had been hard and annealing, and he was twitchy from hunger and looking forward to the soup and bread waiting for them in their headquarters in Suippes.

He gathered up the few personal items he had found—the remains of a fountain pen, a torn photograph of someone's mother, a single key—and took them over to the pile at the base of the monument in the German cemetery.

The monument was hideous—a relief sculpture of a naked man with his hands on the hilt of a massive sword. The man was squat in stature, his hair cropped short, his expression a disdainful frown. Above the man's head were the words *"GOTT-MITT-UNS"* and below the sword point *"Gewidmet, 18. June. Div. 1915–1916."* It struck Arthur as interesting that two years before the fight here the Germans had been so sure of their possession of this part of France they had buried their war dead in its soil and erected this scowling angel to watch over them.

"It's ugly, is it not?" Jérôme said to him in French. He was lighting his massive pipe while sitting on the curving bench in front of the sculpture.

"I don't like it," Arthur agreed.

He tossed the fountain pen and the key and the photograph onto the pile of personal effects. The pile had grown during the day and there were perhaps a hundred items there now, nothing of any obvious consequence and certainly nothing of any value.

"To be a sculptor, to have that gift, and to produce something so wretched as this."

Jérôme was shaking his head in theatrical disdain, waiting for Arthur to reply in the same spirit. But Arthur had stopped listening. He was looking at a small rectangle of metal that gleamed a little in the failing light and looked familiar. When he picked it up out of the pile he saw that it was what he had thought: a rectangle cut out of a mess-kit lid, with a crude relief carving of a horse standing on a Texas mesa.

NINE

Gil and Maureen returned to the Clayton ranch in late November, bringing with them suitcases with enough clothes for a week's stay and a wooden packing box containing the clay maquette of the statue.

As soon as they had set down their luggage, Gil carried the box to a side table in the parlor and asked for a clawhammer. When George's Mary brought it to him he went to work, prying out the reinforcing strips of wood with a deliberate lack of ceremony. Lamar Clayton was a man who would want things presented to him plain, particularly a clay sketch of his dead son.

"I'd like the curtains open, if you don't mind," Gil said, after he had removed the sides of the box. The maquette itself was still shrouded in hay and egg cartons and newspaper, and he was anxious that it be presented in an advantageous light. The windows in the room were small, but when George's Mary opened the curtains the plane-flattening dimness disappeared, and Gil and Maureen peeled back the layers of newspaper with confidence.

Clayton grabbed a hardback chair from the corner of the room and sat himself down in front of the clay model. His little dog, jealous of the attention he was giving it, tried to jump up into his lap, but Clayton swiped her away. The smell of the clay filled the room.

"I still ain't sure about him not being on the horse," Clayton said after a moment.

"I am. The piece will be more powerful if he is standing beside it."

Gil disregarded Clayton's skeptical and slightly perturbed glance.

"I can tell it's him but there ain't much detail," Clayton said. "Not in the face anyway."

"The details will come later. You can be confident it will look like your son before it's finished."

"Something about the horse ain't right either. Legs are too long maybe."

Gil merely nodded. He wasn't worried. The sculpture was strong. He knew that Clayton understood well enough that the model before him was only a starting place. He had seen this look of dour inspection in other clients who regarded immediate enthusiasm as a sign of weakness.

"Well, *I* like it, Mr. Gilheaney," George's Mary said. "I look at that and I see Ben for sure, and Poco too."

"I didn't say I didn't like it," Clayton growled. He turned to Maureen. "What do you think?"

"I think it will be extraordinary."

"Don't want to see him in the saddle?"

"No, Mr. Clayton. I don't think so. This is better."

"Well, I guess it's good the two of you are thinking alike."

And that was his last word on the subject. His lack of any further comment evidently meant that the concept was approved. All through dinner he kept glancing at the maquette, silently assessing it. Afterwards, when Gil and Maureen were sitting with him on the porch, staring out at an orange moon, he unbuttoned a shirt pocket and handed Gil a check.

"That's your commencement money."

"Thank you," Gil said. "As soon as Maureen and I get back I'll begin work on the scale model. Then we'll begin building the armature for the full-size clay. In the meantime, while I'm here, the more I can learn about Ben and the sort of life he led, the better the quality of the work will be."

"The sort of life he led," Clayton repeated.

"Correct."

"You say you can ride a horse without falling off?"

"I can, though it's the best that can be said for my horsemanship."

Clayton smiled, liking his guest's candor. He glanced at Maureen, who replied with an amused shrug, then turned back to Gil.

"We've got some calves in a pasture over on the other side of the ranch that need to be checked for screwworms. I'll tell Ernest to put Ben's saddle on Poco, and you can ride over there with us on the boy's own horse."

"That would suit me fine."

Clayton tossed his cigarette off the porch and stood up. "All right. We'll leave after breakfast in the morning."

The old man said good night and walked into the house. Maureen waited until she thought he was out of earshot before gently confronting her father.

"You know, it's rough country out there, Daddy."

"I suppose the horses are used to it. Don't worry, I'll come back in one piece. And what better opportunity could there be for soaking up authenticity?"

FRANCIS GILHEANEY did not make a particularly authentic-looking cowboy. Just after a hideously early breakfast, Maureen followed her father and Mr. Clayton out of the house to where Nax and Ernest were waiting with the horses saddled. Her father wore his Abercrombie and Fitch hunting clothes, with a stout pair of city boots. His spruce outfit was crowned with a hard-used cowboy hat that he had borrowed from Clayton. Underneath its drooping brim, Gil was grinning with delight. He clapped his hands together and said good morning to Clayton in a hearty voice.

He was the sort of man who could wear anything and make it his, Maureen reflected, the sort of man who strode onto an unfamiliar scene with confidence and purpose. As a young girl, watching her father at work in his studio as he heaved on pulleys, built massive armatures, carried around bronze busts as heavy as cannonballs in a single hand, she had naturally formed the conviction that to be a monumental sculptor you had to be a monumental man. He had been that, and was still.

The seventy-year-old Lamar Clayton mounted his horse with no more effort than it required him to take a seat at the head of his dining table. Maureen knew her father to be a fit man, but he was fit in the wrong way for ranch work, and for a moment—as he tried to lift one long leg high enough to set his foot into the stirrup—she worried that he would need assistance from Ernest and hence die of embarrassment. But he managed finally to heave himself into the saddle and when he did so he looked down at Maureen with an expression that suggested she keep her doubts about his riding ability to herself.

They set off at a walk along the road leading from the house and over the shallow creek. Maureen watched them long enough to satisfy herself that her father was not going to immediately fall off his horse, then she went inside to help George's Mary with the breakfast dishes.

"Oh no, don't you dare even think about that," George's Mary said, pretending to slap her arm away when she brought in a few dishes from the table. "You and your daddy are guests here, and that's all there is to it."

Maureen stayed in the kitchen, thinking that the least she should do was keep George's Mary company as she went about her housework. The housekeeper scrubbed the dishes and placed them in the drying rack with a precision and efficiency that Maureen found compelling, a lifetime's expertise behind the work. George's Mary's face was big and blunt but Maureen supposed that in her youth her features had been agreeably strong; maybe there had even been a period of beauty. She was rather fat now but there was tensile strength in her forearms, which bulged with muscle as she wielded the scrub brush.

"I hope my father survives this outing," Maureen said.

"Oh, I expect he'll be wore out when he comes back, but Mr. Clayton'll look out for him. I ain't never cared much for horses, myself. They had their way they'd keep biting you till hell ain't bigger than a minute."

"You must have done your share of horseback riding, growing up in this country."

"I did, but I also made sure to find a way around it whenever I could."

"And tell me about—"

George's Mary laughed. "You're polite, so it took you about a minute longer to get around to asking about my name than most folks."

"I'm sorry. I hope it isn't forward of me."

"To ask somebody about their name? Don't see what's forward about that. I got it because my daddy and my uncle Dan both had little girls named Mary. They were partners on some land over on the

Salt Fork, and we were all piled on top of each other in a sod house there for a while with everybody calling out Mary and nobody knowing which one they meant. So it came to be Dan's Mary and George's Mary."

"Does your family still call you that?"

"No, they was all killed by Indians a good long time ago."

Since George's Mary said this with no particular inflection while she went on scrubbing the dishes, Maureen did not think it her role to gasp with horror, as she most certainly would have done among her own set. Of course, no one among her own set would have the occasion to let slip in a matter-of-fact way that her whole family had been wiped out by Indians.

"So it's just the two of you—you and your dad?" George's Mary asked.

"Yes. My mother died last year of the flu."

"Well, I'm sure sorry to hear that."

"Thank you. Are you sure I can't help you with the dishes?"

"You just go on about your business," George's Mary answered, "and maybe I'll let you help me get supper on a little later."

The problem was that Maureen had no business to go about. She walked into the parlor and looked wistfully out the window, irritated at how casually her father had left her behind, and how neither he nor Lamar Clayton had even thought to ask if she might want to accompany them on their screwworm expedition to the far reaches of the ranch. She had had no desire to do so and, unlike her father, nothing to prove, but the assumption that none of this was any of her real concern left her deeply annoyed. Here on this ranch the witless primacy of men was in its fullest expression.

With this on her mind she became aware, standing idly in the parlor, of another female presence. The late Mrs. Clayton's clothes were doubtless all packed away or given away, and her personal effects were not on display. But there was the elegant china in its glass-fronted cabinet, and several nicely framed prints on the walls. They were nothing special—just a wintry sketch of a sleigh ride and a watercolor of distant strollers on a windswept beach—but they had obviously been chosen with a woman's eye for balance and color, as a vital assault upon the dim functionality of the house where she had come to live. And next to a battered rolltop desk was a single anomalous specimen of furniture, a corner piece of polished cherry decorated with ormolu script. On its surface someone had thoughtlessly set down a rusted crescent wrench and an old coffee can full of nails and screws. Maureen hesitated for a moment, satisfied herself that George's Mary was still busy in the kitchen, and walked over and bent down to open the small curved door at the front of the chest. Inside, on a shelf, were stacked subscription copies of *Harper's Bazaar,* the *Atlantic Monthly,* and several other magazines she would not have expected to find in this barren stretch of Texas. There were respectable novels as well, and catalogs from fashionable department stores, and news stories about museum exhibits and New York theater productions that had been clipped out of the Dallas newspapers.

She had understood from talking to Mr. Clayton that day on the mesa that his wife had been more worldly than he was, but Maureen glimpsed in this hidden reliquary a heartbreaking yearning for a sophisticated life, for news from the distant capitals of culture. She tried to imagine this woman lying in bed next to Lamar Clayton. She tried to imagine her chatting with George's Mary, setting down her copy of *Harper's Bazaar* to listen to the story of the massacre of her housekeeper's family.

Maureen wondered what aspirations Mrs. Clayton would have had for her son—had she survived his childhood, had he survived the war. Perhaps she had loved this wild country as much or more than any man; it was certainly not impossible. But it was more than a guess on Maureen's part that it could not have been enough for her, and that she would not have accepted that it would be enough for Ben. If she had lived, perhaps he would have too, propelled by her unfulfilled dreams to attend some eastern school or laze about in some foreign capital where neither duty nor the draft would have found him.

But there was barely a hint of the woman who might have presided over this alternative future, just a stack of magazines and books and a few pictures on the wall. And, perhaps most tellingly, no statue to her memory.

"YOU DON'T NEED to worry about them reins so much," Clayton told Gil as they rode across a vast open pasture, golden with winter grass. "Poco's got a pretty good notion about where we're headed and how fast we need to get there."

Gil loosened his grip and let the reins slacken a little, grateful for the chance to concentrate just on keeping his seat in the saddle. He decided not to feel perturbed by Clayton's implicit comment on his riding skills.

"I didn't mean to interfere with my horse's pursuit of his professional duties," he said.

Clayton chuffed out a laugh. Ernest and Nax were a half mile ahead of them, dismounting to open a wire gate that led away from the easy prairie flats onto broken ground. The weather had closed in a little, a moist fog hovering above the grass and in tangles of wiry mesquite. Gil buttoned his jacket up and wished he'd brought gloves or that somebody had thought to bring them for him. They had gone maybe three or four miles and the novelty of riding a horse across the Texas prairie had long since fled. They were moving at a fast walk, and he was having trouble finding a rhythm in the erratic tremors the pace created in animal and rider. Stretching out his legs to absorb the shock had already given him intimations of cramps along the insides of his thighs.

Gil had never had instruction in riding and, unlike his companions today, he had not been born to the saddle. But he had learned to sit on a horse, more or less, during one particularly heady period in New York, when he was a young sculptor on the rise and was frequently invited to Mrs. Gilder's salon. Mingling with various Sedgwicks and Frelinghuysens and Morgans, he had been invited often enough for country weekends involving tame equestrian rambles.

He was a long way from those well-kept trails today, he thought, suppressing a wave of concern as they passed through the wire gate and Clayton—without a word of warning—led them into a plunge down a steep creek bank. It may not actually have been steep, but to Gil it seemed like a cataclysmic drop. He surrendered the pretense of controlling his horse and just grabbed the saddle horn with both hands and prayed that Poco would get them out of this. The horse picked his way carefully downward, along a rude path bordered with jagged rocks, but when he got to the bottom of the slope he hopped forward into the shallow water and then lurched out again on the other side. The horse clambered up the opposite side of the slope with what seemed to Gil—just before he was pitched off—like malicious exuberance.

Clayton heard the note of alarm in his guest's voice and turned around in time to see Gilheaney land on his back on more or less flat ground between a clump of sharp-sided rocks and the pads of a prickly pear. He clucked his horse to a stop and waited to see if the sculptor was going to need help to move.

"*That* was invigorating," Gilheaney said. His breath was short but he was already on his feet, grinning as if he had fallen off the horse on purpose.

"You might've busted something," Clayton said.

"Might have, but I don't think so." He grabbed Poco's reins and launched himself back into the saddle. "Lead on, Mr. Clayton," he said.

Clayton spurred his horse and Poco picked up speed to follow before Gil could instruct him to do so. Gil was rattled and horse-shy now, thinking of the rocks he had barely missed in his fall. He flexed the fingers of his hands in the cold. He might easily have broken both hands when he hit the ground, an accident which could have put an end to his life's work as decisively as a broken neck or a cracked skull. But only his vanity was injured, and he knew that the best cure for that was to bluff his way exuberantly forward.

"Frost is late this year," Clayton was saying in a conversational tone as they ascended to level ground again and Gil finally relaxed his grip on the saddle horn. "Once we get ourselves a good hard freeze it'll take care of them screwworm flies but until then there's always hell to pay."

The sun was higher now, burning away the fog, but the temperature held steady—in the mid-thirties, Gil guessed. Wind swept down from the bluffs and mesas and feathered its way through the winter grass. Gil's shoulder was sore. There would be a many-hued bruise when he took off his shirt tonight. His toes were growing numb in their city boots, and he was hungry and did not know if they would be eating.

"Pretty fair view of it from here," Clayton said, nodding in the direction of a shallow mesa. At first Gil did not recognize it as the summit upon which the statue was to be placed, but once he did he was entranced all over again by the thought of a distant lone horseman standing there, iron-still and vigilant. To a passing rider like himself—and perhaps one day a passing motorist—it would not be clear at first that this apparition was a statue at all. Silhouetted against a far horizon, utterly unexpected, utterly unexplained, it would give the impression of a conscious watcher, someone who had merely paused in magnificent contemplation.

"I believe this will be my masterpiece, Mr. Clayton." He had not planned to say this. He was unlike many of the other artists he had known, pompous and excitable men who had neither the interest nor the ability to keep the breadth of their ambition a strategic secret. But when he had sighted the mesa summit from this vantage—cold and hungry and sore as he already was—a gust of creative exuberance had come out of nowhere to claim him.

"Well," Clayton replied, "I'm pleased you think so."

Poco exhaled and wagged his head and shifted his weight, still bearing his rider along at a plodding walk. Gil gave some thought about what to say to Clayton next.

"I wonder if you would tell me something about your experiences with the Indians."

They rode along, five paces, ten, Clayton not answering. Had he heard?

"I ask because of natural curiosity, of course," Gil explained, "but also because it would help me understand the particular heritage to which your son was born. I've found that the more deeply I can understand a person, the more authentic a sculpture I can create."

Clayton said nothing. He did not nod his head or grunt in response, did not smile or scowl or give any other sign that he had heard.

"We're gonna take a look at these calves up in this here pasture," Clayton said at last, blatantly evading the topic as they rode through another wire gate that Nax was holding open for them. They entered a big pasture, filled with young calves that were ignoring the grass for the most part and roaming up and down the fence line, bleating in anxiety.

"Bawling for their mamas," Clayton explained. "Ain't the happiest time of their lives. We castrate them and brand them and then put them over here to get weaned. Screwworms'll get started wherever there's an open wound, and these calves got plenty of those. Not just from the branding and castrating but from rubbing up against the wire like they do looking for their mothers."

Clayton spurred his horse into a trot and Poco followed at the same pace. Gil grabbed the saddle horn again and pushed against the stirrups with the soles of his feet and did his best to take the irrhythmic shocks in his legs.

With a stern eye, Clayton inspected the miserable lonely calves as he rode among them. Ernest and Nax were doing the same thing far away on the other side of the pasture.

"Over yonder—there's one down," Clayton announced, and this time they broke into a gallop, or at least what felt to Gil like a gallop. They rode for a half mile or so and then Clayton reined in and roped the calf just as it stood up to run.

His horse planted its feet as the old man dismounted and walked along the taut rope to the downed calf. He was agile enough getting off his horse but in no hurry.

"Care for some help?" Gil called to him.

Clayton shrugged. Gil climbed down and let Poco's reins drop, assuming the horse knew not to run away. By the time he got over to the calf, Clayton had already thrown it to the ground and was wrapping its rear legs with a pigging rope.

"Grab ahold of this here hind leg," he said. Gil did as he was instructed, pulling one hind leg and bracing his foot against the other as Clayton held the calf down with one hand and inspected an oozy, bloody scar on its stomach.

"He was bleeding from his belly button," he said. "That's how the flies got in. They been eating at him three or four days now, I reckon. That's how he come to be lying on the ground—just too weak to stand anymore. You keep holding him down and I'll get the medicine."

The calf bawled in distress but lay compliantly still as Gil held him. The stench of the wound came to him now, and he turned his head away.

Clayton untied a boot from the side of his saddle and brought it back and set it down by the calf. From the boot top he pulled out a bottle of chloroform and a jar filled with what looked like black tar.

"First we got to get them worms out," Clayton said, setting to work. He used his fingers, gouging out the white pulsing worms from the open wound on the calf's belly and flicking them away onto the grass. The calf thrashed in pain. The smell of suppurating flesh blossomed.

"Whiffy sonsofbitches, ain't they?"

Lamar saw the sculptor gag as he nodded in agreement. He'd been pretty game up until now, but Lamar wondered how much of his enthusiasm was show and how much was real. He didn't like the pushy way he was about Ben, prying into the boy's life as if it was his private business as much as it was Lamar's. He had his Kodaks, he had Ben's clothes, he was riding his goddam horse. How much did you need to take a likeness of somebody?

He didn't say any of that, of course. But he couldn't help pushing back a little.

"Want to take a turn?" he asked Gilheaney.

He had to give the sculptor credit. He just took a breath and started digging around in the wound with his fingers while Lamar took over holding the calf down.

"They're slippery little creatures," he said, turning his head off to the side, away from the smell.

"They eat live meat," Lamar said. "We didn't put a stop to it, they'd pretty much eat up this poor animal from the inside."

He watched as Gilheaney scooped out another few wiggling handfuls, then leaned over and inspected the wound himself.

"That ought to about do it," he said. "You been a good friend to this little cow today, Mr. Gilheaney. Not that he'd ever admit it to you."

GIL SAT BACK, breathing clear air again, and watched as Clayton poured chloroform on the wound. After that he reached into the can and spread the tarry black medicine on the wound to keep more flies from settling in.

When he was through he nodded to Gil to let the calf go. Weak as it was, it sprang to its feet and trotted away, back toward the fence line, hopelessly bellowing for its mother.

The two men remained on the ground, watching it.

"Well, that's ranch work. You want to know what Ben was up to most of his life, this is it."

"I suspect he was very good at it."

"Most of it he was. Not this part especially. He was softhearted, didn't like to see things in pain. But hell, when it comes to ranching, some critter's always going to be mad at you for some damn reason or other."

"Where'd the soft heart come from? His mother?"

"Could be," Clayton said. He pulled himself up from the ground, and Gil could see from the arthritic effort that the feat of roping the calf had cost him. Had he done it for his benefit? To show the dude in the Abercrombie hunting jacket that a seventy-year-old man was more vital than he was?

Twenty yards away, Poco was calmly grazing. The horse made no objection when Gil picked the reins up from the ground and launched himself back into the saddle. Off in the distance Ernest and Nax had another calf down.

"As far as that other thing goes," Clayton said, as he tied the medicine boot back onto his saddle. "I don't generally talk about that part of my life."

"All right," Gil said.

"I know you say you're looking for something more than what the Kodaks show he looked like, but seems to me that's enough to catch his likeness."

"All right," Gil said. "But I thought *you* wanted more than a likeness."

Gil was tired and hungry—and irritated. His tone had been stern. Clayton caught the bite in it and responded with a tight smile.

"All I want is sixteen thousand dollars' worth of your best work," he said. "Ain't neither one of us going to bring him back to life."

TEN

They were back at the house by late afternoon. Gil offered to help Ernest and Nax put away the tack and take care of the horses, but they refused, as he had secretly hoped they would, and so he was able to stagger into Ben's room and lie down on the floor. He was so covered with dust he could not consider lying on the bed, and anyway the floor suited him, since his body was so dramatically sore and cramped.

Maureen knocked softly on the door and asked if he was all right, and he called out that of course he was, he was just changing his clothes. But it took him another ten minutes to gather the will to pull himself off the floor and remove his jacket. He went to the basin and washed his grimy face and neck as best he could and admired the bruise spreading across his upper back. Then he painfully bent down to unlace his boots. Gil was used to brutal physical labor but the chronic discomfort of riding a horse for most of the day was new to him. As he was pulling off his trousers, cramps began in both his legs at once, and he sank to the floor again until they had passed.

He was starving. Lunch had been a boiled egg and a piece of bread eaten on horseback as they left the far pasture with the weaning calves still crying piteously for their mothers. So far, a city man's muscle and stomach pangs were the only insights he could conclude he had gathered from the day's exertions, but he was confident that on a deeper level something important had registered in his imagination.

The smells of leather and sweaty horsehair, the damp cold, the sere winter grass, the cramps in his thighs, the numbness in his fingers, his growing hunger as they ventured farther and farther into a country that was trackless and unknowable to him, the indifference of his horse to his existence as it took its deliberative steps over difficult terrain, the sight of the screwworm flies teeming in open wounds, the terror of the abandoned calves, the boundless but oppressive sky, Lamar Clayton riding beside him in silence, his expertness in every gesture and deed, his immemorial presence: these things could not be sculpted, but they could be called upon. The hands that shaped Ben Clayton's form would have at least held the reins to his horse, would have turned themselves for a day or two to the work that the boy had known.

He walked stiff-legged into the parlor. Maureen was the only one there. She was setting the table while George's Mary was busy in the kitchen. Gil could smell chicken frying and bread baking.

"She finally gave in and let me help her set the table," Maureen whispered. With a glance, she assessed her father's stove-up condition. "I hope it was worth it. You look like you've—"

"It was worth it," he said. He stood with his hands on a chairback, watching as she set down the plates.

"Why don't you sit?" she said.

"I'm all right. What was your day like?"

She glanced at the kitchen to make sure George's Mary did not hear her.

"Long. Maybe even longer than yours."

"I doubt that."

She came around from the opposite end of the table and whispered in his ear.

"It turns out *her* family was killed by Indians too. We're really in the wild west, Daddy."

Gil was about to respond when Clayton walked into the room. He had taken off his jacket but was still wearing the clothes he had spent the day working in. There was calf's blood on his blue jeans where he had wiped his fingers after gouging out screwworm flies, and though he had washed his hands there were still traces of the black gunky medicine on his fingers.

"Well, your father did his share of work today," he said to Maureen. "Didn't know any better, I'd have thought he'd been riding horses and doctoring calves all his life."

"Mr. Clayton, you get them settled at the table before this dinner gets cold!" George's Mary called from the kitchen.

"You're in charge of cooking the food, not telling me when I've got to eat it," Clayton yelled right back in what might have been a tone of real hostility if he hadn't been smiling when he said it, and gesturing in a courtly way for Maureen to sit.

George's Mary came in with platters of chicken and carrots and rolls, which she laid down heavily on the table as Clayton acknowledged their bestowal with a grunt. It was just the three of them again tonight, Ernest and Nax presumably banished to the bunkhouse for the evening meal. Maureen had the impression that when visitors were not here—and when there was no need to make a show of hierarchy—Clayton had supper every night with his ranch hands, and maybe George's Mary even joined them too, instead of dining by herself at the little kitchen table after all the others had finished.

"It must have been lively around the table when Ben was a little boy," Maureen decided to say. She was determined that there be some kind of conversation.

"Oh, I expect so," Clayton said. "That was a long time ago. I remember his mother would hold him in her lap and feed him with a spoon, and he'd wave his arms and smile and so forth the way little children do."

"When he was older," Gil said, "did he have strong opinions? About the war, for instance?"

"Well, he wasn't the sort to get his bristles up generally, but he was all for fighting it, I guess. I can't say if he had any particular feeling about why it needed to be fought—any better reason than anybody else. People around here weren't happy about that telegram the Mexicans got. We'd had our share of wars with Mexico and didn't appreciate the Germans putting them up to another one. You care for the gizzard, Miss Gilheaney?"

When Maureen said no thank you, he looked mildly disappointed and said he guessed he would just have it for himself then. He put the gizzard in his mouth and silently chewed it. Perhaps he was caught up in his thoughts or perhaps he had just reverted to that state of unvexed silence that seemed to be his natural mood.

"Ben didn't wait to get drafted," he said after a moment. "He just went out and joined the Guard and never told any of us a word about it till a week or so before he was supposed to go. Maybe he just wanted to see a new place or two. He took after his mother that way."

"Not after you?" Gil asked.

"No, I seen all the places I care to see. I know this part of the country pretty well and I been up the Western Trail a time or two, and I'm satisfied with that. But Sarey had her wandering side. If she'd been alive, it would have broke her heart to send her boy off to war, but she would have liked the idea that he got to see France. You folks ever been over there?"

"I haven't," Maureen said, "but Daddy studied in Paris, and in Rome as well."

"Well, I guess Paris and Rome have got Shackelford County beat all to hell."

"That's true in some ways," Gil said, heartened by the way Clayton seemed to be falling at last into an easy conversational frame of mind. "But certainly not in all. For instance, as I was watching you rope that calf today, I had the impression that—"

But Clayton was no longer paying attention. He was staring past Gil, looking out the front window, his eyes suddenly narrow and wrathful. His alarm was intense and public enough that there was no reason for Gil and his daughter to pretend they had not noticed it. They both turned to look out the window themselves, where a beat-up, dust-covered Model T had just rattled down the road and pulled to a stop in front of the house.

Clayton set down his napkin, got to his feet, and walked out the front door without excusing himself. Gil and Maureen watched through the window as he climbed down the porch steps and walked toward the car with a combative stride. An old Indian man with long, graying braids and a shapeless campaign hat sat behind the steering wheel, but it was the woman next to him that Clayton clearly meant to confront. She was old too, her face long and sagging and almost toothless, and like the driver she wore her hair in stringy braids. She was opening the door to step out when Clayton intercepted her and called out, loud enough to be heard inside the house, "You two can just turn that car around and go home right now!"

"Oh, Lord," said George's Mary, who had just come in from the kitchen holding a pitcher of iced tea.

"Who is it?" Maureen asked.

"Oh, honey, that there's Mr. Clayton's sister."

She filled their tea glasses while all three of them watched the standoff outside as it grew in intensity. Clayton had lowered his voice, and they could no longer make out what he was saying, but as he argued with his elderly sister he pushed against the car door, holding her in place as she tried to get out. The Indian man who was driving got out of his side of the car and walked around to intercede, but Clayton pushed him away with his free arm and for a moment it appeared that the two old men were about to lunge at each other and fall grappling onto the dirt. But the Indian seemed to grasp the absurdity of that proposition and backed away and got behind the wheel again. As Clayton stood there scowling at the intruders with his hands in his back pockets, the car tore off down the road, spitting gravel from its rear tires.

Clayton came back inside and returned to his chair and sat down.

"Those people are not welcome in my house," he blurted out by way of explanation.

Neither Gil nor Maureen saw any reason to respond. George's Mary said nothing either, but her mouth was set tight and Gil could see her glowering at her employer.

"Well, what the hell did you want me to do?" Clayton said to her.

"You know I don't give a damn what you do."

"Well, then that about takes care of it, don't it?"

George's Mary turned and walked into the kitchen and pulled the swinging door forcefully behind her. It swung in and out for a minute, squeaking on its hinges.

"You folks finish your supper," Clayton said to Gil and Maureen. "This business don't have nothing to do with you and I'm sorry you had to—"

He was looking up at the window again. The Model T was back. Through the window Gil could see the woman getting out of the car and running up to the porch. Clayton stood up, trembling with anger, and pulled open the door just as his sister hurled something through it. The object struck his face and landed on the table by the late Mrs. Clayton's china gravy boat.

"Don't you ever come back to this house, you god-damned squaw!" Clayton called after his sister as she ran back to the car and drove away.

Maureen reached out to pick up the thing the woman had thrown. It was, she saw, a primitive bracelet, thick strands of sinew supporting a row of glistening animal teeth. She handed it to Mr. Clayton. He accepted it from her with a grim nod and stuffed it in his shirt pocket. This time he did not bother with the pretense of sitting down to finish his meal, he just walked out of the parlor and headed toward the corral, yelling for Ernest to saddle his god-damned horse.

ELEVEN

"Don't ask me," Ernest declared as he drove past the ranch gate and out along the Albany road. "All I know is that there ain't no law that brothers and sisters got to tolerate each other."

"You know more than that," Gil said.

Ernest did not answer. Maybe he was pretending not to hear. They were heading for the general store at Fort Griffin. Gil had eagerly accepted the invitation for him and Maureen to go along on the errand to buy groceries and to pick up a part that had been ordered to repair a windmill. His legs were still so stiff from yesterday's riding that he had barely been able to pull himself out of bed, and he had not been looking forward to another day on horseback. Nor was the prospect of a day at the ranch house an enticing alternative. Clayton had not appeared for breakfast, and judging by George's Mary's skittish mood as she served her guests his turbulent anger still enveloped the household.

Gil had spent a mostly sleepless night in Ben's room, kept awake by leg cramps and by a sudden worry that Lamar Clayton was unstable and unpredictable enough to simply cancel his commission. Such things had happened to Gil before, bringing months of work to nothing and subverting his financial well-being with irrecoverable expenses. A man who was capable of throwing his own sister off his property was certainly capable of having second thoughts about a contract with a comparative stranger.

"I've begun to be annoyed by all this mystery," Gil said to Ernest. "I've been hired to make a credible likeness of Ben Clayton and my attempts to understand my subject have been met with confusion and evasion."

"Well sir," Ernest said, a little testiness in his voice now as well, "I understand some about Lamar Clayton. I've worked for him for twenty-two years. But don't be thinking I can tell you everything you want to know about that man and his boy because I can't."

Gil said he supposed that was fair enough but Ernest was still chewing over his complaint as he drove. Eight or ten buzzards were hunched over something in the center of the road ahead. Ernest did not bother to slow down or swerve around them, and at the last moment the birds sluggishly took flight, revealing the bloody carapace of an armadillo.

"He ain't never told me much," Ernest said as Gil looked back to see the buzzards patiently descending on the carcass to resume feeding. "But there used to be people all over this country who knew him back then in one way or another, and I could sometimes get them to talk about it a little, the way you're doing with me now. I believe he was twelve or so and Jewell a year or two older than that when they was taken. It was a Comanche raiding party, Quahadas as I understand it, over there in Wise County.

"There was an old man who died here a few years back. He'd been on the trail drives with Mr. Clayton and he got him to talk some. He said Mr. Clayton had told him it was about dinnertime when this Comanche fella just walked through the door like he owned the place and stuck Mr. Clayton's mama with a knife before she could even complain about it. There was about a dozen of them altogether and some of them wrestled with Mr. Clayton and his sister while the rest went through the place. They killed all the stock and they'd already killed Mr. Clayton's father and brother. I heard it that they scalped the mama while she was still alive."

Ernest turned to look at Maureen. "You let me know if this kind of talk upsets you, Miss Gilheaney."

"Thank you. I can bear it."

"The militia followed those Comanches all the way to the Red, but they never could find them. They beat up on Mr. Clayton a good bit, trying to see what he was made of, I suppose, and the girl got treated pretty rough herself. I mean treated rough in other ways, if you understand my meaning. The way I heard it, Mr. Clayton had to watch that business along with everything else. After a month or so she got traded away to the Kiowas, but the chief decided to keep Mr. Clayton. He was only with the Comanches a couple years before he got ransomed back, but he took to that life the way a lot of those boys did that got taken captive. It's funny, how after watching what happened to his mother and sister he could turn into a Comanche himself. But he did. He was pretty wild, they say, all painted up and everything. This here's the store."

Ernest pulled up in front of a solitary general store and post office sitting off the road at the edge of a broad floodplain. There was a bluff just above it, and Gil and Maureen could see the ruins of buildings scattered at its summit.

"That there's old Fort Griffin," Ernest said. "There ain't been no soldiers there for fifty years or more."

He swept his arm across the empty floodplain. "And you can't hardly tell it no more, but this here was a town once. They called it the Flat, and it had all sorts of goings-on. Saloons and gunfights and whorehouses—excuse me, Miss Gilheaney."

Maureen was touched by the way Ernest's face suddenly flared into a bright blush.

"It's all right, Ernest. I've heard the word before."

"Anyway," he said, looking off toward the vanished town to avoid meeting her eyes and blushing again, "when Mr. Clayton was a young man coming up the Western Trail he stopped here a time or two. They bedded the cows yonder and I expect they got themselves into some trouble in the town the way those young cowboys did. All them buffalo hunters used to come here too to sell their hides. They say there was always a terrible stink from them hides. But it's all gone now. The grass done grown over it all except for this little store."

Gil and Maureen went into the store with Ernest but there was such a tedious search for the misplaced windmill part that they ended up taking a walk across the site of the vanished town. They made their way through brittle wild grass toward a squat stone building with bars on it that they guessed must have been the jail. The remnants of a main street led past occasional piles of rotting lumber that were all that was left of the saloons and sporting houses that Lamar

Clayton as a young drover might have frequented. The street ended in a screen of brush and hardwoods but Gil, in an exploring mood, found an open path that took them to the banks of a shallow river.

"I believe this is the Clear Fork of the Brazos," he said to Maureen.

"Yes," she replied, "and I believe that's a kingfisher."

She had been studying bird life for her San Antonio River sculpture, and the industrious blue bird fluttering down the center of the stream was a bright note of familiarity in a world that was still hauntingly strange to her.

Gil smiled at her as he might have if she were still a little girl satisfactorily reciting some school lesson for him and Victoria. And then he looked down at the steep-banked Clear Fork, so vital to this parched country but no more substantial than a creek.

"I wonder what sort of a father he was to that boy," he said.

"I don't think he's eager for us to find out. Besides, I suppose in the final analysis such things are unknowable."

"Are they? Do you mean, for instance, that it's unknowable what kind of father I am to you?"

"Maybe a little," she said, with a teasing smile. "We keep a few secrets from each other, I should think."

"Such as what?"

"I don't know. That drawer in your desk, for instance."

"What drawer?"

"The one that's locked. Where you seem to put things that you want out of my sight."

"That's absurd. I have no such intention."

"What's in it, then?"

"Why, I don't even know precisely, to tell you the truth. Bills and correspondence and that sort of thing. And if we're talking about secrets, what about the one you keep from me?"

"What do you mean?"

"This Vance fellow."

"He's hardly a secret. You've met him. He's written about your work. Admiringly, by the way."

"I've shaken his hand a time or two. I read his article. But I can't say I know him, and you hardly bring him up."

"That's because there's nothing to talk about. I don't see him that often myself, you know. Only when he comes to San Antonio."

Gil kicked a loose stone off the bank with the toe of his shoe and watched it clatter down into the shallow water below.

"You would have talked to your mother about him," he said.

"Maybe, but maybe not. Anyway, so what? She was my mother and you're my father. There's a difference. It would feel awkward confiding in you about personal matters like that."

"Tell me what sort of things you and your mother talked about."

She laughed, then saw from the steady look on his face that he was rather serious.

"I talked about silly things with her, if you must know, Daddy. Or at least things that you would consider silly but women consider vital. Such as, well, my figure."

"Your figure? There's not a thing wrong with your appearance."

She laughed again, cruelly this time, cutting him off for his dishonesty. But the mood had been set, and here they were suddenly, flailing about in deeper conversational waters than either father or daughter had ever had occasion to enter.

"She was so beautiful," Maureen said. "I must have been *something* of a disappointment to her, don't you think?"

"Stop it," Gil said. "You were all the world to her."

Confused tears were brimming in her eyes. She took a step away from her father before he could reach out to comfort her.

"There's nothing wrong, Daddy," she reassured him. "Absolutely nothing. Maybe I'm having an emotional reaction to last night. Seeing that poor old woman turned away from her own brother's house. Why would he do that?"

"I don't know, Maureen."

"It's unimaginable, isn't it? What happened to her. What happened to them both."

But it was all mixed up in her mind with what had happened to her own family, and to the world at large. She remembered sitting in the hospital with her father during that last, desperate surgery to drain the pus off her mother's lungs. There had been an odd comfort in knowing that she and her father could very easily die as well, carried off by a disease that seemed of a piece with the apocalyptic convulsion that had generated the war. The gauze masks people wore in the streets had struck Maureen at first as almost comically useless, the meekest possible protest against the world's driving urge to annihilate itself.

Even before the epidemic had claimed her mother, she had guarded herself with steely fatalism, an unsentimental preparation for death that was sometimes dangerously close to a longing for it.

But she had been so unprepared. During the operation, she and her father had sat in a waiting room at the end of the hospital hallway, with nothing to look at but a large crucifix on the opposite wall. Its contorted, agonal Christ seemed to confirm that they were in a nightmare world where anything could happen. The nurses were all nuns, treading about in medieval silence, only the whisper of their footsteps and the clacking of the beads of the oversize rosaries they wore about their waists making any sort of sound. The surgeon who finally came to see them was old and stout, with wispy white hair hovering as if by static electricity at the margins of his bald head. There was a smile on his face and Maureen did not recognize it at first as a nervous smile; she thought he was going to tell them that the operation had been a success. But instead he told them that he had hoped for a better outcome, and was sorry that it hadn't worked out that way. Then he just stood there saying nothing else until her father had to ask him pointblank, "Do you mean she's dead?"

The doctor replied that, yes, this was unfortunately the case. Then he shook her father's hand and offered Maureen a pat on her arm as he walked away, past a nun carrying a tray of quivering orange jello into a patient's room. Maureen did not cry but she clung to her father like a child, holding on to him as if the floor had dropped away and if she let go she would fall into the blankness below.

THEY HEARD the car's horn honking, and turned to see Ernest waving to them, holding the windmill part in the crook of his arm.

"If this was close to spring," he told them when they reached the car, "you two wouldn't have any business walking through that grass."

"Why is that?" Gil asked.

"Oh, there's rattlers all through here. Sometimes you'll see them in the winter, if it's warm enough, but I expect they was mostly denned up today."

"Mostly?" Maureen said.

Ernest laughed as he closed the car door behind her. After he had turned the crank and vaulted over the driver's side behind the steering wheel, he adjusted the accelerator and sat there for a moment in deliberation, then turned to look at both Gil and Maureen.

"I wish you wouldn't tell Mr. Clayton what all I told you."

"We won't," Maureen promised.

"I can tell you something else about this place, but I don't know if I ought."

Gil and Maureen said nothing, allowing him room to make up his mind.

"Well, you know George's Mary," Ernest said. "I expect you know she ain't had it that easy in her life."

"She told me about what happened to her parents."

"Yes, ma'am, that was a terrible massacre. They have a plaque up about it over in Aspermont, I believe. Well, she was an orphan after that and she made her way as best she could. There used to be a saloon here called the Beehive. And that's where George's Mary used to work. You understand the sort of work I'm talking about?"

"I believe we do," Gil said.

"Well, one time these teamsters got a little rampageous and beat her up pretty bad. They say Mr. Clayton come across her lying bleeding in the street the next morning and took pity on her and hired her as a cook without ever knowing if she could even make biscuits or not. So there's that side to him, is why I'm telling you this. What you saw last night with Jewell, that don't necessarily mean that old man ain't got a kind heart."

THE SOUND of coyotes wailing in the black night worried its way into Maureen's dream, and she woke with the sense of malevolent beings near the house. The dream, as she sat up shaking in bed and reflected on it, had been about Indians, about their silent approach and her paralyzed compliance. At first, the Indians had seemed no more threatening than costumed bit players in the pictures, but gradually the dream tightened and grew darker and they became predatory wraiths who moved as softly as a spreading gas. Her father had not been there. There was a sense that he was either lying dead outside the house or had abandoned her in terror. She had seen the years of captivity looming ahead, the pain and defilement and loneliness that would be her life from now on.

She looked out the window at the corral, where a solitary night horse shivered in the cold. The pasture grass and the spindly mesquite branches shone with frost. She was cold, and still unsettled from her dream. When she looked at her travel clock she saw it was four thirty in the morning. She could try to go back to sleep but she did not like the idea of lying here alone in the dark, and she knew that in only a half hour or so the household would be stirring anyway, George's Mary getting out the biscuit pan and Lamar Clayton clomping along the floorboards in his boots. So she dressed and walked out into the parlor and then into the kitchen for a glass of water. It was dark but there was moonlight enough to see, and what she saw was Mr. Clayton sitting alone at the little kitchen table, fingering the strap of rawhide that his sister had angrily hurled into the house two nights before.

Maureen whispered good morning and he looked up at her with a start. He set the bracelet aside and turned his attention to a little notebook that was sitting on the table.

"George's Mary ain't up yet but I put some coffee on," he said.

"I don't want to bother you if you'd rather be alone."

"No bother."

He stood up, scooted a chair back for her, and went over to the dish drainer to get her a cup. The coffee he set in front of her smelled strong and burnt. She could hear the wood crackling in the stove. She took a sip of coffee and watched him writing in the notebook with a pencil.

"What are you writing?"

"Nothing. Just figuring. I got a bunch of white-necked cows and a few linebacks and it ain't easy to see what they'll be worth, the way the market is right now. So I'm calculating it every which way."

"Are these cattle a special breed?"

"Oh hell no, they ain't nothing but throwbacks. I've been doing my best to work my way up to pure Hereford. You get a white neck, a line going down their backs, it means there's a pretty strong strain of another breed. Buyers don't care for that—they'll downgrade those cows like they was in a beauty contest."

He saw her looking at the rawhide bracelet on the table.

"I'm sorry you and your dad got caught up in that business the other night," he said. "There's a woman that pesters me from time to time."

"Your sister."

Clayton said nothing, just nodded.

"What does she pester you about?" Maureen asked.

"Oh, nothing worth talking about. You're up pretty damn early."

"Not as early as you."

"That's just me being an old man. Too agitated to sleep sometimes."

"You must miss your son terribly."

"I believe I do, yes ma'am."

He closed the notebook and let his fingers stray to the sinew bracelet. There were six teeth dangling from the strap. They were as white as porcelain.

"I didn't have the chance to shake his hand and say good-bye before he left for France. That troubles me a good deal."

"Why couldn't you say good-bye?"

"Oh, Ben and me was a little crossways around that time. The way parents and their children can get."

Maureen wondered if he meant her to press him on this point, but something in her shied away from asking another direct question of this evasive man. She watched as he took up the bracelet and held it up to the window, closer to the moonlight.

"Those are buffalo teeth," he said. The teeth were big and vaguely shovel-shaped, with a hole drilled at the root of each one through which a thin loop of sinew secured it to the bracelet.

"They're beautiful."

"Oh, I don't know about that," he said. "They're just teeth. You and your father—you get along pretty fairly, looks like."

"Most of the time."

"You like working with him?"

"Yes. And not just because he's my father. He's a real artist, a great one maybe."

"I wouldn't have hired him if he wasn't."

He took a long sip from his coffee cup. It had been sitting unnoticed next to his elbow from the moment Maureen encountered him in the kitchen; no doubt the coffee had grown cold while he sat there turning over his secret thoughts.

"I always expected Ben and me would be working together too. I had this thought of the two of us. We'd be standing up there on that mesa, looking down at the cows in the big pasture yonder. We'd be talking about ranch work, when we planned to start the roundup this year, whether it'd be better to trail the stock to Abilene or to Albany, where the fences were sagging and where they needed fresh posts. We'd just be talking ranch talk between us, making decisions together. I don't know why, but that would have felt like a big satisfaction to me. Now you want to know what I think about?"

Maureen nodded.

"I think about the same thing, only now him being a statue. I believe I'll spend a lot of time up there, talking to a damn statue."

He laughed before he could cry. "I believe I'll have another cup of coffee, even if it tears my stomach all to hell. How about you?"

"I'm fine, thank you," Maureen said. She noticed that as he stood and turned to the stove he picked up his empty cup in one hand and the sinew bracelet in the other.

And she noticed that as he was standing with his back to her, pouring his coffee, he dropped the bracelet into the firebox.

TWELVE

Before he and Maureen left for home, Gil went out riding with Lamar Clayton and his hands twice more. It had been difficult to force his sore leg high enough to reach the stirrup, but once he was in the saddle and on the move the discomfort began to recede to the point where he could imagine himself at ease and competent, just one more cowboy out on the range. This was vanity, of course, nothing but his hopeful imagination at work. But if an artist began to allow himself to be embarrassed by his imagination he was through.

During those last few days on the ranch, he probed no further into the obviously complicated issue of Lamar Clayton's relationship with his son or his estranged sister. There was no point in endangering the commission, and he had studied the boy's face in those few Kodaks with such absorption, had taken so many measurements with his calipers, that he was certain he could produce a more than credible likeness.

He had turned his attention to horses—watching from the saddle as the heavy muscles in Poco's neck and scapular regions shifted under his weight, observing and sketching the horses at rest in the pastures, and then when he was home poring over his anatomy books and studying photographs of equestrian statues, from Marcus Aurelius to Falconet's Bronze Horseman to the familiar form of the horse that A. P. Proctor had modeled for Saint-Gaudens' Sherman.

It was the horse he was working on now. Not in full scale, not yet, but a scale model a third the size of the finished statue. In this model, gesture and proportion and likeness had to be as accurate as his hands and eye could produce, since it would serve as the basis and reference for the larger-than-life-size final product, upon which all flaws would be stupendously magnified.

He had built the armature for the scale model of plumber's pipe, T-joints, and heavy-gauge wire, and fastened it to a thick wooden base with a floor flange. Tacked to the wall of the studio all around him were the photographs that Maureen had taken of Poco on their visits to the ranch, showing the horse from every angle. Gil would not have the same crucial abundance of views when it came to the human subject of his grouping, but in the week since returning from West Texas he had once again recruited Rusty Holloway as a model, dressed him in Ben Clayton's clothes, which fit well enough after all, and had him pose with his hand resting on the saddle horn of a horse he had rented for the afternoon from the stables in Breckinridge Park. As Gil sketched in clay, Maureen took photographs of Rusty and the horse, and when these were developed and enlarged at a downtown photographic studio they were tacked to the wall. He had borrowed Ben Clayton's saddle; it sat off to the side on a sawhorse, ready to be consulted when it came to the detail work of the model. Near it was Ben's low-crowned Stetson hat, another relic, whose battered, sweat-stained appearance Gil was eager to attempt to reproduce.

Maureen had spent the morning helping him with the armature and setting up the gallery of images that now enclosed him. In the afternoon she had seen to her own work, the Spirit of the Waters column she was modeling in full scale in her corner of the studio. She worked out of his line of sight and covered the piece with wet cloth whenever she was away from it for more than ten minutes—not just to keep the clay moist, he knew, but to keep her work private. She had not asked Gil to inspect her progress and he had decided not to ask. She had spent her life in her father's studio; it was natural that she should have developed the desire to become a sculptor in her own right and on her own terms. But what Gil could not discern was how strong that desire was and how much she was willing to endure to satisfy it.

His own ambition was bold; at times it had been almost ungovernable. He could not recall a time when the first purpose of his imagination had not been to gauge the weight and heft of objects in his hands, to try to make them conform to some ungraspable template in his mind. He had stared at objects with an almost mystical hunger, trying to divine the forms they held within, or to factor out the ways they controlled his focus.

"The sculptor's hand can only break the spell to free the figures slumbering in the stone." His mother had known Michelangelo's famous dictum and quoted it to him when he was a young boy, and he had grasped its meaning at once. It confirmed what he already knew and already felt. At eight or ten years old, he had carved faces out of turnips, figures out of blocks of wood. He knew how to do it; it came to him. As a young man he had earned his keep by cutting cameos. He had studied at the École des Beaux-Arts in Paris, and had later worked for six months at a sculpture studio in Rome, where he carved miniature knockoffs of famous statues for tourists. Carving pleased him, it was elevated and heroic, but it was working with clay—the haptic art—that finally claimed him. It meant more to him to create something that had not been there before than to chip away at a piece of marble to discover what might have been there all along. He liked the feel and smell of clay, the resistance of it, the idea that his medium was the abundant, alluvial matter of the earth itself. But he still worked with Michelangelo in mind. Whether you labored with a chisel to uncover a shape or modeled it with your hands out of pliant material, sculpting was still an act of discovery, a drive to reveal something hidden, something lurking below the surface of the artist's imagination.

At five o'clock Maureen covered her work again and went back into the house to see Mrs. Gossling off and to answer the mail and pay the bills. The full light of day was past, but Gil kept working. When it grew darker he turned on the electric lamps, his experienced eye compensating for their imperfect illumination. Whatever he got wrong this evening he could fix tomorrow when daylight flooded his studio once again. He did not want to stop, now that he had covered the armature with clay and was sketching out the form of the standing horse. The imperative to keep working until it was finished was almost intolerable, and as a young man he had surrendered often enough to this blinding, accelerating need, staying awake for days at a time, working so feverishly it felt as if he was racing against some looming catastrophe that could destroy everything he had accomplished. Age had tempered that anxiety to some degree. He no longer feared that the world would end before he could finish his sculpture, only that his life would.

It was time for dinner, time to step away. He had mastered his creative appetite as he had mastered all the others; it was crucial that he remain in command of the rhythms of his art. But he gave himself a few more minutes to build up the mass of the hindquarters of the horse. He had just grabbed a handful of unworked clay and was squeezing it to make it pliant when the pain struck, an out-of-nowhere jolt at the base of both thumbs. It had not happened for a while and he had half convinced himself that working with clay, continually exercising the muscles and tendons of the hands, did not contribute to arthritis but instead held it at bay.

The theory was not holding up, however. The pain in his thumbs tonight was sudden and intense, and it flared up again whenever he flexed his hand against the clay. He sat down, irritated—no, terrified, the way another man might be terrified of a heart attack.

He walked into the house and opened a cabinet and took down a jar filled with gin-soaked raisins, the ancestral arthritis cure propounded by his father's family, most of them drunkards but none of them, so far as he knew, crippled in the hands. He ate ten or twelve of the raisins and tried not to think about the twinges of pain that still shot through the meat of his hands whenever he rotated his thumbs.

At the dinner table he was preoccupied with worry, both over the pain in his hands and over certain vexing problems with the horse that he had yet to solve. Maureen did not press him for conversation. She had eaten innumerable meals at the family dinner table in deferential silence, aware of the mighty aesthetic struggles raging in her father's imagination.

"I think I'll take a stroll," he declared as she was clearing the table.

Maureen turned to him and he saw the surprise in her expression. It had been his and Victoria's custom to walk after dinner on the neighboring grounds of the old mission, their private time together during which they had confided to each other and conducted their marital debates and negotiations. The walks had been Victoria's idea and her demand, her way of ensuring that his preoccupied mind would not thoughtlessly seal itself shut against her and the concerns of their domestic life.

He had forsaken these strolls after her death, out of grief perhaps, or something more complicated: a reluctance to locate himself in the irrecoverable past when his dreams for the future were still raging. But he remembered what a confidante his wife could be sometimes, how much her quiet, grounded presence meant to him when he was stirred up or confounded by his work.

"You could use the air," Maureen told him as she scraped a dish into the kitchen trash bin. "You've been cooped up in the studio all day."

"Want to come with me?"

"No, you go ahead. I'll just do the dishes."

What she meant to tell him, Gil understood, was that she had no plans to become his surrogate wife as well as his daughter by taking her mother's role in a nightly ritual that had meant so much to her. He sensed that Maureen's decision to enter the sculpture competition had something to do with escape, a subtle probing of just how tightly her own life had become ensnared in her father's needs.

He put on his hat and coat and walked up the street to the vacant lot he and Victoria had used to cut across to the grounds of the old mission. It did not feel so odd without her. He was used by now to her being gone, and anyway he was accompanied by the echoes of the old conversations he had had with his wife, conversations that inevitably fell back onto two themes: her distress at living so far away from home and her continuing worry about her daughter.

"It's just that your mind is always so full of wonderful distractions," he remembered Victoria saying one night as they walked together. "Your work. Your clients. The foundry. What grade of clay to use. And the only hope I have of distraction is her happiness."

It was a beautiful night tonight, no trace of the oppressive South Texas humidity, the temperature at a sharp sixty degrees or so, Spanish moss clinging picturesquely to the limbs of the live oaks and the collapsed remnants of the old mission walls, overgrown with grass, giving the illusion of ancient hedgerows.

He made his way across the weedy plaza of the mission to stand in front of the crumbling church. The great doors of carved oak that must once have been here were gone, stolen or taken away for safekeeping or splintered into nothing by time and neglect. He had not stood here for a while, and he craned his head upward to reacquaint himself with the saints in their niches: Saint Francis, Saint Dominic, the usual cohort of cherubim, the parents of Mary on either side of the doors, Saint Joaquin rendered in a strangely insouciant pose, his hand cocked on his hip. Acanthus leaves, pomegranate leaves, and other forms of sculptural spinach vined around the ledges, columns, and abutments. All of it carved by hand from raw limestone in actual scale. The height at which the statues were set, and the moonlight streaming down upon them, rendered their imperfections—chipped-off noses, eroded chins—in grotesque relief. People thought of stone as ageless, but nothing lasted as long as bronze, nothing stood so strong against the tide of time.

Time was on his mind so starkly tonight. He remembered standing here with Victoria two years ago, staring up at Saint Joaquin. On that night Victoria had silently brushed past him and walked into the interior of the mission church. She had sidestepped the rubble from the collapsed dome and bell tower and stood there in the open nave, looking up at the stars, the night flattering the stark planes of her face. She was entering her mid-fifties, her hair still not completely gray, though its luster had faded and it was shot through with silvery tendrils that he rather liked. They had been arguing, he remembered, but not with any particular bitterness. And whatever petty resentments he might have held toward her that night evaporated as he watched the starlight play across her face. The commonplace signs of age and decay that had begun to undermine his wife's visage stirred him as deeply as her flawlessness had in her youth.

When he had first met her, he was newly home from Europe and sharing a grim little studio on West Fourteenth Street with a young painter fresh out of the Art Students League. The painter had the study during the day and Gil had it at night, after he had finished working at the Eden Musée wax museum, sculpting queens on the way to their executions and writhing victims of the Spanish Inquisition.

He won his first commission that year, an allegorical tablet that was the gift to itself of one of the smaller New York gas companies that was scrambling to secure a place in the electrical future. The tablet was to depict Womanhood Released from Drudgery, following the Spirit of Light toward the horizon of the new century. Gil needed daylight for serious paying work, so when he received his commencement money he quit his job at the wax museum and paid the painter an extra portion of the rent so that he could take the daytime shift.

She came to him on a Tuesday morning, entering his life with a hesitant knock. She allowed him a cautious smile and met his eyes only briefly; it occurred to him later that she must have habitually been wary of what she would find on the other side of a studio door. He knew she modeled at the league occasionally and the painter who shared the studio with him had friends who had used her from time to time, but he had never seen her before until she walked into the room and stood there at the north-facing window in midmorning light.

He explained the piece to her—the Spirit of Light gliding forth with arms raised, one hand supporting a gas flame and the other a stylized burst of electricity. She nodded briskly with professional comprehension. He had the feeling she knew what he wanted more clearly than he did. Her features were clean and sorrowful. Her manner was evasive. He had to struggle to meet her on the businesslike plane she had established, because he was already in love with her and when she began to remove her jacket and blouse and crisp blue skirt he fled to the other side of the room and took up his station behind his sculpting stand as if seeking protection from a blast.

He had a pair of old oars he had scavenged from the North River after a storm, and he gave them to her to support her upraised arms as she posed naked and striding for the better part of two hours. Her sense of privacy and reserve was as powerful as her bare flesh. As he openly studied her body, as he formed it in clay with his hands, he felt a thrilling intimacy with this unapproachable woman. She was entirely professional, holding the pose without complaint, anticipating his requests to shift position slightly as the changing light played across her bare skin.

He felt she trusted or respected him no more nor less than any other artist she had posed for. His lustful stupefaction had to have been plain to her, and perhaps that was part of the reason, in those first few sessions, that she deflected his solicitous questions—Was she cold? Was she thirsty? Did she need a break?—with a shake of her head and an unrevealing smile. It was only after three or four sessions that she finally felt comfortable enough with him to hold a conversation. He learned about how her father had died in a knife fight when she was twelve and the family was thrown onto the mercy of the Settlement Society. Her mother had gone to work in a shirtwaist factory and so had she, trimming off stray threads from the garments seven days a week, working till nine o'clock most nights, being paid for the overtime with a slice of apple pie. When her mother had fallen ill with tuberculosis she was taken to a poorhouse ward on Blackwell's Island and Victoria never saw her again.

She did not expect much from life and it had been hard going at first to be in love with her. It had been hard going all along, as the weight of her grievances toward him began to accumulate. The grievances all sprang from the same poisonous source: his insistence that his mother never know of their marriage, or even of Victoria's existence.

It was strange to think now that she had once loved him enough to agree to such a bargain. She had even listened with some sympathy when he had first explained the situation to her, when he told her that it would destroy his mother to learn that her only surviving son had married outside the Church and that his soul was condemned to hell. He could not think of doing that to her, not after everything she had already endured.

Gil thought he had a faint memory of his father before he went to the war, a hurried, balding man in an apron fussing with the shelves in his grocery store. Whatever patience and optimism there might have been in his nature had vanished at the Bloody Lane or in the slaughter fields below Marye's Heights. He had survived both, and Fair Oaks besides, though shrapnel had badly scarred the nerves in both arms. He probably would have been a drunk anyway but maybe not so much of a tyrant if he had not been literally crazy with pain for the last twenty years of his life.

Gil's mother sought refuge from his beatings in prayer, huddling with her two boys and whispering an Act of Contrition so that they would go to heaven in case he came against them with a knife. The dangerous rages did not happen that often, but often enough that clouds of terror loomed over them all even when Gil's father stayed silent and tame. It was the threat of martyrdom, Gil supposed, that kept steadily raising his mother's investment in the sheltering promise of the Church, that made the goal of preserving her sons' souls for heaven even more compelling than saving their lives.

Gil's brother, Michael, left as soon as he could, apprenticing himself to a fossil hunter in the New Jersey marl pits, then a year later dying of appendicitis on the train on his way to the bone beds of Wyoming to hunt for thunder lizards. The fossil hunters had been a rough bunch, and Gil's mother was tortured by the thought that Michael might not have had a chance to make a good confession before he died. In her grief she prayed incessantly for his soul in Purgatory and could not utter her fears that he might have died in a state of mortal sin.

Gil's father felt the pain of his son's death too, though he was intolerant of the religious ravings of his wife. He himself mourned in drink, in a deepening hostility over the Germans, or the blacks, or the goddam Republicans. As his anger widened, his targets narrowed, to his shaken wife and remaining son. When Gil was thirteen he noticed the malicious look building in his father's eye and stood up against him as he heaved drunkenly across the parlor toward his wife. His father tried to swat him out of the way and when Gil held his ground he threw him hard across the room, sending him smashing against his mother's easel and smearing her half-finished portrait of Saint Catherine of Siena with the blood spouting from his torn forehead. Gil got back to his feet and there was an ugly, clumsy melee that ended with his father running out of the room weeping with shame.

The shame was strong enough to send his father straight to confession, and with the guidance of the parish priest he was able to remake himself for a time. He was a good businessman when he was sober and for several years the grocery store thrived, but he had a glowering nature even when he wasn't drinking, and anyway it was too late for Gil to feel any affection for him, or confidence enough in his continued sobriety to ever let down his guard. When the storm broke again, Gil was older and stronger and the shoving match went his way. After that his father was an increasingly bitter and weakened figure in the household, no longer seeking reprieve in the Church but instead shunning the sacraments and mocking his wife's devotion. He died at forty-eight of a heart attack on the floor of the Golden Swan Saloon.

There was enough money from the sale of the grocery to keep them from immediate distress, though they were soon gone from the apartment on St. Luke's Place and much of the money Gil earned from his talent went to the support of his mother—as it would for many decades to come. She moved to Chicago to live with her sister at about the same time that Gil began attracting notice in New York and winning his first commissions. With his mother at such a distance, the deception he had proposed to Victoria seemed sustainable. And it was vital, of course, to his mother's well-being. He believed this at the time and he believed it still. Victoria was a non-Catholic, a term that in his mother's world was an all-consuming negative. To marry her, to marry outside the Church, was to live in sin, and to live in sin was to die outside salvation. He did not believe this, he never had. But his mother did, with a fervor that only grew more rigid as her life's misfortunes compounded.

To preserve the illusion that his soul was not condemned he had few options. He could end his connection with Victoria and seek out a wife who was Catholic or who at least would convert, which Victoria was too proud and offended to consider. And it was Victoria's defiance, her provocative disdain of convention, that stirred him as much as her beauty. She was unlike other women he had known. She was subservient to nothing, unafraid of God and uninterested in commands of conduct that did not arise from her own heart. But that did not make her like the morally confused and ready young women who swarmed around the New York art scene. She was wonderfully grave. There was a sense of purpose and direction about her that heartened Gil as he embarked on his own trackless quest for artistic greatness. He could not consider giving her up.

So the only other option was to conceal all knowledge of her from his mother. It was not difficult at first. The deceit grated on Victoria and tested her patience, but she went along with it, trusting in her husband's belief that it was an act of kindness. But when Maureen was born the whole thing began to seem more cruel than kind. It was no longer an innocent secret to deny to both grandmother and granddaughter the knowledge of one another's existence.

But what could he do? By that time the deception had already been in place, setting down intricate roots, for years. It was the worst decision he had ever made, could have ever made—he understood that now, but there was no going back. Even at the time he had astonished himself. He had not known until then that he could ever be capable of such a blatant, breathtaking falsehood. And there was never a moment when revealing everything to his mother would not have meant expanding and deepening the original betrayal. So he continued to conceal everything meaningful in his life from her, everything but his work, sending her newspaper accounts whenever a new statue was unveiled, and letter after letter detailing how his furiously paced but deeply satisfying career left him no time for thoughts of marriage. He did not talk about his mother to his circle of friends and they assumed without asking that she was dead. The lie to Maureen had been more direct: her grandmother had died before her birth, killed by a sudden brain hemorrhage as she walked home one Sunday after Mass.

Gil remembered the disgusted, tight-lipped forbearance with which Victoria had allowed this lie to claim their lives. They had argued about it for years on end, and he could see in her filmy, red-streaked eyes that she was edging from grudging complicity to something like hatred. She could never forgive him now, but there was no tolerable way to stop the branching deceit.

When the sister she was living with in Chicago had died, Gil's mother had decided to come home to New York. To continue the subterfuge in such close proximity would have been difficult and damaging, and part of the reason he had agreed to move to Texas was so that the elaborate deception could go on.

Victoria had not wanted to go. She wept at the thought. She would be greeted in this new life only by loneliness while he would be welcomed as the world-famous sculptor who out of all the fair places he could have settled chose San Antonio.

And this fraudulent triumph that he had insisted upon for himself had brought her, as she predicted, nothing but homesickness and isolation and, in the end, a very real death.

Gil walked into the mission church, following the ghost of his wife. The memory of the way she had stood here that night two years ago was still so strong that he had an urge to rush back to his studio and sculpt it, just as he remembered: Victoria standing alone staring up yearningly through a church's broken vault. Her expression that night had looked untroubled and accepting, the worry and anger smoothed away in a wash of moonlight. It was the way he would like to remember her, but he sensed that capturing her like that would amount to nothing more than another betrayal.

THIRTEEN

Dear Mr. Clayton,

My name is Arthur Fry and I served with your son in the 36th or as it is known by us Arrowhead Division over here in France. Ben and I were good friends. We met at Camp Bowie our first day there while waiting in line to fill these empty bed-sacks they gave us from a big pile of oat straw. Ben made a joke that when we went to bed that night we would hit the hay for sure. I trained with your son all the way through at Camp Bowie and sailed with him to France on the Lenape. It was an unpleasant trip, a lot of us were sick most of the time, and we were worried we might get sunk by a U-Boat. But Ben had a way of putting everybody at ease and everybody liked him and wanted to be around him and I told myself when we stepped onto the pier in Brest "I believe I'll stick with Ben."

I don't know if he mentioned my name in any of his letters home to you but we were good friends. I come from Ranger over in Eastland County where my late mother taught school and my late father worked for the County Clerk's office. I liked to hear Ben talk about growing up on the ranch. I grew up in town mostly. He said you had driven cattle up to Kansas back in the old days and I was always interested to hear about that and other adventures you had in pioneer times.

I was there at St. Etienne when Ben was killed and will tell you more of that battle if it is something you would care to learn. I know you have delicate feelings toward your son and may not want to hear the details of his death but I will just say here that it might be a comfort for you to know that it was quick and I do not think he suffered very much. Write me with your questions if you care to using this address. We move around a lot but this French outfit I work for—the STE—is pretty good about getting letters to me, though I don't get much mail and don't care that much about it.

I got wounded pretty bad in the same fight that Ben got killed in. I don't think I'll be coming home to the United States anytime soon. I like it in France well enough and my wound is such that people might get upset to see me. If I were coming home I would come to see you and bring you this in person, but as it is I will put it in this letter and hope it arrives safely. It is something that Ben made out of a mess-kit lid. I guess you could say it is a kind of charm or the like. As you can see there is a picture of a horse on it. Ben told me that the horse's name is Poco and where he is standing is a place on the ranch that Ben said he felt particular affection for.

Ben was looking at this picture he had made of his home place just before we jumped off for the attack on St. Etienne. He put it in his pocket and I guess it fell out when the stretcher bearers lifted up his body. It laid there in the dirt for a year or more until I came across it when I was doing reclamation work for the French government. This part of France is called The Devastated Zone and that is the right name for it because hardly anything is there anymore except shells and barbed wire and blown-up towns. It is a miracle I came across this little piece of tin but I did and I thought you ought to have it to remind you of your son. I hope that seeing it does not add to your grief but subtracts from it instead.

Please write to me if I can be of service to you. For now I will close with my best wishes to the father of my friend Ben Clayton.
Yours sincerely,
Arthur Fry

Lamar Clayton folded the letter back into its envelope. It was the fourth time he had read it, and for some reason this time it made him angry. He goddam well did not want to know the details of how his son had died. Maybe other people would, that was their own business. But he didn't have to be thinking about such things at his age. He had seen enough killing of one sort or another in his life and there wasn't a thing in the world productive about looking back on it.

It was bad enough, holding this little square of tin in his hand, having to think about Ben scratching the image of the ranch and his horse onto it, probably eaten up with homesickness in the very hours before he died. Lamar kicked out hard at the baseboard of the parlor with the toe of his boot, and then rocked irritably in his chair as hot tears came to his eyes. Goddam it to hell. Had the boy even thought of his father in those last hours? Had he thought of him with hate?

Peggy woke up with a whimper in her little basket, startled awake by his kicking the wall. She looked up at him with a bewildered, entreating expression, her left front leg bandaged and swollen up double. He had tied a little tourniquet above the bandage to keep the poison from traveling up to her heart, but he didn't know if it would have any effect. He figured it was just wait and see. Everybody had their own ideas about how to treat snakebite and Lamar's was to swab the wound with kerosene and then to bind to it the head of the snake that bit you. That was how the Quahadas had taught him over fifty years ago and it worked well enough except when it didn't. He didn't see much point to start cutting on Peggy and he didn't care to suck the blood out of a dog anyway. He'd once met a doctor in a Fort Griffin saloon who told him with drunken authority that when a rattlesnake hit you with his poison it was like ink spreading into a wet sponge. You could suck all you wanted but there was no way that poison was coming back out.

"Don't think I have any sympathy for you," he muttered at the dog. "It's your own damn fault."

Peggy was twelve years old. She ought to have known better by now than to nose around in rock crevices the way she had been doing this afternoon when they rode in from the horse trap. When she was young he'd had to whistle her away from brush piles and prairie dog holes a hundred times a day. If she hadn't got the idea by now that there were rattlesnakes in such places, she had nobody but herself to blame. The problem was dachshunds were burrowers. They cared about crawling into narrow unreachable places more than they cared about any other thing in the world. It was a stupid sort of dog to have on a ranch, but Sarey had seen a picture of a dachshund pup in a magazine and there had been no point in trying to talk her out of it.

The dog had been imperious from the beginning and had assumed she had the right to sleep in their bed with them, wiggling down through the bedcovers to warm herself at Lamar's feet. He'd put a stop to that, but the pup just migrated to Ben's bed instead. He tried to stop that too, but the whole household stood up against him and after a while he didn't have the energy to fight about it anymore.

Looking up at him from her basket now, the dog kept whining in pain and bewilderment and he told her to hush. His voice must have been sharp enough because she moved her head and looked past him at the wall and in a little while she was asleep again. Or dead. He leaned forward and put his hand on her rib cage until he felt her breathing and then he settled back in his chair and read the letter again and smoked another cigarette and sat there awake as another hour or two passed.

His mind was agitated. He did not want the dog to die, but there was a part of him that wanted everything over and done with, for every person and every creature that had a claim on him just to be gone and leave him alone. And while he was at it, he didn't see much point in not being dead himself.

He recalled how when he was with the Comanches, when they would be coming home from a raid or a hunting party, they would follow the trail up to some bluff or high point of rock. They would find stones there placed by the party that had gone before. The stones were arranged in a manner to suggest the phase of the moon when the first party had passed by, and there were other stones telling you which direction they had gone. It had been so simple and so calming to him to see those stones like that. Here you might be out in the middle of the llano with nothing but grass and emptiness all around you, and it was like somebody was speaking to you, telling you there were others out here, letting you know how close or far they were, showing you the way home.

He felt lost now, alone in open country with no sign to guide him. Worse, far worse, he felt—he could see—that his son's ghost was lost and wandering, somewhere in those horrible French battlefields, amid the mud and slime and stinking shell craters and twisted dead tree trunks. He sensed that Ben was expecting to discover some sign from his father, some indication of how to get back to Shackelford County. But Lamar had left nothing for him. He had not thought to. He had not wanted to.

He jerked upright and opened his eyes. He had fallen asleep, or close to it. The image of Ben staggering alone through the hellish western front had been a kind of dream, one of those furiously vivid dreams that he had sometimes before settling down into real sleep.

He sat there alone in the room, awake and alert again. The dog fussed and whimpered in her sleep. Lamar did not like being at the mercy of his waking mind at three in the morning or any other time. Lonely hours such as this had never been a problem for Sarey. She had had her books and her magazines, the letters she was always writing to her three sisters. Like Sarey, the sisters were inquisitive, industrious, and chiding. They had grown up on a ranch over on the Clear Fork with a big stone house and rich pastures that back in those days were untouched by mesquite. He had met her at a dinner at the old Stockyards Hotel during one of Fort Worth's first fat stock shows. Sarey's father had brought his four daughters with him, joking to everyone who would listen that he was almost as proud of them as he was of his Hereford bulls. They were an exuberant family, always singing around the organ, organizing croquet matches and boating parties on the deep pools of the Clear Fork.

When he married Sarey, Lamar had been almost fifty, a damaged, silent man she had coaxed out of solitude and drawn into her welcoming family. He had picnicked with them and gamely done his untutored best on the croquet lawn, but the sociability had always been a strain, a price he knew he had to pay for the peace he found at home on his own ranch with Sarey. Studying her in bed as she slept, staring at her in the parlor as she read or wrote letters or cradled their drowsy son in her arms, he had felt a calm he had not known since the days of his own childhood, when he would go to sleep at night listening to the hum of his mother's spinning wheel. In those suspended moments, it was almost as if the child he had been had grown into the man he was meant to be, as if the Quahadas had never walked through the door that day, as if he and his family had been left alone to live out the future that it had once seemed God intended for them.

He had last seen Sarey's family at Ben's funeral service. It was at the Methodist church in Albany that Lamar had allowed Sarey to drag him to six or eight times during their marriage. There had been no casket, no graveside service, since Ben's grave was far away in France, just a morose reception afterward at one of the church members' houses, the house of a stranger. Lamar had talked beef prices and tick medicine with Sarey's father as the women from the church handed them plates of lemon cake. Each of his late wife's sisters—Ben's bereaved aunts—had kissed him on the cheek and told him to let them know if there was anything at all in the world they could do for him. He reckoned he would run into some of them again from time to time, but there was nothing left to bind that vibrant family to him. Like his dead wife and son, they had come and gone through his life like a fast-moving norther.

It surprised him now that he hadn't started drinking again. He just never thought to. Maybe it was Sarey, still lingering on in his mind, still holding him up to her standards. Probably it was just that drinking seemed like another damned thing to do, and he didn't feel like doing anything except being out with the cattle.

And if he had held himself to Sarey's standards after she died, things would have been different with Ben. The gulf between living father and dead son would not now feel so dismayingly, impossibly wide.

"You been awake all night?" George's Mary's voice startled him. Was he asleep again? He looked over to see her standing there in her housedress, tying on her apron.

"What time is it?"

"Four in the damn morning. I was about to start the biscuits."

She squatted down and stroked Peggy's head. The dog opened her eyes and craned her head upwards, staring at George's Mary with a woeful look.

"Well, she's alive," George's Mary said. "You think she's going to have to lose that leg?"

"I doubt it. It wasn't a big snake and this early in the winter it probably didn't have that much poison stored up."

He started to stand up but he did so too fast and inside his head it felt like a flock of birds had just flown up off the ground all at once. George's Mary reached out and grabbed him and helped him back into the chair. One by one, the birds started to return.

"You better not be having a heart attack."

"No, I was just dizzy for a minute."

"Well, that's what you get for sitting there in one place all night. Stay here and I'll get you something to eat."

She went into the kitchen and came back with a handful of crackers and a glass of milk.

"What's that letter there in your lap?" she said as he was eating the crackers.

"It's about Ben."

He handed the letter to her. She was a slow reader and it took her a long time to work her way through it, but there were tears coming out of her eyes soon enough. When she was through reading the letter she held the piece of tin in her hand and stared at it. Her face had grown fleshy, and her thick gray hair was coarse and tangled and she didn't seem to take much care of it. It was hard for Lamar to conjure up anymore what she had looked like when she was young. Pale and thin, the best he could recall. He remembered her shivering in the wagon when he brought her home from Fort Griffin, even though it had been summer. She had probably thought he was going to rape her and beat her the way those teamsters had who had left her lying in the mud in front of Conrad's store. He'd had no thought along those lines at all—he just needed a cook—but it took her a long time to accept that fact, and when she did she went right from fearful to bossy. She'd never thanked him for his good turn and it didn't matter to him whether she did or not.

"Well, hell, Mr. Clayton," she said now.

"Well, hell is about it."

"You be sure to write this boy back and thank him."

"I will, but it's no business of yours if I do or not."

She handed him back the letter and walked into the kitchen. He heard her opening the cupboards, getting down her mixing board and the flour and lard and starting the cooking fire. She shut the steel door of the stove with a hard shove, and when she struck a match it seemed there was fury in that too. She made enough noise for Peggy to forget about her snakebite and get curious, and he had to give the dog a harsh look to stop her from getting out of her basket and limping over to investigate.

He stood himself up—the dizziness was gone now—and bent over and picked up the dog so she wouldn't follow him. Then he carried her into the kitchen and stood there holding her as he watched George's Mary knead the biscuit dough as if she was trying to strangle it.

"What the hell are you doing?"

"I'm making your damn breakfast, is what I'm doing."

"Well, be quiet about it."

She took the mixing board with the dough still on it and threw it hard on the floor, where it broke in two.

"I loved that boy," she said.

"I never said you didn't."

There was a little hardback chair in the kitchen she used as a stool and she sat down on it and began to wail in a way she never had, not even when they first got the telegram that Ben had been killed. She cried so hard she had trouble getting her breath, and Lamar couldn't think of anything to do except to stand there with the snakebit dog in his arms and watch her.

It went on for a minute or two and then she was over it. She picked up the dough and threw it in the trash, along with the broken mixing board.

"I had that for forty years," she said.

"You would have had it for another forty if you hadn't thrown it on the floor like that."

She laughed at herself and smeared the tears from her cheeks and then got down a mixing bowl and reached into the coffee can where she kept the lard.

"Look at that dog," she said. "She's trembling. We ought not to have got her so excited, not with that snake poison in her."

Lamar reached out and got a dish towel off the rack and wrapped it around the dog, careful not to touch her bandaged and swollen leg.

"I guess I'll go sit on the porch till breakfast's ready," he told George's Mary.

He walked with the dog out onto the porch and sat down on a weathered wooden chair whose legs were so uneven it was close to being a rocker. The sun was almost up. The night horse, a little roan called Chesty, was chuffing at him from the fence line. He could hear mourning doves calling and there was a hawk silhouetted at the top of a tree across the creek, preening itself for its morning hunt. Soon he could smell the biscuits cooking in the wood oven. He reflected to himself that if he had ever been at peace, this would have been his favorite time of day.

FOURTEEN

The grand ballroom of the Gunter Hotel was filled with men who looked, in one way or another, like Lamar Clayton. The members of the Old Time Trail Drivers Association were indeed old trail drivers. Some were small and wiry and bow-legged, some had grown mountainous in the decades since they had herded cattle along the now-extinct open range. Those that did not trust the young women at the coat check sat with their Stetsons in front of them on the banquet tables, making life difficult for the waiters trying to serve plates of well-done ribeyes and anemic salads. Many of their faces were hidden behind cascading white mustaches and chin beards. Some wore expensive clothes and looked like they were accustomed to being seen in them, some like Lamar Clayton wore shapeless suits with the lingering scent of mothballs. But they were mostly men who still bore detectable traces of vigor. No matter how broken down they looked, they still had a dogged physical bearing. Their eyes were keen with nostalgia.

"We deplore the loss of these old pioneers," the speaker at the podium declared after reading off the names of half a dozen "Old Trailers" who had died during the previous year. "And it would be the father of all mistakes to allow their daring and valuable efforts in taming this country to be forgotten by future generations. And so I ask that we bow our heads and vow always to remember our old partners on the trail."

Gil bowed his head, as did Maureen and Vance Martindale, who kept scribbling in a notebook as he pretended to pray, determined to get everything down. Only Lamar Clayton, who had invited them to the dinner, kept his head upright. When Gil glanced up during the moment of silence, his eyes met Clayton's. Gil could not read the look he saw there. Maybe it was amusement, maybe it was a hard-headed disdain for being instructed on the manner of how to show his feelings.

Gil responded with an ambiguous half smile. They were at a delicate stage of the approval process for the sculpture and he didn't want to risk a careless reading of his patron's mood. Clayton had wired him only three weeks before that he was coming to San Antonio for the Old Time Trail Drivers annual meeting and that as long as he was in town he would be pleased to come by the studio to check on the progress of his statue. This news had sent Gil into a frenzy of effort to complete the scale model, since he wanted to take advantage of an opportunity to get Clayton's approval of the work so far. He had still not quite finished by that afternoon, but had to leave off to give himself time to get dressed for the banquet that Clayton had insisted he and Maureen attend as his guests. When Maureen mentioned the event to Martindale, who happened to be in town for some reason or another, he immediately bought himself a ticket, eager for the chance to mingle with some of the old pioneers who were the subject of his research.

After the dead had been remembered, another old drover who looked near-dead himself was called to the podium to discuss, in halting speech and numbing detail, the vanished cattle trails of Texas. He went on for forty-five minutes, ponderously recounting the various river crossings on the way to the Red.

"Now after crossing the Llano," the speaker mumbled about a half hour into the talk, fortifying himself with a long drink of water, "it went up Saline Creek, up there to the head of McDougal Creek over in Menard County, and down to Pegleg Crossing on the San Saba."

He looked out at the white-haired audience until he found Lamar Clayton. "That about right, Lamar?"

"Near as I can recall," Clayton growled back.

"Well, I reckon as near as you can recall is about as accurate as we're going to get."

A ripple of knowing laughter passed through the audience. Clayton brushed off the recognition but called back at the speaker.

"About how soon you gonna finish, Bud? You ain't even got to the Brazos yet. We could have driven a herd of cows all the way up the damn trail by now."

The room erupted in laughter and applause. The cattlemen and their stout wives turned in their seats to grin at Lamar Clayton, who looked across the table and winked at Gil and Maureen.

"You think you can give this damn speech any faster, Lamar," the ancient speaker said, "then by god you get on up here and do 'er."

Martindale beamed in delight, still scribbling. If there was a heaven for the academic study of old-time Texas, he was in it. Meanwhile Clayton jokingly halfway rose out of his chair as the audience kept laughing, but he settled back down again and after a few more good-natured interruptions the speaker was droning on once more, cataloging endless feeder trails and minor watercourses, until he came to Doan's Crossing on the Prairie Dog Town Fork and began a sentence with the words that the audience had been longing to hear: "In conclusion . . ."

When the dinner was over, Gil and Maureen and Martindale waited in the lobby while Clayton shook hands with some of his old trail-driving friends and their wives. There was an air of convivial vitality about him that neither Gil nor Maureen had seen before, and a strange kind of urbanity too. He seemed oddly more at home in this hotel ballroom in San Antonio than he did in his own house. And Gil noticed the way he talked to the wives of those tremulous old cowboys, the way he held their attention with a steady, undistracted look. It was the sort of look that men naturally interpreted as challenging but that women saw as flattering. Seeing Clayton in this company helped Gil to understand how this temperamental and solitary rancher had ended up marrying a beautiful and sophisticated woman twenty years younger; and at the same time how he might have ended up driving away his only son.

"Sorry that dinner took so long," Clayton said when he returned to them. "That fella always was a little long-winded. I recall that three or four months on the trail with him was about plenty."

"It was a privilege to hear it, Mr. Clayton," Vance Martindale said. "A privilege just to be at a gathering like this."

"Well, I don't know about that," Clayton said. Gil could tell that the old rancher didn't know what to think of Martindale. Gil felt a little bit the same way. Martindale knew how to listen, his interest in the subject of trail drives and pioneer ranching was impressively deep and unabashed, and he was not a fake. One look at his blunt, beat-up hands told you that he was as much a product of the South Texas brushlands as he was of the university. Gil understood why Maureen liked him. But still, there was something put on about him, the cowboy boots he wore with his rumpled suit, the battered hat he wore pushed back on the top of his head. He wanted you to notice him, he wanted you to appreciate the character he had invented for himself.

"If it's agreeable to you, Mr. Clayton," Gil said, "we'll meet at my studio for lunch and you could have a look at the scale model then."

"That's agreeable."

Gil turned to Vance Martindale. "Will you join us for lunch as well?"

"With the greatest pleasure. But only if I'm not in the way."

IT WAS LATE. Her father drove home alone in his own car, after Vance had asked if he could have the honor of dropping her off. They were now heading aimlessly through the almost empty downtown streets.

"I have the feeling your father invited me only because I happened to be standing there," Vance said to Maureen. One of the senior professors in Austin had lent him his car while he was at a conference in New York, and Vance had gleefully taken the liberty of driving it all the way down to San Antonio.

"He invited you because he likes you."

"I'd like to think so. But he's a little suspicious of me, don't you think?"

"Why would I think that?"

"I don't know, a rough character like myself, lurking around his daughter."

"You're hardly a rough character."

"As if you would know. You didn't see me get into a saloon brawl the other day over Spenser's use of the Petrarchan sonnet. Seriously, what does he think of me?"

"He hasn't said much about you."

"Do you realize how crushing that sounds to an egoist?"

"Yes, and it serves you right. Where are you taking me?"

"I thought we could have an ice cream sundae."

"There's no place that would serve us an ice cream sundae at eleven o'clock at night."

"Must you wave the banner of reality in my face like that?"

He had had maybe a little too much to drink. Maybe she had too, with that second glass of wine. The Old Time Trail Drivers—with the exception of the grimly abstemious Lamar Clayton—had unsurprisingly proved to be a group of serious drinkers, and with prohibition looming on the horizon after the beginning of the year there had been an end-of-the-world spirit of indulgence at the event. Even her father, so crushingly moderate in his habits, had been a little mellow by the time it was over.

Vance drove to San Pedro Springs and they got out and walked through the deserted park, across a footbridge spanning a small, mostly dried-up lake. A boat, built in the shape of a swan, lay rotting on the bank. Its peeling white paint was visible in the moonlight.

"It's a great pity," Vance declared as he stared into the water from the bridge.

"What's a pity?"

"These springs were Texas' Garden of Eden once. Utterly glorious, endless clear water rushing out of the limestone. San Antonio wouldn't be here if it weren't for these springs, Texas wouldn't be here. Now they've been pumped nearly dry."

He told her about the mastodons and dire wolves that had once watered here, the Lipan Apaches and Spanish explorers who had camped here, Sam Houston speaking out at this very spot against the idea of Texas leaving the Union. She listened as they walked on, entranced by his enthusiasm, the bottomless depth of his knowledge, but most of all by the way, as he lectured, that he had made her his audience of one. He paused at an old stone blockhouse that he declared was the oldest building in Texas. He patted the stone with such worshipful attention that she thought he would kiss it.

"So you have the history of Texas," he said, turning to her again, "all compressed in this one spot. But history is boring, or so people seem to think. Let's talk about you."

"My history would make a very slim volume."

"Well, you must add a chapter or two."

"Not so easily done, I'm afraid."

"Why not?"

"I don't know, Vance. Because things are not easily done in general."

He leaned against the ancient stone and looked at her, studied her. He was not in a hurry and his glance did not waver. She was stirred by his scrutiny. She had never been looked at in quite this way, slowly assessed and appreciated with such frank interest. It thrilled her, the way she seemed to be holding this man's attention. She wondered if this was how her mother had felt when she modeled for her husband.

"What do you want for your life, Maureen?"

"Don't ask me such a big question. I suppose I want a little independence, to start with."

"And after that?"

"After that I'll take what comes."

He nodded and seemed to ponder this, then he looked her in the eye again and said, "May I?"

"May you what?"

And so he finally kissed her. Whatever shyness or delicacy had restrained him from declaring himself before now had finally evaporated, helped along no doubt by liquor and by the stimulative effects of being in proximity to so much Texas history. He held her rather chastely as they kissed, his hands on her shoulders as if they were dancing. Nevertheless she could feel the bulk of his body against her, and take in the smell of his cologne and his pipe tobacco, and the nervous sweat that dampened the underarms of his suit. He recovered himself perhaps a moment or two sooner than she would have preferred and backed away from her, grinning widely, staring at her.

"Well," he said, "we better get you home before your famous father suspects foul play."

AS SOON AS Gil got home that night, he went straight to work. To anyone else's eye the quarter-scale model would have appeared complete, every detail conscientiously rendered without appearing too precise in a worked-over way. But Gil was unsatisfied with an unspecified something around the boy's mouth—were the lips too full?—and the attitude of the horse's left hind leg was subtly wrong. He could correct this latter flaw, he realized, by veering a bit from the imaginary line he had conceived from the rear tendon to the ischium. He had relied too much on textbook proportions there, and as a result the leg looked amateurishly rigid. He worried a bit about the jugular grooves in the horse's neck as well. They looked too deep all of a sudden, but he deferred a decision about whether that was a problem until he could see the model again in daylight.

He attacked the human figure's face first, very slightly planing away some of the material from the upper lip and strengthening the tension at the corners of the mouth, pausing now and then to study the imperfect Kodaks of Ben Clayton through a magnifying glass. He used tools he had bought in Rome almost forty years before, their heartwood handles still strong after all the decades of use, and soothingly familiar. But as he gripped them now the pain in his thumbs flared up again, and he had to set the tools down, cursing under his breath. In angry defiance he took them up once more and worked in spite of the pain, shearing away a bit of clay from the hock of one of the horse's rear legs, building up the thigh to help create a more authentic illusion of muscle flexion. But he could not work for more than a few moments without pausing and cursing. The inflammation in his hands made holding the tools feel like gripping a live electrical wire.

It was after midnight. He walked around the model as the pain ebbed away, studying it from every vantage point. He would not be able to gauge the effect completely until he had natural light in the morning, but he thought he had done his job well. Ben Clayton stood next to his horse, gazing off into what to a viewer would be an imaginary distance, but which to Gil's mind was almost as real as it had been to Ben, since he had studied the landscape from the heightened vantage point of the statue and ridden a horse—Ben's horse—across miles of open pasture. The human figure and the horse were thrillingly real to him. He had done as well once or twice before, with the Pawnee Scout perhaps, or the model for the never-cast General Gómez, but he had never done better.

In the kitchen, he chipped some ice out of the icebox, wrapped it in a dish towel, and pressed the heels of his hands against it. Restless, he walked back out to the studio. He lifted the moistened cloth off one of Maureen's almost-finished reliefs. He turned on a desk lamp and held it close as he studied her work. It was excellent, and yet slightly lifeless. It depicted a bird in the foreground, a yellow-crowned night heron sailing on outspread wings, about to land on the branch of a cypress tree. In the distance a modern-day voyager with a pair of binoculars around his neck stealthily paddled a canoe. What worried Gil was the over-researched precision of the heron. Maureen had done her homework, he knew. She had taken the train up to Austin and spent time in the specimen collection at the university, sketching the bird in its inert form, and she had studied it in life as well, along the banks of the river.

The bird, and every other detail on the various panels, was more than competently rendered, and the overall idea was strong and unforced. He was quite sure the ladies who had commissioned it would be pleased. But in the end there was not much power in it, nothing that would stir you or confound you or command your attention as you glanced at it while walking across the bridge where it was to be placed.

As they had worked together in the studio, he on the Clayton model, Maureen on her relief sculptures, she had openheartedly sought his advice and criticism, and he had given it, and the work, he believed, was stronger for it. But there was no way he could advise her past the threshold between a sculpture that was competent and professional and one that somehow breathed with life. The pieces of his that were successful in this way were mysteriously so. He did not know how he did it, only that every so often he had managed to vault past the barrier of skill and technique into the realm of magic. It was painful to admit to himself—and unthinkable to suggest to his daughter—that she did not share his gift.

He had just finished replacing the cloth when Maureen walked into the studio. It was midnight. He could see just from the way she opened and closed the door that she was in a buoyant mood.

"Did you hurt your hand?"

"It's just a little stiff."

"Sorry to be coming home so late," she said.

"You're not a little girl, Maureen. It's no business of mine what time you come home. Did you enjoy your drive with Mr. Martindale?"

"I wish you would call him Vance, Daddy."

"All right. Of course I will."

"Because 'Mr. Martindale' sounds a little frosty and disapproving, the way you say it, anyway."

"I don't disapprove of him. I don't really know him."

That wasn't exactly true. Gil had met Martindale enough to gather more than a sketchy impression, and he had a sense of the man through his writing as well—not just the enthusiastic study of Gil's own Alamo sculpture that had been published in the *Southwestern Historical Quarterly,* but a number of other essays he had written for the publication. In print, Martindale seemed to be always spoiling for a fight, drawing scholarly lines in the sand, throwing down provocative challenges to the timid and conventional thinking with which he imagined he was surrounded. He chastised Texans for their grandiloquent insularity and pride even as he went about romanticizing and mythologizing the place himself, celebrating everything from the rapacious Spanish explorers to the lowly prairie dog.

Gil did his best to hold his reservations aside as he looked at his daughter. She was glancing around the studio, afraid to meet his eyes, afraid to break into the delighted smile he sensed she was suppressing for his benefit. He assumed something had happened with Mr. Martindale tonight. Vance. Something had gone right. Once more he was stung by Victoria's absence, because it was impossible for him to be the maternal confidante that the situation called for. He could only do his best.

"Should I know him better?" Gil asked her.

"If you'd like to. He's very interesting, you know."

"There's no need to convince me of that. It's obvious he's got a brilliant mind, that he's ambitious. He could be a match for you."

"Daddy, it's hopelessly premature to even suggest such a thing." But she was beaming when she said this. "Anyway, he's very grateful that you allowed him to come along with us tonight. He got so much out of it."

"I'm glad."

She smiled again and looked past him, at the scale model of Ben

Clayton and his horse. She walked up to it as if she were noticing it for the first time, instead of having been an intimate part of its creation.

"What do you think?" Gil asked Maureen, after a moment or two. "Will he like it?"

"I think so. He ought to, of course. But he's unpredictable, as we well know. Did you do something to the mouth?"

"Tightened it a bit."

She uttered a little grunt of approval, then made a sweep around the model, studying it from every angle.

"Why do you think he invited us to go to that dinner with him tonight?" she said as she made her inspection. "It wasn't as if he didn't have plenty of people there he knew already."

"He was just being polite, I suppose."

"I think he wanted to impress you. To let you see that there are people who know him and like him. Maybe he's a little in awe of you."

"Are you serious? Clayton?"

"Why shouldn't he be? Everyone's a little bit in awe of you, Daddy. Didn't you know that?"

She kissed his cheek and went inside to bed. He lingered for a moment more in the studio, savoring his daughter's happiness, wishing Victoria were here to witness it.

FIFTEEN

He arrived exactly on time in a chauffeur-driven car he had hired through the hotel.

"I thought we'd have lunch first and give you a chance to inspect the model at your leisure afterwards," Gil suggested when he met Clayton at the door.

"Well, leisure don't have much to do with it but that sounds all right to me."

He shook hands with Vance, who was dressed in the new suit Maureen had helped him pick out, his thick, wayward hair respectfully plastered down. A notebook and pencil peeked touchingly from his jacket pocket, and helped to frame in Maureen's mind what she liked about him. He had a passion for recording and cataloging these old-time tales that was as strong as her father's passion for modeling in clay.

Mrs. Gossling did not work on Saturdays, so Maureen had gotten up early to prepare the meal herself, drawing from a dozen or so recipes that her mother had, at Maureen's urging several years ago, finally written down on file cards. She decided on pot roast with potatoes and onions and carrots and a devil's food cake for dessert. From the time spent on his ranch and the fare served at his table, Maureen had guessed Clayton would not be a hard man to feed. Plain food would do just fine.

He was far more talkative than he had been when presiding at his own table. As they ate, Vance peppered him with questions about his experiences on the cattle drives and he rambled on pleasantly, impressed and, despite himself, maybe even a little flattered by the younger man's precise interest.

"I didn't care for that country up around the Stinkingwater," Clayton said, in answer to one of Vance's questions about the land north of Dodge City to Ogallala. "The creek had a safe bottom but that's about all I can say for it. Nothing but bad grass and sandhills and ever now and then a little bitty pond about the size of a teacup. I remember when we finally got through that country we come to a ranch where a little girl was waiting for us. She'd been milking the cows all morning and had that milk cooling there in the spring waiting to sell it to us. You never did see a happier bunch of cowboys than when we got to drinking that milk."

Vance was writing as fast as he could, shoving a bite into his mouth when there was a pause, occasionally looking up and grinning at Maureen like he could not believe his good fortune.

"You must have been a young man on that drive," Maureen said to Clayton as Vance scribbled to catch up.

"Oh, yes, ma'am, just a kid, though I don't recall thinking of myself that way. They say people grew up faster in those days but I don't know if that's true or just something you hear. There's a lot of boys buried over there with Ben in France that grew up pretty fast if you ask me."

In the subdued silence that followed this comment, he ate the last bite of his cake and then looked at Maureen and said it was as fine a cake as he'd ever eaten. He toyed with the silverware a moment and then set his napkin on top of his plate.

"Well, I expect I better take a look at what you done," he said to Gil.

VANCE INSISTED on staying behind in the dining room, sensitive enough to appreciate the fact that the rancher's encounter with a sculpture of his dead son ought to be a private moment, off-limits to his curiosity and note-taking.

Maureen smiled at him in gratitude as she followed her father and Mr. Clayton into the studio. When they entered, the midday winter light was strong. The model stood in the center of the room, hidden by a simple cotton drape.

"As I believe I explained to you," Gil said, standing in front of the draped model, "this is a scale model, a third the size of the final sculpture. Assuming you approve it, I'll then begin to build the armature and model the statue in full size. It will look very much like this, so if you have any hesitations or concerns it's important that you make me aware of them now."

Clayton nodded. Gil pulled back the cloth to reveal the model. Clayton took a step toward it and then stood there sweeping his eyes across it.

He did this for a long time, a very long time. Gil had been in this anxious position many, many times in his career, waiting silently for approval. People were different. Some were over-effusive, some were embarrassed or strategically disinclined to register a reaction, some—a very few—were disappointed. Usually the person assessing the work was a member of a board or committee, sometimes they had known the individual whose likeness they were studying, but most often not. Once or twice he had silently withdrawn as an old lady had wept at the image she had commissioned of her long-dead father. But he did not know what to expect from a grieving, complicated man studying the face and form of his son.

As even more time went by, Maureen caught her father's eye: should you say something? But he thought not. He thought it best just to wait.

When Clayton finally did speak, he seemed to have forgotten all about what he had been staring at so raptly for so long. He looked around the studio for the first time, picked up a few of Gil's tools and hefted them in his hands, inspected some of the busts and figure studies lining the walls. He took a handkerchief out of his pocket and wiped away a line of sweat that had started to seep down from his hairline. His face looked flushed, but his features were composed and when he finally spoke his voice was eerily conversational.

"So the next step is you build yourself one of these armatures and cover that up with clay."

"That's right."

"How do you know it'll come out the same as this little one?"

"Well, a lot of sculptors—most, I'd say—go to rather elaborate mathematical lengths to ensure that that's the case. They build a kind of chassis for each piece, the model and the full-scale work, with corresponding measurements, so that when it's time to model the larger piece it's just a matter of adding so much more clay between the points you've marked. It's very efficient and generally very accurate, but it doesn't suit me. I build the armature to the correct proportions, of course, but when I cover it with clay I want to feel like I'm still sculpting, not just filling out spaces."

Clayton nodded. Gil didn't know if he had quite understood, and perhaps it had been a mistake to explain himself so elaborately. He thought about sketching out the whole pointing process on a piece of paper and letting him see how it was about as creative as building a fence. But Gil knew that Clayton wouldn't give a damn whether Gil felt creative or not when he was doing his job. All that would matter to him was that the job was done to his satisfaction.

And this was where he was irritatingly impossible to read. Was he satisfied? It had been almost ten minutes; it was extremely odd not to express any opinion at all. Gil was about to press him when Clayton seemed to wobble a bit on his feet and his face grew even more flushed.

"Is there something the matter?" Gil asked. "Would you like a glass of water?"

"I'll be back in a minute."

He turned and left the studio. Gil and Maureen went to the door and watched as he wandered out of the open yard behind the house and out into the street and headed east with a determined gait.

"What's he doing?" Maureen asked.

"I don't know. Going for a stroll to clear his head, I suppose. He'll be back in a few minutes."

But an hour passed and he had not returned. Maureen cleared the table and did the dishes while Vance and her father waited in the parlor. She heard them talking about Ghiberti's doors and arguing about Michelangelo, Vance maintaining that the Bruges Madonna was superior to the Pieta and that the Pitti Madonna was superior to both. When she came in from the kitchen, drying her hands on a dish towel, her father was amiably holding up his end of the banter, but she could tell he was too distracted by Clayton's disappearance to pay much attention to the conversation.

"Something isn't right," Gil finally said. "He's not the sort of man who just takes off walking. I'm going to get the car and look for him."

As he sprang out of his chair, he spoke to Vance. "Want to come?"

"Of course." Vance picked his hat up from the table and set it on his head, glancing with sly surprise in Maureen's direction: her father was sizing him up.

"You better stay here in case he comes back," Gil said to Maureen.

"Yes, obviously," she replied. He probably didn't even detect the annoyance in her voice as he headed toward the door. She didn't mind him bolting off on his urgent business, and she didn't mind him taking her guest along without consulting her. She just wearily minded how it had always been this way, all her life: her father making decisions, seizing on solutions, she and her mother automatically falling into their supportive places behind him.

GIL DROVE NORTH, toward downtown, he and Martindale scanning the sides of Roosevelt Avenue, peering each way at every intersection.

"Well, this is an odd damn thing to happen," Martindale ventured.

"He'll probably be at home by the time we get back. But I can't guess what got into him."

"He might have gotten a taxi somewhere and gone back to his hotel."

"Yes, that's what I was thinking. I'll go downtown and have a look there."

They drove on a few more blocks, Gil continuing to brake at each corner so they could inspect the side streets.

"I take it that you and my daughter have gotten to be pretty good friends," Gil said. "At least that's the impression I've had from her."

"I'm pleased to hear she thinks so. It's certainly true from my point of view. Turn here. I think I just saw him crossing the street."

But it wasn't Lamar Clayton, it was a Mexican man in a suit and a straw hat, walking along the sidewalk with a bag of groceries, who glanced at them suspiciously as they cruised slowly by. Gil drove around the corner and then up the next block, back to Roosevelt.

"How long have you been at the university?" Gil asked him, realizing as he spoke that the question had come out of his mouth like an interrogation. Oh, well, if Martindale didn't know that Gil was trying to probe his background and character he was dim to begin with.

"Seven years. They've rather enjoyed keeping me in limbo there."

"Oh?"

"They don't seem to know what to do with a man who won't get a Ph.D."

"Out of principle?"

"Out of a refusal to waste my time."

"Can you advance in a place like that without one?"

"Oh, I'll advance."

A disdain for institutional propriety, an independent mind, the unswerving pursuit of a personal ambition: all of these traits in Martindale should have appealed to Gil, since they all corresponded with his own outlook and the way he had fashioned his own life. But it was one thing to be the way he was and another to think a similar sort of man would make a worthy husband for his daughter. He had never allowed himself to examine what kind of husband he had truly been to Victoria, what kind of father he was to Maureen. Selfishness, maybe even ruthlessness, was one of the starting places of art. He had not been a bully like his father, but he had made sure without ever saying so directly that the overriding work of his family would be the viability of his career, the furtherance of his vision. It was possible that this Vance Martindale was just as quietly imperious.

He didn't dislike the man, but he didn't quite trust him. Martindale had been the picture of confidence and ease until now, but alone in the car with Gil he seemed nervous. Gil asked him where he had grown up and he said on a small ranch in South Texas, but as soon as Gil started to ask more questions about his background, Martindale called out that he thought he saw Lamar Clayton again, walking into a bank on Commerce Street. Gil parked the car and ran into the bank, but Clayton was nowhere in evidence.

When he left the bank, he pulled in front of the Gunter. He sent Martindale to check out the downtown streets while he went inside and had the desk clerk call Clayton's room. There was no answer. He asked a few of the Old Time Trail Drivers who were checking out of the hotel if they had seen him in the last couple of hours. None had, but with the hale attitude that seemed to distinguish the men of this convention they assured Gil that he would turn up.

"I haven't seen him," Maureen said when he telephoned home. "He seems to have just vanished. I'm a little worried, Daddy."

"I'm sure he's fine," Gil said. "Maybe he just felt pressured for a reaction and wanted to get away to settle his mind."

"He's been gone a long time for somebody who's just settling his mind."

Gil hung up the phone in the hotel lobby and went around to the garage, hoping to talk to the driver who had taken Lamar Clayton to his house. The driver was out, but his supervisor told him they had received no calls from the old man asking to be picked up.

"No sign of him out on the street," Martindale reported when he joined Gil in the lobby.

"Well, let's just head back home. Maybe we'll come across him on the way."

They drove away from downtown in the general direction of Gil's house, veering off the main thoroughfares onto side streets, now and then stopping at places of business—a feed store, a hardware store—that he speculated might possibly have attracted the curiosity of a visiting rancher. Gil didn't bother to continue his fatherly interrogation as they drove back to the house—both because Martindale's artful evasiveness had started to irritate him and because by now his puzzlement over Clayton's whereabouts had turned into real worry.

The more he searched without result, the greater his agitation grew. Had Clayton somehow been so offended by the model that he had just thrown up his hands and disappeared? He had not seemed angry before he took off on his mysterious walk. He had been shaken, perhaps: in the best case by a reaction to the disturbing fidelity of his son's image; in the worst by a contemptuous realization that Gil had failed. In either case he might very well be disinclined to carry on with the project. The lost revenue would be bad enough, but even worse would be the abandonment of a commission that Gil had come to recognize as a work of art, a piece that would not be ignored or dismissed this time by the arbiters of fame, even though it would reside forever in a remote location far from the salons of New York. The Clayton statue was what he had always silently believed he had come to Texas to create—a work that would have its own power, that owed nothing to proximity and critical jabbering but would simply announce its presence to the world as steadily and quietly as a beacon.

When they got home and heard from Maureen that Clayton had

still not returned, the sense that something was really wrong began to take hold.

"Maybe we should have checked the train station," Martindale said.

"Not likely. Would he have gone to the train station without his luggage? Without checking out of his hotel first? Of course, there's nothing likely about this whole thing."

He grabbed the hat he'd set down on the table only moments before. "You're right, I should check the train station. And the hospital too."

"Want me to come again this time?" Martindale asked.

"No, you stay here with Maureen."

Maureen knew there was no point in suggesting that he telephone the hospital instead. He was already out the door again, desperate for any active gesture.

"I have the feeling I'm in your father's way," Vance said when Gil had driven off.

"There's nothing going on for you to be in the way of. We're just sitting here. What did you two talk about?"

"Nothing. Just small talk. Trying to solve the case of the fugitive patron. Listen, as long as you're not going to kick me out, do you mind if I take a look at the work in question that's causing all the anxiety?"

SHE TOOK VANCE into the studio and the two of them stood staring at the scale model. Maureen tried to see it through Lamar Clayton's eyes—how it had moved him, how it had failed him. But she could only see it through her own. It was her father's most assured work in many years. It was even better than the Pawnee Scout. His own heart was revealed in it. In the posture of the young man's body, in his focused gaze, in the unforced mysterious comradeship between him and his horse, there was a welling sorrow. The sorrow came from nowhere that she could discern, from no particular detail. It came instead from the sculptor, from her father.

"What a gift he has," Vance said.

"I know."

He got out his pipe and was about to light it, then seemed to remember he was in another man's working sanctum. He slipped the pipe back into his pocket and regarded the Ben Clayton model again.

"How old was he?"

"Twenty-one."

"Poor bastard."

"Here. Help me cover it."

She handed him a wet cloth and together they draped the model again so it would not dry out. Then he gestured to her little corner of the studio, where the panels for the Spirit of the Waters were likewise hidden beneath layers of moist cloth.

"Is this your piece here? May I see it as well?"

"Not tonight."

"Why not?"

"Because I'm not happy with it. And because even if I were I wouldn't want you to judge my work after looking at my father's. It wouldn't be fair."

"I wasn't planning to 'judge' it. Anyway, you're not in a contest with him, so why should it matter?"

"I don't know why it should, but it does. And your nosiness is unbecoming."

"I agree that it's a character flaw. One of my favorites."

He walked up to her and kissed her, but the moment didn't feel right to her and neither did the place. She kissed him back and briskly patted his lapels.

"We should get back to the house in case he calls."

Her father did call, fifteen or twenty minutes later, with the news that Mr. Clayton wasn't in the hospital.

"Maybe we should tell the police," she told him over the phone.

"All right. I'll go over to the station now. While I'm there, maybe you and Vance should take over the search. I don't want to let any time go by without somebody looking for him."

"I BELIEVE this is the first time in my life I've ever been enlisted into a posse," Vance declared as they drove away from the house in his friend's Chevrolet, with neighborhood dogs sprinting out of their yards and snapping at the tires.

They drove slowly up and down Roosevelt, passing ramshackle cafés and boardinghouses, dry goods stores and warehouses. It was as drab a commercial strip as San Antonio had to offer, and reminded her once again how far she was from the places in the world where things that mattered to her were happening.

"By the way," Vance said, as they peered down alleys and side streets, "I got out my copy of Wilbarger the other night to see if your friend might be in it."

"Wilbarger?"

"*Indian Depredations in Texas.* The Bible for this sort of research. You said it was on the Salt Fork, didn't you, where Clayton's housekeeper lost her family?"

"That's what she said."

"It seems to have been a fairly famous massacre, at least to the folks in Stonewall County. Do you think she'd talk to me about it?"

"George's Mary? She'd probably hit you over the head with a skillet if you pried into her private life. Or maybe I would."

"Too bad. It would have made a good article for the *Quarterly.* But I suppose it's for the best. It would only give my overlords another reason not to take me seriously."

He drifted into a monologue about his endless travails at the university. "A lot of these professors, they're intimidating, all right. A farm boy from Waxahachie or someplace will take one look at some crusty old medievalist in his bow tie and think he's face-to-face with God. But the truth is half of them don't have enough brains to fry an egg in. And when it comes to being open to new ideas—"

He braked, inspecting a group of men gathered at an icehouse, but Clayton was not among them.

"A host of golden daffodils!" he went on. "Fine! No complaints. Everyone should know their Wordsworth. But when I gently suggest that poetry can also be written about mesquite beans and turkey buzzards, that it can come from the native soil, out of the old rock, so to speak, well, that's when they look at me like—"

"Slow down!" Maureen said. It was dusk now and they were passing a garage where in one of the open bays she could see two mechanics in coveralls sitting at a table. There was a third man at the table wearing a suit and a white stockman's hat: Lamar Clayton.

"There he is," she told Vance. "Stop the car."

She approached them carefully, Vance following a few discreet steps behind. Mr. Clayton had not seen them and was engaged in a leisurely conversation in Spanish with the two mechanics. They were all drinking orangeade and the table was covered with butcher paper, upon which sat a pile of greasy barbecued meat and stacks of tortillas.

Clayton was not eating, just sipping his orangeade while the two mechanics helped themselves to the food. They were the ones who saw her first, and she heard one of them say, "Señor." Clayton turned to look at her and said nothing and the expression on his face was blank. He remained seated while the two mechanics stood and offered her a chair.

She turned to Vance.

"Would you please drive back to our house and let my father know that we've found him? He'll probably be home before too long."

"You'll be all right here?"

"Of course."

He gave her hand a warm squeeze and then got in the car and drove away.

Maureen took a seat. The mechanics offered her some of the meat but she politely waved it away and they gathered it up in the butcher paper and went inside to the office so that she and Clayton could be alone.

"They're both from Chihuahua," Clayton said. "They don't say it but I bet you a dime the older one there rode with Villa."

"We've been looking for you all afternoon, Mr. Clayton."

"Oh, hell," he said. "I don't need people looking for me. You want to do that, that's your business."

"We thought something had happened to you."

"I told you I was just going to go out for a minute. I ran into these men here and we got to talking and I went next door to that barbecue place and bought them some dinner. So if anything happened to me that's about what it was."

He took a sip of his drink. He had spoken to her in the same surly, annoyed tone she had heard him using with George's Mary. A trace of temper in her own voice, she decided, would be a good thing.

"Don't be so selfish," she told him, "and please don't speak to me that way."

Her tone caught his attention. He came swimming back from his crotchety self-absorption and looked at her as if aware of her presence for the first time.

"We've all been very worried," she went on, "and it will be a great relief for my father to hear that you're all right. But he's also very concerned about your reaction to the model. He's worried that it might have offended you, and if it did, I think you at least owe him the courtesy of telling him why. If you want to cancel the commission, of course that's your right, but for decency's sake—"

"I don't want to cancel the goddam commission!"

The outburst seemed to startle him. He looked around uneasily, staring at a moldy sign on the wall for Goodrich tires as if it were some difficult text he was trying to decipher.

"To tell you the truth," he said to Maureen, "I ain't all that sure how the hell I got here."

"You walked out of our house."

"I remember that, and I remember being here. I don't remember anything in between. How long have I been gone?"

"About five hours."

She had never seen fear in his eyes before, but it was there now.

"Do you think I'm losing my mind, Miss Gilheaney?"

"I very much doubt it. Maybe seeing the model gave you a shock. That happens to people."

"I've had plenty of shocks and I ain't never forgot where I was before."

He stared at the Goodrich sign again. "I seen my own mother lying on the floor of our little house with an arrow through her. I'd say that was a shock, wouldn't you? And I ain't forgot a minute of any of that."

Maureen was careful not to say anything. But she reached out and touched his arm and he didn't flinch as she supposed he would.

"If I get to where I'm losing my mind I believe I'll just go out and shoot myself."

"Please don't talk that way."

He said it was nobody's business how he talked, but he said it as an observation, not a rebuke. Then he sat there in silence for almost a full minute. Through the window, Maureen could see the two mechanics arguing with each other, and she guessed they were trying to decide whether or not to ask the old man to leave so they could close up for the night.

"When I was with the Indians," Clayton said at last, just when Maureen thought he had decided to turn obstinately mute, "the Rangers used to chase us all over hell. One time we was running from them across the desert for days without any water, and when we finally come to this lake we was counting on, damned if it wasn't dry, nothing but dead fish lying out there in the sun. And so we kept on going west. We had to kill a few horses just to drink the blood. We finally got to some better country and found a spring, but you know what? I started to drink that water and it wouldn't go down. My tongue was swole up so bad the water just came back up out my nose. There I was at that spring, dying of thirst with all that cold mountain water, and it didn't do me a damn bit of good."

He was looking at her now, and speaking to her. His air of confusion and distance had slowly evaporated during the time it had taken him to tell this story, and there was a direct look in his face again.

"I guess you might say I had that same kind of feeling when I saw what your dad had made. It was Ben, all right, or close enough. Closer than I'd thought it would be, to tell you the truth. I thought it would make me feel better to see it, but it didn't. And a full-size statue ain't going to neither."

Moved as she was, she could not quite keep her self-interested alarm at bay, and he must have seen it on her face, because he smiled at her and said, "Don't worry. I ain't going to back out of the contract with your dad."

"He wouldn't want to complete it if it caused you pain."

"It won't cause me pain, Miss Gilheaney. It just won't make the pain go away, and I ought to have knowed that already."

He reached into the pocket of his suit coat and removed a much-handled envelope. He took a letter out and handed it to her. The letter had been repeatedly folded and unfolded and the creases were almost worn through.

"I got this a while ago. I know I ought to write this boy back but I can't make myself do it."

Maureen read the letter.

"This here is what came along with it," he said, taking the little homemade medallion out of the envelope and setting it on the table between them. Maureen studied it for a long time—it was crude but not bad, and rendered with such longing it almost brought her to tears. She carefully folded the letter back again.

"Would you like me to write him for you?" she said.

"All right," he said.

"What would you like me to say?"

"Oh, I don't know. Anything you say would be all right with me, I guess." He handed her the envelope. "You'll need that for the address."

She heard a car pulling in and turned to look. It was her father. She waved to him to stay in the car and wait for them, and then she gently suggested to Mr. Clayton that it was time to go.

SIXTEEN

After Lamar Clayton went home to his ranch, it took Gil, with Maureen's help, a week and a half to build the armature for the full-scale statue. Ben Clayton had been five feet, eleven inches tall, but because a life-size statue invariably appeared oddly puny to a viewer, Gil had increased the height of the human figure to a full seven feet, and had scaled up the proportions of the horse as well. As a result, the armatures for man and horse looked like oversized mechanical beings from another world. The forms were made from old water pipes Gil had scavenged from junkyards, reinforced in vulnerable load-bearing areas with plaster. He had formed the torsos with odds and ends of lumber from his scrap pile, and applied a patchy covering of hardened burlap that he soaked in plaster. After he had brushed on a coat of shellac, the skeletal figures had seemed to spring to life on their own terms, and it was always at this point that he paused for a moment in amusement. He could send it off to the foundry to be cast as it was and call it "modern."

He wondered what Clayton would think of people like Picasso or Gaudier-Breszka. He supposed that at least on the subject of so-called modern art he and Clayton might see eye to eye on what a statue was supposed to be—a work that was about its subject and not about itself. As it was, the old rancher had said almost nothing after Gil picked him up at the gas station and drove him back to his hotel. Maureen had told Gil what Clayton had said to her, how the sight of the statue had thrown him back and sent him on a disoriented odyssey through the streets of San Antonio. But he had been too ashamed, or too scared, or just too surly to say anything to Gil himself. He had gone back to West Texas without ever explicitly approving the work, just had sadly decreed as Gil dropped him off at the hotel that it was to go on.

He would never be able to please him; Gil knew that much now. Clayton was a different sort of client, someone who was looking for something—redemption, perhaps, or some deeper, sharper pain—that no artist would have any way of providing.

"Should we start with the clay now?" Maureen asked on the afternoon they finished, staring up at the armature in its mummy wrapping of burlap. Her hair was pinned back and she was wearing her smock and beneath it the faded dress she usually wore for work.

"No," Gil decided, after glancing at the miniature clock on his worktable. "It's three o'clock. Let's start fresh in the morning. I think we've earned a few hours off."

The Menger Bar was crowded when Gil arrived, and Urrutia and Sutherland were out of sorts because their usual table in the back was taken and they were condemned to sitting near the front door, exposed to gusts of cold air every time a patron entered.

"We were just talking about how much whiskey we can stockpile before January, when this goddam amendment goes into effect," Sutherland said, biting a hard-boiled egg in half. "I was thinking about fifty barrels or so ought to tide me over till people come to their senses again."

"Fifty barrels?" Gil asked.

"Well, I don't want to call attention to myself, but I do like a drink or two in the evening. How's the statue?"

"We'll start packing on the clay tomorrow. Then I'll begin the modeling next week. A couple of months and it'll be ready for the plasterers."

"And how's your client?" Urrutia asked. "The Indian captive."

Gil turned to Sutherland. "What else do you know about him? Is he stable?"

"Stable if he ain't drunk. Why?"

"He took a strange turn when he saw the model. Wandered off and didn't come back and claimed he didn't remember a thing about what happened."

"He ain't trying to cheat you out of your money?"

"No, I don't think so."

"Well, as long as you get your money I guess it don't matter what sorts of crazy things Lamar does."

Urrutia reached into a bowl of peanuts and cracked one open. Then he fixed Gil with a weary, wounded look.

"Is something the matter?" Gil asked him.

"I'm just very disappointed in you, my friend. You have a great secret. You've kept even your good friends in the dark. But now, at last, your secret has been exposed."

Gil froze, uncertain about what sort of information Urrutia might have found out. Had he somehow uncovered the fraudulent story about his mother?

The look on Gil's face startled Urrutia for a moment, but then he broke into a relaxed smile and laughed.

"Don't worry about him," Sutherland said to Gil. "He's got a secret or two himself."

"Yes, very dark ones. I've heard all the rumors. But, Gil, there's no reason for you to keep such wonderful knowledge hidden from us. You should be very proud of your daughter. She was entrusted with the new sculpture for the Commerce Street bridge. Or am I wrong?"

"No," Gil replied, hollow with relief. "I am very proud of her. And she did it all on her own. She didn't even tell me she'd entered the competition. How did you find out about it?"

"Oh, my spies are everywhere, even among the members of the San Antonio Women's Club."

Sutherland spotted someone he needed to talk to, a young man from Kerrville who he said was trying to move in on his grocery business. He walked over to slap the kid on the back and buy him a drink.

"He keeps his enemies close," Urrutia said.

"What do you know about arthritis?" Gil asked him.

"I'm a doctor. I know everything I'm supposed to about it. Why?"

"I've started getting this pain at the base of my thumbs when I'm working."

Urrutia reached across the table, grabbed both of Gil's hands and roughly examined them.

"No crepitus," he said. "That's good. No Heberden's nodes. That's good too. Are you eating enough meat?"

"I think so."

"Eat more. Take smaller portions of bread and potatoes, or even better eliminate them. Take aspirin for the pain. Come around to the office and I'll make you splints to wear at night. Most important, rest your hands. A few weeks."

HE TOOK all of Urrutia's advice except for resting his hands, worried that those few weeks of idleness would leave him cold on what could be his most important commission in decades. He wore the splints at night, and they helped well enough to get him through the mornings as he and Maureen covered the armatures of the horse and then the man with clay. They worked mostly in silence, packing the clay tight into the crevices, then building it up to a thickness of two inches or so throughout the entire surface area. Before he had begun to worry about his hands, it was the sort of brute work that Gil enjoyed, kneading the stiff clay in his powerful fingers and then jamming it in place without any particular creative demands plaguing his mind. For a good part of the three days this process took he stood on a stepladder fashioning the head and shoulders of the human figure as Maureen handed up buckets of moist clay.

Lately he had taken a dislike to being on the ladder, not as secure in his balance as he used to be. When he reached down to Maureen for another bucket he sometimes felt light-headed and unanchored. He knew that these intimations of vertigo, along with the more recent twinges of arthritis, had to be accepted as harbingers of other inevitable complaints. How long could he remain vital before something crucial began to fail? His eyes? His joints? His mind? His heart? He thought that with exceptional luck he might have as many as twenty more productive years, but he knew that it would become increasingly difficult to convince potential clients that he was the man for the job the more his age began to show and miscellaneous infirmities began to undermine his bearing.

But at the moment he felt inexhaustible. At noon one day, Mrs. Gossling brought a tray of sandwiches into the studio but both Gil and Maureen were so seduced by their work rhythm that it was midafternoon before they were hungry enough to pause for lunch. They finally ate their sandwiches sitting in the studio's rickety wooden chairs, the two of them staring without comment at the work they had done so far, the human figure almost sketched out, with a featureless globular head beneath a flattened mound of clay that Gil would later fashion into a hat.

As they ate, he shifted his attention from the crudely emerging sculpture to the face of his daughter, a face that nature had already defined and completed. He could see himself in the shape of her head, in the bold prominence of her features. He had sadly concluded long ago that there was no case to be made that she was pretty, but there was something about her, he believed, that an open-minded man might find attractive, even beautiful. Her brown eyes were large and warm and frank; people did not turn away when she looked at them. She was not fashionably slender, and never would be, but she was not overly stout either. Her body had density and strength, her forearms, exposed by the rolled-up sleeves of her blouse, were visibly muscular from the hard work of manipulating clay and carrying lumber and lengths of pipe. Character, resolve, physical power, and shining intelligence—how could she have all this and not have, on some level, to some discerning eye, beauty as well?

Indeed, something in Maureen had obviously attracted Vance Martindale, kept drawing him back down here from Austin, which was eighty miles distant. Intellectually and temperamentally, he was a fit for her. He had a solid sense of humor and a mind that bristled at academic caution. But it was the bristling itself that still gave Gil pause. An impatience with convention was a problematic thing when it came to the courting of his daughter—if indeed Martindale was courting her and not just amusing himself with a woman who was sufficiently strong-minded to tease him and spar with him.

And the man took up a lot of space, with his cowboy-professor costume and his rebellious opinions and verbosity. Gil could not escape the feeling that Martindale's winning manner carried within it hints of empty promises and dashed expectations. Or was this just the assessment of a guarded father whose daughter's heart had already been broken at least once?

"Were you there when either of my grandparents died?" Maureen abruptly asked him, after they had gone back to work.

"No," he said. "I was studying in Paris when your grandfather had his heart attack."

"And my grandmother? How old were you?"

"Let me think," he said. "I would have been in my late twenties."

"So back in the States?"

"Yes," he said, amid a hidden frenzy of calculation, "but in Washington."

"She just collapsed? Walking home from church after Mass?"

"Yes," he lied.

"So your father died of a heart attack, and your mother of a brain hemorrhage. Should that concern us, that these sorts of things run in the family?"

"Not necessarily," he said. "You and I are both hardier than they were. And my father, of course, never looked after himself. The drinking and so on."

"And your mother?"

"Well, I suppose it was just one of those things that happen."

"It must have been very hard on you, to be away when it happened. I'm grateful I was with Mother when she died."

"Yes," he said, "it was hard." He hoped that she would now move on to another subject, or, even better, turn her attention back to their work. His mother had lived on into her eighties. He had been there when she died, watching as Monsignor Berney prayed over her and anointed her. But the alternate story seemed oddly just as real, and Maureen kept boring ahead.

"What was she like when you were growing up? My grandmother?"

"Religious, if you want a single word for it. Great, unwavering, relentless faith. Holy water founts in the bedrooms, rosary every night, lectured us on not letting our teeth touch the host during communion. That sort of thing."

"You make her sound more superstitious than devout."

"You can be both. Or, in our case, maybe, you can be neither."

"Speak for yourself. I'm superstitious, a little. I think you are too. And devout in your own way."

"Maybe, but not in hers. An old woman, still believing in guardian angels."

"Old woman? If you were in your late twenties, she can't have been much more than fifty when she died."

"I meant she seemed old to me," Gil rushed to say and then, before she could ask another uncomfortable question, stood up from his chair, clapped his hands together, and decreed that it was past time to get back to work.

The work continued, and the working silence now made Gil wary, because Maureen must surely be turning over the conversation they had just had about her grandmother. From the concentrated look on her face, he worried that she was brooding about inconsistencies and uncertainties, checking them against comments on the same subject that he might have heedlessly offered in the past. He could not be sure after all these years of duplicity why he had gone to such lengths to protect his mother from an intolerable truth, when the cost of that protection amounted to the betrayal of his wife and daughter.

"I wrote to that boy," Maureen said, after half an hour of saying nothing as she packed clay onto the armature under the horse's head. The remark surprised him, but any reprieve from the interrogation about her grandmother was welcome.

"The boy? You mean Ben's friend in France?"

She nodded as she continued working. There was a drop of sweat running down her face in front of her ear. Even in December, in San Antonio you toiled in the heat.

"I didn't know how much I should say," she went on, "and I certainly didn't want to tell him about Mr. Clayton's breakdown or whatever it was. I just told him he had asked me to say how grateful he was to him for writing, that sort of thing. And I thought it would interest him to hear about the statue."

"That was kind of you," Gil said.

He stepped down from the ladder to judge his work for a moment.

"Tell me something," she said.

"What?"

She nodded toward her own nearly finished panels in the corner of the room.

"My work's not any good, is it?"

"What are you talking about? Of course it's good."

She walked over to one of the panels and stared at it, aggressively adjusting the moist clay with a finger as she spoke. "Look at it—it's lifeless. Look at the way the water moves across that cypress trunk. It looks like syrup or something. Why did I put a tree trunk in there in the first place?"

"This is nonsense," he said. "You're making this up out of nothing."

"Not exactly nothing," she said, as she walked back to the armature and began to pack clay onto it again. "I'm making it up out of the way you look at it, that smile of approval you work so hard at. And I hear it in your voice too. You know, it would really help me if you would say what you truly think. How else am I supposed to improve?"

"Maureen, I'm not going to allow you to maneuver me into saying that I don't think it's good enough. And why does my opinion have to be the only word on the subject anyway? You could ask—"

"Because yours is the opinion that counts!"

She said this with such ferocious finality that he thought for a moment she was going to storm out of the room, but instead she went placidly back to work. He watched her, her face set, her eyes red but no tears falling, her hands kneading the clay.

"I'll admit that it's not a work of genius, if that will restore your trust in my honesty. But I'm not going to say it's not worthy. It's ready to go to the foundry and it's ten times better than most of what passes for public art in this country."

"I'm sorry," she said. "That was an unfair outburst."

"It certainly was," he said, though with a needling fondness. He had been as honest with her as he could, but like so many truths he found himself proclaiming to his daughter, it was darkened by the shadow of a lie.

SEVENTEEN

Dear Miss Gilheaney," Maureen read aloud to Vance, who sat across the table from her in Schilo's, his spoon poised over his split-pea soup.

"Thank you for your letter, which took a while to catch up to me as we are on the move most of the time cleaning up the battlefields here and we don't know when we will get our mail or even if. I don't get a lot of mail anyway so I guess it's all right. I understand if Mr. Clayton doesn't want to hear more about Ben's death at this time. I guess I wouldn't want to either but I thought I better write to him about it so I did. It was strange to hear from you that there's going to be a statue of him. I would like to see it someday when it gets put up but I don't have any plans to come back to the States. I like it here in France and think I will stay, as I now understand the language and can speak with pretty much anybody, though some of the men's accents are harder to understand than others. I'll be through with my work with the Service des Travaux in a few weeks but they say I can have a job in the little town of Somme-Py helping to rebuild the city hall. I think I will take the job because I can do some good for the people of France and it reminds me some of home though the country is rolling not mostly flat like Eastland County where I'm from.

"You said in your letter that people would be happy to see me and I ought not to worry about coming home. But you would have to take a look at me to see what I mean. My face is mostly gone and would be a shock for most folks to look at and I don't care to spend the rest of my life having people run away at the sight of me, little children especially. You may think I'm exaggerating Miss Gilheaney but it really is pretty bad and it's easier to be in France because the people here are used to wounds such as I have and they don't think too much about it. I hope you do not think I am a complainer, that's just the way it is and I am getting used to looking like this and I want to live a quiet life where I can do some good and not think about myself all the time.

"I can tell from your letter you are a very kind person and if you want to write to me again I would be glad to hear from you. It feels good to me to read words written in english. That way I don't feel so far from home and even though I have friends here I still feel alone sometimes and the people don't understand me like people from my own country do. Please tell Mr. Clayton I'm sorry he feels so bad about his son but I guess saying sorry won't help him much. They say time heals all wounds but I don't know if that's true if you're old like he is and don't have much time for them to heal in the first place. I don't think time will heal my wound either but that's another story and I don't expect it to anyway.

"When you get that statue done or close to it maybe you could take a Kodak of it and send it to me. I would surely appreciate that and would like to see what Ben looks like after your father has done his work.

"I will close by saying thank you again for your kind words to me and by wishing you and your family much happiness in the years ahead. Sincerely, Arthur Fry."

She folded the letter back into the envelope and put it in her purse.

"Are you crying?" Vance asked.

"Shouldn't I?"

"I saw men like that over there," Vance said. "Those kind of wounds. Poor devil."

"It happened in the same battle where Ben was killed. Saint-Étienne. Do you know of it?"

"Of course. It wasn't the Marne, but the boys in the 36th say it was pretty bad."

"I think I'll write him again. He seems to want me to."

"It would help to keep his spirits up. He's bound to be pretty homesick."

She watched him eat his soup, his tie tucked between the buttons of his shirt. He had a lusty appetite and did not make a fuss about manners. She could imagine him eating alone in his boardinghouse or in the university cafeteria, reading Milton or Donne as he spooned up his food with one hand. Schilo's, where he had brought her for dinner, was a noisy saloon on the river that now, after prohibition, would have to survive solely on its hearty peasant food and its home-brewed root beer.

The conversation shifted to his frustrations with the university administration and the hidebound deans for whom real literature was still centered in the old dead world of Europe.

"Look at what's happening in America, not just in New England—and just how long, by the way, do we have to celebrate Hawthorne to the exclusion of every other American writer?—but in Harlem, in Chicago! Music, poetry, women standing up for themselves, Negroes deciding they've finally had enough, Reds poking the country in the eye, everything getting a second look. Well, see, I'm going on again."

"Yes, you are."

He grinned at her as he slurped up the last of his soup.

"Want some schnitzel?"

"No."

"Want to get out of here and go for a walk?"

She waited for him by the door as he paid the bill. She watched him exchanging small talk with the waiter and the men behind the bar, captivating everyone he met, guilelessly selling himself to them. He took her elbow as they walked out onto Commerce Street and down to the bridge crossing the river.

"We must pause and pay homage to the future site of your sculpture," he told her.

There was a bench on the bridge and they sat down and looked at the water below, flowing so modestly it was almost still, reflecting the stars from the clear winter night overhead. They sat casually close together, as if chance had deposited them there.

"Is there a date set for the unveiling?" he asked.

"Early September, depending on the foundry schedule, and on the granite company that will make the base."

"You'll be the toast of San Antonio, Maureen."

"Oh, I don't know. I suppose it will be just one event among many."

But she was excited. Even though her misgivings about her Spirit of the Waters were still vivid, her concerns had not been shared by Mrs. Toepperwein and the members of the Arts and Beautification Committee, who had visited the studio and enthusiastically approved the piece for casting. Just last week, her father had taken two days from his own work to help her cast the original clay tablets in plaster, so they could be shipped to the foundry to be cast again in bronze. She had been careful not to press him again for an opinion on their quality, and she had seen the relief in his face at not having to offer one.

"You haven't even let me see it yet, you know?" Vance said.

"When it comes back from the foundry."

"Don't you trust me? Are you afraid I'll crush you with my merciless opinions?"

"I don't know. Will you?"

"I could never crush you. You're too strong-willed. You'd brush my petty objections aside."

"I don't brush things aside, Vance. I take them to heart."

The comment caught him up for a moment, as she supposed she had meant it to. He smiled slightly, and looked off down the river in a reflective silence.

"Come up to Austin one of these days," he said.

"What for?"

"What for? To see me, I should think. After all, I've made plenty of visits to San Antonio to see you."

"I thought you'd been coming here on business."

"Well, sure. Research, interviews, that sort of thing. All of it legitimate. But you've been an added enticement, as I hope you might have noticed by now.

"We could have a picnic at Mount Bonnell," he went on, as she pondered this proposition. "Maybe go to a lecture or two, hear some fiery rhetoric about something or other. There's always something happening in Austin. How about giving it some thought?"

"All right, Vance, I'll give it some thought."

THE HOUSE WAS DARK and empty when she came home at eleven thirty, but the light was still on in her father's studio. Maureen walked into the yard and opened the studio door and found her father standing on a stepladder working on the upper body of the human figure. He wore his usual old ratty blue shirt with the sleeves rolled back, flecks of clay on his arms, doing fine work on the figure's collar with a wire-ended modeling tool. He had not heard her come in and she did not interrupt him right away, just watched the swift and practiced movements of his hands as he carved the clay and smoothed it with his thumb, movements that had bewitched her since her early childhood. The sight of her father creating something bigger than himself was bound up in her memory and in her present life as an emblem of her own well-being. The night after her mother's death, when Maureen was howling inside with shock and bewilderment, feeling the punishing weight of the empty universe, she had stood here in her father's studio and watched him as he went back to work on his latest commission. The stillness of her mother's body, the piercing finality of her absence, all the intolerable visions and sensations of that week had been smoothed down to a manageable degree by the sight of her father defiantly turning to his life's task.

Tonight her mood was vastly different. Tonight she tremblingly believed she might at last be on the path to love and happiness and independence. Vance had asked her to come to Austin, to visit his world. And why would he want her to visit his world if at least some part of him did not want her to share his life?

"I hope you weren't waiting up for me, Daddy," she said.

He turned in surprise at the sound of her voice, then went back to work. "No. Just wanted to get this part of the shirt right before I quit."

He made a few more careful swipes with the wire tool and then climbed down off the ladder, standing beside her to study his work.

"What do you think?"

"It's strong."

She meant it. Though it was still very rough, it registered in a striking way, with more force and momentum than had been possible to conjure in the scale model. Even if he were to leave off tonight and never finish the modeling, her father had still captured something essential about Ben Clayton: the ease and physicality of a boy who had grown up working with horses and for whom manual labor was not an imposed condition but a way of conforming to the world. The impression had something to do with a kind of looseness in the arms, an unconscious strength waiting to be called on as the boy stood next to his horse, one arm at his side, an open hand holding yet-invisible reins.

"I need to go back to the site," he said.

"You mean to the ranch? Before you've finished?"

"I'll get the lion's share done, but I think I need to stand on top of that hill one more time, just to make sure there's something I haven't missed. There's something about this one, Maureen. I must get it right."

He turned to her, wiping his tools with a rag.

"Write to Clayton, will you? Tell him we'd like to come up in a few weeks."

"He may not want us to, after what happened."

"I don't care. We're going."

He rolled down his shirtsleeves and turned off the lights as they walked out of the studio and into the house. As she was about to tell him good night and go to her bedroom he asked her how her evening with Vance had been.

"We had a good time. He took me to some place on the river. We had split-pea soup."

"Not too romantic."

"I had the impression he thought it was."

She kissed her father good night, but some hesitation she had caught in his bearing caused her to linger in the hallway for a moment, and then to come back to him in the kitchen, where he sat with his back against the sink, opening a box of Hydrox cookies.

"Do you like him any better by now?" she asked.

"Is it time for me to offer a final opinion?"

"Maybe."

He set the box of cookies aside. The weight of his reflections showed on his face.

"I think he's an interesting fellow. Intelligent, witty, hardworking as far as I can tell."

"But you still don't care for him."

"I didn't say that. I like him just fine. If I have any hesitation about him, it's that maybe he tries a little too hard to make an impression. To put himself across, I suppose you'd say."

"Since when is that a crime? Where would *you* be if you didn't have that sort of ambition? *I* don't, and look where I am!"

"What do you mean, 'where I am'?"

But all of a sudden she was too agitated to compose any sort of coherent answer. She could feel confused tears beginning to form in her eyes. Her father tried to maneuver his way out of the emotional trap he had caught himself in.

"Tell me what *you* think of him," he said. "Yours is the opinion that counts."

"Well, it should be obvious to you that I like him quite a lot."

"In love with him, you mean."

"Maybe. I don't know. And I don't know what he thinks about me. At first it seemed there was some sort of hesitation on his part, but that's—oh, this is ridiculous! I shouldn't be talking about this with you. It's my own affair."

She picked up the box of cookies and put it in the cupboard, struck by an angry impulse to tidy up as a rebuke to her father, who was generally too distracted to put things back where they belonged.

"He's invited me up to Austin."

"For what purpose?"

She laughed outright at his prosecutorial tone.

"Well, for a change of scenery, of course. To see him in his native environment. To get to know him a little better."

"Just by yourself? No—"

"Chaperone? Daddy, I'm thirty-two years old! It's nineteen twenty! Do you honestly think I have no judgment?"

He gave her a direct look, thought about what he was going to say, and then said it. "I'm not sure about your judgment when it comes to this man."

The words shocked her. When had he assumed the privilege to deliver such a decree, to degrade her considered affection for a man and turn it into a witless childish fancy? He was a tyrant in his own subtle way, throwing her happiness back in her face.

"I'm sorry," he hurried to say, because he could tell by a glance at her expression how wrong his words had been. "I only meant that when—"

"You only meant precisely what you said."

"I don't like the way he seems uncomfortable in my presence."

"What does that mean? And why wouldn't he be uncomfortable, the way you treat him, as if you think there must be something wrong with him for being interested in me at all!"

"Now just a minute, Maureen. That's unfair, and completely wrong."

"And this pretense of yours about how things would look if I went to visit him, as if you cared at all for conventional thought."

She was wrong on that point, and knew it. Her father was, as a man, almost stuffily conventional—moderate in his habits, punctual in his routines, faithful in his relationships with his clients, his friends, his wife. He walked a narrow line, somehow following the bold path of his artistic journey while never straying too far from society's course.

But he could be a hypocrite all the same. He had arranged his own life so that everyone in it—Maureen and her mother especially—almost unknowingly were put to the task of serving him and his noble work. She had given him enough already; she would not listen to him stand in haughty judgment of her conduct or of Vance's character.

Gil sat there bewildered by the turn the conversation had taken, by the hurt he saw in his daughter's eyes. But Maureen wasn't going to allow herself to remain in her father's presence and explode in angry tears. She turned without a word and walked down the hallway and quietly closed the door to her bedroom. She sat on the edge of her bed in defiant silence and would not speak to him when he knocked on the door. She had agitated him and confused him. Good. She listened to his footsteps as they wandered aimlessly back and forth in the house, then finally retreated toward the back door that led to the studio—though it was the middle of the night.

EIGHTEEN

Lamar Clayton studied the sky from the summit of the flat-topped hill where the statue was to be placed. It was cold already but it was going to get much colder, judging by the sealed-up sky to the north. His fingers were growing numb in his thick work gloves and he faced the wind for only a moment or two before turning his back to it. The thought of all the hard weather he had dealt with in his life used to be a minor source of pride to him, but now that he was old he did not care one bit for being miserable when he didn't have to be.

He stood there watching Gil Gilheaney, who was facing directly into the north wind with his fancy jacket buttoned to the throat and his gray hair blown back. The wind seemed to be carving the sculptor's face as Lamar watched, paring away any loose and inessential flesh until it was as sharp as a hawk's. His teeth were chattering and he seemed to be thinking hard. They had been up here for almost half an hour now and neither of them had said much, Gilheaney just pacing around like he had done before and sketching or writing something in a hard-backed notebook with a rippled surface.

"Your daughter might be getting pretty cold down there in the car," Lamar said at last.

He thought for a moment Gilheaney hadn't heard, but then the sculptor slowly nodded his head and turned to Lamar and smiled.

"Sorry," he said. "We'll go down. You must be cold too."

Lamar shrugged, pretending he didn't care whether he was freezing or not. He understood that Gilheaney and his daughter liked the idea of him as a tough old bird, and every now and then to his own annoyance he caught himself playing along.

They turned and started carefully making their way down. Lamar hoped Gilheaney had gotten what he needed today because by tonight these rocks would all be sleeted over and he reckoned there would be a hard freeze for the next day or so. The cattle would be drifting with the storm and Ernest and Nax would need to go out tomorrow to check their feed and look for any poor stock that might be in trouble. He debated whether he would need to go out himself. He didn't want to, but the thought of sitting around the house with company to have to talk to didn't please him much either.

At the base of the hill, Maureen Gilheaney was shivering in the open car with a blanket up to her chin. Lamar could see Peggy's head poking up out of the blanket. Since getting bitten by that snake, and surviving it, the dog seemed to be thinking ahead a little bit, and she had quickly realized that staying in the car tucked up against Miss Gilheaney's body would be more comfortable than climbing up to the top of the hill in a biting winter wind.

"I ought to have had George's Mary send some hot coffee out with us," Lamar said to Maureen as he turned the crank and got behind the wheel.

"We've been perfectly fine down here, Mr. Clayton. It's the two of you who are bound to be frozen."

"Well, I expect it won't do us no harm to get warmed up."

On the drive back it was too cold to talk. Lamar glanced at Gilheaney from time to time. He was chewing on his bottom lip, thinking about the statue. Miss Gilheaney had the same sort of look. There was some kind of trouble between the sculptor and his daughter, but Lamar didn't know what it was and anyway it was none of his business, no more than it was Gilheaney's business about what had gone wrong between him and Ben. They had looked to be a team when they had first come out to the ranch and you could tell she admired her father, but Lamar figured you couldn't admire someone all your life without getting annoyed by him too, especially if you were unmarried and not all that young and starting to feel this was the way your life was going to be from here on out. Annoyed or not, she still seemed to believe in him. She had told Lamar as soon as they arrived that the statue was going to be a work of genius.

Lamar didn't think the statue had to be a work of genius, it just had to look like Ben and give value for the money he was paying. And he didn't even know anymore why he had wanted the damn thing in the first place. The night he'd gotten the telegram about Ben's death he'd thought George's Mary's silent grieving was going to drive him crazy, so past midnight he had gone out and saddled the night horse and ridden out in the moonlight with the bewildered little dachshund running behind frantically trying to catch up. He'd hobbled the horse at the foot of the hill and walked up to the top with the dog and sat there for the rest of the night saying he was sorry out loud over and over again, his voice so monotonous and rhythmic that after a while he reminded himself of the Comanches singing their songs after a hunt or sometimes their dirges after a raid that had gone bad. It had been more like muttering than singing to him; he never did get used to it. But at times in his life he had taken a nostalgic comfort in those strange cadences, and maybe that's what he was trying to work up on the hill that night, calling out his dead boy's name and saying he was sorry as if the words were part of a chant that might have the power to undo what had been done.

He never told anybody about how when the sun was rising that morning and his throat was raspy and he was trying hard to stay awake; he had had a shivery feeling and the sense he ought to turn his head. And there were Ben and Poco right beside him, looking east across the pastures where hawks were hunting above the dewy grass and the streaks of sunlight on the horizon were as bright as if they were flashing off a mirror. Ben took no notice of his father. He sat there on Poco without moving and his stillness and the horse's stillness were indistinguishable from peace. Lamar realized he was seeing things and as soon as his mind registered that fact the image of his son and his horse was gone. They hadn't really been there—he knew that with cold reason; and that momentary note of peacefulness did not mean that Ben was content in his death, or that his father had any more account to live. But he kept turning to it nevertheless, turning to it and turning to it until he was afraid he would use it up, that if he didn't make it real somehow it would disappear forever.

He didn't know what had happened to him in San Antonio. There was still nothing in his memory between the time he had walked into Gilheaney's studio to look at the model of the statue and when he was eating barbecue with those two mechanics at the filling station. There were plenty of blank spots in his life, times when he had passed out drunk in a bar and woken up a day later on a street bench in Fort Worth or in a livery yard in San Angelo with no idea how he'd gotten there. But that had been a different kind of absence, a different kind of shame. It was one thing to drink away your awareness; it was another just to lose it.

The small sculpture that Gilheaney showed him in his studio had been adequate. It was a close enough rendering of what Lamar thought he had seen on the mesa that morning after the telegram came, though Ben was not mounted but standing beside his horse as Gilheaney had decreed. But at the same time he knew it was more than a rendering. It wasn't Ben, but he was unprepared for the force of the artist's idea of Ben. What had stunned Lamar like an electric shock was the thought that Gil Gilheaney had somehow understood his son better than he had. The statue that Lamar had commissioned to remind him of Ben had so much power and presence on its own that he worried that it would end up stealing the memory of Ben away.

"MAUREEN TOOK PICTURES," Gil said as they sat in the parlor after dinner, their chairs pulled in close to the fireplace as the wind rattled the windows and freezing rain clattered against the roof and the north side of the house. "If you like, we'll show them to you, though it isn't finished quite yet."

"All right," Lamar said.

Maureen went into her room to get the Kodaks, then came back and handed them to him. In one of them Gil was standing next to the full-scale figure of Ben, and Lamar could see how big it was, towering over the sculptor by a head or more. The two figures, the boy and the horse, were not yet arranged in the right way, but he could see pretty well how it would look. This time he was not stunned, as he had been in San Antonio. He knew what to expect. In an odd way the full-scale statue looked softer and more intimate than the model had, but maybe that was just because he was familiar with it by now.

"It would be ideal if you could come to San Antonio in the next few weeks after I've put on the final touches to take a careful look at it. If it meets with your approval, I'll call the plasterers to make a mold that we can then ship to the foundry for final casting."

"I approve of it now," Lamar said.

"Now? Without seeing it?"

"I'm seeing it in these pictures. I approve of it. You can call the plasterers and I'll write you the next check."

He thought this would please Gilheaney, but he could see it didn't. A log in the fireplace popped and the sculptor stood up and walked over and scooted the embers back into the coals with the toe of his shoe.

"I'm having a hard time understanding your reaction to this piece," he said to Lamar.

"That's fair enough. It ain't been that easy for me to figure out neither."

"You're spending a lot of money, Mr. Clayton. It's important for me to know that you're getting what you wanted."

"It ought to be plain enough. I said I'd write you the goddam check."

Maureen started at Lamar's belligerent tone and Gilheaney turned his head from the fire to look at him. The look had a challenge in it, and a condescending scrutiny that Lamar had seen too many times in his life already: from the Indian agent at Fort Chadbourne after the Comanches turned him in for the ransom; from various policemen and deputies into whose custody he had drunkenly been taken; from a few of the guests at his wedding who clearly thought him too old and damaged to be a husband to Sarey; from his own son, the last time he'd seen him.

"Did I offend you?" Gilheaney asked, in a surprised and reasonable tone that infuriated Lamar more. The sculptor was a big man with long arms and powerful hands, but Lamar wondered if he'd ever been in a real fight and whether he would know what to do if he suddenly found himself in one right here and now. It was a crazy thought, but

Lamar found himself thinking it. It came out of nowhere, erupting from the anger of a past he thought he had left behind.

"I ain't offended," he answered. "But around here people just do their work and collect their pay without expecting to be congratulated for it all the time."

When he heard that, Gilheaney stood up straight at the fireplace. Lamar didn't care to get in a staring contest with him, so he just looked into the fire and concentrated on the sounds of the norther that was screeching past the house. He didn't look up till after Gilheaney had turned and walked into his room. Ben's room.

Maureen Gilheaney was still sitting there on the other side of the hooked rug, holding a book in her lap, looking at Lamar like he'd just slapped her in the face. Whatever anger she'd been nursing at her father had just been transferred to her host.

"Do you really think he could possibly depend on your good opinion of him for his self-respect?"

"I didn't mean to upset either of you. That's just what came out."

She stood up and grabbed the Kodaks out of his hands and waved them in his face.

"Look at these. Really look at them. Then tell me if you think he's doing this commission just for your money. But I can emphatically tell you one thing right now: he's certainly not doing it because he needs your praise."

"I said I didn't mean to upset either of you."

"If that's supposed to be an apology, you should offer it to him, not me."

"I never said it was an apology."

She was halfway to the door leading out of the parlor when she remembered the photos in her hand and turned and walked back to him and set them down on the arm of his chair.

"Look at them," she repeated.

She went to her room and he put the pictures on the coffee table in front of him. He was damned if he was going to study them just because he'd been ordered to. Peggy jumped down out of the chair where she'd been curled up with Maureen and walked over to him and reared up on her hind legs in that prairie dog pose of hers till he relented and picked her up and settled her next to him.

•

HE WAS HARDHEADED and he knew it. There had been no reason to get into a pointless argument with Gilheaney and no excuse for being cross with Maureen, who had been kind to him and was right to stand up for her father. He ought to call them both out here and apologize, but he wasn't going to do it.

It had been a burden to Sarey, how inflexible he was. At Christmas parties with her family, he would not allow himself to sing at the piano with the rest of them. She said it didn't matter if he had a terrible voice or not, but he wouldn't let her talk him into it, even after her affectionate coaxing turned to confused pleas. He remembered the tears in her eyes when she finally learned she couldn't talk him into it and gave up. To this day he didn't know if he could sing or not. He had just gotten it into his head that it wasn't something he was going to do, and he never did it.

When Ben was born, Lamar had had that same instinct to hold himself apart, to leave unrevealed to his son the satisfaction he took in being his father. He didn't know why he had been that way. Maybe that had been his nature from the beginning or maybe it was some caution that had come into his life during his time with the Comanches or in the hard period afterwards. Maybe it was because of his own father, who as much as Lamar could recall had been so preoccupied with work and worry he never had time for a spare word.

Nevertheless, he remembered moments of ease with Ben. The boy was always desperate to be outside with Lamar and the hands when they were at work. Even when he was only six months old, before he could walk or speak, he tracked every move Lamar made and seemed to be studying how he did things. Lamar had to get himself used to the idea that the boy just wanted to be around him, that he regarded his father as a figure of fascination. On the back of an old bankbook in his desk drawer, Lamar had written down Ben's first words and noted the day he first walked and when he first sat a horse, or made note of odd things he had said when he was learning how to speak. Lamar had felt a need to keep this accounting of his son's life secret. He never mentioned it to Sarey and he doubted she had ever come across it, since she wasn't the type to go rooting around his desk without asking. He wondered now why he had ever thought those little penciled scraps of dates and phrases needed to be hidden from anyone. The bankbook was still there in the desk drawer. He had not looked at it in years, and would never have the heart to now. After he died George's Mary might find it and toss it away without looking at it when she cleaned out his desk, assuming it just belonged with the piles of bills and give-away datebooks from feed stores that it was buried under.

All his life he had treated the things that brought him pride and comfort as if they were shameful secrets—even his love for his own son. There were times when Ben was older, when they were riding fence together or camped out during the roundup, that he had felt such contentment in being with him that he thought he ought to say something out loud about it. But he never had, not that he could recall. He had expected Ben to know his own value to his father just as he had expected Gilheaney tonight to know the quality of his own work. You shouldn't have to tell people what ought to be plain to them already.

He remembered sharply and with regret how Ben had looked toward him after Sarey had died. He had wanted something from his father that Lamar didn't have the will or the imagination to give him. That night after they'd buried her he couldn't think of anything to say to the boy, or at least anything that sounded right. And after that, the subject of Sarey hardly ever came up between them. They just kept on living their lives without her there.

Lamar supposed he would have been a different sort of man if the Comanches hadn't taken him, but it was a hard thing to factor because now he could barely remember the boy he had been beforehand. In an instant, that part of his life had just been sheared away.

They just walked through the door like they had lived there all their lives and were coming home from a day's work. Lamar's father and his older brother, Emory, were already lying dead and scalped along with their big Newfoundland dog two miles out on the Decatur road where they had been looking for a stray calf. That was the reason there was no warning.

Jewell was setting the table and his mother was cutting dough into strips for a cobbler crust. He remembered the fine hairs on her forearms dusted with flour and the concentration on her face as she cut the dough with a paring knife. The knife's handle was worn and water-streaked and was as familiar to him as the smells of his mother's cooking or the sound of her voice. There was a glass pickle tray on the table that she was proud of because it had come from New Orleans with her own mother and survived the Runaway Scrape after the Alamo fell and Sam Houston was on the run.

That afternoon the half-wild horse that his father had bought from a Tonkawa Indian had bolted with Lamar on it and jammed Lamar's foot against the trunk of a bois d'arc tree. That was why he was in the house and not out looking for the calf with his father and brother. The little toe on his left foot had split off from the other four like a bent twig on a sapling. It was swollen tight and his mother had heated some water on the stove and poured it in a pan for him to soak his foot in. The pain was still strong and it felt personal, as if the pain itself had done this to him and not the horse or his own neglect.

When the Indians walked in, the water in the pan had started to cool and he was looking down at the almost-detached toenail floating out from his blackening toe.

His mother said, "Well!" when she saw them. Jewell screamed and his mother set down the knife and hurried in front of her daughter, nudging her back toward Lamar. Lamar grabbed Jewell's arm and drew her to him. His foot was still in the pan of water. He thought about striding across the room to grab his father's Hawken above the door but before he could make himself move one of the Indians had already beaten him to it.

His mother did something strange. She held out her hand to the one who had come in first. Maybe she thought a handshake would help calm them down and be the start of a civil discussion. For just a moment, there was a confused expression on the Indian's face. He was painted for war and it made the momentary puzzlement in his eyes more vivid. But instead of shaking hands he stabbed her under the ribs with a butcher knife and she collapsed onto the floor so promptly and compliantly it was like something the two of them had rehearsed.

Jewell screamed and seemed to run in place as she sobbed. Lamar didn't know what to do except to go to his mother, but before he could reach her they grabbed him and threw him against the stove. Three or four more Comanches streamed into the house and started stripping the linens off the beds and drinking the milk that had been set out on the table for supper. His mother was still alive and screaming his name, but the Indians beat him down with their quirts when he tried to reach her again and another one shot an arrow into her and he could hear it passing through her body and burying itself with a thunk into the plank floor.

Three of the Indians grabbed him and pulled him to his feet. He fought and bit at them but they had him tight in their arms and he couldn't get loose. He could smell his mother's blood and could feel its slick warmth on his bare feet as they dragged him across the floor. He called out to her as they were wrestling him out the door and they hit him with their quirts again and his mother raised her head and looked at him and told him not to fight anymore or they would kill him.

"Be a good boy and go with these Indians," she said.

He was bleeding from his head and he couldn't wipe away the blood because his hands were bound behind him, but he blinked enough of it away when they pulled him outside to see that his sister was already tied down on a horse, still yelling out for him and his mother. They hit him again and threw him up onto one of the other horses and started tying him down to an old Mexican packsaddle. He held on as best he could as they rode away. He could hear his mother screaming back in the cabin as they scalped her, and when they had gone a few miles he saw the bodies of his father and brother with their arms cut off and hanging from a tree.

THE MAN who captured him was named Kanaumahka, which Lamar learned later meant "Almost Dead" in Comanche. Looking back, he guessed Kanaumahka had been in his early forties then. He had a wide, muscular frame and a dish face whose bottom half that day was painted in black. There were two fingers missing on his left hand and on the side of his face his teeth didn't meet up right because he had been kicked in the jaw by a horse when he was a boy, an accident that had also taken off the tip of his tongue. It took a few days for Lamar to understand that he and Jewell were in Kanaumahka's keeping. They were so disoriented at first that Lamar did not even think to try to tell one Indian from another.

They rode almost without stopping for three days. At first they tied Lamar's and Jewell's hands to the packsaddles and ran a rope between their feet beneath the horses as well. But after Jewell kept slipping down sideways and they had to stop and re-rig the ropes, they finally untied their captives' hands and let them hold on to the saddle so that they could stay upright. It was clear enough to Lamar that if he tried to get away or fell off his horse they would just shoot him or put an arrow through him and move on.

His mother's hair was reddish with gray streaks and he recognized her scalp tied to one of the Indian's lances, but he looked away and pretended to himself he didn't see it, pretended so hard that to this day he wasn't sure he actually had. The packsaddle wasn't a proper saddle for riding and it was hard work to keep his seat as they rode all that day and through the night. When they finally untied him and Jewell and let them off their horses it was because one of the Indians rode up trailing a bellowing cow. They shot the cow and cut open its udder and shoved his head into it and made him drink the milk. He didn't want to, and Jewell didn't either. The milk was full of blood. He didn't think either of them could keep it down, but they both managed. Afterward Kanaumahka noticed Lamar's little toe pulled off to the side where he had jammed it and he went over and consulted with a few of the other Indians about how to doctor it. They finally decided to pull it up and back into place and tie it to the rest of his toes with a splint. They didn't mind how much it hurt him and he tried not to cry out when they did it. It was the first time he had any hope that they hadn't captured him just to kill him but that they had some reason for keeping him alive.

There must have been people in pursuit from the beginning because the Comanches were nervous and from time to time Lamar could hear dogs baying in the distance. Once they set fire to the prairie to throw the dogs off the scent and rode even harder, stopping from time to time to look behind them through field glasses. Lamar could tell that the Indians were worried because the grass was dry and when they rode across it the trail was easy to read.

The insides of his legs were rubbed raw by the packsaddle. When Kanaumahka saw the blood he ripped off Lamar's trousers and put some sort of salve on his legs that helped the sores scab over. They passed within sight of farms and settlements but the Indians didn't stop to raid anymore, and after a week or so Lamar got worried that they would end up so deep in wild country that he could never find his way home.

Lamar was twelve and Jewell was fourteen. For the first few days the Indians kept them apart at night, but once they were beyond the Brazos they relaxed the rules. As his older sister, Jewell did her best to comfort him but she was so scared she could barely speak, and he did not know what he could say to her to ease her fears. Sometimes the Comanches would pitch them strips of raw horse meat or a piece of the liver of a dead steer they had come across. They were hungry enough to eat anything, but Jewell gagged and choked on her tears as she tried to force the meat down and wailed for their mother.

Lamar figured they were headed up toward the Canadian River. They no longer heard dogs howling in pursuit, and the Indians were growing more relaxed and joking with each other. Lamar knew that their chances of being rescued were almost gone, and that the farther they advanced into the treeless prairies the harder it would be to escape and find their way back. The expanding openness all around them, the billowing grasslands crowding the horizon, unsettled him deeply. He did not know this country; he did not belong in it. Every day that they traveled made the possibility of reaching home less real as they traveled into country more and more foreign and unwelcoming.

Sometimes they came for Jewell at night and dragged her over to the edge of the camp. The first time they did this he fought them but it did no good, because they wrestled him to the ground and made him watch what they did to her. After that, she told him it would go easier for her if he didn't try to stop them. But he tried anyway, and she had to plead with him not to interfere. When one of the warriors came the next night and ordered her to stand and follow him, Lamar did as she had asked and did not try to stop it, just as his sister got to her feet and walked away with the Indian whimpering quietly, her hands trembling..

He resolved that they should escape while there was still some possibility of finding their way back. Their hands and feet were no longer bound, either on the horses or in camp, and the Indians had taken a less guarded attitude toward their presence, treating them more like dogs that were just part of the caravan than like prisoners that might turn on them or disappear into the wilderness. The horses were always picketed not far from camp and the bridles and saddles were nearby in open sight. All of the Comanches slept soundly and Lamar did not think it would be very hard to grab a bridle and a skin of water and maybe some food and slip away to the horse herd. He was only a boy and his plans were not sophisticated, but he had a desperate confidence that if they got away in the middle of the night and rode hard enough, heading east, that they could find their way back to the Brazos and the settlements downriver. Just the thought of slipping away and being on the run was bewitching to him. He daydreamed about it all day long in the saddle and at night in his great terror and loneliness it was his only consoling thought.

But when he whispered his plan to Jewell she sobbed and shivered with fright and said she would not go. She said they would be rescued soon and the Indians would kill them if they tried to get away. Night after night he tried to convince her, but she only grew increasingly upset and begged him not to try. He saw that she had let herself slide into a state of terrorized passivity and he knew that with every passing mile the chances of a successful escape were growing more distant.

One night as the Indians were lying down to sleep he told her he could not wait anymore. He was going that very night. She grew hysterical and said she wouldn't come. He said he was going anyway and would come back with soldiers or rangers to rescue her too. He was seventy years of age now and the memory of her face as he told her this still haunted him with dreamlike force and clarity. She had the dark hair and olive skin that came from their father's side of the family. Her chin quivered uncontrollably as the tears flew out of her eyes and glistened in the light of the fires. She pleaded with him to stay with her. She said that the Indians would kill her when they discovered he was gone.

He did not think they would kill her. He thought that if they were going to kill either of them they would have done so already. In the end, he lied to her just so she would go to sleep and not give his plan away with her crying. He told her he would not leave her after all. Then, when she was finally settled down in sleep he broke his promise and crept away, stealing a length of rope to make a hackamore because he worried that the clink of a bridle would wake the Indians. Most of the time since his capture he had been riding the same mare and she let him come up to her and slip the hackamore over her nose and ride her away.

He followed a draw that he thought might lead him eventually to one of the forks of the Brazos. In that country at night the bands of the Milky Way were almost solid in their brilliance, bright enough to silhouette the shapes of the owls and nighthawks hunting in the high prairie grass. He was sorry to leave his sister and he tried not to think about how he had lied to her, but he was confident now that he would escape and he tried to think instead of the moment when she would see him riding into the camp along with the rescuers he was guiding. She would forgive him once she understood that he had done this so he could take her home.

The Indians tracked him easily and overtook him several hours after daylight. Kanaumahka pulled him from his horse and beat him and kicked him and when they got back to the camp the other Comanches felt free to do the same. Then Kanaumahka put his Colt's pistol to Jewell's head and cocked it and looked sternly at Lamar to make sure he got the idea that if he tried to escape again his sister would pay for it. Jewell was a quaking heap afterwards and when he tried to comfort her and explain himself she screamed at him to get away and leave her alone and never talk to her again. This drama between the two captives seemed to suit the Indians. They laughed and talked to themselves, as if it were a play they were watching.

Later the raiding party met up with another group of Indians. They looked similar to the Comanches but there was something different about their dress and attitude that he could not quite pin down. They also seemed to speak a different language, judging by the way the two groups talked to each other in signs. It was not until he could speak Comanche himself that he found out from Kanaumahka that they were Kiowas.

For most of an afternoon they argued about something, though it was good-natured arguing as far as Lamar could tell. Kanaumahka checked the mouths of half a dozen different Kiowa horses and rode several of them off onto the prairie for an hour at a time, then finally went off by himself to think about something. When he was through thinking he stood up and walked over to Jewell and grabbed her by the arm and handed her to the Kiowa warrior he had been negotiating with.

It was over almost before either Lamar or Jewell could understand what was happening. The Kiowas threw her on a horse and tied her down again and rode off at a gallop below a grassy swell. Although he heard her screaming his name for quite a while, that was the last he saw of her. The Indians beat him again when he tried to run to the horse herd to ride after her, and when they saw him scanning the landscape hoping she would reappear they poured sand in his eyes to get him to stop. After a few days they managed to convince him that it was hopeless to get her back and pointless to try to live his life like it could be any different than it was.

Jewell getting sold was the turning point for him, when he was forced to begin looking ahead and not back. By the time the raiding party joined up with the rest of the band, somewhere in the Palo Duro country, he had picked up a few words and phrases of Comanche, and Kanaumahka began to treat him less like someone to be abused and more like someone who required instruction. In the camp, the women jeered at him at first and the other boys wanted to fight him, but he soon learned he had nothing to lose by ignoring the women and using every grain of his rage and indignation in defending himself against the boys. When he broke a boy's wrist there were no consequences, not even from the father, who had a calm talk with Kanaumahka afterwards. From the tone of their conversation Lamar guessed that they had bet on the fight and that the man had lost and was good-natured about it.

He learned that the Comanche band that had taken him was called the Quahadas and that they had contempt for any other band or tribe who signed treaties with the whites or depended for their sustenance on the Indian agency at Fort Cobb. It didn't matter to them if it was Union or Confederate soldiers who were in control of the fort, they were convinced that all white men were the same and wanted to push them off the buffalo grounds. They were friendly with the Mexican traders who sometimes came into the camps leading caravans of mules burdened down with implements and firearms and other trading goods, but they were independent-minded and aloof and thought their way of life was superior to anyone else's.

For five or six weeks they made him haul wood and water for the women, but then Kanaumahka decided to put him to work herding his horses at night and guarding them against Tonkawa horse thieves. Kanaumahka had over a hundred and fifty horses and the nights were long and worrisome to Lamar because he didn't know how far the horses were allowed to stray or what the punishment would be if any were lost or stolen. But Kanaumahka had no words of rebuke or praise, so Lamar took that to mean that he was satisfied with his work and he began to relax. He herded the horses most of the night and during the long, inconsequential days, when the Indians went out hunting, or gambled, or just gossiped outside their lodges, he slept and no one bothered him.

It was during those solitary nights, though, that he felt himself becoming a Comanche. He calmed himself by singing in a low voice the songs his mother had sung in the house, "Believe Me If All Those Endearing Young Charms" and "The Rose and the Briar." But the songs began to seem strange to him, the words—"And around the dear ruin each wish of my heart"—making fainter and fainter sense as the direct Comanche words he was learning supplanted them in relevance and urgency. As the nights passed, some sort of contentment began to steal up on him. The fear of losing the horses had subsided, and the constant overpowering confusion drained away.

The life he had known had disappeared in one bewildering instant, but the life before him gradually began to seem beckoning and limitless—a life without any of the rules he was used to, and none of the angry strictures of work and propriety that had defined the limits of his father's existence, that had kept him rooted to a farm in Wise County like a snake in its hole when the whole world stretched out before him. Lamar's new life was at first life without human warmth and kindness, but that changed in imperceptible degrees, with an approving glance from Kanaumahka or an unexpected cordial greeting from one of the warriors or an invitation from some of the boys to range with them on long horseback adventures across the grasslands.

Kanaumahka was a patient teacher and in his way a kindly man. He told Lamar that years earlier, at the invitation of the U.S. government, he had traveled to Washington and met President Polk, and he still wore a medal around his neck with the president's profile. He had eaten crab cakes in a restaurant and played whist. Lamar could not keep a firm grip on the idea that this man had killed his mother with a butcher knife, and eventually he had to let it go. His confusion extended to his sense of himself, and as he let that go too another self rose up to take its place. No one had to beat him anymore to make him comply or yell at him to make him understand. He complied. He understood. He belonged and could be trusted.

He was with them for almost two years, but it might have been twenty, so profound was his absorption into the Quahadas. He was with them on buffalo hunts and trading expeditions and on their nomadic excursions deep into the far mountains and beyond the Rio Grande into Mexico. He was with them on many horse-stealing raids and on many bitter reprisals against the Mexicans and the Texans.

He did not like to think about what he had done on those raids.

He encountered other captives occasionally, as the bands and tribes came together in their wanderings. They were white boys like him or more often Mexicans. Sometimes they had just been recently taken and were pale with fear and he would turn his eyes from them. But if they had been with the Indians for a period of months they were as proudly wild as he was, some of them so savage and heedless they had to be spoken to quietly by older warriors before a raid to cool their raging tempers. There were girl captives too, usually more frightened and miserable than the boys, but he trained himself not to think of Jewell when he saw them.

In the second spring of his captivity, Lamar joined a raid on a Mexican sheepherders' camp near the Devils River. The herders turned out to be cool and experienced fighters and the raid went bad. Two Comanches were killed outright and six were wounded, including Kanaumahka, who was shot through the belly and lived in hellish pain for two days. They buried him on a scaffold looking down on the Pecos and Lamar rode away from the site feeling empty and orphaned once again. He had friends among the Quahadas who spoke to him in consolation but there were others who saw him now only as unclaimed property. Had he been a few years older and more acquainted with human treachery he might have suspected something when five or six men he did not know well asked him along on a hunting trip up on the llano.

He suspected that it wasn't just a hunting trip, that he would be subjected to some sort of initiation trial along the way, and that he would emerge from this ordeal with the full confidence of the tribe and new standing as an adult warrior. So he was not greatly surprised when they set upon him while he was sleeping one night and tied him up with ropes. But then they rode into Fort Chadbourne with him and handed him over without ceremony to the Indian agent. He never did know what they got for his ransom, because he was taken at once to the guardhouse, where a soldier with the Texas State Troops took a pair of sheep shears and cut off the hair that had grown down past his shoulders and that he had wrapped in otter fur. They tried to get him to talk in English but he couldn't. It took a week or more for the words to start to come back.

The sound of his own name when he finally spoke it in answer to their questions was unsettling to him. He knew it was his name but the syllables attached themselves to nothing he could truly remember or understand. They kept him in the guardhouse and then in one of the officers' homes. He was compliant. He sat at their table at dinner and bowed his head in prayer and answered their questions about who his people were and what had happened to them, but it was as if he were performing in a play.

"Well, Lamar, you are going home," the officer said to him one day. They put him in a wagon and sent him in a supply train with an escort of troopers. It humiliated him to ride closed up in the coach with a woman who lectured him on the importance of his education while the soldiers rode outside on horseback. He thought it might be easy to steal one of the horses and ride off, but he didn't know where to go. The Comanches had stolen him away and then cast him out. There were other bands who might take him in, but as the shock of his recapture began to wear off he understood that his future with the Indians would never be as secure as he longed for it to be. And he was willing to believe that at the end of this long journey back to Texas there might be some form of happiness waiting for him in spite of the fact that his family was gone.

But they didn't take him back to his home in Wise County. They took him to San Antonio, where he had never been in his life. There was a band playing when they brought him into the town, and somebody made a speech and later he was taken after closing hours to a candy store and the owner told him he could have as much candy as he could carry out.

His father had a cousin who claimed him and took him in. She was a weepy sort of woman who was married to a German doctor twenty years older than she was who practiced the French horn at night and collected beetles in a little study that no one but him was allowed to enter. They had no children and the woman had no notion of how to talk to a boy of his age, especially one who was still wild and confused with yearning. The doctor confined his interest in Lamar to interviewing him at great length about his life with the Indians. He nodded with excitement as he took down with his pen the things that Lamar told him, about how in the desert country the Comanches would find tortoises and cook them alive over the fire and eat from their shells as if they were eating from a bowl; or about how trailing a rope on the ground was bad luck; or how Kanaumahka was always careful to pluck out the stray hairs around a wild horse's eyes before he tried to ride it. The doctor wrote up these notes and sent them off to be published in Europe, but he showed no appreciation for the information and treated Lamar with the same cold scrutiny he gave to his beetles.

He was sent to school and found somebody to fight there almost every day. When it was explained to him that he had been expelled, he felt satisfaction, as if being thrown out of school had been a conscious aspiration. When the doctor found out, he yelled at him and raised a threatening hand, and Lamar made sure that he ended up on the floor with a broken jaw.

Before the police could come for him he had stolen a horse and ridden south out of San Antonio. He wandered without purpose for years. He trailed cattle to New Orleans and worked on the docks in Galveston and as a hand patrolling for Mexican rustlers on various ranches in the Nueces Strip. He was in his early twenties when the big trail drives started going up to Kansas and he made the trip three times. He liked being on the move again in open country, on horseback, working himself into exhaustion every night and every day, thinking of nothing but the cattle and the next river crossing and the earth spread out endlessly in front of him. The Indians had all pretty much been hunted down and starved out by then. Even the Quahadas had come onto the reservation. Sometimes, driving the cattle beyond the Red, they could see the Comanche and Kiowa camps in the distance, and once when he rode into Fort Sill he saw people he thought he knew lined up for rations. They were dressed in cheap sack suits and wide-brimmed hats like farmers and the women sat in the backs of the wagons holding parasols and waiting to butcher the cattle that the men would be given to shoot. None of them looked in his direction. They looked down at their feet as they shuffled obediently forward in line.

He saw a group of young Kiowa women walking out of the Red Store. Their backs were to him and he could not see their faces, but there was something familiar in the posture and stride of one of the women that made him go slack. He kept watching them as they walked toward their wagons, wishing they would turn around so he could be sure the woman was not Jewell. But they didn't turn around, and after they had gone a few more paces they disappeared into the crowds waiting for rations.

It had been eleven years. He had never looked for her or asked about her and he had pushed the painful thought of her as far from his haunted mind as he could. He had made it his purpose to get on with his life without letting the past come back to grab him. And he tried to continue to do so, but all the way to the Kansas railheads he was tortured by the thought that he had seen her after all and done nothing.

A year later he came back. The name Jewell Clayton was not on the Kiowa rolls, but he had not expected it to be. The agent at Fort Sill told him that there were many Indians on the agency lands that he had not personally seen or met, and that if she had had dark hair to begin with and had been with the Kiowas for as long as Lamar said she would probably not now seem out of place. He kept asking after her, and after a few days in Fort Sill he met a man in his fifties who had been Kanaumahka's friend and had been one of the Indians who had captured Lamar and Jewell. He was now gaunt and solemn with anger. When he saw Lamar again after so many years he began to weep. He did not know that the men who had invited him to go hunting had sold him back to the whites. They had come back to the camp saying that Lamar had just forsaken the tribe on his own and had left them during the night to go back to live with his own people.

This man remembered the day that Kanaumahka had sold Jewell to the Kiowas. He remembered the name of the Kiowa man who had bought her, and what band he belonged to. When Lamar checked the rolls again he found the man's name and learned that he was probably camped with his family along Medicine Bluff Creek.

It was a small camp, with two or three traditional lodges and a half-dozen agency tents and brush arbors strung out along the banks of the creek. The Kiowas shuffled together suspiciously when he rode in on horseback, but before he could even state his business Jewell walked out of one of the tents and began to wail at the sight of him. He got off his horse and walked over to her and said what she already knew, that he was her brother. She didn't look nearly the same. Her skin was tight and coarse from years out in the sun, her hair was drab, and she was missing a couple of teeth in her upper mouth. There was a blue tattoo of a half-moon on her forehead. They did not embrace but just stood there talking. Jewell was weeping and all the Kiowas around them were teary as well. Lamar wished he could feel something else, but all he felt was anger and waste and shame at what had happened to them, and he couldn't help blaming her in his mind for refusing to make an escape with him when they had the chance. In fact, he found himself starting to wonder if she had woken the Comanches up that morning and told them that he had gone just so they wouldn't take their wrath out on her.

He did not say this to her, but he could not help thinking it when he saw what a complete Indian she had become, not just in dress or in language but—he knew almost at once—in thought. She could still speak English, but not without thinking about what she wanted to say beforehand, and the words when she said them were slow and ponderous.

She served him a meal of gristly agency beef and fried bread. She had a husband who went by the name of Eli Poahway. He was stringy and quiet and she said he was good to her. He was a medicine man and he wanted to set up a sweat for Lamar but Lamar said he would rather not. He didn't know Kiowas, and their manner and rituals were strange to him and he didn't want to linger among them.

Jewell told him that the Kiowas had treated her with great kindness, particularly a woman, now dead, who had adopted her as her own child. Several years after she was sold, a group of Texas Rangers rode into the camp and saw that she was white and tried to make a deal to ransom her. Jewell had become such a Kiowa by then that the thought of riding off with these strange men filled her with panic. She and her Indian mother crept out of camp that night and hid in the high grass across the river until the Rangers had given up and left. When Jewell and her mother came back they expected the chief who had made the deal with the Rangers to be angry, but he was so touched by their attachment to each other that he just chuckled softly and let the matter go.

Her Kiowa mother died before they came onto the reservation, but Jewell married Eli soon thereafter and had lived with him and his two sisters and their husbands ever since, moving camp frequently and mixing with the soldiers and Indian police at Fort Sill only when she had to.

As she was talking, Lamar looked around at the shabby camp and the people in their cheap white men's clothes, at the frayed tents and the trash heaps and the overworked horses that were so few in number compared to the great herd he had once tended on the open prairies. These people were poor, and as they moved from place to place on the reservation lands they were pent up in a way that seemed almost comical when compared to the infinite license they had once enjoyed in wandering across the earth.

She wanted him to spend the night but he wanted to be away from there. He told her he was leaving and he was taking her home. He hadn't thought any farther than that and he didn't even know where home was, but he knew he was taking her. Eli didn't speak English in those days and Jewell was careful not to translate what Lamar had just said. She looked at her brother in astonishment. This is where I live, she told him. These are the people I live with. What are you talking about?

Something got into Lamar when she said that. She had been unwilling to come with him years ago when they had a chance to escape their bondage, and now she was unwilling to do so again, even though the bondage this time was of her own making. All these years Lamar had carried within himself an anger he could not suppress or explain, an anger that had been brewed out of being a captive and an exile both. He had been taken by the Comanches, beaten and humiliated and then gradually educated and formed to their ways, and then when he thought he was one of them he had been cast out and thrown upon the mercy of a people he no longer understood and who had no patience to deal with him.

He told her that if she didn't come with him then by God that was the end of it as far as he was concerned. She was crying and Eli was looking agitated. Lamar got into an argument that ended with him sitting on his horse and riding away alone while Eli and three or four other men trotted along beside with rifles and knives in their hands. He heard Jewell crying behind him in the same high-pitched wail of grief and confusion he remembered from the day the Kiowas had taken her.

If he had had his way he would never have seen her again. But decades later, he made the mistake of mentioning to Sarey that he had once had a sister and that as far as he knew she was still living in the Indian Territories. Sarey took it upon herself to write Jewell a letter through the agency at Fort Sill and invite her to their wedding, but Lamar saw it before she mailed it and tore it up. They had a fight afterwards that almost put an end to everything. They made up and got married after all, but Sarey would never let up on the idea of Jewell. Family meant everything to her and she would not tolerate Lamar being on bad terms with his sister. The letter she made sure he did not have a chance to tear up was the one she sent after Ben was born inviting Jewell to come meet her new nephew.

Lamar did not learn she was coming until the day Sarey told him he had to go meet the train. Jewell stepped onto the platform with Eli behind her, paying no attention to the hostile stares of the other passengers or the people at the station. Sarey paid no attention either. She walked right up to them and gave them both a warm handshake and put little Ben in Jewell's arms.

They stayed for three days. Lamar did not have much he cared to say to his sister and she was the same with him. She was in her fifties then and looked no different than any other old Kiowa woman, deep lines around her slack mouth and her stringy hair in braids and a ragged dress whose muddy hem trailed around her ankles. The blue moon tattoo on her forehead was faded now and cross-hatched with wrinkles. Her English since he had last seen her had become halting and uncertain, and perhaps the reason they stayed civil with each other was because she knew she could no longer hold an argument with him in their native tongue.

She stared down at Ben in his crib as if she had never seen a baby before in her life. She had no children of her own, at least none that Lamar knew about, and the silent claim she seemed to be making on his child disturbed him in ways he could not fathom or tolerate. He put up with it until Eli opened his satchel and pulled out a bundle of sage and lit it right there in the parlor. He said he only wanted to bless the child and Sarey said it would do no harm, but Lamar shouted at all of them that Indians had ruined his life and ruined Jewell's life too, even though she wouldn't admit it, and he would be damned if he would allow any of that business around his son.

Jewell and Eli were gone before sunrise the next morning. He didn't hear them leave and he never did learn how they got themselves to the train station. Sarey took the baby the next day and moved in with her folks and left him alone there for two weeks to think about things before she would do him the favor of coming home.

He was still thinking about things. There was a whole hell of a lot he could have handled differently in his life, starting with him moving faster to get that rifle from above the door when the Comanches came into his house and ending with the way he had spoken to Gil Gilheaney tonight for no good reason other than to get the man's bristles up. On nights like this he had a habit of working his way back through those regrets one by one as if he was looking for some sort of answer or satisfaction. But there was no answer to anything, and no satisfaction, and no one left to apologize to except for the sculptor sleeping in his dead son's room.

NINETEEN

By six o'clock the next morning Gil had dressed and packed his bag and set it against the wall of the parlor. Clayton did not join him and Maureen for breakfast, and George's Mary served them with wary discretion until she grew too curious to be silent any longer.

"So what did he do?"

"It's nothing," Gil said. "A slight disagreement."

"Go ahead and tell me," George's Mary said to Maureen. "I ain't going to be surprised."

"He was rude and insulting. My father treats his clients with respect and is accustomed to—"

"Maureen," Gil told her, "you should pack."

"I'll pack when I'm through with my breakfast."

Gil set his napkin on the table and walked over to the front window. The winter storm of the night before had sheathed the tree branches along the creek in ice, and as the wind gusted he could almost hear them tinkling like the glass in a chandelier. Clayton, Ernest, and Nax were all standing on the frosted ground by the corral fence. The two younger men stood next to their saddled horses as they talked to their boss. It looked like they were arguing with him about something—probably, Gil supposed, about whether they actually had to go out riding in this weather. The argument ended when Clayton turned his back on them, and Ernest and Nax, with a shared look of annoyance, mounted their horses and rode them off into the face of the wind.

Clayton walked into the house and when he saw Gil standing at the window he said good morning and walked over to the dinner table for a cup of coffee. His face was flushed with the cold and as he walked he left a melting trail of ice droplets on the rug.

Gil followed and stood in front of Clayton. "When I get back to San Antonio I'll immediately put a check in the mail, reimbursing you for your last payment to me."

"What for? I ain't canceling the damn commission."

"No, but I am. If you read the contract, you'll find that either party has the right to terminate the agreement."

Gil saw a look of real hostility in Clayton's eyes now, and he took some satisfaction in it.

"You need to talk some sense into your father," Clayton said to Maureen.

"I do?"

It warmed Gil to realize that his daughter was taking his part, if a little bitterly. After their tense conversation about Vance, their manner with each other had been brittle and formal, especially during the long train ride to Abilene. But now Clayton's surliness had brought them back into their natural alliance.

"Well, if that's the way you want things to be I guess it's all right with me," Clayton said. "I see your bags packed there. I expect you want to get out of here on the next train."

"If it's convenient," Gil said.

Clayton laughed and pointed toward the window, at the icy aftermath of yesterday's storm. "That look convenient to you?"

"We can wait till tomorrow," Maureen said.

"No," Gil declared. "We'll go now."

Clayton met his guest's eyes. "Ernest is out riding fence, so I'll have to drive you myself."

"You ought not to be out driving in this, Mr. Clayton," George's Mary said.

"Well, that's your opinion and you're welcome to it." He turned back to Gil and Maureen. "You folks are welcome to stay another day or so till this weather clears or take your chances in the car with me."

It was a miserable, dangerous trip to Abilene, Clayton wrestling the steering wheel of the flivver as it slipped along on the icy road. Several times Gil was on the point of telling Clayton to turn back, but he thought better of breaking the already irritated driver's concentration. So Gil and Maureen just stared silently ahead, hoping the journey wouldn't end in a spinout on the side of a desolate road where no help or rescue would be forthcoming.

When they finally made it to the station, they learned the train would be an hour and a half late.

"I'd better stay around and make sure it comes," Clayton said. "Don't want to leave you stranded here."

"We'll be fine," Gil said. "If we end up having to spend another night, we'll stay at the hotel."

"No, there's no point in waiting for the train here," Clayton said after a moment. "Let's go on across the street to the Grace and at least have a decent lunch while you wait."

"We'd be happy to," Maureen said, before Gil could contradict her. They left their bags with the porter and walked quickly across the street to the warmth of the Grace Hotel, where they sat down in the dining room—full of stranded passengers like themselves—and Clayton scowled at an overworked waiter and demanded menus.

They ate in awkward silence, Clayton and Gil ignoring each other, Clayton taking only a few bites of his club sandwich before pushing the plate away. Maureen introduced a few neutral remarks but the conversation went nowhere and neither man cared to nudge it forward.

It was snowing outside now. As Gil watched the flakes descend upon Abilene he had to fight back a wave of unwelcome nostalgia. He did not need to be reminded just now of the wintry New York streets of his boyhood and adolescence and exuberant twenties, the sense of rejuvenation and mystery he had felt with every new snowfall. When he was young he had taken it as a certainty that artistic greatness awaited him, but now his best work was either destroyed or stillborn and he sat on the verge of his old age waiting for a train that would only carry him deeper into obscurity.

"I want you to keep the money I paid you and finish the job," Clayton said.

"What for?"

"Because I made a deal with you and you've held up your end of it and I want you to finish."

"I appreciate you wanting to honor your contract even though I'm not holding you to the obligation. But it's better if we just—"

"Is your father always so damn prideful?" Clayton asked Maureen. "Do you think you could talk him into giving me a chance to say I'm sorry?"

He turned to Gil again. "I want you to finish the statue and don't pay no attention to me."

"All right," Gil said. "I'll continue working on the piece and when I'm satisfied with it I'll contact you for your approval."

"That settles the matter, then," Clayton said.

But it didn't seem settled, at least not judging by the way Clayton sat there folding and refolding his napkin in deliberative silence. There was clearly something else he felt the need to say, but a lifetime of keeping his thoughts to himself had made sharing them an unaccustomed burden.

"You saw that woman who came to my house," he finally said.

"Your sister."

"Well, she's part of what came between my son and me. Or maybe I ought to say I caused her to come between us. I know people have told you how I got taken by the Comanches when I was a boy. I've had newspaper writers and such show up at the ranch and want me to tell them all about it, but I don't care to speak about that part of my life and the reason is it's confusing to me and there's a lot of it I'm ashamed about."

"It's not necessary for you to discuss this with us," Maureen said gently.

"Well, no, I think maybe it is."

He paused while the waiter took away their plates, including his nearly untouched club sandwich, and waited until he was out of earshot on the other side of the dining room to continue.

"I meant to keep Jewell away from Ben because she had taken to Indian ways and I didn't want any of that around my son. The way I looked at it, the Comanches took away my life mostly. For a good long time I didn't know who I was or how I ought to behave around people and there wasn't a whole hell of a lot of good that came my way except for Sarey and Ben. I didn't want that boy confused like I was, or like Jewell was. Sarey took a different view of the subject and we had an argument or two about it. She may have been right but it seemed to me that Jewell was trying to turn my boy into a damn Indian and I wasn't going to stand for it.

"I didn't know until after he got killed and I went through his room that she'd been writing him pert' near all his life. Sarey was in on it with her. Jewell didn't understand how to write in English anymore, but there was a woman up there at the Fort Sill Indian school that wrote down for her what she wanted to say. She'd heard that Ben lost a baby tooth once and she wrote back and told him to go out and face east right before daybreak and make a wish and throw the tooth into the sun and his wish would come true. That was the kind of thing she filled his head with. When I came across those letters it irritated me a good deal and I threw them all in the fire. I didn't care if they were his property or not. Anyway, he was dead so it didn't matter what I did with them. I believe I'll have an ice cream sundae."

He turned in his chair and summoned the waiter with an impatient wave of his hand.

"You saw what happened that night," he went on when the waiter went back to the kitchen with his order, "that night when the two of you were at the house and Jewell showed up. She knew damn well she wasn't welcome there anymore and there she was anyway."

"Maybe she had something she needed to say to you," Maureen said.

"She could have said it in a letter if it was that damn important. No, she just wanted to agitate me about Ben. You saw that bracelet she threw at me. She and Eli probably wanted to do another one of their useless ceremonies with it like they did last time."

"What do you mean, 'last time'?" Gil asked him.

Clayton didn't answer until his ice cream sundae had been delivered and he had consumed two or three spoonfuls of the confection with as much mechanical indifference as a horse eating feed.

"She and Eli showed up at the ranch a few days before Ben went off to the war. I don't know how she knew he was going. I guess he had written to her about it. They set up their tent down by the creek and I didn't make too much of a fuss about it at the time. I figured I owed it to Sarey to be hospitable. Ben spent a lot of time with them down there but they seemed to be behaving themselves so I just let it go on.

But the night before he was supposed to leave I heard a lot of singing coming from that tent. I remember some of those Comanche songs but I didn't understand a word of what they were singing about in Kiowa and it made me suspicious.

"So I just walked into the tent to see what was going on. It was the three of them sitting around a fire, Jewell and Eli doing the singing and Ben just staring into the coals like he'd lost his wits. I'd heard about that peyote church that Quanah Parker got started up there in the Territories and I knew right away that was what they were up to. I walked around that fire circle to grab Ben and get him out of there. Eli stood up and started yelling at me that I was going in the wrong direction, but I didn't care about what he had to say one way or the other. The two of us got into a scuffle and then Ben got into it too. I saw that bracelet on his wrist and I tore it off. It ended up with me dragging him out of there somehow and the two of us yelling at each other. He'd eaten enough of that damn peyote to where he didn't make a bit of sense, but maybe I didn't either. I didn't care."

"What was the purpose of the ceremony?" Gil asked. "To protect him in the war?"

Clayton nodded wearily. "That's what Jewell kept yelling at me. That was what the bracelet was for too. But I already told you I wasn't going to stand for that nonsense. And it wouldn't have made a bit of difference. You tell me what you think: you think a buffalo tooth bracelet's going to stop a German artillery shell?"

He was staring at Gil with aggressive intensity, as if he really meant for the question to be answered.

"You don't need my opinion about any of this," Gil said. "You already know what sort of a mistake you made."

"I guess I do."

Clayton looked down at his melting sundae in its glass tulip dish. He took another bite of ice cream and then set down the spoon and watched the snow brushing softly against the windows.

"Anyway," he said finally, "that was the last time I ever saw Ben."

EVEN AS THE TRAIN traveled south to tropical San Antonio the winter storm held steady. Gil and Maureen lingered after dinner in the dining car, passing ice-sheathed tree branches that shone in the moonlight and fields whose shallow coating of snow made them eerily luminescent. The dispute with Clayton had thrown them briefly into a lively alliance that seemed now to be fading. The revelation about his break with his son should have provided them with plenty to discuss on their trip home, but perhaps it was too raw a subject so soon after their own argument about Vance.

"I had a letter from the Louisiana Historical Society before we left," Gil said to Maureen, in the careful tone they seemed to be using with each other lately. "They want a La Salle for the riverfront in New Orleans."

"A competition?"

"No, it's mine if I want it. But they want to meet me and draw up the contract while I'm there. I hate to leave the Clayton before it's off to the foundry, but they want me in New Orleans in the next few weeks."

"So you have a major commission in your pocket. No wonder you were so quick to give Mr. Clayton his check back."

"It's not about money and you know it."

"Yes, I know it, Daddy."

"I had no intention of letting that man push me around. It seems to be his way of doing things, judging by how he drove off his own son, but it won't work on me."

"I feel sorry for him," Maureen said.

"Of course. It's a pitiful situation all the way round."

They resumed looking out the windows as the Texas night rolled by. The disquiet that had arisen between Gil and his daughter over Vance Martindale still lingered, and he had been unsettled by hearing Clayton's story of open hostility toward his own son. Their situations were hardly comparable, of course. Clayton was a hard and naturally disapproving man, his confused grief just another means of angering people and pushing them away. But Gil could recognize traces of that overbearing man in himself. He too was a father who expected his child, even his grown child, to behave in a certain way, an expectation that, as in Clayton's case, was no longer countered or softened by a motherly influence. But didn't all fathers, if they were worth anything, expect something of the sort?

It would be several hours before the train arrived in San Antonio. Maureen excused herself to go back to the parlor car to finish the

Sherwood Anderson novel she was reading. Gil stayed in the dining car, thinking about his statue of Ben Clayton. The trip to Clayton's ranch, for all its unpleasantness, had been worth it. Now with the piece nearly finished and so strongly lodged in his imagination, it was almost as if it had already been in place when he stood again on that lonely summit. He had seen at once that by placing the statue six inches farther to the west than he had originally planned he could bring the whole landscape into conformance with it. The statue would in some mysterious way define the world that surrounded it. And he had also seen that a delicate shift of Ben Clayton's eye line would make him appear to be looking not just at some distant hill but beyond the horizon itself, giving the piece an additional measure of sadness and lofty yearning.

He was glad he had made the trip, an extra step he would not have taken for a less crucial sculpture. And confronting Clayton had been necessary, both for his own pride and for the sake of the statue. The work was now his in a way it had not been before. He had claimed it as his own, he would fight for his vision of it. He owed Clayton nothing except the promise to toil in the service of his own imagination, to create a work that had a chance of transcending the demands of the client, perhaps even the vision of the artist.

What he had learned from Clayton in the dining room of the Grace Hotel, the anger and heartbreak and never-to-be-healed rift between father and son, would now work its way into the statue. He did not know how exactly, but it would. The new information residing in his mind would be transferred to his hands as he modeled the clay, and would be present in the final image of the boy's face.

TWENTY

Dear Miss Gilheaney,

I am sorry to trouble you again by writing to you. I hope you don't take it wrong I just have to talk to an American every now and then and though this is not talking but writing it feels kind of the same. You have been very kind to answer my letters and tell me about the statue and to give me news of the States. I don't know what I think about prohibition, I guess it is all right. My uncle Cloyce was bad when it came to drinking and my aunt Verna had to live with it. When it got out of hand once, Cloyce got into a fistfight with his own son, my cousin Phil when Phil was about fifteen. He couldn't live with his dad anymore after that and moved on down to the Concho country where he is presently working sheep. They could never have passed that law in France if you ask me. The French people drink a lot of wine and put a lot of store by it. I have drunk a lot of wine since I've been here but it seems a natural thing to do and I do not think I will end up like my Uncle Cloyce.

People here are asking about the treaty and when the Americans are going to sign it. I don't know much more than they do though. I don't see any American newspapers. Everything is pretty hard to get in Somme-Py but that is okay because I don't need much and don't really need to know about what the Reds are up to or what President Wilson has to say about this or that matter because when I am busy with my work the world doesn't concern me too much.

Somme-Py you may remember from my previous letter is the name of the little town that is near St. Etienne where I was wounded and Ben was killed. I am not working with the Service des Travaux anymore. There is a man here in Somme-Py named L'Huillier and when he found out I was an American he said I had to help him rebuild the town and he hired me away just like that. L'Huiller is a lieutenant Colonel in the French Army. He was born in Somme-Py and was a big hero in the war and they sent him to the States to raise money for reconstruction. There is a lot of work to do, since there's almost nothing left of the town, and decent pay. L'Huiller likes Americans and even wants to rename the place Somme-Py les Marines because the marines helped liberate it. I told him that was all right with me as long as he named it Somme-Py les Marines et La Garde Nationale because the Guard was in that fight too and we don't care to be left out! He likes having me around to practice his english I think. Also he doesn't mind the look of my face too much. He was wounded two or three times himself and has seen a lot of boys in my condition.

So I am not roving all over the Champagne anymore but am in one place Somme-Py and I will call it my home for now. People are moving back in and we are working hard to build a new town where the old one stood. We already built the church back. Well it is only wooden and just temporary but it is satisfying just the same to have built it and see the people go in there to worship.

Well I will close by thanking you for your patience in reading another letter from me and hoping you will write me back again even though you don't have to. It is good to have an American friend. I know you don't think we are friends because we have never met but maybe you don't have to see somebody in person to get a good idea of who they are and whether that is a person you would like or not. Therefore I like you Miss Gilheaney. I think you are a good lady. You are welcome anytime in my new "home" of Somme-Py where I will show you the "sights."

Sincerely,
Arthur Fry

It was the third letter she had received from Arthur Fry in three weeks. She read it sitting on the bed in her room with the door closed. Her father was gone to New Orleans and she had the house to herself, but the habit of reading her mail in solitude, in her own private space, had taken root when she was a girl and had grown to be an imperative for a young woman living in a house with her parents. When she was finished reading she sat at her desk and answered the letter immediately, haunted by the thought of this boy as he waited plaintively in his bombed-out village for the appearance of the postman. She did not want to keep him waiting, did not want to disappoint him. It had become her responsibility somehow to keep him from succumbing to despair in a strange land.

She told him about the full-size clay statue of Ben Clayton that was now finished and waiting for the plasterers to come take the molds, which would then be carefully packed and shipped to the Coppini Foundry in New York, one of the few foundries in the country still employing the venerable lost-wax technique her father insisted upon. There it would be cast in bronze, the pieces welded together, the patina applied. Her own work—the Spirit of the Waters—was there already, waiting to be cast, a far simpler job than that of a monumental statue.

Arthur would be very impressed with the statue of Ben, Maureen ventured. He would recognize his friend but he would also surely recognize something much larger. As she was about to name this larger something—the futility of war, the stolen promise of a generation, irrecoverable youth—she hesitated. She did not want to burden Arthur Fry with her own somber speculations about the statue's meaning, nor did she want to lecture him like an art professor. She wanted him to hear her genuine voice, her plain thoughts.

But her thoughts, as usual, were far from plain. As much as she was moved by what her father had accomplished with the Clayton, she was still furious about what he had said about Vance, and this fury had quietly grown in the weeks since. They had not discussed the issue further; she did not care to. But in the meantime letters from Vance continued to arrive, erudite and lively, sometimes with copied-out poems or bizarre newspaper cuttings—a boy being struck in the foot by a meteorite, the wife of the director of the New York Aquarium waking in the middle of the night with an octopus next to her in the bed—for which he charmingly offered no commentary at all. And each letter repeated his plea that she come visit him in Austin.

She was irritated by her father's absence and by his overbearing assumption that, for propriety's sake, she should stay in place. Men in general and her celebrated father in particular had no such restrictions on their freedom. No doubt at this moment he was being lionized in New Orleans, and finding his creative energy renewed by the promise of a new commission. The destruction of the Pawnee Scout had been a great wound but it was behind him now, receding in the face of new accomplishments and new opportunities.

This sort of dynamic renewal was a man's birthright; it was his to lose. But a woman had to fight every day to escape the narrow domestic stasis that threatened to utterly define her. Maureen was unmarried, childless, stranded in a widening pool of uncertainty. Her most ambitious work—her Spirit of the Waters—was admired by the Arts and Beautification Committee of the San Antonio Women's Club but not really by herself, and clearly not by her father, the towering artist she could not help measuring herself against, the sole critic she could not help being desperate to please.

With the modeling on the Clayton finished, her own work off to the foundry, and her father out of town, she had little to do in the next few days except to pay the bills and look after the studio, putting things in order after the months of disruptive work on the statue and keeping an eye open for sudden shifts in temperature that might damage the clay. But the weather was clear and the temperature mild again after the passage of the last winter storm, and it occurred to her, as she was finishing her letter to Arthur Fry, that Mrs. Gossling could certainly watch over things for a night or two.

What was holding her back from picking up the telephone and dictating a telegram to Vance? There were boardinghouses and hotels and probably even university facilities for visiting women in Austin. There was no reason to feel self-conscious about abruptly accepting Vance's invitation. Concern about her father's approval was something she could no longer allow herself to feel. If she felt a hint of hesitation on her own behalf about Vance's sincerity or suitability—well, that was just another argument for traveling to Austin to find out once and for all.

She picked up the telephone and arranged for the telegram, asking if it would be convenient to visit tomorrow on short notice, and three hours later the Western Union boy came to the door with the one-word reply: Yes!

Vance was grinning and waving his hat when the train pulled into the Austin station the next morning, and he grabbed her suitcase before she could step down onto the platform.

"I've found you a very good hotel near the campus," he said as he led her to his friend's car, which she saw was packed with a picnic lunch. "The woman who owns it is a raging suffragist, so of course she is appalled by the idea of a curfew. You can be as scandalously late as you like, and you may consider me your accomplice."

They drove down Congress Avenue and skirted the Capitol building and the university campus that stretched behind it and then headed out west toward open country, Vance rambling on excitedly all the way about their plans for the day.

"I canceled all my classes when I heard you were coming," he said.

"You can just do that? Won't you get in trouble?"

"Who cares what some top-lofty dean thinks? I work three times as hard as most of the men in the department already. Anyway, are you in the mood to scale our local Alp?"

The local Alp was called Mount Bonnell. It took them only five minutes to climb up to the summit but when they arrived the view was sumptuous, the Colorado River cutting its way through a deep limestone valley below them, tree-covered hills swelling and subsiding toward the horizon on the opposite bank, and to the east the gleaming granite dome of the Capitol rising in isolated splendor from the heart of the town. Austin was more emphatically scenic than San Antonio. This view from Mount Bonnell of rocky declivities rising above water, of wild primeval mystery, stirred homesick memories in her of the Hudson River Valley, where her father would take her sometimes when she was a girl to visit his artist friends in New Paltz or Peekskill.

The day was brisk and clean, a little cold, with a cloud front gathering in the north. Vance spread a blanket out for them and dug into the picnic hamper for the lunch he had ordered from the wife of a colleague in the Classical Languages Department who baked and cooked for pin money: chicken sandwiches on thick-sliced bread and bean salad and sugar cookies almost as big as dinner plates.

"They say that Bigfoot Wallace met with some Indians up here and—"

"Oh, please stop," she told him. "I don't think I can stand another lecture about Texas history."

"All right," Vance said, shearing off half of his sandwich in one bite, "I'll intrude upon your ignorance no more."

They sat close together on a limestone rock that had been carved into a bench. She felt the wind on her face and his rough hand touching hers as they ate. They were not the only people here. Twenty yards away some students from the university were taking turns standing on the edge of the precipice, standing there with their arms outstretched, the girls' skirts filling with wind.

A young mother stood holding the hand of her two-year-old son as he stared at the students. The little boy watched their raucous antics with such total innocent absorption that it almost moved Maureen to sudden tears. Noticing this, perhaps, Vance squeezed her hand. There was some sort of message in this gesture, she thought, some attempt on Vance's part to reassure her that his character ran deeper than its witty and blustery surface.

She felt she had to believe this, otherwise she might just as well sweep away the whole idea that it was not too late to fall in love and be married and have children, to join at last the world that existed beyond her father's studio. From her early girlhood she had been aware that boys tended to treat her with kindly indifference, and that her father's steadfast love might be all that the world would allow her. She trained herself to accept the idea that she was undesirable, to accept it with a wounded pride. Her life would find a higher purpose. The nights of her youth that might otherwise have been thrown away to bohemian abandon had been defiantly spent in her father's studio, helping him with the thousands of last-minute sculpting details of some piece that absolutely had to be ready the next day for the moldmakers, or the foundry, or the patron's inspection.

He had not pressed her into his service; she convinced herself she had been called to it. From the cocoon of her father's studio she would emerge someday as a full-fledged artist in her own right.

But that had not happened. She was a skillful sculptor but not a blazingly intuitive one like her father. She now understood that the years of monastic apprenticeship had been for nothing, that they had been years not of focused advancement but of craven withdrawal.

Maybe it had been Arthur Fry's letters from France, with their portrait of a young man so much more justifiably paralyzed by self-consciousness and faint prospects than she. Maybe it was her father's blithe dismissal of Vance, which implied such poor judgment on Maureen's part that it was at the same time a dismissal of her.

It would end here, on this trip, with this man. There were strictures to violate but she was happy to violate them. They were not so strong. Her common sense told her that it was an insult to nature to remain a virgin at her age. Her father had feigned outrage that she wouldn't be traveling with a chaperone, but he himself had long ago forsaken conventional propriety by becoming an artist and marrying his nude model. Maureen's mother had grown far cooler than her husband to risk and new horizons, but she had been up-to-date and matter-of-fact on the issue of sex, and it was this practical attitude that Maureen now seized on as a legacy.

"Shall we break the law?" Vance said after he had finished off his gigantic cookie and half of hers. He looked around—the young students and the young family had trailed off along the sloping summit—and withdrew a flask from his jacket pocket.

"Bourbon and branch water," he announced as he poured some in a cup. "Thrillingly illicit, as of last month."

She drank it down, recoiling a little at the taste but savoring the way it seeped into her body and made her just that much more alert to the steely beauty of the clouds coming in from the north. A cold wind began to sweep across the summit and Vance gathered up the remaining picnic things and led her back down to the car.

They spent the rest of the afternoon in the parlor of the little house he rented on Nueces Street, lying in each other's arms on his tattered sofa while he read aloud T. S. Eliot's Prufrock poem.

"Let us go then, you and I," he almost whispered, her head resting against his soft belly while he stroked her hair with his free hand. She scanned the room as he read, the hatrack by the door filled with artfully battered hats, the longhorn skull with its horns spreading above the mantelpiece, the cheap portrait busts of Shakespeare and Tennyson, the books spilling out of the warped shelves and stacked against the walls, his pipes secured in their circular rack like war implements, his cowboy boots on the floor, their worn leather tops sagging toward each other. "And indeed there will be time," he went on, reading the poem now into her ear, as if he were making up these words on the spot just for her. "Time for you and time for me."

They went to a party that night at another professor's house. The house was on the edge of a park near the campus, and despite the cold the party spilled outside almost at once. Maureen had the impression that most of the guests were renegade faculty members like Vance, disgruntled at this or that stifling dictum of the administration. There were students as well, the worldly coeds all smoking, wearing bobbed hair and gunboat shoes, the men in sweaters and patched jackets, their hair spilling into their eyes as they passed around their flasks with outlaw abandon. There were poets and sullen bolsheviks and a visiting professor from Serbia who said he was sick of people asking him about the assassination of the archduke, and a young folklorist who had spent last summer traveling through South Texas collecting cowboy songs and *corridos*. He had brought his guitar and set up shop against the drooping limb of a live oak. Ten or twelve of the partygoers, entranced with the idea of hearing authentic working songs, sat in the grass to hear him out, but he had no idea how bad a singer he was, and the louder he attacked the choruses the more of his audience members he drove away.

Vance dropped her off at her hotel past midnight and the owner handed her the room key without comment. They spent the next day strolling in the bracing winter air, all the way from the main building of the university through the rotunda of the Capitol and along the downtown streets to the river. They had no agenda, no one to meet, nothing to discuss except what occurred to them. He took her to dinner at an open-air beer garden that now sold only what it called bone-dry beer and afterward they walked into an adjacent room where a German singing club had built a bowling alley. He knew everyone there. He insisted on teaching her how to bowl. The bone-dry beer had no alcohol in it but she felt intoxicated anyway, and disturbed by her own happiness. Could all this really be happening to her at last, or was it some sort of cruel delusion?

When they left the beer garden they walked north, toward the university. She was leaving tomorrow. It was time for him to take her back to the hotel, but she did not remind him to do so and he did not propose it. They walked on beside a meandering creek, her arm in his as she huddled close to him. The wintry tree limbs creaked above them, every now and then a car passed on the street that bordered the campus. They were walking toward his house and she said nothing. She let him take her there. They fell onto the sofa again, though she was willing—she was expecting—to be guided into his bedroom. He kissed her and she kissed him ardently back, wordlessly complying, not just with where his desires were leading them but with some new and long-delayed envisioning of herself.

But after a few minutes the pitch of their lovemaking did not seem to be progressing. They were stalled, and she realized it was him, not her. He pulled away from her and sat against the arm of the sofa, his suit still on, his boots still on. There were no lights on in the room but there was moonlight from the uncurtained window and she could see his eyes gleaming as he looked away from her toward a blank wall.

"Well," she said, hurrying to salvage her dignity, "I should go. No matter how progressive you say that woman is, she won't like me coming in at three in the morning."

"All right," Vance said.

She was thunderously confused. It was ridiculous to think that he was appalled at her loose behavior, but his usually open face was so blank and so unrevealing as to be hostile.

She would be damned if she would demean herself by asking what was wrong. She stood up, straightened her clothes, and thanked him for the evening with a bitter tremor of laughter she could not suppress.

"I am married," he said.

"Oh."

"It's hardly much of a marriage."

"I didn't ask you to what degree you were married." The rage she was feeling now was better than the stupefaction she had felt a moment ago. There were, at least, words to employ.

"It was a mistake to marry her in the first place, but I was only twenty and didn't know anything. We didn't have that much in common, and then she got sick with some sort of stomach thing they've never been able to figure out. Couldn't travel, couldn't do anything, resented me because I could—and because I just couldn't condemn myself to spending the rest of my life on her parents' farm in Falfurrias. I know that would have been the noble thing but I couldn't do it. We send each other letters every now and then—very proper and careful letters. That's about all there is to it. I can't divorce her because she's sick, you see. Some of my friends know about her, some don't."

She hated the way he looked now, the tense satisfaction in his face, as if he thought he was explaining himself perfectly well and was congratulating himself for being patient while she absorbed what he had just told her.

"Why did you wait till now to tell me?"

"Well, we were crossing the Rubicon, so to speak. I couldn't leave you in the dark about it any longer. I know you're questioning my character right now, but I couldn't very well do that."

"No, you very well couldn't, could you? I'm going to the hotel."

He insisted on walking her. It was very late, so she let him, but she walked with her arms tightly folded in front of her and she would not look at him. She half listened as he besieged her with explanations and excuses, but all his words were like water swirling around the base of a great ragged boulder of betrayal. It was colder now and the sky was overcast and sleet was collecting on the tree-buckled sidewalks.

"So there have been other women, I suppose," she said, "who didn't mind that you were married."

"Let's not talk about that sort of thing."

"All right. It's rotten of me to make you feel uncomfortable."

"Stop it."

"My father was right about you. I hate to admit it, but he was. What sort of game were you playing?"

"It wasn't a game. I wish you could believe me about that."

She stopped and turned to him, her tears brimming on her cold face.

"So why me?"

"What do you mean?"

"What did you see in me? Why did you even bother?"

"Do we have to talk about this like it's completely a thing of the past? I know it's a shock, but the idea we would never see each other again is—"

"Did you just want to hurt me?"

"Please don't be ridiculous."

"Then what was it? I know I'm not beautiful. I'm not even pretty. Why bother with me?"

"Because I like you. Because you interest me. You don't bore me. Because you're intelligent and serious and funny. And I happen to find you attractive no matter what you say about yourself."

"But you didn't love me."

"I wasn't in a position to love you or anybody."

He tried to reach out to her, but she took a step back and batted his arms away before they could envelop her. He begged her forgiveness and she could see that it genuinely troubled him to hurt her so much. But his discomfort was nothing, something he would recover from, learn from, and leave behind. Her hurt, by contrast, was something final, so deep and so defining it seemed to nail her in place on the street. If he had told her that he had loved her, she might have gone back to his house and begun something scandalous with him. In this new age after the war when everything was upside down anyway it would not have mattered so much. She would not have minded people talking about them, not if he had loved her. But he didn't love her and she had guessed it all along—or should have allowed herself to guess it—and now there was nothing to do but let him continue to escort her through the sleet back to her hotel.

TWENTY-ONE

She had a name that was bewitchingly apt for a beautiful New Orleans widow: Therèse. Her grandfather had come to New Orleans as a young aide to General Butler during the Civil War. Her husband was a prominent lawyer who had dropped dead in his office four years ago. She was almost fifty but saw to it that she looked twenty years younger, and was so securely a part of New Orleans society that she cared not a thing about it or what it thought about her.

She was the sole woman on the committee that had chosen him for the La Salle statue, and by far its most opinionated member. She knew quite a bit about art and was full of interesting prejudices about it, but during Gil's get-acquainted meeting with the committee in the boardroom of a New Orleans bank, she said very little, letting the men expound on what an oversight it was not to already have a statue of La Salle standing on the bank of the Mississippi in the heart of the city that owed its existence to his explorations.

"We want something grand," one of the committee members said, a plump young man still in his twenties who was in a hurry to make his mark on the city, having just inherited his family's bank. "La Salle standing there at the mouth of the Mississippi, his sword in his hand, his armor shining. Maybe a few of his men with him."

"That's not my idea of the piece at all," Gil told him.

It seemed not to have occurred to any of the committee members that the sculptor might have his own opinions, and Gil's blunt dismissal left them hanging in silence, their cigar smoke gathering weight in the room's stultifying atmosphere. Therèse, however, shifted in her chair, interested.

Gil told them he had no interest in depicting the Sieur de La Salle as the usual triumphant conqueror of the wilderness, or even less as the bewigged nobleman attired for his audience with the Sun King. He saw his subject as a gaunt and ravaged explorer staring at the Mississippi as much in wonder at the fact that he was alive as that he had finally discovered the river's mouth.

"Anything else would be a cliché," he told them. "We must catch the human La Salle in this figure or it's not worth doing in the first place."

It did not take much discussion for them to endorse his idea. Gil simply held back and answered the occasional question as they weighed the merits of his conception. He held firm and they came around, as he was pretty sure they would.

"Well, that's settled, then," one of the older men, the committee chairman, said after a few minutes. "We'll haggle with you on a price, and assuming we can reach an agreement, then you're our man."

"Would you be willing to go to France?" Therèse asked him.

"France?"

"Yes, should have mentioned that," the chairman said. "The man who's putting up half the money, whose idea this statue was—celebrating American and French friendship after the war, that sort of thing—is this Monsieur something-or-other."

"Du Prel," Therèse said.

"He's some sort of descendant of La Salle's. Has some family portraits he wants to show you. It's a formality, really. He probably just wants to get a look at you, talk your ear off about his famous ancestor. Of course it goes without saying your expenses would be entirely covered."

After the particulars of the deal had been ironed out and the letters of intent signed, the committee took him to a celebratory dinner at Commander's Palace. When it was over, Therèse insisted on dropping him off at his hotel, but when they were alone in the car she told the chauffeur to head to Lamothe's instead.

"It's a pity we've already had dinner," she said, "since Lamothe has the best étouffée in town, but I insist on showing you at least a little of the interesting side of New Orleans before you go home. I don't care how much you protest or how tired you are. Do you mind going all the way to France?"

"No. I haven't been overseas in years."

"They say Paris is livelier than ever. Funny to think it would be that way after all that's happened over there. Half the young artists I know are already there and the rest are packing their bags."

They stood on a restaurant terrace overlooking the park. Therèse whispered to a waiter and he brought them manhattans. Prohibition apparently meant nothing here. She drank a lot and held it well. She pointed out several elegantly dressed prostitutes. From the terrace Gil could see her driver standing at the side of her touring car, patiently reading the paper in the tavern's porch light.

"You certainly spoke your mind today," she said. "I'd heard that you do that."

"You must have done some checking up on me."

"Of course I did. It was I who found you in the first place. Do you think those men in that room know anything about sculpture? Why do you live in San Antonio, of all places?"

"I like it there," he said. "Why aren't you living in Paris with all your artist friends?"

"Oh, I'm far too old for cafés and nightlife. Can't you see I'm ancient?"

He knew where it was going with her. They left the restaurant and walked alongside Bayou St. John with the car following behind. The bayou docks were crowded with dilapidated houseboats and squatters' shacks, and the lamps from the boats shone imploringly across the dark water. She told him amusing details about the committee members he had met, their sham marriages, the scandalous stories behind their wealth, their ties to the political ring that ran the city.

After a while she waved for the driver to pick them up and they drove up to the lakeshore and then back along Old Shell Road to the center of town. It was one in the morning by then. The whole world must have known her at the St. Charles but she strode boldly through the lobby with Gil and then up to his room, and in the morning came down with him and they walked together to her waiting car.

Nothing but good-bye needed to be said when she dropped him off at the train station. She patted his knee, a little wistfully, and straightened his necktie in a mock wifely way, but the night had been what it was and they parted cheerfully and with no expectations for the future.

The legacy of his marriage to Victoria had haunted him during the evening, but in his rational mind he knew there was nothing to square and no point in looking back. Even so, on the long trip back to San Antonio, he wrestled with unsettling thoughts. The undemanding interlude with Therèse was of a piece in his mind with the commission he had just been handed by her and the rest of her committee, something that could engage him without the risk of defining him. The truth was that he didn't care much about the La Salle statue. It was a fitting subject and his conception lifted it above the dutiful public monument that the committee had envisioned, but he had done enough explorers and statesmen and grandees by now. The La Salle would be a good strong piece of work, something that in a generation or two from now several passersby out of every thousand or so would look up at and admire and then go on with their day. But there would be nothing in it to shake them or startle them, and nothing in its creation to do the same to him.

That was why he was so anxious to get back to the Clayton. He had been away almost five days, and the thought of the sculpture standing in his studio, only days away from completion, was intolerable. This was the piece that had captured him in a way that the La Salle never would, the work that would outlive him, and not just in the literal sense of bronze outlasting flesh. He thought of it the way physicists were now thinking about light, a steadily traveling beacon, carrying forth the boy's memory, and along with it his own, through the darkness of time.

The arthritis came again as he cut his steak in the dining car. He put Urrutia's splints back on after lunch and tried to push away the fear that the disease brought to his thoughts. He would simply have to endure the pain while he finished the Clayton. After that he could give his hands a rest for a few months before he started modeling the La Salle.

Another bitter norther had swept through San Antonio in his absence, but as he got into a taxi at the train station the temperature was steadily rising. There was sludge in the streets and the wintry tree branches were dripping with melted ice. Gil had the driver stop at the post office and he went inside to collect the mail. In his private post office box there were the usual church bulletins and Catholic newspapers, but also a package containing a small book so worn and leafed-through it was almost falling apart at the binding. The book was also searingly familiar to him at first glance: his late mother's daily missal.

The letter inside was from a Father Dewey, who said he had come across the missal while going through the effects of Monsignor Berney, who had recently died after serving as the pastor of St. Joseph's parish for many decades. Father Dewey supposed that Margaret Gilheaney had given the missal to her great friend the monsignor as a keepsake before her own death, but now that he was gone as well it seemed fitting that it be given to her son, the renowned sculptor of whom she had always been so proud.

He leafed through the ancient book on his way home in the taxi. It was as much a scrapbook or a diary as a missal. The paper on which the prayers were printed had been almost worn away by her hands as they had turned the pages, decade after decade in a life of unbroken daily communion and observance of the sacraments. Interleaved between the thin pages were dozens of holy cards, the holy cards she herself had painted, that he had watched her paint as a boy in the tiny parlor of their Leroy Street apartment. And for every holy card in the missal there was a faded newspaper cutting announcing the unveiling of one of his statues, or the awarding of a commission.

He could not bear to look at it for long; he could not endure the innocent belief that rose from its musty pages. His mother had lived a hard life but she had managed to hold on to an untarnished faith in God's purpose. And she had believed in her son with the same shining conviction, even as Gil had lied to her and sealed her out of his real life.

He put the missal into his jacket pocket to hide it from Maureen when he got home. But Maureen was not there, nor was Mrs. Gossling. It was six in the evening, but there was no sign of anyone preparing dinner. He set his suitcase down on the floor. He was weary from the long trip and hungry, and was puzzled by Maureen's absence.

He walked out to the studio, but she was not there either. He took the missal out of his jacket pocket and set it on the desk while he unlocked the drawer where he kept his mother's mail. In that moment something struck him as wrong, something to do with the temperature in the room. He walked over to the woodstove and felt the door. It was cold.

He looked at the almost-completed full-scale clay statue of Ben Clayton and his horse and gave it closer inspection than he had when he had walked into the room. For a moment it seemed that there was nothing wrong with it. It was intact, still supported by the armature, the details of human face and animal musculature still sharply defined.

If he stood there and did nothing he could still make himself believe that it had survived the cycle of freezing and thawing to which it had apparently just been exposed. But he could not sustain that hope forever. He took a few steps forward and put his trembling hand on the flank of the horse and watched as it began to crumble like a sand castle.

TWENTY-TWO

Maureen had planned to be back in San Antonio by late morning, well before her father's scheduled return from New Orleans that afternoon. But the ice storm that swept through Austin during the night of Vance's confession delayed her train for hour after hour as she sat miserably in the station, too shattered to do anything but stare vacantly at the advertisements on the walls.

She did not arrive in Austin until after dark. It had seemed important once that she return before her father did, so that he would never have to know she had gone to visit the man he distrusted. It gave her no comfort, of course, to know that her father had been right. It only made the wound deeper. And since she was past caring about pretty much everything, she was also past caring whether he knew about her trip. Maybe she would tell him everything, maybe she would tell him nothing, just declare that her life and her whereabouts were her own business and close the door to her bedroom. None of it mattered. She had no more interest in being comforted by her father than in being lectured by him. She missed her mother rather desperately but all her mother could have offered in this case would have been soothing lies.

She should get out of San Antonio, away from Texas and its heat and cold and corrupting mythology, and go back home to New York. Her mother was dead and she was tired of her own deadening life as her father's prized assistant. But her deadening life now seemed to spread out everywhere in front of her. She wished she could summon more anger toward Vance, a liberating energetic fury, but instead she felt queasy and smothered, her soul buried under something that was as static as a fogbank. Escaping to New York or anywhere else would mean willing her body to move, and she was not sure she would ever be able to bear the weight of her own existence again.

When she walked into the house her father was sitting in the front room. Except for the light from the lamp beside his chair, the house was dark. His suitcase was on the floor. He had not unpacked, and he was still wearing his suit jacket and tie.

"What's the matter?" she said.

"Where were you?"

"What's the matter?"

He handed her a folded note. "I found this on the entry hall table. It's from Mrs. Gossling. Her brother died yesterday. She says she's very sorry she had to leave in such a rush and hopes we can look after ourselves for dinner."

"Well, of course we can."

"Yes, of course we can."

"What's wrong, Daddy?"

"Well, as it happens, dinner was only one of the things she wasn't able to get around to doing."

It took her a moment. Then she remembered the freezing night and morning in Austin, the steadily warming afternoon as she had waited for her train.

"The stove," she said.

But before he could answer she had already raced out the back door of the house and into the studio. She turned on an electric light and saw the magnificent sculpture that would have been her father's greatest work cracked into hardened pieces, some of them still clinging to the armature, some crashed to the floor. She had been explicit with Mrs. Gossling when she left for Austin. If it grew cold, she was to be sure to light the stove in the studio to guard against the danger of the clay freezing. But in the shock of her brother's death Mrs. Gossling had clearly forgotten.

"It's pretty remarkable sometimes, this Texas weather," her father was saying from behind her in a dead voice. "It can be freezing in the morning and in the afternoon you're sweating through your clothes."

"I never thought anything like this would happen."

"Obviously not. I'm not saying you did it on purpose."

She turned to look at him, understanding in a glance that she and her father were pretty much at the same pitch of despair.

"But you are saying I did it."

"I'm saying nobody was here to light the stove. I suppose you left that to Mrs. Gossling while you went to wherever you went. Austin, I suppose, to visit your cowboy professor."

He walked up to the ruined statue and peeled a piece of hardened clay off the horse's nose, then shook the dust off his hand.

"It's interesting you felt you had to do that in secret."

"I'm sorry, Daddy."

"Yes, I know you're sorry. And if you were still a little girl, saying you were sorry might even have been enough, as colossal as this loss is. But by God, Maureen, you're not a little girl and I counted on you."

"You have no right to speak to me that way!" she declared, surprising herself with the force of her resentment. "I made arrangements with Mrs. Gossling. I did nothing wrong. I had as much right to go to Austin as you did to go to New Orleans. You needn't act like a child by looking for someone else to blame."

"Act like a child?" He was too stupefied by her defiance to say anything more. He looked away from her, perhaps silently accepting her argument, though too wounded and proud to say so.

"We can start over," she suggested, in a much softer voice.

"We?"

The sarcastic laugh that escaped from him was a terrible sound to her. She had never heard it before in her life.

"And, by the way, do you think I have *two* of these in me? Do you think I can just order up a copy?"

"No, but—"

"It might seem like a mechanical enterprise to you. It might seem like re-creating a statue you've poured every bit of yourself into is no more of a problem than replacing a sewer line or rebuilding a collapsed porch."

She seized on his hectoring, belittling, self-pitying words and threw them back in his face. She couldn't help herself, though she didn't know where her anger was coming from or whether or not she even had a right to it.

"Well, I think it *is* somewhat similar. As a matter of fact, I think it's exactly like replacing a sewer line. It's just work. You always told me you had contempt for artists who sat around and waited for inspiration. Isn't that what you're talking about all of a sudden?"

But he was paying no attention. "You have no conception of what it is to be sixty years old," he said, "and to see your work come to nothing."

"I have a conception of what it is to be thirty-two years old and to be trapped in this house with you with no hope of escape. I have a conception of what it is to see my *life* come to nothing."

She had shocked him, and was glad.

"What happened with Martindale?"

"I don't want to tell you. I don't *need* to tell you, because in your superior wisdom you already know."

"Did you and he—"

"Leave me alone!" She was almost screaming now. "I'm sorry about your statue, it's my fault. But just please leave me alone, Daddy, please!"

Without quite realizing it, she had ordered him out of his own studio. He left, slamming the door behind him. She was alone in the studio, in her father's sanctum, the place that had been her refuge as well as his. Here she had always felt wanted, had always felt herself working toward the goal of not just pleasing her father but becoming an artist in her own right.

Now she saw the studio only as a prison, where without ever quite realizing it she had settled more deeply day by day into a life that was too careful and too dependent. When her heart had been broken in the past it was here she had come, after she had purged herself of tears in her mother's arms. It was here she had put herself back together, working in concert with her father to create the great works that would stand through time. But it was not just her heart that was broken now, it was her judgment, her purpose, her worth. Coming back here now, settling into the once-comforting routines—the physical labor of building armatures and hauling clay, the clerical satisfactions of cataloging, invoicing, and correspondence—would mean nothing but the final surrender of her spirit.

But where should she go? What could she make of herself? Would she live here the rest of her life in defeat, trying to make some sort of peace with the knowledge that no man had ever really wanted her and never would?

She stared at the ruined statue, the armature showing through in places like the bones of a decaying corpse, the powdery clay gathering in piles on the floor. Beneath the weight of her own pain and anger she could not help feeling pity for her father. To have this happen to him in a year when he had already lost the Pawnee Scout, the work of which he was the proudest and which he had thought would endure the longest. She knew that dying in obscurity was his greatest terror, greater than the loss of his wife, greater she was quite sure than the loss of his daughter. He was one of those men who were born to look beyond the horizon of his own existence, who instinctively valued his legacy more than his life. She was not like that. She wanted happiness. She wanted love. She could give up her own artistic aspirations for just the normal things that people had.

If she had not left for her secret trip to Austin she would have kept the stove going in the studio and it would not have mattered if Mrs. Gossling had been called away. But she had too much justifiable anger toward her father at the moment to feel guilty. She looked away from the statue and her eyes settled over his desk, his fountain pen, his reading glasses, his sketch pads, ledger books, his old anatomy books with their spines cracked from decades of use. Among the familiar objects was something she had never seen before, an old prayer book with cracked leather covers, stuffed with holy cards and newspaper cuttings. She picked it up and thumbed through it—puzzled, increasingly puzzled. When she put it back on the desk she saw that the drawer her father had always kept locked was half open. In her current mood she did not feel the need to ask herself if she had the right to take advantage of this oversight. The drawer was full of letters, her father's name and address written in a woman's careful hand. The return address read "Mrs. T. L. Gilheaney." She slipped the most recent letter out of its envelope and read: "My dearest son."

GIL KNEW his accusations were unjust, and the anger and hurt that had ruled him a moment before were now smothered in a blanket of shame. He had not been able to stop himself from lashing out at her about the statue, when it had been clear to him as soon as he saw her that something was desperately wrong. Something had happened in Austin with Vance Martindale. Now the possibility of her confiding her own sorrows to him, of him being able to stand by her at a difficult time as a father should, was gone. She had turned away from him and he could give her nothing.

He went for a walk in the dark streets. The neighborhood dog that usually lunged at his car tires when he drove by trotted out and walked alongside him with silent complicity, as if the two had previously agreed to meet. The temperature had dropped a little and Gil kept his hands in his jacket pockets. He had still not changed his clothes or eaten. He was too agitated to do either.

He knew what he should do: set things right with Maureen as best he could, and in the morning pry the rest of the clay off the armature and start all over again. But he could not start all over again. He knew it; it wasn't there anymore. He was sixty years old. He had come from nothing, had escaped from the tenement streets of New York, from the violence and iron strictures of his upbringing, and had made a brilliant start. His talent had been recognized by important people, he had studied and worked in Paris and in Rome, he had been poised more times than he could remember on the cusp of greatness, one statue away from being ranked with Saint-Gaudens or Ward. Now he was a minor celebrity in San Antonio, Texas, his two best works destroyed, his wife embittered and then dead, his daughter apparently betrayed by a deceitful suitor and blaming Gil for his cruel foresight.

When he walked back into the house it was ten o'clock at night. He had not eaten since his lunch on the train. His hunger seemed out of keeping with his deflated spirit, but that was no reason not to eat something. He found a box of graham crackers in the pantry and took them over to the kitchen table. He broke each cracker into four pieces along the perforated lines—even that simple action summoned the arthritic pain in his thumbs, a mocking pain that foretold the hastening end of his career. He ate each section of graham cracker in one bite, shoveling them into his mouth as if he was feeding a machine. He tried not to think as he ate, but he could not stop his mind from reminding itself of the months of work he had spent on the Clayton piece and the decades-long hopes he had poured into it.

Maureen appeared at the door and pushed in the light switch, flooding the kitchen with harsh illumination.

"I thought you were in bed," Gil said.

She didn't answer. Her face was pale and he could see a pulse beating in her throat above the neckline of her dress. She seemed so unsteady that he stood in alarm, took her elbow, and guided her to a seat across from him at the table. It was not until then that he noticed the envelopes she held in her trembling hand.

"You said she died when you were in your twenties. Before I was born. But these letters, the postmarks, the things she writes about . . ."

She did not say anything more, just stared at him with a question in her eyes that he had no option but to answer. But it took him a moment to find his own voice, to understand that the reckoning he had dreaded for all of her life had finally come.

"I'm so sorry," he said, but the volume of what he had to apologize for now was so huge, its appearance so sudden and unexpected, that the words came out in a muttering way as if he was talking to himself.

"Sorry about what, Daddy? So it's true that you've been lying to me all my life?"

"Yes."

"Why?"

He stared down at the surface of the kitchen table, moved a silver napkin ring around like a chess piece.

"I've told you a little bit about her," he said. "About my mother. Very Catholic. Very, very Catholic. Guardian angels, feast days, novenas, always saying the rosary, always—"

"You said she was *dead*!"

He nodded. The graham cracker box sat absurdly on the table in front of them.

"In her world, marriage outside the church was a mortal sin. I was in love with your mother. She was a Protestant. You have to understand, my mother wouldn't have been able to accept it. It would have destroyed her. I had to protect her."

"You had to protect yourself!"

"Yes. Maybe. I don't know."

An odd buzzing started up in Maureen's head. She felt like a machine that had fallen off a track and was now senselessly grinding its gears.

"I don't even know what questions to start asking. I don't understand how it was even possible—all these years, to keep it a secret."

"I had to work at it. I had to think ahead, all the time. It was cruel, I know that. But I had to think of her and what it would do to her if she found out."

"If she found out that I *existed*? That she had a granddaughter?"

She stood up, walked around the kitchen in agitated circles, not knowing what to say, torn between her angry desire never to set eyes on her father again and the flooding curiosity that only he could satisfy.

"It's late," Gil said after a few moments. "And we've both had a terrible day. Maybe it would be better if we talked about all of this tomorrow."

"No, it would *not* be better! Putting off talking about it will just make everything easier for you."

"There are reasons I did what I did. They may not make sense to you. They may not make sense to me anymore, I don't know, Maureen, but I was thinking of my mother, of how to protect her so that—"

"And what about *my* mother? She had to know about this, didn't she?"

"You shouldn't blame her for anything. She wanted to tell you. We had terrible arguments about it."

"You made her lie to me."

"Yes."

In one brisk stride Gil's daughter walked up to him and struck him across the face. He had never been slapped by a woman, had only seen it in the moving pictures, and the theatricality of the gesture astonished him more than the blow itself. It was so out of keeping with his daughter's temperament, so out of keeping with everything.

She was gone now, down the hallway and into her room. He had nowhere to go so he stayed where he was at the kitchen table, gripping its enamel sides in his powerful sculptor's hands.

TWENTY-THREE

Lamar Clayton sat in a corner booth of the Manhattan Cafe on First Street, eating soup and crackers while he read the *Abilene Daily Reporter.* The news was about the treaty and the Lansing business and the Reds threatening to take over Eastern Europe, all the confusion left over from the war that nobody was ever going to settle. Especially not Wilson, who Clayton hadn't ever thought was worth a damn. He remembered the craziness when the war ended, people bursting out in tears, the paper full of blather about everything the boys had accomplished. It was like people really believed the world had been put back together and everything was going to make perfect sense from now on. It had made him sick, all those furniture stores and tire dealers taking out ads with poems welcoming the soldiers home, all those illustrations of women in flowing gowns holding torches and olive branches hailing the victors and blessing the noble fallen. He hated that goddam word "fallen." Like they'd just slipped to the ground instead of being blown into pieces by shells or getting their guts ripped out by machine-gun bullets. There had been one illustration that had really torn at him, an advertisement for Farmers and Merchants Bank showing a boy in uniform running through the front door of his parents' house, his arms extended, his mother sitting in a chair, surprised in her knitting, gasping in joy, the boy's father standing behind his wife, about to drop his newspaper in astonishment. The wondrous reunion, all the tests passed and all the trials behind them. You could look at that picture and imagine the boy sleeping in his old room for a day and a night, wrung out, bursting with stories yet to be told, woken at last by the smell of his mother's cooking, the morning sun streaming through the window.

It would not have been like that if Ben had come home, he knew. There had been no mother for him to come back to, just George's Mary. He had left for Europe without a word to Lamar and he would have come back agitated and resentful and scarred, with new grievances to take up with his father. But there might have been a moment at least, a welcome-home moment not too far off from that illustration in the paper. Lamar had imagined it often enough while Ben had been overseas. A simple tight-gripped handshake at the train station, him saying "Welcome home, son," and Ben looking off to the side so his father wouldn't see the tears in his eyes. Maybe they would have sat out on the porch after dinner, neither of them saying much, Lamar making a point not to quiz him about what he'd seen over there, Peggy asleep in Ben's lap, George's Mary opening the door with her hip and bringing out two big dishes of cobbler.

Lamar finished the last of his watery soup and looked around the diner. It was two o'clock and most of the customers had left by now. The waitress had a pan of biscuits just out of the oven and was about to put them in a warming tray. It seemed odd they would be making a new batch of biscuits after lunch was over but it was no business of his.

"Bring me a few of those before they get cold," Lamar called out to her.

She put a couple of the biscuits on a plate and walked over to him and plunked it down. She was about sixteen, skinny and homely and no life to her at all. There was a waitress over at the Ideal he liked better, but it was closed on Tuesday and it didn't matter anyway. He didn't come to Abilene often enough for the waitresses to remember him. He had a few friends here in the cattle business but he saw them mostly at stock shows and the like. He didn't generally visit people just to pass the time. He wouldn't have been in Abilene at all today if George's Mary hadn't taken a dislike to the dentist in Albany and insisted on being driven all the way to the city just to get a few teeth out. Lamar would have left the business of driving her to Ernest or Nax but there was a fence down in one of the far pastures and he was feeling his age this week. There was a stabbing pain in his knee that came and went and a creak in his hipbone. He figured he'd rather be in a motorcar than on board a horse, but it aggravated him that he had to drive so damn far because George's Mary was squeamish about dentists.

He ate the two biscuits while they were still hot and then paid his bill and walked next door to a dry goods store and bought six new shirts, for seventy-nine cents apiece. They were all the same, khaki work shirts with flaps on the front pockets. He disliked buying new clothes and didn't care for the feel of them until George's Mary had washed them six or eight times, but the rest of his shirts were worn out and needed to be replaced. He looked around the store to kill time, but there wasn't anything else he needed. He thought about buying something for George's Mary, just to cheer her up after getting her teeth out, but he didn't know anything about women's clothes or what size she was.

A half hour later he picked her up in front of an office building on Pine Street. She was standing there looking miserable with her mouth swollen and full of bloody cotton swabs. She gave Lamar a cross look and held up four fingers when Lamar asked her how many teeth the dentist had taken out. He got irritated with himself for not thinking of having that waitress pack up some soup for her, since she wasn't going to be eating anything that needed much chewing for a while.

"Don't you worry about cooking dinner tonight," he told her, doing his best to feel generous. "We can open a can or two of chili."

"I already cooked your dinner ahead," she mumbled. "Think I don't have the sense to do that?"

"I was just trying to make things easier on you," he said. "No reason to bark at me about it."

She took one of the blood-soaked cotton wads out her mouth, inspected it for a moment, and threw it out of the car before replacing it with a fresh one from a paper bag she had on her lap.

"Hurts like hell," she said.

"He didn't give you any aspirin or anything?"

"He did, but it still hurts like hell. Is my mouth all caved in now?"

"I can't tell," he said. "It looks all swole up to me."

"I hate losing my teeth," she said. She was silent and glum for another ten miles, until the left front tire went flat and Lamar, cursing, pulled over to the side of the empty road. When he looked over at George's Mary, she was crying.

"Take some more aspirin if it hurts that bad," he said.

"It ain't that it hurts." She could still barely open her mouth when she talked and her words were slurry and hard to catch. "Maybe I don't like it that I'm an old ugly toothless woman."

"Well, I can't fix that and fix this tire both," Lamar said. He got out of the car to get out the tire irons and the air pump. Fortunately there was a spare tube, so he didn't have to patch the damn thing, but it was hard work all the same, bad on his knee to bend down and harder still on his scarred and stiff hands as he pried the tire off the rim. As he worked, George's Mary got out of the car and walked off a little ways to be by herself, which suited him fine as well. The only good thing he could say about anything was that it was a warm enough day, over fifty degrees. He'd hardly needed his coat when they started out and now as he squeezed the new tube back into the tire there was sweat in his eyes just like it was August instead of February.

He pumped up the tire and put the old tube and the tire irons back into the toolbox, and then he was ready to go. But George's Mary was still off by herself, sitting on a rock and looking out over the open land that stretched off from the road. He started to yell at her to come and get back in the car, but he decided he'd be more gentlemanly about it. He walked over to join her. She was watching an armadillo root around in a shallow little draw about twenty feet away. The creature hadn't caught their scent and was too deaf even to hear Lamar's boots shuffling through the rock chips that covered the ground.

"You get back in the car and we'll get you home," he told her.

She didn't say anything in reply and didn't move. Lamar decided what the hell and sat down on the rock bench next to her. She threw another bloody cotton swab down onto the ground and said she missed Ben.

"I know it," he said.

"I'm a fifty-eight-year-old woman with half my teeth gone."

"They'd still be gone whether Ben was alive or dead. Wouldn't make no difference."

"I know, but I cared about that boy and he cared about me and now I got nothing."

"Ain't you a little late bringing all this up?"

"Didn't know I'm supposed to feel things like I'm on a train schedule."

She reached down and picked up the bloody cotton she had thrown on the ground and put it into her pocket instead. She turned to him and asked him if he thought about his folks much.

"Not much, I guess. I'm old and that was a hell of a long time ago."

"I think about mine."

She didn't seem to have any more to say about the matter, so he just sat there with her without either of them saying anything. It wasn't a bad place to sit on a mild February day, and he was tired from changing the tire anyway. He figured he would just give her whatever time she needed to get out of this mood she was in.

She didn't pity herself for the most part, but every once in a while the idea that she'd missed out on something got ahold of her and wouldn't let go for a few days. The first time he ever saw her she'd been beat all to hell and looked a lot worse than she did now. It had taken days for the swelling to go down enough to where you could see the natural shape of her head and the look of her face. He had come across her one morning when he was walking through the Flat looking for someplace to eat breakfast. She was sitting out in the dirt in front of Conrad's store groaning and staring off into space and holding her split lip together. None of her bones were broken, but they had worked her over pretty good in all sorts of ways. Lamar talked to the sheriff in the Flat and the duty officer at Fort Griffin and even a man on the vigilance committee but he couldn't get anybody interested. The teamsters that had done it had left in the night and had a good start, and anyway they were carrying freight for the biggest merchants in town. Even the other whores didn't care about her. She was new in town to begin with and she wasn't friendly. She'd been rude and pouty with the customers and it was no wonder somebody finally treated her like that.

Lamar was in his late thirties then, getting a good start for himself finally after too many years of wandering and drinking and not doing much worth a damn. Quanah Parker, the Quahada chief whose own mother had been a white captive, was the big man on the Comanche and Kiowa reservation in those days, and Lamar had talked him into leasing him some land for six cents an acre, a better price than even

Burk Burnett had got. He made enough money on that Comanche land grazing longhorns that he was able to buy a few thousand acres in Shackelford County and gave up the lease years before the government would have taken it away anyway for nothing. There was a homesteader's abandoned blockhouse on the land and he built his house around that piece by piece, and brought in Durhams and Herefords and worked on getting them right. He kept a few longhorns for nostalgic reasons but otherwise the hell with them. You could lose money thinking the years hadn't passed and the country was still wild.

When he came across George's Mary, he was living in his house on the ranch but he was as likely as not to be out in the line camps with the hands. He asked her if she could cook and keep house and she said she could do both. He decided that even if she was lying she would do a better job than he did, and it made sense to him to have somebody in the house when he wasn't around. So after she'd healed up a little he took her back. He wasn't sure why he trusted her, he just did. She was young and in those days was not bad-looking, but he never had anything to do with her that way, and it didn't matter to him if people thought he did. She turned out to be a better cook than he thought, though she was starchy and opinionated and acted like she was the one who'd done him a favor by coming to live with him and not the other way around. She was a little resentful at first when Sarey came into the picture, but she softened up soon enough, and when Ben was born he brought the feelings out of her that she'd been hiding away all those years. It was hard to look at her now, because the grief at losing Ben had never really left her face. She was old in a way that wasn't just old, but broken and angry and even kind of righteous, as if she meant for you to look at her and see that there was no such thing as being happy after all and you were a fool to have ever believed otherwise.

Lamar thought he probably gave the same impression to people. He and George's Mary were more alike than they were different. There weren't too many people who could say they'd lost their family to Indians, even back in those days. And they'd both been coaxed back into the world before having it close down on them again.

"I guess I'm about through sitting on this rock," she said at last in her tight-jawed mumble.

When Lamar stood up, he had to take a minute, because there were jabbing pains in his knee from kneeling in the dirt to change the tire and he was not all that sure it would even support him. But he worked it out enough to hobble back to the car.

"You're getting too decrepit to sit a horse," she said, goading him again after he'd been nothing but kind to her the whole day.

"To hell with you," he said, but he was glad she was getting some of her bite back.

When they got home she went straight to her bed and he opened the mail. One of the letters was from Gil Gilheaney. There was a check inside reimbursing Lamar for the money he had paid out. The letter said "unforeseen circumstances" had made it impossible for Gilheaney to continue the project after all. He wished Lamar well and thanked him for his patience and said he would be happy to recommend another sculptor if one was desired.

Clayton picked up a chair and threw it against the wall. George's Mary came out of her room and wondered why he didn't have the decency to give her even a moment of peace.

"Because the sonofabitch went back on his word is why!" Clayton said, thrusting the letter at her.

"Just tell me what it says. My teeth hurt too bad to read."

"It says he decided not to do the statue. Says it all calm and business-like, like it don't matter a dime to him. Probably got a commission that paid him more and he just decided mine wasn't worth the trouble. By God, I shook that man's hand and looked him in the eye."

"Well, that's too bad but there ain't nothing you can do about it. We don't really need a statue of Ben anyway if you want my opinion on the subject."

"Who the hell wants your opinion?"

Her jaw was throbbing too hard to take the insult personally. She just gave Lamar a dismissive wave and padded back to her room. He stood there in the parlor, too mad to sit down, not sure what to do with himself, just knowing he by god wasn't going to stand for being treated that way by some self-important artist who couldn't even keep his seat on a horse.

TWENTY-FOUR

Show me your goddam gas mask!" the inspection officer was yelling in Arthur's dream. It was night and mustard gas had pooled all around them in the shell craters, and the officer was staring down with disgust as Arthur tried to claw his way out of a putrid slurry of liquefied human remains. If he did not get his mask on in the next few seconds the mustard gas would kill him, but for some reason his fear of the officer's disapproval was greater than his fear of a hideous death.

Then the officer was gone and Arthur was on another part of the battlefield, horribly alone now in the foul blackness, listening to the Boche machine gunners laughing at him from their lines, taking their time with him. His mother and father and brother had just arrived. They were part of a group of battlefield tourists that was picking its way across the craters with their Michelin guides. His mother was calling his name. He tried to call back but before he could open his mouth a German soldier grabbed him from behind and was squeezing his face so hard with his big hands that he couldn't breathe. The man was breaking his face apart and the broken pieces were choking him.

Waking up did not stop the panic. The prosthesis had shifted in his sleep. It took him a moment to realize that it wasn't totally blocking his breath and that if he was calm he could guide it back into place along the bone-grooves in his jaw. He decided, when he had stopped shaking, that he must have turned over on his side while he slept and knocked the prosthesis against the wooden frame of his cot.

It was cold but there was no wind blowing and he was too shaken by the dream and the treacherous prosthesis to stay in his hut. He put on his coat and gloves and walked outside. He lived alone in a little *abris* he had built himself out of scavenged wood and *tôle*. It was just down the street, or what used to be the street, from the old *mairie* that had been destroyed in the bombing. In its place was the *mairie-baraque*, the temporary city hall that was merely a grander version of Arthur's own hut, and which he and the rest of the workers had hurried to finish for the visit of Poincaré the day before. The president had been traveling through the Devastated Zone, stopping at each destroyed town to marvel at the resiliency of the inhabitants and to promise that aid was on the way.

Much of the aid that the village had gotten so far, though, had come from America, where Lieutenant L'Huillier, who had grown up in Somme-Py, had been sent to raise funds. He had arranged some sort of fashion show in New York and enough money was starting to come in that in a few months they would be able to start building in earnest, not just *baraquements* but real stone buildings like they used to have before.

It was two in the morning, he supposed. He stood alone in the center of Somme-Py, his hand to his jaw, making sure he had worked the prosthesis back into place. It had been the worst dream he had ever had. The most horrible part had been his placid acceptance of the decaying human sludge in which he had been trapped as if it were quicksand. His mother's voice, helplessly calling his name, was still echoing out of the dream. He could hear it now, and he had to convince himself not to try to answer it.

They had brought him up Baptist but he had never taken to any of it that much. He didn't know about heaven but he had a pretty good idea that if there was one his mother would be waiting for him there and not looking for him in France like she had in the dream.

The night was moonless and the stars in their brightness only made it darker and caused him to feel more alone. The two hundred or so villagers who had moved back to Somme-Py to rebuild their homes were all asleep and so were the workers like himself who were being paid by the government to help them. There were still tables set out in front of the *mairie-baraque* from yesterday's rally, and their emptiness heightened his desolation. He had stayed in his hut while Poincaré spoke, even though Madame L'Huillier and her husband had tried to talk him into attending, saying that people would be grateful for the chance to honor a young American soldier who had already given so much for France. Maybe even Poincaré himself would want to shake his hand.

But Arthur hadn't wanted to shake the president's hand, or to meet any of the people flooding into Somme-Py from other destroyed villages, people he did not know and whose horrified and piteous glances he would have to endure. He only wanted to be around people who were used to him. The thought of traveling even to another village, let alone to Reims, or to Paris, with its throngs of gaping strangers, or especially back home to Texas, was as much the material of a nightmare as the war memories that hounded him in his sleep.

He walked behind the waist-high wall of a bombed-out house to piss. Dogs were barking, but at each other, not at him. The village dogs all knew him and he liked their company because they did not try to cheer him on or encourage him. He liked speaking to them in French.

Except for the barking dogs the silence in the village was consuming, not an absence of noise but the presence of some aggressive deadening force. In the bombardment before the attack on Saint-Étienne he had felt something like it, all that unbelievable commotion reaching at its most intense pitch a crescendo of nothingness, the ruling silence of the universe bearing down, taking control.

Standing alone tonight in the center of the village, in the cold air, he felt the horrors of the dream slowly dissipating. But the darkness all around him and the foreign cosmos overhead greatly amplified his loneliness, and finally he had to retreat back into his *abris* so he wouldn't be exposed any longer to that crushing emptiness. He put a few more sticks of wood into the stove. He was still too scared and too alone to sleep, so he lit his lantern and pulled out the letter he had received that afternoon from Maureen Gilheaney. He had read it three times already but he had not yet memorized it like he had the others. It was still new enough that he felt a sense of keen anticipation as he slipped it out of its envelope.

Dear Arthur,

Please, Maureen from now on. "Miss Gilheaney" makes me feel old, and this has been the sort of week when I don't care to feel any older than I already am. Some rather puzzling and painful things have happened—personal things which fortunately are much too complicated to explain, so you are hereby spared the spectacle of my self-pity. (Sorry—I just realized I'm sounding breezy and dismissive, and that's not a tone I mean to strike. I don't know what sort of tone I mean to strike, in fact. Honesty, I suppose, but not if that means detailing my trivial troubles to someone who has suffered so much *real* pain.)

There is one disappointing piece of news about the statue I must tell you. Almost at the moment of its completion, before it was to be cast in plaster and then sent off to the foundry to be finally cast in bronze, the piece was destroyed. The stove in the studio went out and the clay froze. There was quite a discussion in our house about whose fault this was, though neither my father nor I is in a mood to accept the blame, and it doesn't matter anyway. The point is that the statue of Ben won't happen now. I'm not sure my father has the will anymore to start all over again. When he was younger this would have been a terrible setback but he would have gotten over it soon enough, in fact it might even have invigorated him. But he's not as resilient as he was. He's sixty now. His hands are hurting him, arthritis I think—though he doesn't talk about it and I'm sensible enough not to ask.

I know you were enthusiastic about seeing the statue of your friend and I'm sorry. Daddy told me that he wrote Mr. Clayton to tell him that the deal is off and to return his money. Fortunately there is another commission so the bills will be paid, although I don't think my father has much interest in the subject, not the sort of interest he had in portraying Ben.

Yesterday a delivery truck pulled up to the house and unloaded four big wooden crates from the Coppini Foundry in New York. I think I told you about my "Spirit of the Waters" sculpture. Well, here it was, or at least the four panels—the granite base is still to be contracted for and manufactured. I know I should have been thrilled when I looked at the finished bronze but I just felt terribly flat instead. Maybe it's just because of the last few weeks, but I wonder if it's something more, the idea that nobody cares about this kind of thing as much as we pretend they do. I've done a nice decorative piece but that's all it is, just decoration. Just something to relieve the plainness that would be there without it. But maybe we're all mistaken in thinking that plainness—or even emptiness—is something that needs to be relieved. I suppose you could even say that about the statue of Ben. It could be that Ben's absence is memorial enough and that the best thing you could have said about my father's statue, even if it was a great work of art, was that it was beside the point.

Well, it's very late—I can't sleep tonight—and I see that Miss Gilheaney is making no sense. Is it very cold there? Do you need anything that we could send you, like a warm coat or gloves? Now I'm sounding like your mother instead of your friend, but I'd like to send you something. Something that could be useful to you in your new life in France or remind you—in a good way—of your life back here in the States, in Texas. I know you said you aren't ever coming home but you're very young and sometimes young people think that when they decide something they're bound to it for the rest of their lives. I guess that's an example of the cheap unasked-for advice you get from someone who managed to set a trap for herself but hasn't quite managed to find the way out.

I shouldn't even mail this but I probably will.

Maureen

When he'd first read the letter, he hadn't known what she was so upset about and he still didn't. Something seemed to have gone wrong between her and her father. He was pretty sure there was more to it than just what had happened to the statue. She had never sent him a photo so he couldn't picture her one way or the other. But he had a sense of her through her letters, somebody who was unhappy and lonesome, who was too proud to come out and say it but needed somebody to know it just the same. It was odd that he was the person she had chosen to tell, somebody she had never seen and would probably never meet, somebody she would look away from in horror if she ever saw his face.

It was funny to think she was the only person in the whole United States he wrote letters to and got letters from. Somebody he didn't even know. He felt that if she were here he could talk to her in a way he couldn't talk to those girls from Smith College. Maybe it was because she was old, in her thirties; maybe it was the way something was gnawing at her, something that she wouldn't say or maybe couldn't even name. Nothing seemed to have been gnawing at those college girls. It was like they had been born into the world already knowing what it was all about and how to make their way through it.

He didn't want to try to go back to sleep after that dream. He took out one of the school tablets that had come in the boxes of supplies from the States and sharpened a pencil with his pocketknife over the stove, watching the tiny shavings flare up as they hit the fire. He sat at the edge of his cot with his jacket still on and a piece of scrap lumber for a writing desk and wrote Maureen Gilheaney back.

He said he was sorry to hear about what had happened to the statue and sorry to hear she was out of sorts. He said he had been having a bad night himself, starting with the dream about his folks. Now he was sitting here afraid to go to sleep again and feeling pretty lonesome. He told her it was like he could see all at once the emptiness of the Champagne fields and the rest of France beyond it, and past that the whole dark ocean. All of it seemed to exist just to separate him from the home he had once had and the person he had once been. He understood what she said about setting traps for yourself but he still didn't think there was any point in ever going back to Texas. He'd had some childhood friends in Ranger, and he'd had some other friends he'd made in the army, but it couldn't be the same with them now and he knew it. All of them looking at him, or trying not to, and remembering how he had been. She was his only friend now. He didn't mean that like it sounded, like he was feeling sorry for himself, it was just true. And he'd never even talked to her or seen a picture of her. He asked her would she please just keep writing even if she felt bad like she had when she wrote that last letter. It made him feel like somebody was really talking to him, not just trying to be kind.

TWENTY-FIVE

The outright anger between Gil and Maureen had lasted no more than a day. It had quickly shifted to a tone of heart-sick civility. They spoke to each other, they ate their meals together. Mrs. Gossling was not yet back, since she had to sort through her dead brother's belongings and deal with his many creditors. Gil had written to her to take as long as she needed, had sent her a week's wages, and had not mentioned what had happened to the Clayton statue because of her abrupt departure. The poor woman was distressed enough.

He would sail for France in two weeks and he and Maureen would have a respite from each other's company, each other's silent resentment and despair. She had never told him exactly what had happened with Vance Martindale, except to say he had turned out to be married and for complicated reasons had not been able to tell her so. The complicated reasons, Gil assumed, had amounted to nothing more than his selfish wish to take advantage of her ignorance, but there was no point in railing against him. She knew now the kind of man he was, she had suffered enough from that knowledge without her father driving the point home.

He wanted to comfort her somehow but of course that was out of the question. She was too proud and too hurt, and his own angry and wounded spirit was still in the way of his truly reaching out to his daughter. Gil knew no other cure for despair than to work himself through it, but even as he made his preliminary sketches for the La

Salle he was losing faith in the old remedy. He was closing in on the end of his career with no works to his name that he thought would truly last, nothing visible in the future but dispiriting works for hire.

She had many questions about her grandmother and he answered them as clearly as he could while they cleaned the brittle clay off the armatures of the man and the horse. Much of what Maureen had learned as a girl about Margaret Gilheaney still applied. She had been a talented, loving, enterprising woman of great intelligence and conviction, independent in her thoughts except for her inflexible fidelity to the Church and its teachings. She had been married to a failed and damaged man, had raised two boys, one of whom had died. Gil had misled Maureen only about the date of her grandmother's death, but he could not pretend that this strategic falsehood had been anything other than a poisonous lie, a lie that had shaken her own identity and shattered her trust in the father she had once worshipped.

When the armatures had been cleaned they shoved them to one side of the studio to clear space for the La Salle armature he would build when he returned from France. It would have made more sense to simply dismantle the Clayton armatures but he did not have the heart to do that right now.

He went into the house to eat a sandwich. Maureen said she was not hungry. When he came back to the studio he found her standing in front of her Spirit of the Waters panels, silently and ruthlessly appraising their worth.

Gil had been very favorably surprised when they had first lifted the panels from their packing crates, and his initial reaction still held. Something had happened to Maureen's images in their journey from clay, then to plaster, then to bronze. He had seen it many times before, the depth of the bronze and the luster of the patina imparting an authority that had not been there before. He had not expected it to happen in this case, but it had. The forced movement he had seen before in the flights of the birds and the rush of the water now felt more natural, and the draftsmanlike figures were more dynamic. There was some other new dimension as well, something that must have resided in the piece all along. Maybe it had something to do with the fact that the sculptor was a woman. The subjects were not framed or pushed or defined, there was no statement made, no artistic agenda promoted. The artist had nothing to prove, no interest in testing herself against the expectations of the viewer. The piece was simply about what her eye had seen and what her hands had rendered.

He continued to watch Maureen as she silently regarded the panels. There was more scrutiny than worry on her face, so perhaps she had given herself a break. He was cautious about praising her work in front of her now. After the bitter words that had passed between them, she would read his praise as false encouragement, or as a pathetic bid for forgiveness.

"How do you feel about them?" he decided to ask her.

She didn't speak, didn't turn her head to look at him. She just shrugged. Gil went to his modeling stand and back to work on a preliminary clay sketch for the La Salle, though he would not begin working in earnest on the piece until he had met with Monsieur Du Prel in Paris.

"I suppose it will look all right on the bridge," Maureen said after a moment.

"I suppose it will too."

"It was a mistake to do it in four separate panels. If I'd been thinking, I could have made a big relief that—"

She had abruptly broken off because Lamar Clayton had just opened the door.

"I knocked on the door of your house, but there wasn't nobody there," Clayton said.

"Come in," Gil told him. His fingers were moist from working the clay and he wiped them with a rag before offering his hand to his surprise guest.

Clayton cast his eyes around the studio. He nodded to Maureen. He was wearing the same suit he had worn to the Old Time Trail Drivers banquet and in the daylight it looked too big for him, hanging rather than draping on his rangy stockman's body. His shirt collar was a size too large as well, gaping at his sunburned neck. He had lost a little weight, his hair was grayer.

"I didn't know you were coming," Gil said.

"Didn't know I was either till I got your letter saying you weren't going to live up to your part of the bargain."

"I'm sorry. I regret having to cancel the commission. There was no way for me to continue."

"Why?"

Gil directed his guest's attention to the armatures shoved up against the wall of the studio. "There was an accident. The clay froze. I lost months of work."

"So you need more money. Why didn't you tell me that instead of just saying you quit?"

"It's not a question of money."

"What is it a question of?"

"Of my strong feeling that I don't have it in me to do it all over again, to get it right, as I had it the first time."

"You'll get it right in a different way."

"No, it would be a second-rate work."

"How do you know that?"

"Because I know it."

Clayton turned to Maureen. "Is that what you think too?"

"It's what he says, Mr. Clayton, and so I believe it."

It was true, she had come to believe it. Her father was working on the La Salle sketches without heart, without excitement. She had never seen him work that way. At first she had mistaken his despair for an uncharacteristic bout of self-pity, but it ran deeper than that, deep into his broken sculptor's heart.

"I said in my letter I could recommend another sculptor," Gil said to Clayton. "I would be happy to do that. There are a number of excellent—"

"I don't need you to recommend another sculptor. If I wanted another one I would've found him myself. I'm going to hold you to this contract, Gilheaney."

Gil stared at him, seeing not the bereaved father who had wanted to memorialize his son but the angry, unbending man who had driven that son away.

"You're not going to hold me to anything," he said.

"By God, you try me and you'll find out."

"Let's go into the house," Maureen said, "and discuss it there."

"No, Miss Gilheaney, I believe we better discuss it right here."

Gil stormed across the room to his desk, pulled open a drawer, hastily thumbed through a file of contracts, withdrew the one for the Clayton and slammed it on the desk.

"If you would read this, you'd see that each party has the right to withdraw from the deal at any time. The clause is standard in all my contracts. It's there for your protection as well as mine."

Clayton grabbed the document and swept his eyes across it. He set it back down on the desk, silently conceding the point.

"You're right, it's here in the contract, but I never thought you'd use those words to quit on me. I thought I had a better sense of what kind of man I was dealing with."

"You're dealing with a man who doesn't want to deliver to you an inferior product, and for that you should thank me. You should thank me and now that you've had your say you should leave my studio."

Clayton's face was so inflamed with anger that for an absurd moment Gil wondered whether they were going to come to blows after all. But as the standoff wore on, the tension started to drain from Clayton's face and posture. He did not back down, he just looked away and shrugged his shoulders and seemed to decide the hell with it.

"You said it was going to be your best work."

"That's right. I did."

"And you're just going to walk away from it?"

"The piece was destroyed, Clayton. You may not know what a devastating thing that is to an artist, but you'll have to take my word for it. The statue was in my grasp once; it's not anymore. If I continued I'd be taking your money under false pretenses. The only thing I can do is to let it go."

Clayton looked to Maureen, as if she could explain this to him. But there was nothing she could say, or was willing to say, and she saw that he took the blank look she gave him in return as a rebuke.

He turned back to her father.

"This statue's got you scared, ain't it?"

"I don't know what you mean. And if that's what you wanted to tell me, I'm sorry you felt you had to come all this way to do so. Maureen will see you out."

"The hell anybody will see me out," Clayton said.

THE DOOR slammed shut, Clayton was gone, and Gil went back to his La Salle sketch, angrily squeezing the clay onto the miniature wire armature. After five minutes of his industrious silence Maureen couldn't take it anymore.

"Are you pretending that just didn't happen?"

"I'm not pretending anything. I'm simply working."

"I don't understand why you had to be so defiant."

"The man accused me of—I don't even know what. Duplicity. Cowardice. Do you suppose I'd let someone talk to me like that in my own studio?"

"He was giving you another chance."

"I didn't want another chance. Haven't I made myself plain enough on that point? Are you as thick as he is, Maureen?"

"Yes, Daddy, I'm terribly thick. I must be, since I'm so easy to deceive."

"That's not what we're talking about. The man came in and—"

"It *is* what we're talking about. We haven't even started to talk about it!"

He went back to work. He didn't bother to give her the courtesy of firing back. She watched him as he narrowed his eyes, focusing all his attention on his sketch, creating a little clay figure. All at once his mighty vocation seemed absurd, a child's pastime.

"You've thrown this commission away," she told him. "You're unbending and prideful. All you care about is dominating your clients, not satisfying them. That's why we had to leave New York, because of your pride. You made us move to Texas. You made us move here and look what happened."

"Look what happened. I don't know what you mean by that."

"Yes, you do."

"That I killed your mother? Is that what you mean?"

But she wouldn't let herself go that far. She watched him in silence as he continued to work, shutting her out, shutting out what she was saying. He squeezed another fistful of clay onto the armature but he felt such a jolt of pain from his arthritic thumb that he had to pull his hand away as if from an electric wire.

He gave the pain a moment to subside and then went back to the sketch.

"You should give your hands a rest if they're hurting you," Maureen said.

He ignored her advice. Almost at once, his hands were hurting again, but he forced himself to keep working, as if it was the pain he was trying to dominate and not the clay. When he could stand it no longer he pulled away again.

"You're making it worse, Daddy. Please stop working."

"I'll stop working when I want to."

He stared at the sketch with cold-blooded scrutiny, decided he hated it, and began ripping the clay off the armature.

"What about the boy?" Maureen said.

"What boy?"

"Ben Clayton. Did you even care about him?"

"You're not making any sense. Ben Clayton was a subject. I didn't know him, you didn't know him. And he's dead, so it won't matter to him in the slightest if there's a statue of him or not."

Three hours later the two of them sat down to dinner at the kitchen table. Maureen had made potato soup. Gil wore the splints that Urrutia had prescribed for his hands. It was awkward for him to wield his soup spoon, but the effort gave him something to concentrate on as they sat in silence, avoiding each other's eyes. They both seemed to recognize there was no reason to talk anymore about the day's poisonous topics, no point in bringing their seething resentments back to the surface.

"I'm going to France with you," Maureen announced.

"What?"

"You may not care anything about Ben Clayton, but I do."

"I don't understand you. How will going to France make any difference one way or the other?"

"I want to meet his friend. This village he lives in, Somme-Py, it's not far from Paris. There are even tours you can take to the battlefields. I want to go there and meet him."

"Why?"

"I don't have to give you a reason. I don't know the reason. I just have this idea I can be of help to him somehow. I don't have to go with you. I can book my own passage on another ship. I have money from my commission. It's mine to do with as I see fit."

"Go some other time. We'll be terrible company for each other. Why now?"

"Because unlike you I can't just move on to the next thing and forget all about Ben Clayton."

TWENTY-SIX

They sailed from Galveston on the *San Jacinto,* stopping first at Key West and then four days later in New York, where they embarked on a Cunard liner, the *Caronia,* for Liverpool and at last Le Havre. So soon after the war, with so many passenger ships still out of service, the voyage had been the most direct the agent could arrange, but they had still been almost two weeks at sea, two weeks of awkward small talk with her father in dining salons and on promenade decks. But now that Maureen was sipping a *café crème* in Paris on a fiercely cold afternoon, the act of getting here seemed to have telescoped into nothing. It was as if she had simply awakened one morning, blinking with wonder, into a new world.

She sat at an inside table in the Cloiserie des Lilas, studying without much admiring Rude's statue of Marshal Ney on the corner outside. Her father had told her to wait for him in the cafe, which he remembered from his days as a young man subsisting on nothing while he studied at the École des Beaux-Arts. It was still full of artists and writers, solitarily drawing in their sketchbooks, composing stories in their blue notebooks, or huddled together in dynamic argument as the platters piled up on their tables. Some of the arguing voices belonged to Americans, holding forth about this or that in their stridently accented French.

Vance had probably come here, she thought, during his little sabbatical after the war. She could picture him as the center of attention at one of the tables, everyone galvanized by his energetic opinions boldly delivered in imperfect French. It just now occurred to her that while he had been lingering in Paris as a young man mostly untouched by the war, his invalid wife might very well have been wondering why it was taking him so long to come home.

She tried to push the thought away, along with all the anger and futility that went with it. Vance had been thoughtful enough to let a few weeks pass before he wrote her a long letter, apologizing, explaining, castigating himself, hitting all the proper notes, baring his heart with eloquent precision. But he had been a little too enthusiastic in owning up to all the wrongs he had done her. She could feel his satisfaction as he composed his lines, his conviction that she would be moved and stirred by his searing self-criticism. It had taken all her will not to answer him. What could she do? Accept his apology and pick up things where she had left them, on the verge of becoming an occasional mistress to an inconstant married man?

Her bitterness toward him could not quite erase the longing she still felt, particularly now that she had crossed the ocean and had a sense of what it might have been like to be in Paris with Vance. Laughing, licentious Americans were everywhere, with all the time in the world to kill lounging in the cafés or dancing at the Bal Bullier. It would have taken no great effort to convince Vance to run off to Paris, to leave his wife and his job behind. They could have been just another scandalous pair running from convention, and all the more interesting, all the more accepted, for their crimes.

But once again she was alone, sitting here with her *café crème* and Professor Curtis' book about the Venus de Milo. She and her father had plans to see the Venus at the Louvre tomorrow. But Paris itself, for all its vivacity, seemed like a museum to her. You could walk through the crowded streets of Montparnasse without encountering any stark reminders of the war, unless all that frenetic eating and drinking and dancing and arguing had something to do with a collective release of tension. She had seen a few wounded soldiers but not many, and none as grievously damaged as Arthur Fry.

Though she had always yearned to see the Louvre, to stand face-to-face with the great works of art that she had seen only in books, the idea of it felt oddly hollow to her now. The errand she was on was more urgent and personal. Ben Clayton's death, Arthur Fry's shattered face, her father's failure with the Clayton statue, and her role in that failure, and then the hurt and fury in Lamar Clayton's expression when he learned the project was over, as if Gil Gilheaney's artistic defeat was a personal affront—all of this was bound up together.

She was not entirely sure why she had decided she must come to France, but once she had declared it out loud to her father the idea had taken on an urgent logic of its own. She had written Arthur immediately and had received his surprised reply only a day or so before they sailed. Yes, he had said, of course she and her father were welcome to visit, though there was nothing to see in Somme-Py and nowhere to stay and he was nervous about anybody seeing him, especially her for some reason. He said he didn't think there was any way to prepare her for what his face looked like. There was a tone of puzzlement in the letter, more puzzlement really than expectation.

She had written back immediately, full of reassurances and casual comments that she hoped would answer his unstated question of why she was coming at all. They would be in Paris, only a little more than a hundred miles away, it would be a shame to be that close and not have a chance to say hello in person. But she knew there was a deeper purpose; she just did not know what it was. Maybe she wanted to coax Arthur home somehow. Maybe she just wanted to visit the places where Ben had fought and died, so that she could be sure her father's abandonment of the boy's statue did not amount to a betrayal of his memory.

Through the window she saw her father striding down the Boulevard du Montparnasse. She could see the frustration on his face as he entered the café. He was an hour late and he apologized to her as if to a stranger, a symptom of the posturing civility that now seemed to define their interactions. They had established this polite distance as a way of tabling their resentments. They had kept it up on the long steamship voyage, and now they had brought it to Paris.

"As I expected, Monsieur Du Prel was a windbag," Gil said, then turned to speak to the waiter in acceptable French. "I think he approves of me. He ought to. I sat there looking interested while he recited the whole family history through a hundred generations. It took him a long time to get around to showing me the stuff I wanted to see."

"Was it worth seeing?"

"A couple of portrait sketches that might be of some help. And a bust. He says it was taken from life, after La Salle appeared at Versailles when he returned from his Mississippi expedition, but I doubt it. There's some authentic period clothing at the Invalides I should see. He's calling around to the director to arrange an appointment.

"I stopped in at the hotel on my way over here," he said as the waiter brought his coffee. "This was at the desk for you."

The letter he handed her was addressed in the handwriting they had both come to know as Arthur Fry's.

Gil watched his daughter. Her face clouded over as she read, and finally she slipped the letter back in its envelope and put it on the table between them.

"He can't bring himself to call me Maureen. It's still 'Dear Miss Gilheaney.' "

"May I read it?"

"You may if you like. I don't care, it doesn't matter. He doesn't want me to come after all. So that's that, I suppose. More time at the Louvre. Do you mind if I go back to the hotel?"

"Of course not. I'll knock on your door about seven and we'll find someplace to have dinner."

She nodded and walked hurriedly out of the café, meaning to outpace the tears that Gil saw were coming. She had left the letter on the table for him to read.

> Dear Miss Gilheaney,
>
> I sent this to the Hotel Printania. That's where you said you were going to stay in Paris and I hope you get this.
>
> I know you and your dad have come a long way but as you explained to me it was a business trip and you were coming anyway. I hope you don't take this wrong but I decided maybe it would not be a good idea for you to visit Somme-Py. This is not because I don't want to see you but I guess because I'm not ready for people to see me. We have gotten to know each other "through the mail" as they say and that is probably the best way to keep things for now. Maybe someday if I ever get used to the way I look I will come back to the States and say hello to you in person and we can have a good visit. Please do not be offended at this. I do not mean any offense. I am

just "shy" about my appearance, and that is why I am writing this. Please don't be mad at me either, although I understand if you can't help it.

I've been thinking about Ben a lot since you told me about what happened to the statue and that your dad doesn't plan to do it over again. I decided maybe that's for the best. If Ben were still here he'd probably say he didn't need a statue of himself. He was a hero that day if you ask me but I don't think he felt like one. He was mostly just boiling over about something he found out. Well I guess that's the same thing as courage but I don't know. But the more I think about it the more I think he wouldn't want his dad to turn him into a statue so I guess this all worked out all right.

I hope we can still be friends. I just don't like people looking at me especially people who mean to be kind and I should have told you that earlier but I didn't know it yet really.

Yours sincerely,

Arthur

"Boiling over about something he found out."

Gil read the line again, puzzled by it, stirred by it somehow. Then he put the letter back into its envelope and slipped it in his pocket and left some centimes on the table.

He must have already walked five miles that afternoon, from Monsieur Du Prel's flat near the École Militaire into the heart of Montparnasse. He still remembered all the streets—avenue de la Motte-Picquet, rue de Grenelle. He still remembered himself here as a young man, staying long past dark in the studios of the École both because he was in a feverish working mood and because there was plenty of heat, which was not the case in the dingy apartment in rue Saint-André-des-Arts he had shared with two other students. He had had a patron of sorts, the rich son of a Tammany ward boss who had been an early believer in Gil's promise and proposed to pay for his crossing, tuition, and board in exchange for busts of himself and his wife and annual commemorative medallions of his four children. Even with his patron's stipend, he had been hungry much of the time, but gloriously so, a feeling that his body was a raging furnace and that there was not enough fuel in the world to feed it. He had felt that about his work too, which had raged as well, demanding all of him, all of his strength and spirit. He had stared into the windows of the artists' supply shops in the rue de la Grande-Chaumière with as much hunger as when he passed the oyster shuckers outside the restaurants along Boulevard Raspail. There had been love affairs, blazingly brief but remembered now, almost forty years later, in hypnotic precision and detail. He had learned French and part of the intoxication of that time had involved the invention of a new self in a new language.

He walked now toward the Place de l'Observatoire and the Luxembourg Garden. Streetcars and horse cabs passed him by, and though it was cold, young people were scurrying along the street, chattering with each other, alive with energy and expectation, a new crop of human material sprouting up to replace his own generation, which would soon be ploughed under and forgotten. He was an aging, unfulfilled man. The world had changed without consulting him.

The fountain at Place de l'Observatoire had been only a few years old when he came to France, and like most of the other students he had viewed it with disdain. Carpeaux's contorted female figures had seemed hackneyed even then, and Frémiet's horses, rearing from the water in such fury that they seemed to be trying to claw their way out of the fountain, were just more overwrought allegory. The pointless symbolic weight of the whole affair was heavier than the bronze from which it was made.

He was more forgiving of it now—now that he was older and less forgiving of himself. The fountain had been here for decades and would be here for many decades and even centuries more. The nudes standing above the rearing horses, holding aloft a hollow sphere, did not seem quite as awkward to him today. He had once felt free to regard this sculpture with contempt, but now he was not all that sure he could do better. Where were the works of his own that would endure, the works he had so confidently envisioned long ago? All he could think about were his losses, his destroyed masterworks.

He walked past the fountain and along the tree-lined street into the park, listening to his shoes tread upon the gravel paths in the wintry silence. Two women sat bundled in shawls on one of the benches. He could hear fragments of their conversation as he passed; they were talking about their sons who died in the war as they watched a solitary girl and her father push a toy boat on the margins of the shallow lake.

On the far side of the palace Gil noticed a young man in a brown suit, with longish, wayward hair and a cap pulled down on his forehead. He stood alongside the Medici Fountain, his hand resting lightly on the trunk of a horse chestnut tree. The young man was squinting slightly, looking for someone or something in the distance. This trivial act somehow gave his face a look of dawning expectation. It was not just the look in his eyes, it was his posture too. If Ben Clayton were standing like that, Gil speculated, with that slight bend in his right knee, his head notched down a little, it would bring the whole body into a different alignment, a different relationship with the unseen something out there on the prairie horizon.

As Gil watched, the man removed his hand from the tree and called out to someone on the far edge of the park. Then he walked off. He had ceased to be interesting. But for a moment he had been Ben Clayton himself, alive, settled into the future whose arrival he had been glimpsing, the future that never came.

"WHAT DO YOU THINK he means?" Gil asked Maureen at dinner that night. "What was Ben 'boiling over' about? What did he find out?"

"I don't know. It doesn't matter now. I could write back and ask him, but what's the point?"

"I think we should go see him."

"Arthur? You read the letter, Daddy. He asked us not to."

"He was probably just in a bad mood when he wrote it."

"Well, if his mood improves, maybe he'll write again and invite us."

"We'll be gone by then."

Maureen looked up from her turbot and out the window toward the congested carrefour. They had stopped for dinner at La Rotonde, which had been a mistake. Everyone from their fellow passengers on the *Caronia* to the desk clerk at the hotel had recommended it as the place to be in Paris, but it was just a noisy hangout for Americans, the tables jammed together, the air foul with smoke, long-haired intellectual provocateurs insulting one another at the crowded bar.

"Why are you so interested in seeing him all of a sudden?" Maureen asked Gil.

"I had an idea for the statue today."

"You're not doing the statue, remember?"

There was no point in trying to continue a discussion in this echoing café. They ate their meal in silence and Gil paid the bill and they walked down rue Vavin on the way to their hotel on Notre-Dames-des-Champs. It was chilly but there was no wind and the static cold felt good. As the noise from the cafés on the corner receded, they could hear their footsteps on the pavement and the lazy clopping sound of the horse cabs.

"It's possible I might want to take another crack at it," Gil said.

"Well, take another crack at it, then, Daddy. Do whatever you want. I don't care."

It just came out. She had not planned to say such a thing, but after weeks of strained civility between them the raw words just erupted.

He paused for a moment in surprise, then kept walking beside her. She thought of him now as brooding and self-absorbed, almost a stranger. Trust in her father, in his love and consequential strength, had been part of the organic basis of her self. Walking down the avenues of Paris, she thought of the New York streets where she had grown up, like Montparnasse a teeming world of artists and writers and students and all sorts of in-between characters with big opinions. She remembered the colliding cooking smells from the narrow streets off Sixth Avenue, newsboys hawking the afternoon editions, and the haggard poets trying to hand-sell their fiery literary manifestos; the apartment where she had grown up, the sole adored child of her father and mother; the studio on Washington Square South with its wonderful light, especially in winter, where her childhood companions had been the bronze heads of business leaders and politicians who had commissioned busts of themselves from Francis Gilheaney; the patient voice of her father cautioning her to be careful with his tools, but to be heedless with the clay he set before her to model; the statue of Farragut in Madison Square Park that he took her to see again and again, declaring that in its deceptive foursquare simplicity resided all the beauty and mystery of art; the Italian restaurant Renganeschi's, on

West Tenth Street, where her father would take her and her mother to celebrate his finishing an important piece, where the owners and waiters would toast his success and present her with a special dessert; the sense of somehow being chosen to be this great man's daughter, as if of all the children in the world he trusted her alone to share the secret space of his studio, to learn the magic of giving permanent physical form to people who for the most part had already vanished from the earth.

He had lied to her not just about her grandmother but, it seemed to her, about all of this as well. Her whole life felt like an illusion that he had spun, that he was still spinning.

"I don't know what else to say to you," he said wearily. "I've admitted I was wrong, I've apologized as sincerely as I know how."

She looked away, tears filming her eyes, quietly accepting this declaration for what it was as they walked into the hotel and got their keys from the clerk. They climbed the winding stairs. Both of their rooms were on the sixth floor and she watched how her father climbed ahead of her with even strides, each firm footstep lending strength to the next. By the time they reached the top she was winded but he was not. In the dim electric light his face had a shadowy, stricken look.

"As far as the statue goes," he said, "I declared it to be a dead issue, so I suppose it should stay that way. But I think I gave up too soon."

She hefted the heavy key and opened the door to her room. She lingered for a moment in the hallway.

"Even if you decided to start over with the statue, what would be the point of seeing Arthur?"

"Well, I have a feeling there's more to learn. Don't you agree? More to learn about Ben."

TWENTY-SEVEN

They went to a branch office of Thomas Cook near the Opera. Gil told the agent he did not want a conventional tour of the battlefields but wanted to hire a car and a driver who knew the Champagne region and was familiar with the condition of the roads in the Devastated Zone. The agent had to consult with his manager about this out-of-the-ordinary request, but they determined there was a car available, along with a reliable guide-interpreter, and the trip could be arranged for six hundred francs. Gil and Maureen were asked to sign a waiver and warned against touching grenades, shells, or loose wire in the war area. They would also do well to bring mackintoshes and wear strong boots, as the battlefields offered unsound footing. They were given tickets for the morning train to Reims, where the car and driver would be waiting for them at the station.

After making these arrangements they went to the Louvre. In the sculpture galleries they stood before the Venus de Milo, Gil for the twentieth time, Maureen for the first. She read aloud to him from her book about the conflicting theories of Furtwängler and Reinach, about whether the statue was truly meant to be of Venus or, as Reinach contended, the wife of Poseidon.

Gil stood staring at the statue, pestered just as he had been as a young man by its ungraspable beauty. How exactly had the unknown sculptor pulled it off, that gorgeous torsion of the body, the near-blankness of the face, which somehow provoked an idea of ageless serenity and self-possession?

He left Maureen in front of the Venus to wander through the galleries, pausing before the massive Melpomene, and then the Diana with her fawn, and the running figure of Atalanta, both of which he had studied in his Paris days when his own work had been rather stiff and he had been vexed by the mystery of how to convey movement. And once more he stood in front of the thrilling Winged Victory of Samothrace, amazed anew by the drape of its garments, by its bold and urgent momentum, the dynamism with which the weight of the body was shifting in mid-stride from the left foot to the right.

After a few moments Maureen joined him there at the top of the grand staircase. The two of them stood staring up at the Victory without feeling the need to speak about it, just bound in appreciation. It was the first time in weeks there had been an easy silence between them.

They took the train from Gare de l'Est early the next morning and reached Reims before lunchtime. Their guide was waiting for them in the station. His name was Stuart. He was a middle-aged Englishman with owlish spectacles. He briskly took their bags and led them outside, where he tied the luggage to the top of the touring car as Gil and Maureen stared in amazement at the rows of houses hollowed out by bombs and at the piles of rubble that had still to be cleared away.

"As you can see," Stuart said, "Reims was rather knocked about."

"And the cathedral?"

"Quite the worse for wear, sir. Do you know it?"

"I haven't seen it for many years."

"We'll have a look on our way out of town."

The trip from Paris had been mostly unremarkable: fields, winter foliage, country lanes, towns huddled against the railroad siding. The war that had consumed the world and destroyed a generation seemed to have receded before them like a mist. But in Reims it was different.

Here it is, Maureen thought, as she looked out at the shattered streets. Here is the war. Stuart piloted the big touring car around the shell craters as they passed one ruined block after another, half the buildings, it seemed, roofless and empty.

"Good God," she heard her father say as the car turned onto a central street and brought them in sight of the shattered cathedral. "Stop the car."

Stuart pulled over on the torn-up square facing the cathedral's facade. Hotels and government buildings on either side of the square were almost completely destroyed. The cathedral itself still stood, but the facade was blackened by fire, some of the carvings shorn away by blasts, the great rose window above the main doorway empty of its stained glass.

Gil got out of the car and Maureen followed him. He stared at the facade of the cathedral and then turned in a slow circle, taking in the destruction. When he spoke to Maureen, his voice was steady but his eyes were filmy.

"I came here once when I was a student," he told her. "To see the carvings mostly. Just stood here and looked at them for hours. Feeling a kind of rapture, I suppose, as young people that age do."

He did not say what else had contributed to that rapturous feeling—a young woman named Maryse who worked in one of the artists' supply shops near the École. She had been a few years older than Gil, effortlessly slender, a small, watchful face under a towering crest of hair. Breezy and optimistic, she had disapproved of his solemn ambition, his sense that life was a forced march toward a fixed goal, and that an idle hour represented crucial ground lost. What was the point of being an American, she had asked him, if you don't allow yourself the freedom that is your birthright?

She spoke a little English but they talked mostly in French, and though she held forward-thinking and even strident political views it was gossip that truly animated her. She had been for a time the mistress of one of his professors, and she was still fond of him and greatly amused when Gil told her about the man's continuing helpless flirtations with students and shopgirls.

"You must take me to Reims," she told Gil one day. "People tell me my portrait is there."

He took her there. He did not think she looked at all like the famous smiling angel on the facade of the cathedral. The carved angel had a simpering, secretive expression, far from the open delight that animated Maryse's face. But she was amused by the fact that people told her there was a resemblance, and at odd moments while they were in Reims she would do her best to mimic the angel's mysterious and self-satisfied smile.

They had pooled their few spare francs for the train fare and a bare room in a small hotel off the rue Voltaire. They had hardly anything left over for food. They had no meals, just bread and cheese and a bottle or two of wine they had brought from Paris. He had meant to see everything, study everything, but he stayed in bed with her for most of the two days they were there, hungry, drowsy, drained of all earnest curiosity about the world.

On the second morning he left her sleeping and stood alone in front of the great cathedral, staring at the carvings on the western facade as the sun rose behind the twin bell towers. There were so many carvings of saints and angels and bishops and gargoyles, all of it so hectic and dense, that at first he had been repelled. It was too much art. But he made himself look at each portal, at the action represented: an infant Christ touching the forehead of a hermit, demons being cast out, heads being chopped off, the damned being led to hell, a multitude of seated figures with their hands raised in benediction. He was hungry for breakfast, hungry for the life to come, feeling as the sun rose that he was content and confirmed in his calling.

They had gone back to Paris and she had taken up with an ancient painter in his fifties with a spacious atelier. She had broken Gil's heart so cleanly and sweetly he felt almost grateful. The loss of Maryse was another thrilling sensory deprivation that set him on a higher plane and led him deeper into his art.

He stood now staring at the facade of the cathedral, wondering if she was still alive, trying to picture her at sixty-three or sixty-four.

He thought he noticed something and walked closer, scanning the tight rows of saints and angels, some of them intact, some not, that were crowded above the doorways.

"If you're looking for the smiling angel, sir," Stuart said, "I'm sorry to say it was decapitated in the first bombardment, in 'fourteen. But they found the pieces of its head and it'll be back together soon enough."

Gil turned back to the empty plaza.

"There was a statue of Joan of Arc here."

"She came through unscathed. They moved her before the worst of it started."

"It was by Paul Dubois," Gil explained to Maureen. "The Joan of Arc wasn't his best work, in my opinion, but I'm happy to hear it's survived."

Gil walked into the cathedral and Maureen followed, passing below the gables and buttresses thick with their sculpted figures and on into the nave. The floor had not yet been cleared. There were still piles of rubble, some of it made up of fallen pieces of statuary. Light flooded in from the broken vault, and through the open roof far above they could see the winter clouds streaming by.

They walked solemnly through the vast space, down the aisles where great tapestries had once hung, past broken tombs and pulpits and burned walls. As they walked, Stuart narrated in a reverent whisper, telling them which damage had been rendered in which years of the war; the terrible bombardments of 1917 were the worst, he said, with shells raining down on the cathedral for seven hours without a letup, a sustained and targeted assault.

From the expression on her father's face, from the way he nodded courteously but distractedly as Stuart kept up his monologue, Maureen thought she understood what was going through his mind. He was a monument maker confronted once again with the death of monuments, with the annihilating human contempt for what was supposed to be sacred and therefore safe.

For her part, Maureen was stirred by a sense of scale that was new to her. Her own unhappiness, her bitterness toward Vance, her anger at her father, were like some memory from another life. Nothing like that could register here. The cathedral was vast, but the destruction it pointed to had no limit. She had the sense that she and her father had left their world behind.

As they drove out of town Stuart continued his discreet narration: the German invasion, the French offensives that followed, Ludendorff's desperate but failed counterattack, finally the great push that broke the German line that took place after the Americans arrived in the summer of 1918.

"I'm a bit of an amateur military historian," he told them cheerfully. "Just off to the right, you see the great massif of Moronvilliers. Terrible fighting all along here. May I ask, sir, what brings you to Somme-Py?"

"We've come to locate a friend."

"Ah, well, first we'll have to locate the town, I'm afraid. Terrible fighting around there too, as you know. Somme-Py was one of the towns—a thousand of them altogether—that the Germans just wiped off the map. No place to stay there, of course. Nearest proper up-and-running hotel is in Verdun. I believe the company wired ahead for a reservation."

Gil nodded. He stared out at what used to be the landscape: dead fields, dead forests, old women pushing wheelbarrows full of scavenged lumber and wire, families camped out in the cellars of houses that had been blown away down to their floors. Men were at work everywhere in the scattered villages they passed, tearing down teetering walls, building back ancestral stone dwellings out of raw lumber. The dirt road was uneven and in places it simply disappeared, vanishing into massive shell craters that had not yet been filled. They swerved around the craters onto cropless fields, through rows of fruit trees with greasy black limbs, killed by fire or by poison gas. The winter sky was gray and the earth below was unnaturally devoid of color. The clothes of the people they passed were brown or black, or so old and worn that the color had faded into nothing. The only relief in this chromatic dead zone was the red roofs of the warehouses and dispensaries built by the French Red Cross.

The world they were driving through was sobering enough that even Stuart, their chatty, history-loving guide, finally gave up his commentary and fell into silence. They passed other cars going in the opposite direction, more war tourists with their Michelin guides to the battlefields and their box lunches, sightseers swarming over the vast open wound of the front.

He couldn't be too hard on them, Gil thought. Their curiosity was no more naked than his own. Maybe some of them had come to see where their sons or brothers had fallen, to lay a wreath on the ravaged ground. He himself was coming against the wishes of a young man he had never met, but who might hold some secret that would allow him to begin anew the work he had abandoned.

In another hour and a half Stuart announced they were arriving at Somme-Py, the village where Arthur Fry had told them he was living. Where exactly the village was—or had been—was hard to reckon. There was nothing left of it but a few teetering walls that rose above the debris-strewn ground like hoodoos in a desert. Some people were squatting in the cellars of their vanished houses, others were in thrown-together shacks with corrugated metal roofs, others in neatly built wooden shelters. They stared blankly at the passengers in the touring car as it made its way to what Gil guessed had once been the center of town, a crossroad in front of an imposing municipal ruin.

"That's the *mairie,*" Stuart said. "Of course it's nothing now. The new one is just there."

He pointed to a barnlike building made of new lumber twenty yards away, from which a young man in a kepi and blowsy blue coveralls was striding forward to greet them.

Maureen saw the man's welcoming smile and asked herself: could it be Arthur? But almost as soon as the thought formed she knew to dismiss it. This young man's face was whole, and though when he greeted them he spoke in courtly English he had a thick French accent.

"Welcome to Somme-Py. My name is André L'Huillier. You're Americans?"

"Yes," Gil said, returning his handshake, which in the French manner was brief and precise. "Francis Gilheaney. My daughter, Maureen."

"Are you from New York? Are you friends of Harry Collins?"

"We're from New York originally. At present we live in Texas. No, I'm afraid we don't know Mr. Collins."

A brief look of puzzlement crossed L'Huillier's face. "Please forgive me for assuming. Monsieur Collins is Somme-Py's great friend in the States. Last spring he was kind enough to host a fashion show there to raise money for our village. Several of his friends have come here to see the work for themselves."

"We're looking for Arthur Fry," Maureen told him.

"Arthur Fry?" The puzzled look returned. "May I ask—are you his family?"

"No," Maureen said. "Just friends. But we've come a long way to see him."

"Well, of course you must see him then. We hold Arthur in very high regard, along with all Americans. He is a great friend to Somme-Py. But I must tell you, during the war he suffered an—"

"We know about that," Gil said.

"Then let me take you to him. He's in our temporary city hall at the moment. I've set him to work helping us sort out the town records. We were fortunate to save them from the devastation."

They followed him into the wooden building, a drafty hall that looked more like a warehouse, with hundreds of boxes stacked against the walls and half a dozen young men—some dressed in coveralls like L'Huillier, others in threadbare suits—sorting through them.

"Supplies from America," L'Huillier said to Gil and Maureen. "Clothing and blankets and saucepans, that sort of thing. All critically needed here, of course. When the Germans came our people had to leave with only what they could carry, and when they came back everything they had left behind was gone."

He gestured to an open doorway cut into a plywood partition that served as an interior wall.

"Here you will find Arthur," he said. He smiled again and discreetly withdrew to talk to some of the men cataloging the supplies. There was a stiffness in the man's stride that Gil had not noticed before, and a palsied rigor in his upper back where part of his shoulder had been shot away.

Maureen touched her father's arm as they were about to enter the room.

"I think I should see him alone. Just at first. Do you mind?"

"Why should I mind? Please go ahead."

HE WAS sitting alone behind a desk. Like the building in which it sat, the desk was made of new lumber, a broad plank supported by sawhorses. His head was down, bent to the task of sorting his filing cards, and his concentration was deep enough that he did not look up when she entered the room. He wore the same coveralls as some of the other workers. His hair was sandy. When he lifted his head a bit and turned to sort through the filing box she saw his face. One side of it looked like something that had collapsed and then been awkwardly shored up, an assemblage of disproportionate planes that was only a rough structural approximation of the flesh and bone that had been blasted away.

He had not yet seen her; she still had the opportunity to silently withdraw without ever disturbing him. But instead she spoke his name.

He looked up at her and almost instantly shifted his head to the left, trying to hide his damaged face from this unexpected visitor.

"I'm sorry. I know you told me not to come."

She took a step or two forward.

"I'm Maureen."

He stood up politely, his hands at his sides, his face still turned away.

"Is it all right that I came? Please tell me if it's not and I'll go."

"No, ma'am," he said. "It's all right, I guess."

His voice was soft and slurry. The left side of his mouth was lipless and did not move when he spoke, though the joinery beneath the skin shifted in a way that was unsettling to see.

She walked up to him and offered her hand.

"I think we should say a proper hello."

He was wearing a glove with the fingers cut away and he took it off to shake her hand, looking down as he did so.

"My father is outside. He'd like to meet you as well."

"All right. I ought to finish this work, though."

"Of course. The last thing we want to do is get in your way. Maybe we can have dinner together, after you're off work. Are you angry with me, Arthur?"

"No, ma'am. I said I wasn't."

"Do me a favor, then. Call me Maureen instead of ma'am."

He nodded. She was about to go, but something else needed to be said.

"Please let's not be shy with each other. I've seen your face now. That's what you were afraid of, wasn't it? Showing me your face?"

"I expect so. I don't like it when people see me for the first time."

"Well," Maureen said, "the first time is over."

TWENTY-EIGHT

They sent Stuart ahead to spend the night in Verdun. There were no accommodations in Somme-Py, but André L'Huillier, the young man who had greeted them on their arrival, had insisted it would be his great pleasure to set up cots for them in the temporary town hall, and to host them for dinner in the shell of his former home.

"I was born in this house," L'Huillier declared as he poured the wine. They were seated at an Empire dining table, a proud piece of furniture half shattered by shrapnel. Crowded together on mismatched chairs were Gil and Maureen and L'Huillier and his young wife and, looking uncomfortable, Arthur Fry. "Of course when I was born it actually *was* a house and not the ruin you see today. But there were two walls left standing after the war, and that by itself was something of a miracle."

Candles burned on the table, and there was heat enough from the cookstove to make things reasonably comfortable, but the wind pressed against the canvas roof and vacant walls, and whistled wherever it managed to pass through the tied-down flaps. Madame L'Huillier had made a cassoulet, and Gil and Maureen had insisted on contributing to the meal with the baguettes and cheeses that Stuart had packed as a picnic lunch.

"This street was called rue du Clichet then," L'Huillier said. "It is rue Foch now. The war took away everything, even the names of our streets."

He raised his glass in a toast. "But tonight it has brought us new friends."

He was inquisitive, courteous, generous, his good nature intact after somehow surviving the slaughter on Mort-Homme during the defense of Verdun. He spoke fluent English and graciously translated the conversation for his wife, who spoke only French and who seemed vaguely oppressed by her husband's loquacious hospitality.

L'Huillier genially interrogated Gil on what had brought him and Maureen to Somme-Py, and when he heard the story of Lamar Clayton's unusual commission he asked a dozen informed questions about the work of the sculptor and the complicated process for transforming a clay or wax original into bronze.

Gil answered his host's inquiries as he glanced toward Arthur, sitting at the end of the table, carefully spooning cassoulet into the working side of his mouth, attentive but excruciatingly silent. Gil had not yet had the occasion to say more than a few words to him. As soon as Maureen had walked out of the *mairie* after meeting Arthur, L'Huillier had swiftly invited them all to dinner, which had necessitated a hurried logistical discussion with Stuart, who clearly had not relished spending the night in a bombed-out village when there was a warm bed waiting for him at a pension in Verdun.

Gil had barely had a chance to absorb the devastation of the boy's face. It was hard to train his eyes away from it, partly because he was as transfixed by horror and pity as any other mortal would be and partly because as a sculptor his instinct to shape and repair was so strong.

L'Huillier was talking about the fashion show that his friend Harry Collins had put on at the Willard Hotel in Washington for the Somme-Py relief fund.

"Jeanine and I were greeted with such great generosity," he said. "So many people so eager to help our little village. And to walk through the streets of Washington, to see the monuments and the White House! Very emotional for me. And your President Wilson is not well. I'm very sad to hear this."

He stood and raised his glass to Wilson. And then to America itself. His eyes were shining with emotion. He reached out and gripped Arthur by the shoulder.

"Monsieur Fry here, he is one of the Americans who helped save my country. Who is still saving it. Arthur, my friend, we in Somme-Py cherish you as one of our own. To us, you are a citizen of our village and of France. You have paid for this citizenship with your blood."

He was crying openly when he sat down, smearing the tears away and whispering a few embarrassed words in French to Madame L'Huillier, who patted his hand in comfort. He took another sip of wine. He drank too much, Gil suspected, and he also suspected his host was in a great deal of pain from his wounds. L'Huillier seemed like a naturally reticent man whose emotions had come unanchored by the horrors of the war. He hid nothing, his tears flowed easily, explosive pronouncements of love and friendship were elements of ordinary conversation. Surviving the war had left him so raw and grateful that he dared leave no tender thought unsaid.

And then there was Arthur Fry, whose thoughts were secret, whose anchor chains were tight. He was naturally bashful, but his shattering wound made him incalculably more so, his face always subtly averted so that when you looked his way you could get only a glancing impression of him. He responded courteously when spoken to but waited for the conversation to come to him. When he spoke, his voice was obstructed by the brutal device that held his face together, and you could feel the pain that it cost him to form the words.

"And so, Monsieur Gilheaney," L'Huillier declared; pronouncing his name "Zhil-ha-*nay,*" "you must be a remarkable sculptor."

"You would have to see my work to judge, Lieutenant."

"I see it in your face, Monsieur. In the way you move and talk. You reveal your genius." He turned to Maureen. "He *is* a genius, I hope. I wouldn't want to be mistaken."

"You're not mistaken," Maureen said, smiling slyly at her father—a welcome reminder of the warm repartee they had shared until recently. But then her attention returned again to where it had been all evening, to Arthur Fry. Though he was crowded in with them at the table, he seemed to be in a room by himself.

Gil had intruded upon Arthur's wary solitude because ever since abandoning the Clayton statue, he had felt his life going wrong, his work leveling out at a high level of craft that would never again rise to art. The clay crumbling off the armature had seemed to confirm the futility of his quest for greatness. The sight of that young man the other day in the Luxembourg Garden, the look of expectation in his eyes, had given him an idea of a way back in to the Clayton piece. But the door had opened only a crack. He needed to push it open, and his instinct told him that the place to try was here in the Devastated Zone, in the presence of this devastated boy who had been Ben Clayton's friend.

But he had only half-guesses about what Maureen was looking for, why she had traveled so far and reached so far to make a connection with Arthur. Was she trying to prove herself against her father, to let him know that she sensed value and vitality in a project that a disappointed old man had cast aside? Or did she just feel so betrayed by Gil and by Vance Martindale that she needed to be in a place that was already foreign, where there were no established trusts that could be broken?

Madame L'Huillier whispered to her husband. Gil no longer considered himself fluent in French, but he caught what she was saying: "Ask them to tell us something about this young man."

L'Huillier translated for Maureen, who was the only one at the table who did not speak French.

"My wife would like to know about the subject of your statue."

"Arthur is the one who knows about Ben," Gil said. He shifted his eyes to the young man at the end of the table. Arthur looked down at his plate. Everyone else had finished dinner, but eating was such a painstaking process for him that he had only made it through half his serving of cassoulet, and he seemed to regard the remaining portion as an unfinished chore.

Arthur looked up at Maureen, as if asking for instructions.

"Please," she said. "Unless it makes you uncomfortable."

"No, I'm comfortable enough talking about Ben, I guess," he said. He turned to Madame L'Huillier and spoke in French, apologizing for having to speak in English. She smiled patiently.

"I don't know what exactly to say, though," he told Maureen. "We were friends, that was pretty much it. I liked Ben better than most of the other boys in the company, and he got along with me fairly well, I guess. I remember we sat next to each other on the train almost all the way from Fort Worth to Hoboken, at least we did when we could get a seat. Some of the time we just had to lie on the floor, the train was so crowded. And of course we didn't know we were going to Hoboken. They wouldn't tell us anything and we couldn't write home about where we were. We crossed through Arkansas. That was the first time either Ben or me had ever seen a pine tree. Some of the boys thought we were going to go to Mobile to ship out for France but then we changed trains and headed up north."

Arthur paused and looked down again at his plate and then looked up again. His mouth was rigid and inexpressive. You had to look at his eyes to know he was smiling.

"But I guess you didn't want to know all about me riding a train and seeing a pine tree. You wanted to know about Ben. We talked a fair amount on that trip. I was pretty homesick already, but he wasn't, not that I could see. He'd already lost his mother and he didn't get along too well with his dad."

"Did he say why?" Gil asked.

"He mostly just said he was a sonofabitch."

"Sonofabitch. One of my favorite American words," L'Huillier said, and tried to translate it to his puzzled wife. L'Huillier laughed, but Arthur didn't laugh along with him. He met Maureen's eyes again. She could tell he knew more about Ben and his father than he was willing to disclose, but she wasn't going to press him.

"He talked kindly about their housekeeper. She had some kind of funny name."

"George's Mary," Gil said.

"Yes sir, now I recollect. George's Mary it was."

He paused and took a painful sip from his glass, carefully sluicing the wine into the side of his mouth.

"Ben knew a lot about how to do things. I guess it was growing up on that ranch. Nothing seemed to surprise him, he didn't get excited about anything much. I grew up in town mostly and I guess you could say I was a little more nervous in general about things than he was. On that train we were all pretty excited but we were scared too. All of us trying to hide it one way or the other. With Ben, though, it seemed like nothing bothered him much, at least not at first."

"Not at first?" Gil asked. "What do you mean?"

"Oh, I don't know what I mean. I was just saying that, I guess."

Gil was about to press him on the point, but he felt Maureen's touch on his arm, silently asking him to desist.

"I remember before we shipped out we had a day's leave in New York City. Most of the boys wanted to go to Chinatown and go to the hop dens but Ben wanted to see the Brooklyn Bridge. He said his mother had told him if he ever got to New York he ought to stand on that bridge and look at the view. I don't believe she ever got up that way herself but I understood from him that she wanted to real bad. So I guess he did that for her. I was glad I went along. We stood up on that bridge for about two hours. It was windier than any place I'd ever been, even windier than West Texas, but it was a clear day and I don't expect there's a better view anywhere else in the world. We watched the troopships sailing down the river and knew in a couple days we were going to be on one ourselves and we started talking about what it would be like. What France would be like and what war would be like. We sure found that out before too long. I remember Ben said we oughtn't to worry none because we were friends and would look out for each other and if we got killed then that would just be the way things turned out. I'd been a little scared and a little blue that day, being so far away from home, missing my folks, but Ben put my mind at ease. I reckon he always did that pretty well. If somebody was to give me back a day out of my life, I believe I might choose that one, 'cause I felt peaceful up there on that bridge with Ben."

Madame L'Huillier began to gather up the dishes. Arthur spoke to her in French, complimenting her on the meal, apologizing that he was unable to finish his portion.

"I'd like to know something about how he died," Gil said. He was aware of Maureen's disapproval at his probing, but he also knew that if he didn't probe, the possibility of learning anything of significance would be lost.

"Why do you need to know that?"

"I'm not sure."

"I thought you weren't doing the statue anymore."

"I'm not sure of that either."

"For some men," L'Huillier explained to Gil, breaking into the silence that had now settled over the dinner table, "it is not a problem to talk about the war. For others it is."

Gil nodded but kept looking at Arthur, who finally spoke.

"He was hit by machine-gun fire in the chest. It was in the town. We'd mostly taken it by then but there were still Germans on the other side of the Arne, this little river they got over here. He got killed and that's about all there is to it."

"I don't think that's all there is to it," Gil said. "You said in your letter to Maureen there was something Ben was upset about, something that he'd just found out."

"Daddy!" Maureen said.

"If I said that I don't recall what I meant," Arthur told him. "I don't see what difference it would make to anybody anyway."

"I'd like to know."

Arthur lifted his head and faced Gil full-on for the first time that evening, as if consciously challenging him with the sight of the wound that had taken away almost half his face. Gil could hear him breathing through the prosthesis, a laboring wheeze that was louder just then than the wind beating against the canvas walls of the house.

"It's pretty late," Arthur said at last, and stood up to go.

WHEN THEY LEFT the L'Huilliers' house Arthur walked alone down the dark main street of Somme-Py. Maureen followed him, not bothering to answer her father when he asked where she was going, just swiping away the question with a backward wave of her arm. She felt her father's eyes on her, the bitter recognition that she had passed out of his control, and then heard him turn and walk back in the other direction, toward the *mairie*, where they were to spend the night.

She caught up with Arthur just before he was about to enter a small wooden hut.

"I know you're angry with us," she said. "You should be. We had no right to come here."

She tried to look him in the eyes but his face was averted again.

"You look pretty cold," he said. "I've been here long enough I'm used to it, but you ought not to stand out here in the wind at night if you're not."

"Are you inviting me in?"

The question seemed to startle him. He didn't know what to do other than open the door to his hut for her.

"Don't go more than about a couple feet," he told her as she entered the dark room. "You're likely to bump into something."

He closed the door and brushed past her and lit a kerosene lamp. He opened the stove and threw a few more scraps of lumber onto the coals that were already glowing there. The room was warm and mostly bare: a cot to sleep on, a patched-up wooden chair to sit on, a few planks of wood to serve as shelves. Tacked to the wall was a wrinkled photo of a stern-looking couple in Sunday clothes staring at the camera lens as if it was something they were trying to identify.

"Are those your parents?"

"Yes ma'am. I carried that in my wallet all the way from Camp Bowie. Glad I did, 'cause they're gone now. Don't know if I told you that."

"Yes, you did. I'm sorry."

"I had a picture of my brother too but I lost that somewhere along the way."

She sat down on the chair while he remained standing against the wall.

"What was your brother's name?"

"Franklin. We called him Little Frank, though. I'd offer you some coffee or something to drink but I don't have any."

"That's all right. I just wanted to talk to you. My father and I have both been very forward, coming here when you asked us not to. And I'm afraid he was rude to you tonight."

"I don't think he meant to be."

"It's just that this statue has gotten under his skin. I'm worried about him. I'm worried about what will happen to him if he doesn't complete it."

"Looks like it's got under your skin too," Arthur said.

"You're right. It has."

She looked once again around the tiny bare room. The ceiling was low, so low that Arthur's head almost touched it. A toothbrush in a glass, a can of tooth powder, a pitcher for washing, a trunk at the foot of his cot that held his clothes, that plaintive crumpled picture of his parents, posed so sternly in life and now dead: the room was as empty as the future he seemed to be expecting. He was so heartrendingly solitary and self-sufficient.

"Aren't you very unhappy here?" she asked him.

"Not any unhappier than I'd be anywhere else. I like it here pretty much."

"Turn your face to me, please."

He did as instructed, still enough of a child to respond automatically to a teacher's tone.

She stared at him deliberately. She knew it made him anxious but she did it anyway.

"There's nothing you have to hide from me," she said. "I'm your friend, at least I think I am. If you still want me to be."

"Yes ma'am, I do."

"Maureen."

"I keep forgetting to say that."

She laughed and stood up and tightened her scarf around the neck of her coat. He opened the door for her and escorted her back down the street to the *mairie.*

"The place where Ben died ain't but a few miles from here. You tell your dad that if he wants me to I'll take the two of you over there tomorrow and show you what that fight was like and what happened. I don't know how that would help him with the statue but if it would I'm happy to do it."

"It wouldn't be hard for you?"

"Doesn't matter. You talk to your dad and tell him I'll meet up with you right after breakfast."

TWENTY-NINE

The gusting wind had swept itself away during the night. The sun was out, presiding over a day of brilliant cold. It was seven in the morning and already the noise of hammering was echoing all over Somme-Py, everyone impatient to rebuild their homes and their village and for the world to return to some semblance of its former reality. Arthur had grown to love the sound, a call to industry as solemn and stirring as the ringing of a church bell.

He shaved at the basin under the glassless window of the *abris,* the crude shutters open, the cold pouring in. He had no mirror. The remaining skin on the left side of his face had been stretched and reconfigured during his surgeries and his beard grew differently there now, like the grass around a stock tank. He shaved by touch. He had not looked at his face on purpose since he had been wounded and did not intend to. Every once in a while, passing a barrel full of water or a window sitting on the ground ready to be framed into one of the new wooden buildings, he would catch an accidental reflection and it would unnerve him for days. The gaping nothingness he saw was even worse than the picture he had constructed in his imagination. He knew it would be better to have a mirror after all, to confront himself with his appearance every morning so there would be no more danger of being taken by surprise. He knew it would be better but he was a long way from finding the strength to do it.

He finished shaving and got dressed and sat down on his cot to eat a piece of bread and sip some of the weak American cocoa that had come in the aid packages. It was during his solitary breakfasts that he gave himself permission to think. If he got the thinking over with before he set out for work he could tell himself that any meddlesome thoughts that came to him during the long hours of the day would just have to wait until the morning. It worked more or less. Sometimes he assigned himself a topic and mostly the topic was painful. He had to remember his parents and his little brother. He had to remember his childhood and the life he had lived in Ranger. It would be easier to let himself forget about all of that, but he knew it wouldn't be right. And sometimes when he bore in on something that he thought was going to be painful it turned out not to be. One morning he sat there thinking he ought to remember the taste of what his mother had called dream bars. They were a sort of cookie with a thick sugary crust and chopped nuts in the middle and shredded coconut on top. Remembering the taste of something he would never taste again had started out as an exercise in punishing himself, but it hadn't turned out that way. It ended up that the dream bars felt more like something he'd recovered than something he'd lost.

Today the topic was Ben, since he'd offered to take the Gilheaneys over to Saint-Étienne and show them the place his friend had died. So he sat there on his cot drinking his cocoa and thinking of him and Ben on the *Lenape.* They had both gotten seasick right away. Almost everybody had, crammed in the hold of the troopship with hardly any air to breathe and no space to move, the bunks four-deep, hanging from an endless three-dimensional maze of iron pipes. They didn't eat anything or get out of their bunks for two days, but one night they were showing a Fatty Arbuckle picture on deck and Ben said he was going up to see it even if it killed him. Somehow Arthur managed to follow him up the ladder. When they got up to the deck they vomited over the side and then watched the picture, an eerie square of movement that looked like it had been scissored out of the black mid-ocean sky. There was no orchestra, but after a time the surge of the water against the ship's bow seemed to accompany the action of the story and to add emphasis to the laughter of the seasick audience. The open air made him and Ben feel so much better that they hid themselves behind a coal cart and slept on deck. They woke just at dawn. There was no wind and no noise except for the rhythmic shushing of the ship ploughing endlessly forward. They could see the whole convoy, the transports and subchasers spread out over the ocean like playing tokens in some board game as vast as the world itself.

They were weak from hunger but not sick anymore and it felt like they had woken into a different life. That was the morning that Ben told him about his father, how he'd been taken by Indians when he was a boy and how he'd missed out on a good part of his life because of it, and how he'd just turned meaner and more confused and more demanding the older he'd got. A few weeks before the order came down at Camp Bowie to strike tents, he and his father had gotten into a fight over Ben's aunt wanting to pray over him in the Indian way. The old man could have gone up to Fort Worth and visited Ben and apologized and said good-bye but he never did. He sent the housekeeper, George's Mary, instead. Nobody knew exactly when the Arrowheads were supposed to leave for the train station but it was common knowledge it would be soon. Ben told Arthur that if you didn't go to see your son when he was about to ship out it was pretty clear you didn't want to, so as far as he was concerned his dad could rot in hell. He had tears in his eyes when he said it. It was the only time Arthur had ever seen Ben cry, the only time he'd ever seemed lonely or lost.

HE FINISHED his breakfast and walked down to the *mairie.* Mr. Gilheaney was standing outside drinking coffee and staring off toward the direction of Blanc Mont.

"Good morning," he said to Arthur. "Maureen tells me you've offered to show us the battlefield."

"Yes sir, I'll show it to you if you want to see it."

Maureen came out of the *mairie* with her coat buttoned against her neck, pulling on her gloves, her breath steaming into the clear air and her skin flushed with cold. They all shook hands the way French people did in the morning.

"Will we need the car?" the sculptor asked. "Our driver isn't back yet from Verdun."

"We don't need a car if you don't mind a stout walk. It's three or four miles from here."

"Nothing would suit us better than a stout walk."

Arthur went to find L'Huillier to explain what he was doing. He knew L'Huillier wouldn't mind, since he had lectured Arthur in the past about his unhealthy and un-French dependency on work, his refusal to uphold civilization by joining with his comrades in their rare days of leisure.

"Of course you must guide our friends," L'Huillier declared, looking up from the writing desk in his makeshift office. "There can be no question of this. I would go with you myself but there are a hundred letters I must write today."

Arthur filled up his canteen and bought a baguette from the *boulangerie* truck that made the rounds of the devastated villages twice a week. He put the baguette and some cheese and wine from the Gilheaneys into a pack he'd found near the summit of Blanc Mont where some marine had dropped it in the fighting. Then the three of them set out walking down the dusty trace that had once been the rue de la Chaussée and followed it north out of town.

He wasn't sure why he'd offered to show the Gilheaneys the place where Ben had died and where his own face had been blown off. He had been over this ground yard by yard in the Service, so it was not like he was returning to it for the first time, not like it was still haunted for him, but that did not make it a place he cared to visit. Maybe he'd made the offer because he'd been so nervous around Maureen Gilheaney and just felt like he'd needed to say something. It had been strange to be alone in the *abris* with her, strange to have her looking at him and talking to him the way she did. She had not been like those two girls from Smith College, straining to pretend that nothing was wrong with him, or like Madame L'Huillier, with her motherly pity. He knew that Maureen felt sorry for him like they did, but there was more to it than that, something she seemed to need from him.

She didn't look like he thought she would. She had told him in her letters that she was thirty-two, and in his mind he pictured thirty-two as closer to fifty than his own age. She wasn't beautiful or anything like that. If she had been, he would have been even more nervous around her than he was. But she had some quality that made you feel you ought to be looking at her and listening to her. And as they walked down the road toward what was left of the Bois des Vipères she and her dad were mostly silent, waiting for him to decide when to speak.

Mr. Gilheaney was tall, with long arms and powerful hands and from beneath the brim of his hat he stared out at the cratered fields like a hawk looking for something to kill. He walked a few feet ahead, outstriding Arthur and Maureen without seeming to be in a hurry, every now and then pausing to let them catch up. Sometimes he took out a sketchbook and made some drawings or notes, holding it close to his chest like it was a secret what he was writing, but mostly he just stared at things, taking it all in, turning it all to his own use in a way Arthur could not quite factor out.

"We filled in most of the trenches and a lot of the big shell holes last year," Arthur told them. "There was a big German trench over here on the left side of the road. This was the front before me and Ben and the rest of the Arrowheads got here. The Germans had machine-gun nests all in these woods and when the marines came down this road to take that hill up there they got shot up pretty bad. They call the hill Blanc Mont, I guess because it snows on it sometimes in the winter. But I've never seen it white. It's always just been dirt-colored."

The hill rose up before them like a cresting wave, a raw heave of earth, no longer full of twisted metal like when Arthur had first seen it but still riddled with unnatural dips and swells from the uncountable shells that had landed here. The Service had done its best to contour the slope back into something that resembled the work of nature, but it still looked nightmarishly wrong to Arthur. There were no grasses, no crops, just hard, black, poisoned soil.

He told the Gilheaneys that when he had first seen Blanc Mont, on the night of October 7, it had been so clawed apart by shells you couldn't even recognize it as a hill, you couldn't get your bearings about whether the land was rising or falling because the ground right at your feet seemed to pitch every which way itself.

They had been at their advanced training camp in Nuisement when the orders had come to roll packs and head for the front. They had stood in line at the scales next to the threshing barn where they had camped, a Percheron horse plodding endlessly nearby on a treadmill. They watched in wonder as the great beast exhausted its pointless life. The scales told Arthur his pack weighed forty kilograms, and it wasn't until they were halfway to Bar-sur-Aube that Ben told him that forty kilograms was the same as ninety pounds. Arthur told him he wished he hadn't said that, because just knowing he was carrying that much weight on his back made the pack feel heavier. They were both stupefied with fatigue and by the time they reached the train that was to carry them to Chalons their arms quivered as they handed up their packs to the other men in the forty-and-eight railcar.

At Chalons they were told to leave their pup tents and dress shoes and extra blankets behind and they marched on from there with their packs fifty pounds lighter. Up above them the big German Gotha bombers were flying west—to Paris, Ben guessed. They ate cold meals of canned salmon and canned hash. They heard the shells of the long-range guns roaring and whining above them, and though none of the shells hit nearby they could still feel the earth shake when they landed. No one told them where they were going.

They had marched to a village named Somme-Suippe and then after a rest they moved north. Beyond Somme-Suippe they came to the heart of the war, the fields in every direction no longer fields, no longer anything, just a heaving infinity of shell craters under the gray winter sky. It was like the ocean he and Ben had seen from the deck of the *Lenape,* except that on the ocean they could watch the waves moving as the wind pushed them, they could smell and sense the throbbing life below the surface. This ocean did not move, it was as still as death. The ground had been so wildly uneven that every step they moved forward took four or five more steps of clambering up and down. In some stretches work crews had come ahead of them to build a kind of road across the shell holes, but otherwise they just had to climb in and out of the craters, their light combat packs growing heavier and heavier, the mud caking their boots and weighing them down even more.

Most of the dead had been removed by French burial crews, but once the Arrowheads came across a burial crew that had themselves been killed by a shell before they could make it back. The soupy corpse they had been carrying lay on its back with its eyes gone and its slack skin pulling away from the skull. But the stretcher bearers were newly dead and looked surprised to be so. The three of them were grouped around a splintered tree where they had stopped to take a break when the shrapnel struck them. One of the dead men was sitting up. He held his canteen in one hand and the opposite arm was outstretched and resting on his bent knee, as if he were still talking to the other men and trying to make a point about something.

Arthur didn't tell Maureen about any of this as he walked along beside her up the slope that led to the long ridgeline summit of Blanc Mont. Her father was ahead of them again, already up to the top, standing with his hands on his hips as he stared off to the west. Maureen stumbled a little on the uneven ground as they climbed. Arthur thought about holding his hand out to her, but she wasn't helpless or frail and he couldn't really see himself doing something like that.

"Is that the Reims cathedral?" Mr. Gilheaney called out to Arthur as he and Maureen joined him at the top.

"Yes sir, that's Reims," Arthur told him.

"I had no idea we'd be able to see so far."

"The country here is pretty open. Even more open once so many trees got blown up in the war."

He joined them in staring across the rolling landscape of the Champagne to the distant cathedral spires on the horizon.

"It's so lovely," Maureen said, and then looked at Arthur like she felt bad about saying it. "But I suppose there's nothing lovely about a battlefield."

"I remember looking out at Reims from up here," Arthur said. "But I knew we were about to get in the fight and I was pretty scared by then, I guess, not really noticing much. By the time we got to the top of this ridge the marines had already taken it, and while we were going up we kept passing them going down. You could see it in their eyes that they'd had a tough time. There were a lot of trenches up in here. They're mostly filled in now, but those Germans were dug in tight and those marines had a time getting them out."

"And that little village there," Mr. Gilheaney said, pointing off to the north a mile or two. "That's Saint-Étienne?"

"Yes sir, it is. That's where Ben and me were headed. We hadn't been told that yet, but we could guess it. The Germans were making a stand there and it was pretty clear somebody had to kick them out."

"And what was your mood at that prospect?"

"We were just tired mostly. I guess a part of me wanted to get in there and do what they'd sent us over here to do. But I was scared too."

"And Ben?"

"Maybe he was scared too but he didn't show it any. He was pretty calm in his mind. That's why I wanted to be around him. He made me feel like I could get through whatever was coming."

They kept walking along the road, down the slope on the far side of Blanc Mont and on toward the plain that led to Saint-Étienne. Mr. Gilheaney strode out ahead again.

"Your dad doesn't look like he ever gets tired," Arthur told Maureen.

"No, I'm afraid he's inexhaustible."

She smiled at him and he nodded his head but didn't smile back. He knew that trying to grin with that prosthesis in his mouth would give him the look of a snarling dog and maybe worse.

"How do you feel coming back here?" she asked him.

"I don't feel that much. It's a whole lot different now than it was then. This stretch here, we came through at night. It was dark and we couldn't see anything. We had these guides who were supposed to know the way but they kept getting lost, so every so often they'd call out 'About-face' and sure enough we had to walk back the way we come. It was poor planning if you ask me but I guess that sort of thing just happens in a war and there's no point to complain about it."

It was true it had been dark that night and he wouldn't have recognized the ground from walking across it now. But he could still remember exactly how it had felt to be walking toward Saint-Étienne, the whole company anxious and silent and exhausted, the captain and the top kick cursing out the useless guides in a whisper. He remembered the taste of the canned salmon he had eaten for dinner still in his mouth, not enough water to wash it away. He remembered the big blister growing on the ball of his foot, and that worried him more than anything, the idea that he would be crippled by it and left behind. There were German patrols out and he knew that at any minute the company could walk in front of a machine-gun nest or that one of the long-range shells vaulting overhead could come down right on top of them. He had walked behind Ben, keeping his eye on the back of his friend's neck, trying to copy the steadiness of his step, the calmness he had told Mr. Gilheaney about. Every once in a while Ben would look back and smile at him, like the two of them were in on a joke together. Arthur was all right as long as he was in step behind Ben, as long as the two of them were pretending this was all just a big adventure and not a nightmare that was drawing them closer and closer into itself.

Arthur was all right until they ran into that damn Indian from Company E. After that, everything changed and Arthur felt alone in the night.

THIRTY

About right here was the jump-off line," Arthur told them. They had walked north for a half hour from the top of Blanc Mont. Now they stood facing the village of Saint-Étienne-á-Arnes, several hundred yards away across an open field. The ground was mostly level, the big craters filled in by Arthur and his colleagues. But the field remained untilled and unplanted, still scarred and bare.

Gil brought out his sketchbook as Maureen took aim at the desolation in front of them with her Kodak. He sketched quickly, the big wooded hill to the right, the long, barren approach to the village, the scattered stone buildings visible beneath bare winter trees whose spreading branches had been sheared off in a lopsided manner by the shelling of a year and a half ago. He wasn't sure why he was sketching all this, what purpose it could possibly serve in the execution of the Clayton statue if he decided to resume work on it. It was only curiosity leading him on at this point. From the beginning he had been vexed by some missing understanding in his portrait of Ben Clayton, and he was intrigued by the idea that this hidden something could be grasped and given life in his statue.

"Better watch your step," Arthur said as Gil put back his sketchbook and the three of them began to walk toward the village. "We got most of the shells out but some of them were buried deep and might have worked their way up to the top. And there could be some wire and rebar and such too."

As they strolled along at a casual pace, Arthur fell silent. This was the killing zone, Gil realized, and he could detect this same solemn awareness in his daughter's face. She stopped taking snapshots and hung the camera by its strap over her shoulder, just walking forward with a respectful stride. Gil had the odd feeling he had just become a kind of proxy for Lamar Clayton, walking across a stretch of ground on the other side of the ocean that the old rancher would never see, could never bear to see.

Gil and Maureen waited for Arthur to speak. As they waited they drew closer to the village. They could make out towering gravestones behind the gray rock of the distant cemetery wall, the shattered steeple of the village church off to the left.

"I expect you want to know what it was like that morning," Arthur said, coming to a stop about halfway to the village.

"We do," Maureen answered. "We'd be grateful if you told us."

"Well, it wasn't too bad at first. They had what you call a rolling barrage in front of us, and we were supposed to be walking behind that. But we got kind of a late start and nobody seemed to know what was going on and by the time we jumped off that barrage didn't do us much good. Right about here was where all hell broke loose. There were machine gunners up on that hill and behind that cemetery wall, and in that steeple in the church. Pretty much everywhere, it seemed like. They didn't open up till we got here. That's where the wire was, where a lot of boys got hit. Ben and I got through somehow and we made it to about right over there. Twenty yards, I'd guess."

Arthur walked to the spot with deliberate strides, as if he was confirming his estimate of the distance.

"There was a machine-gun nest over there," he said, pointing off to the left. "They had us pinned down here pretty bad. But we were in a shell hole and as long as we kept our heads down they couldn't get us, so I was happy right where I was. Ben wasn't, though. He didn't even say a word to me about it, he just took off to go after that machine gun."

"And you stayed here?"

"No sir, I went with him. I didn't want to be left behind here by myself. I wanted to be with Ben."

The ground today looked nothing like it did that October day, when there had been a gray, rainy sky to begin with, and then the shells erupting all around them, shrieking metal and soil and sugar beets flying everywhere, the dirt clods pattering down on his helmet. Arthur remembered how winded he had been, how he couldn't get a good breath because his nose was plugged up with mud and he was afraid to open his mouth because he didn't know whether there was gas or not. He remembered how in the middle of all that terror he had still been irritated by blisters on his feet, by the entrenching tool digging into his groin.

He had followed Ben to the next shell hole, the bullets from the German Maxim guns swarming all around them. Even now, it seemed impossible to Arthur that they were not hit. But neither of them was, not then. They dropped into the hole beside four men from another company they didn't know. One of them had lost his rifle. Another had a Browning but he didn't seem like he was planning to use it. He just sat there crouched over it like he was trying to protect it from the dirt.

"We didn't have any trench mortars to take out that machine-gun nest," Arthur told the Gilheaneys as he stared at the place where the emplacement had been, a gentle mound of earth now. "Just rifles and grenades. There was a French tank wandering around over here to the left, and we tried to wave it over to help us out, but it never saw us."

"So you decided to take out that machine gun yourselves?" Gil asked.

"I didn't decide anything. Ben did."

He told them about the rest of the fight, just setting it out in a matter-of-fact way. Talking about it made the events of that day seem weirdly normal: this happened, then that happened. But at the time the day seemed to be something completely unrelated to the whole rest of his life. It hadn't even seemed to be him who was living through it. It was somebody with no memories or thoughts, somebody with an empty mind and a body that was just a throbbing mass of fear.

They were lying in the shell hole with their heads down, listening to the puttering of the machine gun thirty yards away. The gunner knew they were there and he kept the dirt flying at the rim of the crater.

Arthur didn't see how there was anything they could do except stay where they were, but that wasn't what Ben thought. He turned and yelled at the soldier with the Browning, told him and his loader to get ready and cover for him because he was going after the machine gun. Arthur remembered how hard his face had looked, how hard and sharp and old all of a sudden. Ben didn't care about anything anymore and Arthur knew it. After what he'd learned from that Indian he would just as soon get himself killed as not, and the rest of them with him. Arthur resented it, the way he was suddenly barking orders at everybody. Ben wasn't his friend anymore, he didn't care about anything other than killing the men in that machine-gun nest.

"All right, I'm going!" was all he said. Arthur and the others opened up in the direction of the machine gun and Ben scrambled up over the rim of the crater. Arthur was sure Ben would be cut down before he went a yard but he got far enough to throw a mills bomb into the grass-covered slit from which the barrel of the machine gun was pointing. Before the Maxim could open up again he threw another grenade and then he was charging toward the gun with his bayonet. Arthur had just put another clip into his rifle. He climbed out of the shell hole and started shooting and the other men followed behind him. Two of the Germans ran out of the nest and before Arthur could fire, the soldier with the Browning caught them both in a single burst. Another German came screaming at Ben with his bayonet but he lost his footing in the mud and went down backwards and the sound of his knee popping out was loud enough that Arthur could hear it even above the noise of the battle.

Another machine gun opened up then from the hill to their right and cut down the Browning team beside him. Arthur dove into the scrape behind the machine-gun nest and sliced open his nose on the boot of a dead German. Ben was still fighting with the other Boche gunner twenty feet away, the two of them grunting and yelping as they tried to stick each other with their bayonets. The German was still on the ground with his leg splayed out to the side but even lying there like that he wouldn't quit. When Ben finally managed to drive in his bayonet, the man let out a gasping astonished wheeze.

Ben scrambled into the scrape next to Arthur. His hands were shaking with what he'd done but there was still that look in his eyes that said he didn't care and wasn't finished.

"We've got to get that Browning," he said to Arthur. He was looking behind him at where the two men had been shot down. They were both on their faces, perfectly parallel with their heads pointing in the same direction and the automatic rifle lying in front of them like they were priests and it was something they'd laid down to worship. Arthur didn't know where the other man had gone.

"We can't go out there, we'll—"

But Ben was already gone. He grabbed the Browning and threw it back to Arthur and then he pulled off the dead ammo bearer's webbing and bandoliers. Arthur gave him what cover he could, shooting in the direction of the hill where the machine-gun fire was coming from. He couldn't believe it when Ben made it back into the scrape again.

"You remember how to do this?" he asked Arthur, handing him the ammunition. Arthur nodded. The Browning was a brand-new weapon and they'd had a class on it at Camp Bowie. Mostly what Arthur remembered was how the rifle shot so fast it could hammer you to the ground with each recoil.

He loaded the magazines while the machine-gun fire from the hill kept them pinned down. The support and reserve troops were coming up now. Some of them were attacking the positions on the hill and others filtered their way forward, scrambling for cover along with Arthur and Ben fifty yards in front of Saint-Étienne's cemetery wall. There were three or four machine guns in that cemetery and another up in the steeple and lots of tied-in trenches where the Germans were going to make a stand.

Half a dozen men jumped into the hole with them. One of them was a lieutenant. He glanced at the Browning and told Ben and Arthur to cover him and the other men while they made a grenade assault on the closest machine gun. The men slung their rifles and pulled the pins on their grenades and they ran out of the hole. It was hard for Arthur to see what was going on from his place in the shell hole but it looked like at least a couple of them had made it through.

"Let's go!" Ben yelled. He leapt to his feet and ran forward firing from the hip with the Browning and strafing the top of the wall. Masonry dust, mixed with spraying arterial blood, hovered like a pink cloud. Now there was a surge of other doughboys rising up from cover to join them as they climbed over the wall and into the cemetery. Ben emptied the last magazine and threw the Browning on the ground. The red-hot barrel bounced up against Arthur's shin but he was so busy and scared that the deep burn he felt was only just another streak of sensation, another one of the thousands of things that were happening to him or around him all at once. He had unslung his rifle by then and was face-to-face with a German soldier who had just crawled out of the trench. The German looked old and he thrust uncertainly toward Arthur with his bayonet. Arthur thrust back, and then the two of them looked at each other like they were trying to decide whose turn it was now, until finally the German figured out he could just drop his rifle and spin around and run away.

THEY WERE STANDING in the cemetery now. Maureen and Mr. Gilheaney were walking among the marble vaults and tombstones, reading the names of the dead villagers of Saint-Étienne. Half of the monuments were broken and still lying in pieces, their inscriptions as often as not chipped away by shrapnel or machine-gun rounds.

"The fighting appears to have been pretty heavy here," the sculptor remarked.

"It appeared that way at the time too," Arthur said. He didn't know how peevish that sounded until the words came out. He hadn't meant to feel any anger toward Mr. Gilheaney and Maureen for putting him in the position of tourist guide. But maybe he was just angry with himself, for playing that role, for enjoying it maybe. It was probably his own fault because he couldn't seem to feel any more than a tourist guide would feel in the first place. Here's where Ben went after that machine gun, here's where we charged the cemetery with that Browning. He had led them across the open ground, telling them everything he could remember about the assault against Saint-Étienne, but the more he talked about it the less real it began to seem. You couldn't talk about it without leaving most of it out. He didn't know how to tell anybody what it had felt like to be face-to-face with that German soldier, the unexpected anger in the man's face as he came running toward Arthur with that bayonet. The man had come at him with a hateful grin, the long roots of his teeth exposed in his shriveled gums. It had felt peculiar to be the specific target of this stranger's rage. Why, out of all the people in the world, had this old man chosen Arthur Fry to hate and to kill? But there must have been something of the same murdering spirit in Arthur's face as well, or else why would the man have dropped his rifle like that and run off?

He wasn't the only one who had done so. So many Americans were swarming into the cemetery by then that half of the defenders were throwing up their hands in surrender and shouting *"Kamerade!"* and the other half were trampling each other as they ran away through the interconnecting trenches like cattle in a chute.

"And Ben?" Mr. Gilheaney said. "Where did it happen?"

"Right about here. We took the cemetery but the fighting wasn't over. The Germans retreated to across that stream over there, and there were some still shooting at us from the town. There was a machine gun up in the steeple of that church and Ben decided to go after that, and that's when he got hit."

Arthur gestured toward the village church, rising from the center of the town west of the cemetery. It was still in ruins, the steeple mostly shot away now and shell holes all through the roof. He noticed that some of the villagers were standing there at the edge of town looking toward them in the cemetery, wondering what they were doing there.

"He died instantly?"

"Yes sir, it was pretty quick."

It had been so quick his mind was still trying to catch up to it, almost two years later. He told Mr. Gilheaney that Ben "decided" to go after the gun in the steeple, but whatever deciding Ben had done had happened before that. He had determined something in his mind back before they even jumped off. Whether he lived or died in this fight hadn't concerned him at all.

The machine gun opened up just after the prisoners had been led away, and there was rifle fire from the village as well. The Americans in the cemetery had dived into the trenches and huddled there, the Maxim rounds striking the chalk at the top of the trench wall behind them. A few men from Ben and Arthur's company were with them by now, but there were no officers close by and nobody seemed to be taking charge. Arthur was thirstier than he'd ever been in his life. Somebody had brought up a crate of canned tomatoes and the men were passing them up and down the line. They punched holes in the cans with their bayonets. Arthur cut his bottom lip on the ragged opening but that didn't matter to him. He drank till the juice was gone, then gouged the hole wider with the point of his bayonet and dragged out the moist, pulpy tomatoes. All the time they heard the Maxim firing from the top of the steeple and felt it kicking up white dust behind them.

He saw the look in Ben's eyes and said, "Don't!" But Ben wouldn't look at him or even act like he'd heard. He was in the same state of mind he'd been in all along, shutting Arthur out, fighting some kind of war in his head along with the one that was here in front of them. Ben unfastened the bayonet from his rifle, wiped the blood off on his mud-caked pants, then methodically put it back on. He checked his pockets for grenades. He was still wearing the webbing that held the Browning pouches, so he took that off. All the while Arthur kept saying don't and Ben still wouldn't look at him. Arthur called him a sonofabitch and Ben said he didn't intend to wait around here forever for somebody to do something.

"You need to settle down," Arthur told him. "You're all mixed up. You may think this has all got something to do with your dad but it doesn't."

But it didn't do any good to try to talk to him about it. Ben just looked at Arthur like he was an annoyance. They weren't friends anymore. It was like they'd never trained together at Camp Bowie, or drunk together at Boot's Place in Fort Worth or had dollar steaks at the Westbrook Hotel. It was like they'd never sat next to each other riding a train all across the country, or stood on the Brooklyn Bridge looking down at the harbor with the wind hitting them in the face, or watched the sun come up from the deck of the troopship in the middle of the Atlantic Ocean, or kept each other's spirits up during the march from Nuisement.

"Y'all cover me," he said to Arthur and the rest of the men nearby. One of the men yelled at Ben that they ought to wait for a 37 mm team to take that gun out, but Ben said he was going to do it himself and he was tired of talking about it. They saw he was serious so they opened fire in the general direction of the steeple and Ben launched himself out of the trench.

When he fell right back in, Arthur thought he had just changed his mind. But if he wasn't already dead he was close enough where you couldn't tell the difference. Arthur put his arms around him and tried to pull him up. Half of Ben's back seemed like it was missing, torn out by the Maxim rounds when they went through his body. Blood poured onto Arthur's legs and onto the white chalky soil. Ben's eyes were so fixed and blank it looked like he was willingly dead, like he had decided to shut Arthur out for good and that his death was nobody's business but his own. Arthur didn't remember saying anything, or screaming, or cursing. He had just sat there holding his dead friend, and then he started to shiver like a scared and lonesome child.

"YES SIR, it was over pretty quick." That was all he had said to Mr. Gilheaney. He didn't particularly care to say any of the rest of it. Even if he'd wanted to, he didn't know how. Mr. Gilheaney just nodded and kept looking around at the tombstones. Maureen leaned against the cemetery wall, staring at him. He turned away from her. He didn't want her looking at his face. When she reached out and touched him he shied away from her, but by then it was too late. He wasn't crying; it was worse than that. He was on his knees, barking in pain, his chest heaving, the prosthesis shifting around dangerously in his contorted face. Out of the corner of his eye he saw the villagers walking toward them thinking he needed help, but he waved his arm at them to please go away. He tried to say *"C'est rien"* but the words wouldn't come out and he had to rely on Mr. Gilheaney to go over and tell them he was all right. Maureen sat down next to him and put her arm around him and made shushing sounds like his mother used to, and it didn't seem to him he had any choice but to let her.

The harder he tried to calm himself down the worse it got, until he was stupidly out of control, crouching tighter and tighter against the cemetery wall while the snot ran out of his nose and sounds he had never made before—like the bellowing of cattle—came out of his mouth. While all this was going on he was aware of Mr. Gilheaney withdrawing tactfully over to the German side of the cemetery and staring at the monument there, with its ugly carving of the squat, naked man with his hands on a sword hilt. He stayed there until Arthur was finally calm again, and then came back and sat down next to Arthur and Maureen against the wall.

"We've asked too much of you," he said.

"No, you didn't do anything," Arthur told him. "I guess I just never went over it in my mind that way before."

When he realized Maureen still had her arm around him like he was a little boy he was even more embarrassed. He shifted a little and she got the idea that he didn't need to be comforted anymore. She stood and wiped the dry grass from her skirt and none of them said anything for a long time.

Then Maureen asked: "What about you, Arthur? When did you get hurt?"

"I don't know exactly. It must have been right after Ben got killed. I believe there was a counterattack. We must have fallen back because the French found me out there somewhere, in those fields yonder. But I don't remember any of it, to tell you the truth."

"What you went through, it must have been—"

"It was pretty bad, yes ma'am, but I don't care to talk about it if you don't mind."

"Of course."

"Maybe we should head on back to Somme-Py. You folks are probably hungry for your lunch."

Half the cemetery wall had been blown up in the fighting and nobody had repaired it yet. Arthur stood there watchfully as Maureen hitched up her skirt and stepped over the rubble and then he followed her. He had gone only a few yards when he realized Mr. Gilheaney didn't seem all that interested in going anywhere.

"Aren't you coming, Daddy?" Maureen asked him.

He didn't say anything right away; he was thinking about something.

"You said he was boiling over," he said to Arthur after a moment.

"Sir?"

"In your letter to Maureen. You said Ben was boiling over about something he'd found out. What was he so upset about?"

"I believe I said I didn't want to talk about that."

"Why not?"

"It seemed like a private matter of Ben's."

"Ben's dead."

"Yes sir, I know that. But it still seems private. And I don't expect it would have much to do with making a statue of him."

Arthur saw that the sculptor thought he had an answer to that, something along the lines of what do you know about making a statue? The man clearly had a high opinion of himself and thought he had the right to whatever information he needed. But when he spoke again his voice was softer than Arthur expected it to be. He stepped through the breach in the cemetery wall and walked over to Arthur and stood there next to him, looking out across the sugar beet fields.

"Something happened to him, you said, something that made him not seem to care whether he lived or died. I want to know what that something was. I need to know that because I want this statue to have the truth in it."

"I don't believe you, Mr. Gilheaney, not really. That sounds good what you just said, it sounds like the way an artist ought to talk, but you'd probably be pretty poor at your job if you couldn't put the truth in that statue yourself without needing me to tell you what it was."

"All right. Fair enough."

He moved closer to Arthur and put his hand on his shoulder. He looked him steadily in the eye, something that Arthur wasn't used to. Most people, even those who knew him well, like L'Huillier or his wife, tended to meet his eyes for only a moment and then look away like there was something off to the side that had just happened to catch their interest.

"I didn't mean to be condescending. Leave the statue out of it. Leave art out of it. Maybe I just want to know. For myself, for myself and my daughter."

Arthur glanced over at Maureen. She stood there with her gloved hand at her throat, fingering the top button of her jacket. She didn't say anything, but the expression on her face said it was up to him whether he wanted to talk about it or not.

"I don't think Ben's dad ought to know about it," he told them.

"You can trust us not to tell him," Gilheaney said firmly.

"All right," Arthur told them. "There was this Indian."

THE INDIAN'S NAME was Felix Whiteblanket. Arthur and Ben had met him coming over on the *Lenape,* after they'd gotten past the worst of their seasickness and the men in the different companies had started to mix a little bit, playing cards down in the hold and bragging back and forth to each other about where they were from and what sort of work they had done before they ended up in the army.

Company E was made up of men from the Indian Territories up in

Oklahoma. Most of them were Choctaws and Cherokees, some of them were rich from oil leases on their allotments and had big cars and big houses back at home. There was an Osage boy on the ship that everybody talked about who had supposedly gotten a check before he left Camp Bowie for sixty-six thousand dollars.

There were only two or three Comanches in Company E and Felix Whiteblanket was one of them. He said nobody had bothered to look for oil on his land and he didn't care if they ever did. He didn't care about being rich and he pretended he didn't care about much of anything else. He was silent and a little disdainful of all the rowdy behavior on the ship, and he acted like there wasn't anything in the world that could surprise him.

But he had been friendly to Ben and took a liking to him. Maybe it was because Ben was silent in his own way and didn't make a show of anything. The three of them sat on the deck playing dominoes and talking horses and cattle and watching a group of officers try to shoot flying fish with their Springfields, leading them the way hunters lead ducks. The way the flying fish skimmed above the surface of the ocean, staying aloft far longer than you would have ever thought, reminded Arthur of his own dreams of flying, in which he would suddenly rediscover a magical hovering ability that he had forgotten he possessed.

After Ben had gotten comfortable around Felix Whiteblanket, he told him about how his father had been captured by Comanches when he was a boy. Arthur recalled Felix nodding his head and playing his next domino, like he would lose face somehow if he showed too much interest in anything. He said he was going to write to his own folks to see if they'd ever heard of Lamar Clayton. He asked Ben if his dad had a Comanche name. Ben said he didn't know because his dad never talked about any of that.

They didn't see Felix again for months after that, not until that long nighttime march from Somme-Py when they were crossing over Blanc Mont to get into position for the attack on Saint-Étienne. They had been walking for many hours through the mud and even though they only had light combat packs on their backs they still staggered under the load. Arthur felt his oozing blister with every step. His canteen was empty and all he could think about was when the water wagons would be brought up from the wells. When Sergeant Kitchens told them to fall out and take a break, it wasn't because somebody had taken pity on them, it was because they were lost. They collapsed onto the muddy ground, taking care not to get entangled in barbed wire or to slice open their legs on a shell fragment. They sat there listening to the German long-range guns bombarding Somme-Py and the roads leading out from it. Every time an 88 exploded in the distance the earth shook underneath them, and sometimes they heard the dud shells ploughing into the mud with no explosion but with a terrorizing impact all their own.

Felix had been sent as a runner to tell the captain to have the company stay put and wait until the guides had had a chance to talk and figure out where they were. After he was through making his report he managed to find Ben and Arthur and sat down in the mud with them. Felix had a few sips of water left in his canteen and he drank it down without offering them any. It made Arthur angry but he knew that he wouldn't have shared any of his water either if that was all he had. The three of them were almost too tired to open their mouths and with all those German 88's screaming across the sky it felt unlucky to be talking anyway. Nevertheless Felix told Ben he was hoping he'd run into him again because he'd just gotten a letter from his grandfather up on the Kiowa-Comanche reservation. Felix had written him and told him about meeting Ben and how Ben had said his father was with the Quahadas back in the olden days. The grandfather wrote back and said it was a pretty small world, because when he was a young man he'd known Lamar Clayton pretty well.

"Grandfather said you couldn't hardly tell your dad wasn't born a Comanche," Felix said to Ben. They were all shivering now. They'd been sweating under their packs while they were marching but now that they'd stopped they felt the cold again, one more misery piled up on top of all the others.

"Well, he never was the sort to do things halfway," Ben said. "He never talked about that time of his life to me much."

"Grandfather said he killed white folks."

"No, he wouldn't have done that."

"He said they was on a raid together and Lamar Clayton did his share of the work. Grandfather watched him shoot a white boy with an arrow."

"I don't want to hear that kind of talk about my father."

"Said it happened over on the Salt Fork."

When Felix mentioned the Salt Fork there was a shuddering far-off explosion. The distant shell burst lit up Ben's face for a second like heat lightning, and Arthur could see his friend's eyes turning cold and his mouth growing tight as he figured out the meaning of what Felix had just told him.

"You don't know anything about it," he said to the Indian.

"I just told you I did."

"Shut up about it."

"Your old man was a wild sonofabitch is all. He was a goddam wild Indian, just like my grandfather. It didn't bother either of them none to kill white people. That was just the way things were in those days."

"I told you I didn't want you talking about this."

But Felix was grinning now. They hadn't seen him like this before. He had a cruel, needling side that all the exhaustion and fear was bringing out.

"Don't know why you're upset," he said. "You ought to be proud your old man took a scalp or two. You ought to be—"

By that time Ben was on him and they were rolling around in the mud, but they were both too tired and overloaded with equipment to make much of a fight of it. Neither of them had a chance to even land a punch before Kitchens broke it up and sent Felix back to Company E and told Ben he'd better shut his fucking mouth and behave himself or he'd personally kick out his teeth for him.

Ben didn't say anything. Kitchens left, shaking his head in disgust, and Ben just kept sitting there and wouldn't talk to Arthur anymore or even look at him.

"HE WAS just locked inside his head," Arthur told the Gilheaneys. "He was like that all through the night and during the attack the next day and up until he got killed."

They had been walking for twenty minutes and now they were halfway up the northern slope of Blanc Mont on their way back home to Somme-Py.

"I reckon we can eat our lunch up at the top," Arthur said. But Gilheaney had stopped walking. He just stood there thinking, taking in what Arthur had told him.

"I don't understand," he said. "Ben had always known his father was with the Indians. He must have guessed he might have been involved in a raid or two. Why did it come as such a shock that he'd throw his life away?"

"Well, I believe he was still pretty mad at the old man, on account of the way he'd been treated by him. And the raid Felix told him about, there was something personal about it."

"Something personal?"

But Maureen had already guessed what he was talking about.

"George's Mary," she said.

"Yes, ma'am, the housekeeper. That was her family that Mr. Clayton and those Indians killed."

THIRTY-ONE

They had come to the American cemetery in Romagne early in the day. The weather was still raw and the grounds unfinished, just a flagpole and a paved road and temporary wooden buildings where the staff and groundskeepers huddled around their stoves. And fourteen thousand white crosses massed on the hillside.

The rows of crosses were laid out with such bewitching military precision that Gil had the sensation, walking through them, of being in a trompe l'oeil painting, a landscape ruled by a trickster's perspective. As they made their way up the slope, along the grassy aisles sectioning the burial zones, more white crosses seemed to spring up at the crest of the hill, rank after endless rank of them.

Gil checked the map the American caretaker had given him and led Maureen and Arthur to a row of graves halfway up the hill. They found the cross with Ben's name on it and Gil and Arthur took off their hats. The three of them stared down at the marker in silence for a moment, then Maureen set down a spray of winter flowers on the grave.

"I think we should take a snapshot for Mr. Clayton," she told Gil.

"Of course."

While she took the photo he glanced down at the big elliptical driveway at the base of the hill, where their driver, Stuart, and the caretaker stood smoking and talking as they leaned against the front fender of the Thomas Cook touring car. Then he looked over at

Arthur, who had backed away from Ben's grave as soon as Maureen got out her Brownie, alarmed at the idea of his picture accidentally being taken. The young man stood there with his hands in the pockets of his jacket, staring down at the tombstone of his friend with no apparent emotion on his face. Of course it would have been difficult to detect emotion there in the first place, since his shattering wound had left his face as blank and inexpressive as that of the man in the moon.

Maureen walked this way and that in front of the grave, looking for the best angle for her camera. It was the right thing to do to take a picture for Lamar Clayton, though Gil could not imagine the rancher taking any comfort in receiving it. The old bastard was probably beyond comfort anyway, and that was as it should be. Clayton had not just fought with his son and turned his back on him. It was worse than that. He had killed Ben with the secret of his own long-ago crimes; he had shut the door of understanding in his boy's face and the boy had died because of it.

After Maureen finished taking her photos, Gil got down on one knee in front of the cross and studied the words incised in the marble: BENJAMIN CLAYTON PRVT I CL 142 INF. 36 DIV. TEXAS OCT. 8, 1918.

"Do you want to say something, Daddy?"

"What?"

Maureen's voice had surprised him. He had apparently been kneeling there for some minutes.

"You looked like you meant to say something."

He shook his head and stood up. His daughter was weeping. She was standing close to Arthur now. She reached down and touched the stone.

"Well," she said, "maybe we understand him a little better now."

THEY HAD a late *petit déjeuner* at a café in Romagne and drove back to Somme-Py. Stuart narrated the events of the last year of the war as they passed through the Argonne Forest and out again into the open Champagne countryside, through a succession of bombed-out villages.

"This is the old Roman road we're on now," Stuart told them. "Julius Caesar himself came this way, if I don't miss my guess. You'll find no shortage of history in this part of the country. History upon history, you might say, Mr. Gilheaney."

Gil sat in the front seat with Stuart, distractedly nodding his head. To Maureen, in back with Arthur, the driver's history lectures were an annoyance. She didn't feel like listening to anyone prattle on about anything.

She watched Arthur as he stared out the window at the ruined villages and houses. Somme-Py was not unique. There must have been hundreds of villages just like it throughout this part of France, villages all but erased from the earth by years of bombardment. And then there were the dead, none of them unique either, lying beneath the earth in their uncountable multitudes. There were graveyards everywhere, their crosses spreading across the landscape in crop-like rows, monuments going up at every village crossroads. She had the feeling that there was something futile, maybe selfish, in their attempts to conjure up the last days of a single soldier, in investing so much in the creation of one more statue—a statue that would serve as a monument to her father's art as much as to its subject's life.

She had taken it as a matter of course throughout her life that art was an essentially noble thing, that individual practitioners might be scoundrels but that art itself was exempt from charges of exploitation. But she felt like a predator today. She and her father had come here against Arthur's wishes. He had compliantly allowed them to drag him through memories he might have preferred to forget. It was Maureen who had suggested they should visit Ben's grave, and she could tell Arthur had not really wanted to come along. He only wanted to be left alone to do his work in Somme-Py, among familiar people, like the L'Huilliers, who asked nothing of him. But out of politeness he had joined them on the drive to Romagne and stood there uncertainly at the grave of his friend.

They would go on to Reims tomorrow and take the train for Paris. Tonight they would stay once more in Somme-Py, releasing Stuart again to find more comfortable accommodations. As soon as they arrived in town L'Huillier insisted they dine again with him and his wife, and though Maureen would have preferred to escape his hospitality there was no particular way to refuse. During the dinner Gil signed over a traveler's check and pressed it into L'Huillier's hands for the Somme-Py fund. It was a sizable amount, the cost of their combined Atlantic passages, and L'Huillier beamed with gratitude and promised he would have their names written on the wall of the Salle Mémoriale Franco-Américaine, which would be the great room where the citizens of Somme-Py would congregate when the permanent *mairie* was built.

"Do you suppose Mr. Clayton ever told his wife?" Maureen asked her father after they had said good night to the L'Huilliers and to Arthur and walked back to their rough quarters in the provisional *mairie.*

"Told her what?"

"About what he had done to George's Mary's family. About all of it."

"I shouldn't think so," he said, as he distractedly arranged his blankets on the narrow cot in the big open room of the building. Maureen's own cot was on the other side of the partition, in the small office where they had first encountered Arthur. "We know that much about him. He doesn't share his secrets easily."

"Let me do that, Daddy. You're hopeless."

She stripped off the sheets and blankets and tucked them in properly as best she could.

"It would have made a difference if she had known," Maureen said as she set a rough pillow at the head of the cot. "She would have found a way to tell him."

"You think so?"

"Of course I do. Women don't like secrets."

"Yes, you've made that clear enough."

"Maybe she would have kept him from hating his father. Maybe she would have kept him from dying because of it."

She watched him as he took off his coat and draped it over a wooden chair. He slipped his watch out of his pocket and wound it and set it on the seat. The weather had taken a mild turn and the cold wind had ceased roaring outside. For just a moment there was no sound but the ticking of his pocket watch.

"What about the commission?" she asked him.

"There's no commission. As you recall, I gave Clayton his money back. I doubt whether he'd want to renew a deal I've already walked away from."

"But you're going to do the statue?"

"I owe it to the boy now. Or at least that's how it feels. It was one thing to sleep in his room at Clayton's ranch. It was another to visit that battlefield, to stand at his grave. I thought I had some understanding of this war until I came here, saw that poor fellow's face, saw all those white crosses. I don't care if Clayton wants his statue or not. I'll put it up in our front yard if I have to."

He sat down on the cot and began to untie his muddy boots, but Maureen lingered in the room, staring at the fire in the portable stove.

"You're not going to bed?" Gil asked.

"I want to talk about Arthur."

"Yes, we should do something for him. I could try to give him some money. I doubt he'd take it."

"I think he should come home with us."

Her father stared wearily down at the laces of his boots. She hated the way he seemed to be silently dismissing her opinion, as if it was something a thoughtless child had presented to him.

"And you think he would want to?"

"I don't know. Maybe he would."

"He's a grown man. He's made up his mind to stay here, as far as I can see. At some point he might make up his mind to go back to the States, but I don't see how it's any of our business either way."

"He hasn't gone home because he doesn't have anyone there. He'd have us."

"You want him to *live* with us?"

"You'll need a studio assistant."

"I will? I was under the impression I had one."

"Not forever."

"What is that supposed to mean?"

"Only that I believe I'm well past the point where I should be entitled to my own life."

"And I'm the one who's kept you from having your own life? Is that what you think? Is that what you truly think?"

She whispered no and shook her head—she knew it couldn't all be his fault—but he wasn't looking at her anymore. He was staring at the bare plank wall, quietly furious, fitting something together in his mind.

"By God," he said, "you and that Vance Martindale aren't planning something, are you?"

"No, Daddy," she said, though not immediately, since his accusation almost took her breath away. "I'm not quite so desperate to get away from you that I would run off with a married man."

She bid him good night with far more civility than she felt and retired to her own makeshift bedroom in the office next door. But she was in too much of a stir to think about sleeping. She sat on the edge of her cot for ten minutes, staring at the piles of file cards at the desk where Arthur worked, breathing in the smell of new lumber and feeling the depth of the night outside, a night as lonely and boundless as those she had experienced on Lamar Clayton's ranch. She had come all the way to France in an effort to jar herself loose from her own confining existence, but nothing had changed. She was still as much her father's hostage as his daughter, her life ruled by his ambition, diminished rather than enlarged by his creative power.

Before her mind could quite catch up to her actions, she had pulled on her coat and walked out of the office and then out the front door of the *mairie.* She heard her father, unable to sleep himself, rise up from his cot and ask her where she was going, but he had no right to ask her and she had no intention of answering.

IT WAS ELEVEN THIRTY, the sky mostly clear overhead, just a few torn tufts of cloud against the stars. The temperature was only in the mid-thirties but she had the sense, here in this lifeless land, of an interstellar cold bearing down upon the earth. One of the village dogs who had not yet accepted her presence trotted along behind her, calling down judgment upon this trespasser with a howl that rebounded across the landscape like the voices of the coyotes she had heard in West Texas.

She saw pale lantern light leaking through the wooden shutters of Arthur's *abris.* She walked up to the door and knocked swiftly, before she could talk herself out of it. She was used to the way he looked by now but she was still startled a little to see him so suddenly appear at the opened door, his expressive eyes hidden in shadow so that the distorted remainder of his face seemed to confront her with its hostile blankness.

He swung the door wide to let her in. She noticed an open book lying on the single chair.

"Were you reading?"

"Yes ma'am."

She picked the book up and glanced at the title: *Kindred of the Dust*.

"There were some books in one of those aid packages that came from the States," he explained.

"Is it any good?"

"I guess so. I'm not that far into it yet."

Maureen sat in the chair and held the book in her lap, saving Arthur's place with her finger. He took a seat opposite her on his cot with its neatly tucked-in blankets. He looked away from her as he waited for her to speak.

"Thank you," she said. "For everything that you've told us, and shown us. You've been very patient, letting us intrude on your life like this."

"That's all right."

"We're leaving here tomorrow. Our ship sails in five days. I know it would be very presumptuous of me to imagine that you might want to come home with us. But I have imagined it."

He said nothing. She couldn't tell if his silence was meant to shut her out or to hear her out.

"I'm not trying to make a case that you should come back," she said. "I just want you to know that if you did, you would have friends. We could find you work."

"I've got work here."

"I know that, but you seem lonely. You seem—"

"I don't even know you," he said.

His tone was not just sharp, it was almost violent.

"You keep talking like it's your business to save me from something. But it's not."

"I'll go," she said after an unnerving silence. She stood up and replaced the book on the chair, open to the page he'd been reading.

"I didn't say you had to go."

"Don't worry, the initiative is mine."

He stood up and walked across the room in two strides and put his hand over hers before she could pull the rope latch of the door.

"I didn't mean to sound that way," he said. "It was nice of you to think you could take me back to the States with you but I'm fine where I am. I don't want to go home. I don't need anybody to take me there. If I wanted to go I could get there by myself. I could find work by myself. I could get used to people looking at me."

"I'm sorry," Maureen said. "I thought if you knew you had a friend in the States, if you had someone to count on, that it might make it easier for you to come home. But it's a fault of mine—assuming too much."

"You can sit back down if you want to."

"Thank you, but it's better if I go. I'm sure my father and I will have a chance to say good-bye to you in the morning."

She left and closed the door behind her. But she had gone only a few paces when she heard it open again, and stopped to see him walking toward her, buttoning his coat. The dog that had been barking quieted when Arthur joined her. They walked up the street toward the *mairie.*

Arthur said nothing, and neither did she. With a tilt of her head she indicated her intention to veer away from the *mairie* and to continue walking past the remains of the village church, which stood roofless on a little hill, its doors and stained-glass windows raggedly blown away. In less than five minutes of walking they were at the northern limits of Somme-Py, looking out at the terrain they had covered in their trek to Saint-Étienne.

Maureen took a seat in front of a remnant of wall, all that was left of a house that had once stood here. Beyond a strip of forest that Arthur had told them was called Vipers Wood the open land verged away into the darkness, rising upward to its crest at Blanc Mont, visible tonight only as a suggestion of gathering mass against the stars.

Arthur slouched down against the wall until he was sitting on the ground next to her. They had been committed to their awkward silence for so long now that when he spoke his voice surprised her.

"I wish we hadn't run into that Indian fella. Maybe if he hadn't told Ben what his father did, Ben would still be here."

"He'd be home in Texas," Maureen said.

"Maybe we all would."

Arthur picked up a piece of a brick from the pile at the base of the house and chucked it out into the darkness, where it landed softly in a tangle of winter branches in the ravine below them.

"I don't expect to ever be happy or anything like that," he said. "But I'm getting along pretty well here and I'm learning a trade of sorts, helping to put this place back together. I know you meant it out of kindness that I ought to come back with you, but I took it wrong."

She said nothing, but smiled over at him in gratitude. She stood and brushed the masonry dust off her skirt, ready to walk back, when he looked up at her in the darkness.

"Anyway, seems to me you're the one who's lonely."

"That may be," she said. "Shall we go back now?"

But he didn't move, just sat there and kept looking at her, his eyes hidden in shadow and his shattered face unreadable.

"I don't know anything," he said.

"What do you mean?"

"I just don't know how you're supposed to—"

He shook his head when he couldn't find words to finish his thought. She crouched down beside him, saw the confusion and frustration in his eyes.

"I'm going to guess what you mean," she whispered. "Is that all right?"

He nodded. It did not seem, in the moment, such a daring thing, touching her hand to his face, kissing him, though she would look back on this action throughout all the rest of her life with a sense of amazement. His urgent response saved her from humiliation. He did not have much of a mouth left and so the kissing itself was rather tentative, neither of them knowing exactly how to manage it. But Maureen felt on sure ground anyway, confident of his desire, grateful for the conviction that lay behind his shyness.

After a few minutes he pulled her to her feet and walked with her back past the dark church and to the center of the village. They did not speak out loud or even whisper, and when they passed the *mairie provisionaire* where her father was sleeping she did not pause, but stayed by his side and walked with him to his hut.

She knew very little about lovemaking and suspected the same was probably true of Arthur. Perhaps he had been with women while he was in the army. Her own experience had never taken her further than that dreadful evening in Austin, when she had almost given herself up to Vance beneath the empty eye sockets of his longhorn skull. Arthur bent down and built up the fire in his little stove. He turned down the blankets on his cot, each action confirming that something further would happen, that she wasn't misreading what they meant to do.

They both stalled for a moment at the staggering impropriety of taking off their clothes, until Arthur rather boldly took things in hand and began to unfasten the buttons at her throat. When they were undressed she wanted to stand there for a moment, even though they were shivering, because feeling exposed like this, revealed inside and out, was the most startling sensation she had ever known.

The cot was impossibly narrow, the coarse wool blankets intolerable against their bare skin. But the discomfort she felt, and the pleasure she felt, were fused together somehow. Shaking from cold, itching from wool, quivering from astonishment.

"You don't have to look at me," he told her.

"I want to."

She touched his face, the wrong side, feeling the hard surfaces of the prosthesis where there should have been muscle and bone. He flinched a little in embarrassment, but by degrees relaxed and let her look at him and touch him. Then he shifted carefully and she shifted in response until she was settled beneath him. She made a point to keep looking at him during the most urgent pitch of lovemaking and in the languorous silence afterward. She did not want him to ever see her looking away. But when he closed his eyes and began to doze she allowed herself to do the same. She skimmed along the surface of sleep, her mind taking her back over the battlefield of Saint-Étienne, over that field of white crosses in the cemetery in Romagne, where she stared at her father's face as he stared down in turn at Ben Clayton's grave. He seemed to be trying to summon the dead boy from the ground, trying to see Ben's face and form and spirit as they had been in life, so that he could use his genius to render them in bronze. Tight in Arthur's arms, verging deeper into sleep, she had the sensation of lying beneath that white cross herself, keeping company with all those terrified and bewildered and homesick boys. It would have been a peaceful feeling without the thought of her father still staring down, calling out her name, unable to understand where she had gone and why she was hiding.

The dream was vivid enough to jerk her awake. It had only been fifteen minutes or so. She felt Arthur's fingers lazily circling her forehead. He was awake as well. She told him she had better go back, and so they dressed and stood there in the *abris* holding each other, knowing that except for the formal good-bye they would have in the morning this was almost certainly the last time they would ever see each other. But she was content for this moment to stand alone. She felt it ought to be that way, like a great rock rising from the static lake of her life, visible from every direction.

She walked back by herself to the *mairie.* She could feel her father's wakefulness as she crossed through the dark hall where he slept to her own alcove. He was awake but said nothing. If he had asked she would have told him the truth. There was nothing she cared to reveal and nothing she cared to hide. The neutral comportment she felt, the sense that her secrets were not gravely held but were simply her own business, was satisfyingly new to her.

Stuart was there in the morning with the car. They thanked the L'Huilliers. They thanked Arthur. He stepped forward and kissed her on both cheeks in the French manner. They promised they would continue to write each other but any other promise would have been false and cruel. Arthur waved briefly as they drove away and then, as she watched, L'Huillier gently touched his shoulder and directed his gaze to something on the wooden steeple of the temporary church that needed his attention.

Meanwhile Gil Gilheaney was staring straight ahead, silently fixed in his own thoughts as Stuart continued his historical narration of the events of the war.

THIRTY-TWO

The cattle had wintered well enough, but a late norther had kept the grass down and so there was a fair amount of weak stock that needed to be gathered and fed. After that there was the spring roundup to organize and get ready for. The thought of all that work made Lamar feel even older than he was. Or maybe not the work itself, but the way it came around with the seasons every year, a relentless cycle that seemed to grab his life before it could move forward and haul it back to where it had been the year before. Of course he didn't have any notion about his life moving forward in the first place. You stayed in place and then you died, and that was about it.

He could remember times, though, when it felt like he was headed someplace. When he met Sarey; when Ben was born. And for a while there when he was with the Comanches. Life with them had been just as cyclical and pointless in its own way. The hunts and raids he had been on, the long stretches of idleness when it seemed like the world had stopped—all of that had followed the calendar just like the spring and fall roundups and worming and branding and putting out salt. But when he had been on the move with the Quahada—riding west into the mountains, or down into Mexico—it felt like you weren't trapped in the world and its rules after all, like you were escaping time itself.

Today he was looking for a couple of cows that were heavy with calf and needed to be moved to better pasture. He was alone and happy to be that way. It had long ago gotten to the point where he knew what

Ernest or Nax or George's Mary was going to say before they said it, and that added to the sense he had that life just repeated itself over and over again until it finally wore you out and you could go on ahead and die. His own thoughts were tiresomely familiar too, but sometimes when you were alone with yourself you were just better company.

There was a cramp working in his thigh and he dismounted to stretch it out. That never used to happen, but neither did hemorrhoids or not being able to pass water or a hell's dozen other nuisances of the sort. He took a thermos of coffee from a saddlebag and drank it down. It was midmorning and the coffee was cold. He put the thermos back and set his foot in the stirrup and damned if he could pull himself up into the saddle. It wasn't his crampy leg, it was more like he'd just taken the muscles in his shoulders and arms by surprise. He knew it would pass and that in another minute or two he'd be able to mount his horse like nothing had ever happened, but in the meantime it made him angry and it made him scared too. One of these days he wouldn't be able to get out of his bed or out of his chair. If he wasn't lucky enough to have a heart attack or crack his head open getting thrown from his horse, there was no telling where he'd end up. Maybe in the Abilene hospital, eating jello and staring out the window.

He saw a buzzard sail down out of the sky to the top of a craggy hill and disappear into what looked like a little cave. That interested him for some reason. He figured that climbing up to the top of the hill to see a buzzard's nest would be good for his leg cramp and give his body some time to think about getting back to business and lifting him into the saddle like it was supposed to. He tied his horse to a hackberry trunk and climbed the hill. There was no clear way up and it was steeper than it looked from the pasture, with lots of shady little crevices where it would be easy to surprise a rattler or a vinegaroon.

He was out of breath when he made it to the top. The little hill wasn't nearly as prominent as the one that meant so much to Ben, and he'd never had enough cause or curiosity to climb up on it before. The cave he had seen from the bottom was really only a shadowy seam in the rock, part of a craggy crest guarded by prickly pear. The slope leading up to it was sharp enough that he needed to use his hands as well as his feet, and he didn't like the sensation of all that loose rock under his boots. But he kept climbing anyway, and when he was almost to the opening the mother buzzard burst out of the nest and puffed up her feathers and threw up on the ground in front of him, the way buzzards do when they're trying to defend themselves or make a point. The buzzard vomit was almost as foul-smelling as the spray from a skunk, and Lamar carefully backed away a few paces to keep the mother from getting any more agitated than she already was. Behind her, in the shadowy nest, the two chicks were spreading their wings just like their mother and stamping their feet and hissing at him.

The chicks already had the sharp heads and beaks of adult birds but their feathers were still mostly white. They hissed at him without any variation in pitch or any stopping for breath. It was like the noise that came from a hole in a steam pipe. They didn't seem to know why they were mad or afraid, just that they ought to be.

"All right, calm down now," he told the mother buzzard when she hopped toward him again. "I'm leaving." At another point in his life he might have shot her, and her chicks too, just out of a general feeling that varmints were some kind of mistake that nature had made and that they deserved to be dead. But he didn't have that feeling so much anymore. He had climbed all the way up here just because he had never seen a buzzard nest and at his age there probably wouldn't be another opportunity to satisfy himself about what one looked like. And he wouldn't like to shoot those chicks now, even though they were ugly and evil-looking and hissed at him like snakes. They were helpless creatures, and he thought maybe their disagreeable appearance had something to do with that helplessness. In any case, they pulled at him for some reason, and left him unsettled in a way he didn't care for. The tenderness he felt for those birds was like an accusation. How come you couldn't feel that for your own damn son? How come you let things get to the point where he could go off and leave without even saying good-bye?

He started to make his way down, carefully watching his step on the loose rock, feeling it trickle under the soles of his boots. Sure enough, he fell; not as hard as he could have, but his feet skidded out from under him and he landed on his backside and hit his funny bone on a rock. He sat there for a minute cursing his foolishness and hoping his elbow wasn't broken. He could move it all right, so he guessed it wasn't. That would be a hell of a note, he thought, to fall down up here and not be able to get back down, to have to wait for Ernest or Nax to find him. What if he'd passed out? Maybe they wouldn't find him till the next morning. All because he wanted to see a damn buzzard's nest.

He stood up, his funny bone still humming with pain like a tuning fork. It didn't stop hurting until he was all the way back to the bottom again, and all the good that did was shift his attention to the sore spot on his upper thigh where he had fallen and to his worn-out knees, which hadn't needed a steep uphill climb in the first place. But he'd been right in thinking he just needed a little time to get back onto his horse. His elbow hurt and his knee hurt and his leg hurt but he got himself into the saddle with no trouble this time, and he went on and found the two cows where they were shaded up under some trees and spent the rest of the day moving them along to decent grass, wishing they had the sense to be grateful to him for his trouble.

IT WAS FIVE O'CLOCK by the time he was home and when he rode up from the creek bottom he saw that Ernest and Nax were both on horseback and they were dragging a horse carcass out of the pen by its hind legs.

"We're surely sorry," Ernest said. "It just happened about a half hour ago."

Lamar walked along beside the hands as they dragged Poco to a clearing about fifty yards beyond the house. The horse's tongue was hanging out past its mouth, and as it dragged along it made its own separate trail in the dirt.

"I think it was the sleeping sickness," Nax said. "He was looking a little confused this morning."

"No," Lamar told him, "it ain't likely to be sleeping sickness with no mosquitoes around yet to speak of. Maybe some damn beetle or other got baled up in his hay."

"Or locoweed," Ernest guessed.

"Don't matter now," Lamar said.

Without speaking about it anymore, the three of them began collecting tree limbs and dry brush to cover the horse carcass where it lay in the clearing. Peggy joined them but didn't nose around in the piles of brush like she would have before—that snakebite had taught her her lesson. Lamar kept piling up the fuel past the point where it was necessary. He didn't really want to see Poco when they lit the fire. It was nearly dark when they finished. Ernest left and came back with a can of kerosene and sprinkled it over the brush and tossed a match onto it, and the fire erupted into the sky and then began to settle and crackle as it took hold. Ernest and Nax went back into the house for their supper but Lamar said to go ahead without him and he'd be there after a while.

He hadn't planned to watch his son's horse while it burned but he found he was drawn to the sight for some reason. There was the smell of roasting meat and burning hair. As the night around him deepened, the heat from the fire grew stronger, almost singeing his eyebrows. As it cooked out, the fat from the horse made a puddle in the dirt.

Poco hadn't been Ben's first horse but he was the one that had mattered. Ben had been fourteen that Christmas, Lamar recollected. It was the year after Sarey died and he thought buying Ben a horse would distract him and keep him from being listless about losing his mother. It worked about as well as anything could. Ben broke Poco himself. He was a gentle horse to begin with and didn't need much work before he could be ridden, but the fact that Ben had been the one to do it had gotten the animal's attention. Lamar knew he probably didn't have any business speculating about the things a horse might or might not feel about people, but there was some kind of closeness the horse had with Ben that he never had with Lamar or any of the hands after Ben was no longer around.

He sat there for nearly an hour and then he left the fire to smolder and walked stiffly back to the house, feeling his sore thigh and knee with every step. As she walked along beside him, Peggy still favored her snakebit leg. Like him, she had to probe a bit before she committed to setting it down.

When he got back inside, George's Mary set his supper down on the table without a word, chili and warmed-over corn bread and pinto beans.

"You get thrown off your horse?" she asked.

"I don't usually and I didn't today," he said.

"You're walking like you did."

"I slipped on some rocks."

"What do you mean, slipped on some rocks?"

"That's what I mean."

He didn't tell her about walking up to the top of the hill to see the buzzard's nest. She would have found some reason to disapprove of it. While he ate, she sat in a chair in the parlor and didn't even pretend to occupy herself with anything other than being upset about Poco. When he was through eating she picked up his dishes and gestured to a big parcel sitting on the divan with the rest of the mail.

"It's from that Mr. Gilheaney," she said. "A letter too."

She stood over him, waiting to see what was in the letter, but he wouldn't open it till she went back into the kitchen.

Dear Mr. Clayton,

I should like you to know that I have been to France and seen your son's grave, as well as the battlefield on which he fell. Maureen was with me and took the photographs that I enclose with this letter. As you can see he rests in the company of many thousands of other American soldiers, in the great cemetery in Romagne. It is my hope that these Kodaks will bring you more comfort than pain, but if I'm wrong please forgive my presumption in sending them.

Maureen and I were in France on other matters when I decided to search out Arthur Fry, the young man who wrote you some months ago and who, as you know, was with Ben when he died. I suppose what motivated me was a feeling of unfinished business. The despair I felt over the destruction of the statue—a despair that you yourself of course witnessed—rendered my interest in the project dormant for a time but did not kill it. In fact, "interest" is far too weak a word for the passionate sense of direction that seemed to animate me while I conceived and modeled the sculpture. I told you, while we were riding across your ranch, that this statue would be my masterpiece. I was a little embarrassed at the time by that outburst, particularly since I know perfectly well that an artist's reputation is the result of opinions not his own. But I sensed a defining purpose for me in this work, and though I lost the statue itself in a studio accident I did not want to lose that purpose.

Therefore I decided to take the work up again. Whether I take up the commission again is another matter, one entirely for you to decide. Upon my return from France I barricaded myself for six weeks in the studio, working at a pace and with an intensity I had not known for many years. Another full-size clay version of the statue is, as you can see, now completed. Next week the plasterers will come to take a mold, which will be shipped off to the foundry in New York for casting in bronze. I will be nervous as a cat while the plasterers do their work, hovering over them to make sure no harm comes to the clay. When the mold is taken Maureen and I will follow it to New York, where I will haunt the foundry to make sure everything is completed to my satisfaction.

You may make your own judgment about the success of my work from the photographs. I am satisfied. I have done my best and believe I have succeeded. If you do not recognize your son in the clay, then I have of course failed to satisfy you and in a more technical sense I suppose I have not met the basic requirements of my profession. But I believe this is Ben. I believe this is Ben as you described him to me, and as I encountered and understood him on my own.

If you want the statue you may rewrite the contract and amend the original terms as you desire. I do not care. I will sign what you send me. For reasons of my own I had to finish this piece and I have. Let me know what you want to do.

Sincerely,
Francis Gilheaney

P.S. By separate mail I am sending Ben's clothes, which you were kind enough to lend me. His saddle and hat have been shipped as well and should arrive next week. All have been insured.

Lamar stared at the photographs of his son's grave, at the close-up of his name carved in the marble cross, at the shot that showed his cross among all the others. It looked like there were as many crosses as there were blades of grass on the llano. He looked at the pictures of the shot-up little town—Saint-Étienne—that Ben and his regiment had attacked. He saw the cemetery where his son had died. While he was looking at the pictures George's Mary came out of the kitchen and stood behind him. He passed each one off to her without comment and all she said was "Oh my."

The last photos were of the statue. It was different than the model he had seen in Gilheaney's studio that first time, the one that had startled him so much he had forgotten who he was and where he was. It wasn't like Gilheaney was trying to steal Ben away anymore. Ben was there, in the statue, all by himself. It wasn't like he was put there by the artist, like he was shaped by Gilheaney's hands; it was like he and Poco had just showed up on their own.

It was there in the face, whatever it was: the quality that made Lamar believe that the sculptor had succeeded. He saw the innocence and trust that had been in Ben's eyes when he was a boy, when he had been so proud to ride and work alongside his father. He saw some kind of wanting in that face too, not a lack of anything but an expectation, the bright sort of yearning that Sarey used to have when she talked about what it would be like to see Europe or some other such place.

But there was anger too, and you couldn't miss it. Lamar didn't know how Gilheaney had got it into Ben's expression but it was there. It was the fury that had been in Ben's face the last time Lamar had seen him, a fury Lamar had never been able to erase from his memory and that Gilheaney had somehow seen and understood and sealed into the sculpture.

The funny thing was that from one moment to the next you did not know what you were looking at: the innocence of a child, the buoyant expectation of a young man, or the anger of a betrayed son. They were all bound up together, like they might be in a living face, impossible to pin down or pry apart.

He handed these last pictures to George's Mary. He watched her as she looked at them. She worked her mouth like a jackrabbit, unconsciously sucking and probing the empty places in her mouth where those teeth had been pulled.

"Well, what do you think?" he finally asked her.

"What do I think about what?"

"This damn statue. What do I do about it?"

"I never saw what you needed a statue of your son for in the first place. But that's your business. You spend your money how you want."

"It look like him to you?"

"I don't want to talk about it," she said, throwing the photos into his lap. "It looks too damn much like him. It looks too much like our Ben."

She went into her room and he could hear her sobbing. He thought about knocking on her door after she quieted down a little and trying to find something of comfort to say to her, maybe telling her to sleep in in the morning and not worry about getting breakfast. But he knew from long experience there was no way to be kind to her without stirring her up more. She'd wait on him hand and foot just to spite him, no matter how broken-up she was feeling.

Sometimes he wondered if her resentment of him had to do with more than just her nature and his and them being in the house together for so long. Sometimes he wondered if she knew. She had never told him much about what had happened on her farm when she was a little girl. He'd had to put it together himself, and after he had he'd kept quiet about it. He had made it a rule never to say much about his life with the Comanches to anybody—especially not to the newspaper writers or the college professors who used to come around every few years wanting him to drop everything he was doing and tell them his story, thinking he would be pleased by their attention. Sarey he had told the bare outlines, Ben even less. Enough time had passed that people thought there was romance in it, but he looked back on that part of his life with mostly shame—shame at what he had let happen to his sister and what he had let happen to him. His character, even as a boy, ought to have been stronger. He ought not to have surrendered his soul and turned into a Comanche because Kanaumahka and a few of the others had decided to be kind to him and accepting of him.

The invitation to go on his first raid had been a surprise. Kanaumahka and some of the other warriors had gotten all painted up and ridden their horses through the camp, gathering up recruits. They'd gone around three or four times when Kanaumahka finally reined up in front of Lamar and gave him a look that said: Ain't you coming? It had never occurred to him before that moment that he was a member of the band and that he could decide what he wanted to do along with the rest of them. So he got his horse and followed the caravan around the camp and took part in the dancing that night and Kanaumahka gave him a shield and put it next to his on the rack outside his lodge, where it gathered up power from the sun all the next day.

They rode east for the better part of a week, Kanaumahka building little maps in the dirt at the start of each day's travel, explaining to them all the landmarks they would pass in case any of them got separated from the main bunch. It was all very organized and strategic. Not a bunch of wild Indians whooping and carrying on, but a disciplined and well-informed body of mostly young men moving deliberately across the prairie. At the Salt Fork, the scouts came back with the opinion that a farm up ahead looked like a likely prospect, just a man and his wife, three or four teenage sons, a young girl, six or eight horses in the pen at night and a pasture with thirty head of cattle. Kanaumahka went on himself to see the place and came back and sketched out his plan. They would kill the dogs with arrows first and then whoever was visible in the pasture or in the horse pens and then move on up to the house before a clear warning could be given.

The party attacked on two fronts and Lamar was given the task of holding the horses of the warriors who crept up to the farm from the riverbank. It was late summer and that part of the Brazos was almost dry, the water only ankle-deep between sunbaked sandbars. In the case of a forced retreat, the assault party would have little trouble making its escape across the river to the rendezvous point. He held the reins of the horses while they stood cooling their forelegs in the shallow water. The trees were thick along the riverbank and they obscured his view as the Indians made their way along the grassy slope up toward the horse pens. He could hear the mother in the house calling out to somebody, but in a normal voice. She had not yet noticed anything wrong. He was confused, because the stealth and deliberation of this attack seemed at odds with his own memory of the Indians suddenly bursting into the house while his mother was setting the table. There had seemed no planning at all to the act that had changed his life, just a hair-raising impulsiveness.

He had painted his face black and yellow, and in the midday heat it was a suffocating paste. He could feel sweat running down the mask of his face and tickling the crown of his head, where he had outlined the parting of his now-longish hair with a red streak. He was young and inexperienced and not qualified to wear a feather, but the hair he had gathered into clumsy braids and tied with strips of blue homespun was decorated with beads of glass and flashy triangles of tin. He wore a bandanna around his neck whose ends were gathered into a hollowed-out knob of buffalo bone. He had asked a kindly old woman in the band to pierce the tops of his ears in imitation of the older warriors, and each ear now held multiple ornaments of brass and silver wire whose sagging weight he could feel. All of this he had fussed over. He could feel the power of these signs and markings. He understood them and gloried in them. Although his mouth was dry from fear he somehow did not feel confusion about the raid in which he was about to play his small part. He felt contempt for the Tahbybo, the white people who kept swarming over the horizon to live their demeaning settled lives, rooted to one spot, slaves to their crops and even to their stupid cattle. He no longer clung to his memories of being one of them, he no longer thought of his white family as anything more than unthinking people trying to control a land whose enormity and dominion and ancient memory they could not understand. Their ignorance had swept them away, all but him. In his mind the predation in which he was now taking part was mixed up with a sense of biblical righteousness, a cleansing of all who were presumptuous and ignorant and not fit to abide on the majestic earth.

He heard the abbreviated yelp of one dog and the agonized howling of another and swept the tree branches aside to see his fellow Comanches converging toward the cabin from two directions. The family that was taken by surprise was angry and incautious. An older brother came to the door and shot down an eighteen-year-old warrior named Tosaguera, who lay twisting in the grass with his legs drawn up for the rest of the fight and was dead before anybody could come to his aid. Kanaumahka burst through the door before the shooter could close it and another five or six followed him in. There was screaming in the cabin and not much gunfire. Lamar guessed that the fighting was too close and fast for anybody to reload. In a minute he saw one of the older warriors dragging the mother out by the hair with the little girl clinging to her skirts and trying to pull her away from the Indians. They bashed the mother's head in but before they could do anything else there was rifle fire from a ridge on the other side of the cabin and four or five white men came running into the fight with their teeth bared and not caring whether they got killed or not. Nobody had seen the men on the scout and it was much argued about later where they had come from and how they had been able to take the Comanches by surprise.

The Comanches were in possession of the cabin and the outbuildings and were not in the mood just then to surrender them, so for a time there was firing back and forth from both sides. Lamar had tied the reins of the horses to pecan trunks and he checked them to make sure they wouldn't run off but they weren't as scared as he was and they stayed in place. Through the trees he saw one of the brothers that lived on the farm rise up from where he had been hiding in the grass and run in panic toward the river. He stumbled when one of the Indians shot him but he kept on coming, right toward Lamar. Lamar could hear him breathing and could see his face. It was pale and stretched tight with fear.

Lamar notched an arrow and pulled it tight and pointed it at the man as he came crashing down the bank and flailed wildly at the tangles of branches and grapevine. He was not a man. He was hardly older than Lamar himself. The shot had caught him below the elbow and his arm was flopping like he had no control over it as he ran. He didn't even see Lamar at first, but when he stumbled into the water he saw the horses and then he looked back like he'd missed something. He held up his good arm and said "Please" and it was the first English word Lamar had heard in a long time. It was familiar but he didn't know the meaning of it anymore, or wouldn't let himself.

The boy turned his back and kept on stumbling through the water toward the sandbar in the middle of the river. Lamar could hear the Comanches calling to each other behind him and he knew they had had enough of the fight and were running back to him to get their horses. The white boy kept looking back at him as he ran and waving at him not to shoot him but he did anyway. The arrow slipped into the boy without a sound and it seemed like he was determined to ignore it at first. He made his way to the sandbar and then sat down and looked back at Lamar. He was just breathing and looking at him, like he was trying to figure out who Lamar was. But Lamar turned his back on him and untied the horses just as the rest of the Comanches came running down the riverbank with the rifle balls of the attackers hitting the branches and leaves all around them.

Two of the Indians counted coup on the stunned boy sitting on the sandbar as they rode past him. Another reined up beside him, jumped down from his horse and stuck his knife into his windpipe and then cut away his scalp in practically the same motion.

They met up at the rendezvous point with the men who had attacked the homestead from the other direction, and who had carried away the body of Tosaguera, the only Comanche casualty in the fight. They had killed a number of Tahbybo but because they had been surprised by the men coming over the ridge they had not been able to carry off any stock or any goods, so the raid was counted as more or less a failure. The men who had driven them off would organize their neighbors for a reprisal, and the Rangers would be after them as well, so they decided it was best to do no more raiding along the Salt Fork that summer.

They rode for five or six days before it was deemed safe enough to have a fire, and it was only then that they began to talk about the fight with any spirit. The various members of the party claimed their kills and their coups in that boastful way that was still foreign to him. Nobody had seen Lamar shoot the fleeing boy, at least that he knew. If he stood up to speak about it there would be nobody to back him up and he would lose the respect he was just starting to gain. He was given credit by Kanaumahka for steadily maintaining his station during the fight and that was enough. It was better not to remind himself of the boy's pale distorted face as he raced past him toward the river, and the disappointed look he had taken on as he sat down on the sandbar after Lamar shot him with the arrow.

It was only decades later, long after he had brought George's Mary from Fort Griffin to his ranch house, that she got it into her mind to tell him and Sarey anything about that day. As he recalled it, it was after she had worn herself out cooking one Fourth of July and the three of them were sitting out on the porch after Ben had gone to bed. She said she had had three brothers. The two older ones were Octavius and Marius. Her father had been an admirer of ancient history but after the first two boys were born her mother had said enough was enough with the Roman names and called the next one Andy. Andy had almost gotten away that day, she told them. He had made it halfway across the river.

Lamar sat there frozen in his chair as she told them how they'd killed her brothers and father and uncle and how they were about to kill her when some men who had been building a bandstand a mile or so away had heard the gunfire and come to the rescue.

She said she went to live with a neighbor family after her folks were killed but it didn't take. She was determined to be a wild and willful child in order to punish the world and everybody in it for what had happened to her. She was sent to live with a schoolteacher in Decatur and after the schoolteacher had washed her hands of her she ended up in an orphanage in Fort Worth. She was told that her family's land had been sold and the money put in trust for her, but when she tried to find out more about that they said she had been told wrong.

George's Mary knew of course that Lamar had been taken by the Comanches and lived with them. He knew from the way people sometimes acted around him that it was common knowledge that he had done more than live with them, that he had been a wild Indian in his own right. And one of the things he remembered about that night on the porch was the way her eyes had kept darting to his face as she told the story, like she was trying to see if what she was saying showed up somehow in his reaction. As best he knew, he had not revealed anything to her. He had kept the panic inside, and had carried it there ever since.

There wasn't any reason to bring it out. There wasn't any reason to confess to her. It wasn't like she would be grateful to him for telling her, or more at ease with herself. It would just stir things up more than either of them would be able to stand.

Before he went to bed he looked out the window and he could see the smoldering fire in the darkness where Poco was burning. He saw coyotes start to come in and lick at the grease and so he got his rifle and went down there and stood guard, for no practical purpose he could think of. What did it matter if the coyotes got to his son's burned-up horse? They would sooner or later; that's what they were put on earth to do.

He sat there senselessly in the dark, holding his rifle in the crook of his arm, sensing the coyotes with their intolerable excitement pacing back and forth just out of sight.

If he had any sense he would write back to Gilheaney and tell him to go to hell. Ben was gone and now Poco was gone and a statue wasn't going to change that. But he and Gilheaney were alike in one way, maybe. Once they got an idea in their heads, it didn't seem to come easily to their nature to let it go.

It occurred to him he might take that sixteen thousand dollars he was paying Gil Gilheaney and give it to George's Mary instead. But she wouldn't take it, and if he told her the reason he offered it she would turn her face away from him and be gone the next day. She would go away fuming with resentment, just like Ben had. Just like Jewell too, once he'd run her off. Maybe that's what he had been trying to do all along, just drive people off his property and out of his life.

THIRTY-THREE

The hackmen were all gone. The avenues of New York were jammed with the motor taxis that had replaced them, and crossing the street in the middle of the block was now as hazardous as it was illegal. Women smoked brazenly in the restaurants, the old Elevated still clattered overhead, adding to the traffic and subway noise, and the money the war had brought to the city was visible everywhere, from the streetside demonstrations of expensive cooking ware to the vibrant display windows of the department stores and groceries, to the well-dressed young people with time on their hands queuing up for chop suey or swarming giddily into the wicky-wicky clubs.

He had not been home to New York for five years, not since he had come back alone to his mother's funeral. He realized he was looking upon all the changes with the sort of reflexive disapproval he had always despised in others. Once again he had the sense of the world surging forward, leaving him stranded behind.

Gil had not bothered to notify any of his old friends to tell them that he would be in New York for the casting of his statue, and he had made a point of avoiding the Algonquin or any of the other hotels or watering holes where he was likely to encounter someone he knew. He was not in hiding but he was not in a mood to catch up with people; he didn't know where to begin. He had booked Maureen and himself into a small tourist hotel a few blocks from Madison Square Park, where Saint-Gaudens' Farragut still stood with its foursquare brilliance—no allegory, no sculptural business, just a statue of a determined man modeled with quiet fidelity.

He and Maureen had arranged to meet in the park today at eleven, but he had woken at five a.m., unable to sleep, unable to be still. He had set out walking through the dead streets, all the way down to Battery Park. After so long in Texas, he felt a nostalgic freedom in being a New York pedestrian again, ranging through a cityscape that had been built for walking.

Now it was sunrise and he was standing quayside at the Battery, looking out toward the bay. There was no wind, the water lay flat. The ferries were coming in from Brooklyn and Staten Island, and because it was still so early and the day so calm he could hear the ploshing of the vessels as they neared the quayside and even the voices of passengers bounding across the taut water. He could hear the barking of seals from the aquarium.

The rising sun struck the breastplate of Ettore Ximenes' statue of Verrazano, whose dedication Gil had attended years earlier. Hartley's John Ericsson statue caught the sun as well, though not as dramatically, and across the park at the entrance to the Customs House Dan French's muscular tribute to the continents of America, Africa, Asia, and Europe sat there taking on the morning light with a magnificent indifference to the firefly span of human life. Good for Dan, Gil thought as he stood in front of the sculptures. The sculpture groupings were a little busy and the sinuosity of the minor figures was rather sinister, but they held the eye with honest force and the perspective from below was commanding.

He was pleased that he did not feel the envy and sense of injustice he had felt when he had stood here in the past, surrounded by the works of men who had made more of a mark than he had. The Clayton statue was almost done, it was at the foundry across the river in Brooklyn. It was the equal of anything here, anything in New York. He had no idea if it would ever even be displayed. If Lamar Clayton didn't want it for his desolate hilltop it would be difficult to find another place for it. But he would try. He would never stop trying.

He flexed his hands, just to feel the pain. The arthritis, which had been tentative for so long, was now solidly established. He was not sure if he could ever really work again, not in the same way, not without assistants to take over the greater part of the modeling. It was his own fault. He had worked too heedlessly, unable to stop himself. The voyage home from France had been a kind of torture, all that static time on the ship trying to burn up his energy on the promenade deck, trying to read in the library, politely listening to the talk of strangers in the dining room. He had been desperate to work, to pack clay onto the armature again, to bring to this new version of Ben Clayton's likeness all that he had learned about his subject from Arthur Fry.

When he was finally in his studio again he had worked almost without pause, his mind flaring with urgent inspiration even in sleep. When his hands began to hurt again, he still kept up the pace, attacking the clay in short bursts, using the heels of his hands when the pain in his fingers was too great. Maureen worked alongside him, the two of them hardly speaking, both because they had so little to say to each other now and because the primacy of the task superseded conversation. He had tried to spare his hands as much as possible for the detail work, trusting her with the gross contours of the human and horse figures. But toward the end, when his hands were so inflamed he could barely move them, he could only stand there and watch and instruct as Maureen used his own cherished tools to make the delicate additions and elisions that would spell the difference between a credible likeness and a work of art.

And so it was she who had put the finishing touches on Ben Clayton's face, and in doing so had brought something to it that Gil was quite sure he could not have brought on his own. He had watched her work, he had seen every adjustment she made, but he could not say at what point the piece's defining quality—its shifting tones of heartbreak, and anger, and loneliness—had entered the portrait. All he knew was that it came from his daughter's hand.

HE WALKED back up Broadway to Madison Square Park. Maureen was already there, standing by the Farragut holding a mixed bouquet of spring flowers.

"Shall we go?" he asked, and she nodded. She did not ask him how he had spent the morning and he did not dare ask the question of her. The experience in France had bound them together in a different kind of way. They had walked the Saint-Étienne battlefield together and shared in hearing Arthur's secret story of Ben Clayton's death. Upon their return home they had spent six weeks in the studio together, working so swiftly and harmoniously there had barely been any need for discussion. The flush of power and independence that Gil observed in Maureen seemed to be predicated upon a kind of fluid silence. She was polite, judicious, companionable—but no longer quite his daughter. Or maybe he was no longer quite her father. The balance between them had shifted; a little girl's unquestioning admiration had been replaced by a woman's calculated respect.

They got into a cab at the edge of the park and rode up Fifth Avenue, leaving the Farragut behind only to pass by another of Saint-Gaudens' great works twenty-five blocks farther north, his gleaming Sherman riding A. P. Proctor's horse.

"Proctor has nothing on you," Maureen said, with a hint of the old admiration in her voice. "Your horse is every bit as good."

"I think I'd like it even better if you said Saint-Gaudens had nothing on me," he told her.

"Well," she said, smiling, "why don't we just let history decide that?"

It was as strong a compliment as she could have given, a cool acknowledgment that his Clayton statue deserved to be judged in the courts of history alongside the works of the master. He looked at her but she was turned away from him, staring at the buildings of Marble Row. The scent of the flowers she held in her lap filled the cab and in some odd way seemed to increase the distance between them. She needed that distance today, had been declaring it for some time now, most emphatically on that night in Somme-Py when she had disappeared from the *mairie* before midnight and did not come back until a few hours before dawn. Where she had gone, whom she had seen—common sense pointed only in one direction. He knew she would never tell him what had happened between her and Arthur Fry that night, that she had no more reason to confide in him about Arthur than he did to tell her the story of his night with Therèse at the St. Charles Hotel. He knew that his daughter's quiet self-sufficiency was in part an indictment of himself, of his own failure as a father. His deceit had liberated her.

They crossed the East River on the new Queensboro Bridge and ten minutes later passed through the gates of Calvary Cemetery. The driver took them to the side of a sloping hill from which the buildings of New York were vibrantly visible across the river. Gil had designed his mother's tombstone himself, a simple granite marker upon which he had hand-carved her name and dates, and above them a detail he had taken from a holy card she had painted of the Thirteenth Station of the Cross.

He said nothing and stood back while—for the second time in a little over two months—Maureen set down flowers on the grave of a person she had never met. He watched her read the wording carved into the granite, saw her lips move as she did so, as if she were muttering a prayer.

"How many people were here?" she asked. "When she was buried?"

"Twenty or so. Most of her old friends were dead. People she knew from church mostly."

"And Mother and I were in San Antonio?"

He nodded. "She died just after the plaster molds for the Crockett had been shipped. I was planning to come up here to supervise the foundry work anyway."

"Yes, I remember you leaving. So there was no need for any great subterfuge? Not that time?"

"Not that time."

"Was it a lonely feeling, to be here by yourself, burying your mother?"

"Yes. I missed you and your mother terribly."

She knelt down and traced the carving of her grandmother's name with her fingers, plucked away at the unruly grass at the marker's base. Then she stood and looked at him, not crying but with such a burden of sorrow and disappointment on her face that it took all his nerve not to look away.

FOR ALMOST A WEEK Gil had anxiously watched the plasterers at work in his San Antonio studio, making molds of the finished clay statue. It was a delicate business and there was always the chance it could go wrong, ruining the original work while at the same time making a useless impression of it. But under Gil's demanding supervision the plasterers had done their job well, and a negative plaster impression of the statue had been shipped to the Coppini Foundry in

Brooklyn in eleven pieces that, when cast in bronze, would be welded back together.

At the foundry, the hollow plaster impressions were filled with liquid wax. When the wax cooled and the plaster shells were pried off, Gil was relieved to see the pieces of the sculpture once again in their positive form, though in wax this time, not clay. He spent most of the day at the foundry, as was his custom when an important piece was being cast. He consulted with the workers on the system of hollow sprues that needed to be added to each wax piece of the sculpture through which heated air could escape and liquid bronze could be channeled. He tracked each piece as it was dipped into a silica slurry until it was covered with yet another mold, this time a hard ceramic shell. The process of casting was the process of repeatedly obscuring the original sculptural form, then liberating it from this new chrysalis, each time in a different material: clay to wax and finally to immortal bronze.

Now, on the afternoon after Gil and Maureen's visit to the cemetery, the time had come for the final decisive moment. The ceramic molds had been baked in a kiln, burning out the wax inside, and now they were set in beds of sand as two foundry workers in fireproof gloves and aprons carefully stepped forward from the furnace, sharing the weight of a glowing crucible suspended on an iron frame.

Gil and Maureen stood watching. It seemed impossible to him that that bucket could contain the molten bronze within it, since it was itself so superheated as to be nearly transparent. But the crucible was more solid than the brilliant sludge it held, and as the workers tipped it forward into the first mold the bright lava flowed and flared into the now-empty cavity that, once cleaned and chased and trimmed, would become the bronze hind leg of Ben Clayton's beloved horse.

He could feel the furnace heat on his skin as the pour continued, and see the glow reflected on his daughter's face. They had watched this hypnotic process before, the two of them, back in the old days when she was a girl and her mother was alive and his pride had not yet exiled them from New York. But now they stood together in a new configuration, no longer artist and child but collaborators, as united in accomplishment as they were divided in spirit.

The first piece he inspected, two days later when the ceramic shells were sandblasted away, was the bronze plinth upon which the human and horse figures would stand. The base was as shallow as he could practically make it. It would not be a pedestal, just a utilitarian platform. He wanted the Clayton to be perceived as the heartbroken memorial it was, not a heroic monument.

Maureen was not with him today. She had stayed in Manhattan, preferring to wait to see the statue when it was fetted and assembled, not caring to watch her father fuss over every ongoing detail.

It was one in the afternoon and the foundry workers were returning from lunch. He asked several of them to help him and they built up a waist-high stack of wooden skids. When it was in place Gil joined with four other men in hoisting the heavy bronze plinth onto the top. He pulled up a chair and borrowed a hammer and a point chisel and then—just below where he had incised his name into the pliant clay—he began to add the letters he realized he had left off.

"WELL," HE WROTE, "before it is all over and done with I guess you will be calling me a 'Frenchman.' That seems to be the direction I am headed, as I am off to Paris to see a man Lieutenant L'Huillier knows who says he wants to meet me. This man is trying to put together an outfit of people he calls Gueules Cassées. It's a kind of club or society I reckon. 'Gueules Cassées' means broken faces. I don't know what this man's got in mind exactly but it seems like he figures the more people see us the less horrible we'll look to them and they'll give us jobs and the like. I don't know about that but I guess I'll give it a try as I suppose I have been 'hiding out' a little bit in Somme-Py and should 'show my face' as the expression goes, though as you know it is a poor face to be parading around. But I guess I will do it. Maybe because you didn't mind so much that I looked like a monster it could be that other people won't either."

That was about as close as his shyness allowed him to come to even an oblique acknowledgment of their night together in Somme-Py. She would not have to be quite so evasive in her response. She knew he craved a tender voice, a direct tone. But she would not embarrass him by speaking too plainly about a moment that could never be repeated—only remembered.

She had spent the morning at the art library that had just been opened to the public in what once had been a bowling alley in the Frick home on Fifth Avenue. She had strolled afterward through the park, gazing nostalgically at Ward's Shakespeare and his Indian Hunter, two statues she had known from her childhood; and at Emma Stebbins' Bethesda Fountain, which had goaded and inspired her in her youth because it was the only public monument she knew that had been created by a woman.

Arthur's letter was in the batch of forwarded mail that the desk clerk had handed to her when she came back to the hotel. Among the envelopes was one addressed in the elegant penmanship of Mrs. Toepperwein of the San Antonio Women's Club. The date of the dedication of the Spirit of the Waters was now definitely set for September 9. Would Maureen please meet her for tea at the Saint Anthony as soon as convenient so that they might discuss specific plans for the event, particularly any remarks Maureen might like to make before the mayor officially unveiled the piece? Was it true, as Mrs. Toepperwein had heard, that Maureen was an acquaintance of Vance Martindale, the rustic Texas critic and intellectual? Would she suppose that he might be persuaded, both on the basis of friendship and objective merit, to write an essay on the sculpture in the pages of the *Southwestern Historical Quarterly,* like the one he had written on the occasion of the unveiling of her father's Crockett grouping?

Maureen smiled as she sat reading the letter in the lobby of the hotel. She put it back in its envelope. No thank you, Mrs. Toepperwein. If Vance Martindale wanted to spout off about her talent in print, he was free to do so, but she would be damned before she would "persuade" him. It was odd, though: the fact that she no longer had any use for him made her fond of him in a new way. She could imagine in time moving from icy correctness in her relations with him to a tolerant friendship. But no more than that; never any more.

At almost the same moment that she recognized the spidery hand of Lamar Clayton on one of the envelopes, Francis Gilheaney himself strode into the lobby. He looked like he had walked a long way; he was beaming and sweating.

"I've come all the way from the foundry," he said. "Walked across the bridge."

"You look thirsty. You should have a glass of water."

He ignored her; his mood was too high. "The castings are first-class. I was worried we might have picked up an air pocket or two in the wax, but I believe we're going to be free from disaster. Is that the mail?"

He sat down and she handed him the envelope from Mr. Clayton. He tore it open in suspense and she saw the relief in his face when a check slipped out. He laughed at the letter and handed it to Maureen. It read, in its entirety, "Go Ahead. L. Clayton."

He relaxed into his lounge chair, let out a deep breath.

"Well, at least we have a place to put the damn thing. I doubt Clayton will ever have any use for me but he's going to have his statue. What did you do today? Are you hungry? Why don't we go to Renganeschi's? I wouldn't mind bumping into some people from the old crowd, now that this thing is finally settled."

"All right," she said. "If you'd like."

"Remember when the three of us used to go there? You and your mother and me?"

"Of course I do."

He slackened a little more in his chair, wistful now, regretful. For a moment he was silent, then he drew himself up and leaned forward to face her.

"I put your name on it today," he said.

"What?"

"I carved your name on the plinth with a cold chisel, right below my own."

"Daddy . . ."

"It's your work as well as mine. It's more your work than mine, if you want to know the truth. I couldn't have finished it, not with these hands. Not with this selfish old soul of mine. If there's life in that statue, and I know there is, then you're the one who put it there."

She started to answer but her lips were quivering so much she couldn't get the words out. He handed her his handkerchief while the other hotel guests discreetly refrained from staring. After a moment, he reached out and touched her hand.

"I want you to be a full partner on the La Salle. When we get back to San Antonio and start working on it, you'll—"

"I'm not going back to San Antonio, Daddy. I'm staying here."

The blank look he gave her could have been just momentary confusion, but she thought it was something else: a sort of fear she had never seen in his eyes before.

"This is where I'm from," she said. "This is where I want to be. Not Texas."

"You don't want to work with me?"

"No. Not anymore."

"Then what will you do?"

"Work for myself maybe. I don't know."

"I don't see how you can manage. You have no income, you have no money except for what you got from that commission in San Antonio. You can hardly expect that to last for more than—"

"There's my half of that check."

"What are you talking about?"

"You said you couldn't have done the Clayton without me. I happen to think so too. Give me half the money, Daddy."

For a moment she thought he was going to rise from his chair, wad the check up and throw it at her feet and say, "Here! Take it all!" But the anger in his expression turned instead to a kind of wonder, and then to a sadness so deep she could hardly believe her audacity.

"All right," he said at last. "You and I will go to the bank tomorrow and open an account for you. We'll find you a place to live."

"Thank you."

"The money will only last for a little while. I'd still like to know how you think you can get on."

"I won't be proud. I'll take whatever work I can. If I can't get any commissions, I'll be a clerk. I don't care. I want to be here. I want to be on my own."

"You'll have to at least come back for the unveiling of your Women's Club piece."

"No. I'll write them and tell them that you'll be there to represent me. Will you?"

"Of course I will, if that's what you want. But what about the Clayton? Don't you want to be there when it's installed? Don't you want to see it?"

"I've seen it, Daddy. I've already seen it from the inside out."

His eyes were reddening and he was glancing around the room, looking for someplace for his gaze to settle other than on his daughter's eyes. He was a proud man and he did not want to weep openly in a public place.

She leaned forward and spoke in a soft, emphatic voice to her broken father.

"You know, of course, that it's a magnificent work of art. And no one but you could have done it, Daddy. No one."

Struggling for composure, he answered with a nod. She pretended to look at the mail, giving him the chance to gather the formidable emotional strength that had seen him through every artistic setback, every regret, every disappointment, that had enabled him to keep his mind and his heart trained on the work to come, the shapes waiting to be formed in his studio.

"Well," he said when he had come as far back to himself as the moment would allow, "shall we say eight o'clock for dinner?"

THIRTY-FOUR

There was no ceremony. On a day in late September the statue was delivered to the Abilene station in three pieces—man, horse, and base—transferred to a flatbed truck and conveyed to Lamar Clayton's property. The truck then inched precariously along the narrow, half-washed-out ranch roads to the base of the little hill where the statue was to be installed.

It was hard, sweaty, dangerous work getting the pieces to the top, Gil worrying about the fate of his creation every foot of the way. Clayton had hired a crew to clear brush and rocks and outline a rough path to the summit, where the ground that would hold the base had been carefully graded. They tied a stout rope to the axle of the truck and, as it drove forward, the wooden skids to which the statue's pieces were lashed were lurched upward one by one by means of a block and tackle secured to one of the big boulders at the top. Gil and Ernest and Nax and Clayton himself all took a hand in helping to guide the skids along the cleared trail, two of the men walking behind with thick wooden poles to help lever the skids forward and do their best to prevent them from sliding back in case the rope broke.

They all slipped and fell from time to time as they steered and straightened their burden. Gil gashed his knee on a rock, tearing the new twill pants he had bought in New York, scraping his knuckles as he struggled to regain his grip. But the brute work of lifting did not seem to trouble his arthritic hands nearly as much as the complicated flexion of his fingers that modeling required.

The base was the first piece to reach the top. They secured it in place with steel rods, and then when horse and man were brought up they were removed from their thick cotton batting and lifted by the block and tackle, which had been transferred to an A-frame. Gil called out instructions as the men steadied the swaying forms and gently lowered the feet of the man and the hooves of the horse—all with stabilizing rods protruding from them—into the holes that had been drilled into the bronze base and below into the rock itself.

And there it stood. There was no plaque, no need for one. Everyone knew it was Lamar Clayton's boy. George's Mary drove to the base of the hill in Clayton's Model T and walked up to join them. Peggy was with her and the dog sniffed at the pungent patina on the surface of the statue. George's Mary didn't have anything to say at first and Gil couldn't read her expression. She just stared at the sculpture with what might have been admiration, or sadness, or perplexity.

"Well, I believe you should be happy now, Mr. Clayton," she said at last. "You've got your statue of Ben right where you wanted it."

She turned to Gil. "You did a right good job, if you care to know my opinion."

"Thank you."

"Your daughter ought to be here to see this," Clayton said.

"I think so too."

Three weeks before, Gil had attended another installation, a far more formal affair when the Spirit of the Waters was presented to the city of San Antonio. The mayor had unveiled it. A band had played and Gil had been called upon to make remarks in Maureen's absence. He told the audience he was honored to represent his daughter and they were fortunate to witness the unveiling of the first public work of a major new sculptor, a young woman whose name would soon be known not just in San Antonio but throughout the nation.

The men Clayton had hired stood around admiring their work for a time. They were drenched with sweat and bleeding from cuts. One of them had a Brownie and he told everyone to stand next to the statue. Clayton said he didn't feel like having his picture made and moved off to the side. After the photo was taken the men took down the block and tackle and Clayton gave them their money and shook their hands and they drove off riding on the back of the flatbed truck. Gil and Clayton and George's Mary remained on the summit with Ernest and

Nax for a few minutes more, watching the dust cloud thrown up by the departing truck as it rumbled along the poor road.

"That was a piece of work, getting this goddam thing up here," Lamar said.

"Yes sir, it surely was," Ernest replied.

Nax lit a cigarette and pounded the rump of the bronze horse, a muffled echo sounding from the hollow cavity. After that there was just an awkward silence, everyone seeming to think maybe something ought to be said, but no one knowing what it should be. Gil knew it was not his place to speak. Whatever he had to say about Ben Clayton had been said in the statue itself.

So after a while they walked down the hill and crowded into the lizzie and drove back to the ranch house. Gil spent the night again in Ben's room, the boy's clothes back in his dresser, the saddle back on its sawhorse. He woke to the sound of mourning doves and the smell of biscuits baking. He washed and dressed and made his way through the familiar house to the breakfast table, where Clayton was smoking and drinking coffee and solemnly staring at an equipment catalog. He greeted Gil by asking what time his train was.

"Four in the afternoon." Gil nodded his thanks to George's Mary as she poured his coffee and set his plate in front of him.

"You got time if you want to come with me."

"Where?"

"I thought I'd ride out to that far pasture we went to that other time. See what the statue looks like from there. You want me to I'll have Ernest saddle up Margarita for you. She's a pretty mild-tempered animal. Not that I'm saying you can't ride."

"I'd very much like to do that," Gil said.

WITHIN THE HOUR they were off, riding across the same open pastures and rocky declivities they had traveled last November on their way to search for calves that needed doctoring for screwworm. The summer had been harsh, from the look of the grass and the parched greenery along the creek banks, but there was such breadth to the landscape, such boundlessness in the sun-washed blue sky, that Gil felt surrounded by a sumptuous natural beauty all the same.

He felt more secure in the saddle than he had on that previous occasion. Margarita was a conservative-minded horse, no more eager to take a spill than he was. When they came to the rocky slope upon which Gil had been thrown by Poco, she tested the terrain with such caution that he could almost hear her deliberating thoughts.

Gil and Clayton had ridden for two hours, hardly saying anything to each other, before they entered the open pastureland spread out before the mesa on which the statue had been erected. They both stared at it in the distance but still Clayton did not comment. He just led his horse ahead through the high grass and Gil followed. After another five minutes the rancher reined up and turned his horse toward the mesa and sat there in the saddle staring at the unmoving figures on top.

They were maybe two hundred yards away. The piece looked unnervingly natural, just as Gil had planned it to. Ben Clayton was no colossus. The figures were seven feet tall but looked to be only life-size from this distance, so that it seemed that at any moment the young cowboy on the hill was going to catch sight of them and raise his hand in greeting.

"Well," Clayton said to Gil, "is it your masterpiece, like you said it was going to be?"

"Are you asking me if you got your money's worth?"

He'd meant it in a light-hearted way but Clayton took it as a cross remark. "No, dammit, I'm asking you if you're proud of it."

"I am."

"It don't bother you that hardly anybody's ever gonna see it? After you and me are dead it'll just be standing there with nobody to explain it."

"No, Clayton, that doesn't bother me."

Just as he said this Gil noticed that the statue was no longer a solitary shape on the mesa. There were moving figures next to it, a man and woman. The man was walking around the statue, gesturing with some sort of burning bundle he was holding in his hand.

"That's my sister and her Kiowa husband," Clayton said when Gil turned to him. "They're blessing the statue or some goddam thing."

"I thought you told her never to come back here."

"I was in a hard mood that day. I wrote her a letter a while back. Figured she ought to see it, that Ben would want her to. She and Eli are camped out in town somewhere. She didn't want to stay on my property and have to talk to me and that's just about the way I want it too."

Gil's horse shifted her weight from one shoulder to the other and idly nosed through the grass at her feet. He stretched his legs in the stirrups, working out the stiffness from the ride. He thought about dismounting but liked the sensation of still being in the saddle, of looking up toward his statue with the benefit of the extra elevation that Margarita provided. He could hear Eli's voice now, declaiming some Kiowa song as he blessed the sculpture. When he was through singing, Jewell put her hand against the statue, touching the boy's arm, bowing her head, and then she turned and disappeared with her husband down the far side of the hill.

When they were out of sight Clayton turned to Gil.

"I expect you didn't go all the way to France without asking that boy over there how my son died."

"Yes, of course I asked him. He took Maureen and me on a tour of the battlefield. He showed us where it happened, how it happened."

"What did you find out? Ben wasn't no coward, I can tell you that right now."

"He wasn't a coward. Far from it. He took out a machine-gun nest, pretty much by himself. There was a rather desperate assault against the German position in the cemetery and he was in the thick of that as well. Then they were under fire from a machine gun in the steeple of the church and he decided to take that gun out too. He had just climbed out of the trench when the gunner saw him. He died instantly, as I believe you've heard."

"That all of it?"

"What else do you want, Clayton? Your son was killed trying to eliminate a German machine-gun position. No one ordered him to do it. He just took it upon himself."

"So it was just foolishness that got him killed."

"It wasn't foolishness. By any common definition it was heroism. If you insist on faulting your son then I guess you could call it heedlessness. He was in a big fight and his blood was up."

"I don't care to fault him. I done plenty of that already."

There was just the slightest temptation to tell him the whole truth. Maybe he deserved to hear it, to hear what Ben had learned from that Indian in Company E and how it had led him to throw his life away in a rash assault on that German gun. Gil had told Clayton that his son's blood was up, but he did not tell him his blood was up because of Clayton's closed-up heart and his grudging secrets. Lamar Clayton had been a failure of a father, a man who had allowed his own disappointments and his own seething temper to lead his son to a bewildered death. If Lamar Clayton had had an artist's vision, if he could have detected the fate of his son as it slumbered in the stone of his own tragic life, there might have been a better ending than this forlorn monument. But even an artist's eye, as Gil had learned, could not necessarily detect what was buried in the hearts of the people the artist was supposed to love.

The two men sat their horses and kept their secrets and continued to train their eyes on the statue. Gil had hired a photographer from the San Antonio newspaper to come out in a few weeks to take some high-quality images, since he did not know if he would ever see the piece again firsthand. This would probably be his last chance to study it, to judge what he had done.

He was pleased. It stood there on its promontory with a kind of natural dominion, as if this cowboy and his horse were living beings that had not been painfully winched up onto the top of the mesa but had just happened upon it and had paused to appreciate the view. After so many years it was still a mystery to Gil how he had done it. How he and Maureen had done it.

"Well," Clayton said, "do you want to sit here and look at it all day or do you want to go catch your train?"

Gil knew Clayton meant the needling tone to be friendly-sounding. But neither of them was really in that kind of jousting mood. Gil said nothing. He just wearily pulled his horse's head up from the grass and followed Lamar Clayton back the way they had come. They were not friends and they rode under separate burdens of silence and solitude. Lamar Clayton set his face straight ahead but Gil kept looking back, startled and gratified by how alive the boy looked as he stared off into the cow pastures and beyond them to the plains.

AUTHOR'S NOTE

Francis Gilheaney is a fictional character, so of course all the statues credited to him in this book are fictional as well. But I would like to acknowledge that the initial idea for *Remember Ben Clayton* came from reading *From Dawn to Sunset*, the autobiography of the sculptor Pompeo Coppini, who undertook a commission similar to the one described in this novel, and whose finished work, an affecting statue of a young man named Charles Noyes, stands today in the courthouse square of Ballinger, Texas.

It is always a privilege to thank the people whose generosity with factual information or critical judgment helps to make my work possible. In the case of this novel, it is the usual long list, beginning at home in Austin with my wife Sue Ellen and extending to New York, where I have long had the honor of being represented by Esther Newberg and edited by Ann Close. I'm continually grateful to them and to all their colleagues at ICM and at Alfred A. Knopf and Random House.

Elizabeth Crook's sustaining insight proved, as usual, to be a crucial factor in helping me navigate my way through a complex story. I am also especially grateful to the late Elmer Kelton, who supplied me with details from his own memory of ranching life in Texas during the early part of the twentieth century.

Thanks also to Lawrence Wright, William Broyles, Jr., Gregory Curtis, and James Magnuson; to sculptors Patrick Oliphant, Neil Estern, Clete Shields, Glenna Goodacre, and Jason Scull. And to Alan Huffines, Enrique Villarreal, Tony Noyes, Christina Holstein,

Steven D. Dortch, Michael Hanlon, Eleanor Crook, Betsy Tyson, Barbara Tims, Ann Mount, Laura Lewis, Martin Cox, Kevin Griffin, John Emery, Rich Turnwald, Jodi Wright-Gidley, Mireille Golaszewski, Isabelle Secretan, and Gisèle Dessieux. And since a father-daughter relationship is central to this novel, I can't end this list without a loving acknowledgment of all that I have learned from my own three daughters, Marjorie, Dorothy, and Charlotte.

AN UNFINISHED LIFE

by Mark Spragg

Jean Gilkyson has a history of choosing the wrong men. After yet another night of argument turned to violence with her boyfriend, Roy, Jean knows it's time to leave—if not for herself then for her ten-year-old daughter, Griff. But the only place they can afford to go is Ishawooa, Wyoming, where Jean's family is dead and her deceased husband's father, Einar, wishes she was too. Of course, Griff knows none of this—only that here in Wyoming, with a grandfather she has never known and his crippled friend Mitch, she may finally be able to find a home.

Fiction/Literature